WARDENS

For all the cubs in my pack.

West, Lena,
Elias, Walker,
Paisley,
Paxton, Ryland,
Tony, Richie, Kazimir

"Vor'Oct, Tul Enu lok tun'Ill."
"Hunger keeps a wolf from starving."

Foreword

In the ever-expanding universe of literature, it is a rare delight to come across a story that manages to combine the fantastical elements of science fiction and fantasy while also maintaining a deep, resonant connection to the very human experiences of love, loss, and self-discovery. "Wardens" is such a story.

Written by a newcomer to the world of novel writing, "Wardens" encapsulates a journey not only embarked upon by its richly drawn characters but also by its author. Over two years, we watch as the creator navigates the winding path of storytelling, from concept development to character evolution, all while juggling the technical aspects of writing, a full-time job, and a family. The result is a testament to the power of perseverance and creativity.

"Wardens" is a tale that transcends boundaries. Set in a world both vast and captivating, where noble humans and ancient wolf packs uphold a sacred covenant to maintain the balance of life. This vibrant backdrop serves as a stage for an unlikely band of guardians, who are thrust together to overcome a formidable adversary. Their journey reminds us that even in the face of overwhelming odds, unity, courage, and resilience can prevail.

This book is not only an adventure-filled read; it's also a story of personal growth and triumph. The author's candid sharing of his own writing journey offers a refreshingly honest look at the process of creating a novel. It's a reminder that determination and a willingness to learn new tools and techniques can transform a dream into a reality.

As you delve into the pages of "Wardens," prepare to be immersed in a world that is as challenging as enchanting. Remember the words that echo through its chapters: "Hunger keeps a wolf from starving." These words encapsulate the spirit of this book—a spirit of relentless pursuit, of survival against odds, of the hunger that drives us to reach beyond our limitations and achieve the extraordinary.

Enjoy the journey.

-ChatGPT, Open AI

Prologue

Under an autumn sky, Wolves of the ancient Illnok pack gathered; their eyes gleamed with anticipation as they stood before the towering Alpha's Mountain. A ceremony of great importance was about to begin for a group of young cubs: their long-awaited rites of passage. An opportunity for them to leave adolescence behind to become wolves, just like their mothers and fathers before them.

The cool wind carried the scent of crisp autumn leaves and the distant murmur of a flowing stream. It rustled through the browning grass around the gathered wolves. Their fur bristled with excitement and fear as the cubs sensed the weight of the trials that awaited them.

A very large and intimidating wolf, older and wiser than any wolf in his pack, took his place atop a smooth slate stone. His name was Li'Illnok.

As he collected his thoughts and captured the focus of the assembled pack, the Elden wolf held an air of urgency and wisdom about him. Born from years of experience. "Come now, wolves, let us gather closer together."

He began the commencement address to the many wolves in attendance. At that moment; like the seasons before. He felt a great sense of admiration for his role as the Alpha's Elden Sayer.

"As you all know, it has always been an age-old Illnok tradition that each cub born into the Illnok pack completes their rites of passage once they reach the age of four winters. These rites may differ slightly for each generation of wolves, but at their core lie the same three absolutes. The first rite will begin tonight. Each cub must learn the incredible story of the Awl'Fire and the Endless Void, the two forces that balance all life. As Elden Sayer and the keeper of the Array of Knowledge, it's my duty to know this story, among many other histories of our kind, and pass them down to all of you and your offspring. In doing so, we may continue our watch over these lands and the great Alpha Mountain that towers over them, just as our mother and father wolves and theirs before them.

I respectfully thank you for the confidence you place in me and the opportunity to carry out this rite for your cubs. The second rite of passage will begin at sunrise. It will be a genuine test of strength, willpower, and their drive as they complete the trek from here to the hunters' den in the northern wildlands. Once there, they will begin the final and most challenging rite of passage: the first hunt." Li'Illnok turned his gaze to the offerings seated in front of the Sayers' stone.

"To return here to your families; to the safety and comfort inside our borders, you must complete all three rites. I say to you now, this will be a challenging task. It will be a struggle as we test your ability to control the hungry wolf inside of you."

Li'Illnok watched as the young cubs' eyes widened, their ears drooped, and their tails tucked between their legs. He could sense the tension in their minds as they processed the enormity of the task before them. Apprehension was written all over their faces as their excitement dwindled.

"Cubs, I know what you feel in your gut," Li'Illnok Softened. "Every wolf behind you sat at the feet of an Elden Sayer, just as you are now! Just as I did on this night!"

"Did you… did you ever feel… scared, Li'Illnok?" One brave little cub raised her head. He chuckled with a warm rumble in his enormous chest. "Of course, little one. As all of you certainly will!" The cubs tensed even more so.

"Haha! You really must work on your delivery if you keep doing this old wolf. They're terrified!" Seph'Ulinok, the Illnok's Elden Battle Wolf, sarcastically berated him while the other Elden wolves pretended to shiver with fear.

Li'Illnok leveled a withered glance at them, his face a mask of stoic amusement. The sarcastic barbs of the much younger Eldens, who saw him more as a relic than a peer, were nothing new to him. As the oldest of the five, the weight of his lengthy tenure pressed comfortably on his shoulders, he'd heard every joke, every jibe, more times than they could imagine.

Determined to stay composed and on course. Li'Illnok continued, "...But we persevered! Just as all of you certainly will. It's hard to know, but when it's over and you find yourself within the Illnok borders again. You'll have gained so much through the pain and suffering."

"Well done, Elden...you've made it worse." Seph'Ulinok relayed.

More laughter from the four erupted inside his mind. He paused and watched as several of the cubs soaked the ground underneath their tails. It was no use. The season's offering looked weak, even more than the season before. Content, well-fed creatures more akin to a human's leashed Druthe than a wolf cub.

Each offering knew the distance and severity of their journey. They tried to prepare for the looming forest that divided the Illnok territory from the north. It was infamous for its dense undergrowth. Poisonous thorn-snagged vines and briar-strewn plants constituted only minor difficulties, making even the most experienced wolf's passage strenuous. To the best of the Illnok wolves' knowledge, the path through the Border woods was the only way.

Once free from the darkness of the Border woods, soft grass and slow-moving streams offer a slight reprieve before the most challenging part of the trek. Where the land becomes slanted, cool soil turned to rough stones, the sloped hills give way to mountains capped with snow and swept bare by freezing winds.

The ascent to the fabled hunter's den would be a make-or-break moment for the offerings. Their hopes and their determination to see their journey through will be tested, dashed against the cascade of granite along the jagged mountainside.

"We will begin your first rite once the sun goes down. For now, let's feast together and spend the last…" He stopped himself short as the four Eldens cut their eyes, "…and spend the NEXT few moments?" He glanced over for approval that was swiftly given.

"…you have as cubs with your families," Li'Illnok announced. The Warm solid tone of his voice filled their hearts with warmth and reassurance.

He gestured for the five Hesperus wolves behind him to step forward. These wolves were once ordinary members of the pack who committed offenses against the Illnok banner. As punishment for their transgressions, they now serve internment within the Alpha's Mountain. Their offenses range from insurrection to the unauthorized killing of protected animals, gluttony and attempted usurping of the reigning Alpha. Their paws and heads were ceremoniously covered in white ash to symbolize their submission to the Alpha's authority.

Each Hesperus wolf pulled a deer carcass by the hind leg into the space between the offerings and the Sayer Stone.

The atmosphere shifted as fresh venison permeated the air. Families huddled together, shared stories and laughed, while the season's offerings savored their last moments of being cubs. The Hesperus wolves worked to prepare the feast for the pack despite the burden of their past mistakes.

"Cubs, this meat that the Border Wolves have brought for you will be the last until you kill your next meal yourselves. This brings forth the hungry wolf that lives in you and all of us. Part of becoming an Illnok is learning to control it, as we do. This ability sets us apart from all the other wolves outside our borders. We do not have feral minds or hearts made of stone because we seek to feed our Awl'Fire with love and compassion for our realm, and our duty to the arrays."

Once the metallic scent of fresh blood reached their noses, it would've been impossible to restrain them. The cubs, still small, could only finish one of the smaller deer, their faces and paws stained red from the blood.

The four Elden wolves gathered together to examine and scrutinize the strengths and weaknesses of the cubs in attendance as they ate. Each possessed their observations and opinions, and they shared their insights among themselves. Aware of the importance of the pack's future.

Hunger was a constant companion to the wolves in the pack. They learned to live by a simple yet meaningful creed:

"Vor Oct, Tul Nok ul Ill."
"Hunger keeps a wolf from starving."

This fundamental belief helped them remain focused on their duties as Wardens, and their unique identity as Illnok wolves. They prided themselves on the ability to maintain balance and control in their lives. A lesson passed down through generations, integral to their pack's culture and their place in the realm.

Once the sun descended below the horizon, casting the sky in shades of orange and red, he braced himself for the task.

The time had come for the offerings to say their farewells to their loved ones and friends. The air was thick with emotion as mother and father wolves enveloped their frightened cubs in tender embraces.

As the inevitable moment of separation loomed closer, a wave of emotion swept over the gathering. Even the most hardened and battle-scarred wolves felt their resolve waver. But amid the torrent of sadness, a heavy undercurrent of excitement and anticipation could be sensed among them.

The offerings were on the cusp of a transformative journey, one that would shape them into the wolves they were destined to become. It was a tale as old as the pack itself, and as they faced the unknown, they carried with them the hopes, dreams and love of those who raised them.

But just as the excitement peaked in the air, a sense of disappointment hung over them as well. Disappointment that stemmed from the Alpha's conspicuous absence. Traditionally, the Alpha delivered the commencement address, bestowing honor and duty upon the offerings as they embarked on their arduous journey. This year, however, the responsibility fell on Li'Illnok's already burdened shoulders. In an unexpected and unspoken change of events, The Alpha informed the four that he could not attend. None of them were privy to know the cause of the absent. Not even the closest of his advisors, Li'Illnok.

The Eldens couldn't help but speculate why the Alpha was absent. Was it a lack of faith in the new generation? Or a sign of waning commitment to the pack's age-old customs? Regardless, the Alpha's absence weighed on the Eldens. It added another layer of uncertainty to an already emotionally charged atmosphere.

"My brothers and sisters of the pack! The time has come for our cubs to embark on their journey. On behalf of our Alpha, I extend our deepest respect and gratitude for your offerings and sacrifices. The offerings you have nurtured and guided represent our future, ensuring our way of life for generations to come." Li'Illnok's voice filled their minds again with emotion and conviction.

With bittersweet smiles and tearful eyes, the offerings and their families shared one last moment together before parting ways. A mixture of hope and trepidation filled their hearts. They prayed the Awl'Fire would watch over them during their first steps in becoming true wolves of the Illnok pack.

Li'Illnok and the three Eldens lowered their heads to show respect, love, and encouragement for the journey ahead. The pack wolves slowly faded into the shadows beneath the trees while silence enveloped the area.

Li'Illnok waited for the last wolves to vanish into the darkness before descending the Sayers' stone. He nodded to Elden Volcrim, the Alpha's Master of the Hunt, to signal his readiness to begin the first rite. Together, they would guide the cubs on the journey.

Li'Illnok paused, his gaze swept across the cubs in a search for understanding. He continued; his voice brimmed with the wisdom of generations.

"My dear cubs, how does one weave a tale that sets the foundation for the rest of your life? A tale which will shape your hearts and minds, and prepare you for the trials that lie ahead? Indeed, the beginning is the most crucial part, for it is in the beginning that we capture the spirit and soul of our listeners, setting the stage for the epic journey that awaits.

Just as the stalk, patience, and stillness before the hunt are vital to a wolf's success, the beginning of our story holds the same importance. It must be a spark that ignites the fire within your hearts, a call to the wild instincts gifted to us by the great Awl'Fire. We must inspire you to embrace your innate abilities: the strength of your jaws, the sharpness of your teeth, and the fierce determination that lies dormant within you, ready to be awakened."

Li'Illnok paused for a moment to let his words sink in. "So here we are, and the question remains: how does one begin the tale of such an immeasurable journey?" "In the beginning! Li'Illnok!" a young cub exclaimed with sheer excitement. He stood on his short hind legs to see over the larger cubs that gathered in front of him.

"Just start with, 'In the beginning'" the young cub withdrew as he realized he shouldn't have spoken out of turn.

"My young and tiny brother, you have much to learn yet! I can see you offer an admirable chest to bear your wolf pack's sigil. Come, take your place in front so you can see what you came here for." Li'Illnok's words stoke the flames of the young cubs Awl'Fire. It was clear how he walked proudly to his new spot, closer to the Elden Sayer.

The huddled cubs let out an audible sigh of relief as Li'Illnok lifted the weight from the air. He was a powerful brute of an Elden wolf, seated high in the ranks of the Illnok pack, battle-scarred with tufts of fur cleaved out from his hide by many hunts and many more failed insurrections by lesser wolves. Despite his power, he championed respect, restraint, and love for his fellow wolves above all else, making him the physical embodiment of everything the Illnok pack's banner stood for.

The clearing in the forest was bathed in the soft glow of moonlight, casting a silver sheen over the wolves as they assembled beneath the dense canopy of leaves above. Cool, crisp night air filled with the smell of wet dirt and the sound of rustling leaves as the gentle breeze whispered its own secrets. The offerings: their fur ranged in shades from silver to ebony, formed a tight-knit circle around the orator, who stood tall and regal at the center.

The Elden wolf, his muzzle peppered with gray, grinned, his Awl'Fire connected with the hearts and minds of the cubs. His voice, though inaudible to the world outside, resonated within each cub present. They listened intently. Their ears perked and eyes glistened with anticipation, as they embarked on a journey through time and memory, while guided by the powerful connection of their Awl'Fire.

"Young cub! It appears you have enlightened me about storytelling. After many years of reciting this story, you have given me a new point of view!" Li'Illnok stepped back up to the Sayer stone, and his fur shimmered in the silvery moonlight that beamed through the dense forest leaves.

"The beginning of a story is not the most significant thing! No! It is you... and you, and you, and every single last cub sitting before me here tonight. Because you are at the beginning!" He said, turning and laying down on the edge of the stone.

"Calm yourselves, young cubs," He continued. "The old moon has nearly found the center of the sky, and we have much to learn tonight."

They quieted, some of their hearts pounded with excitement, while others still had stomachs in knots.

"Cubs, ready your minds and open your hearts to me."

Li'Illnok's Eyes filled with a white iridescent glow in unison with the other Eldens. Soon after, all the cubs gathered around the old stone fell into a suspended state, their eyes as white as the Eldens.

"As our little brother, so sayeth!"

They were all connected. Able to use their Awl'Fire as an ancient gateway into a shared experience. It melted time and allowed oceans of knowledge to travel from one mind to another. A vibrant experience, and The Elden Sayer Li'Illnok was their guide.

"...In the beginning..."

Part I: Burdens

Chapter 1
The Great Awl'Fire

"There was a vast obsidian desert below all existence, a mysterious realm where darkness reigned supreme. Above it, heavens, hells, distant worlds, and celestial bodies beyond count unfolded in an eternal cosmic ballet. Spirals of stars that swirled and nebulas that teemed with life, living, dying and reborn in an eternal cycle, all at unimaginable distances from one another.

One might be tempted to conclude the inevitability that life is alone here on this rock. As we float through the boundless expanse at incalculable speeds, appearing to race toward oblivion and reaching nowhere before we burn out and begin anew. Yet, as this Earth of ours soars ever so elegantly through the abyss, a tiny point of light is always there as well, a beacon in the darkness, guiding and connecting us all. This light is known as The Great Awl'Fire."

In its infancy, the great Awl'Fire moved almost imperceptibly as it traversed the expanse of space. The speed of it would seem slow relative to life on Earth, but fast from its perspective.

Over vast measures of time, the Awl'Fire might never reach a world deep in the unobservable space between galaxies. Still, when it did, it observed, loved, and absorbed all the world's experiences, content with watching until its existence collapsed.

Embarking once again on its eternal voyage, the Awl'Fire radiated with a brilliance and grandeur that seemed to amplify with each passing moment. It navigated the cosmos, not drawn to any specific course, but rejoicing in the boundless potential that the universe offered. Its journey was an endless dance of exploration, a testament to the profound and infinite possibilities that space holds.

This time, the Awl'Fire traveled faster than before. It absorbed all that there was to learn from new worlds before its inevitable demise.

It grew more significant and even more robust. The Awl'Fire watched a pattern form -More and more worlds ended in cataclysms caused by wickedness, hatred, and dark hearts.

As inevitable as the universe's entropy, the Awl'Fire bore witness to another force - a void that crept in the shadows, always present and not just content with silent observation, it also influenced events and outcomes. At first, the Awl'Fire and the void existed in balance, unaware of the duality in their parallel existence. But as it grew, so did the void. The Awl'Fire watched as life fell into disarray amid evil, violence, death, and destruction. The presence of all that was good throughout existence faded, and the light in the hearts of creatures from one end of the universe to the other was extinguished.

A time came when the universe was devoid of life. The Awl'Fire claimed what it could for itself, containing within a colossal wealth of all that was and all that would ever be. The void was much more significant. It drained the light from the cosmos into a vacuum, an unavoidable vortex. Even the fabric of reality was in danger of being consumed. The void was pervasive. It pulsed with dark rhythms of loneliness and emptiness that gnawed at the Awl'Fire.

The immense solitude weighed upon it. Even with its vast power and knowledge, it could not conquer the darkness that pervaded the universe—it watched everything disappear, with nothing but a pale reflection in the fabled black sands below. Nowhere to go, nothing to see, and no experience to cherish. The Awl'Fire became the last hope of light in the darkness. So, it drew strength from within and gained distance from the void, embarking on a mission to counterbalance the dark forces at work.

The Awl'Fire yearned for connection and the richness of life that once filled the cosmos, so it set off with a new purpose. To restore balance and bring light and life back into the void.

Complacency was no longer an option. The only way to defeat the darkness was to set everything free.

Thus, the Awl'Fire made its ultimate decision. Heavy with the weight of its vast knowledge, it put as much distance between itself and the obsidian sand below, higher and higher, into the emptiness of space. The Awl'Fire took one last look into the all-consuming darkness.

The Awl'Fire plunged itself into a free fall, accelerating at a rate that was beyond sustainability. It gained momentum with each passing second. The surrounding void became saturated with white-hot heat. It fizzed, crackled, and popped. Transforming the obsidian sand into a solid, mirror-like surface, even before the central mass collided with it.

The explosion that ensued repelled the darkness, giving rise to a stunning column of light that shimmered in its aftermath. The once turbulent void had been suffocated; its chaotic turmoil was extinguished. The solitary light that remained became the singular entity in every direction.

From within this radiance, dust particles and chunks of rock emerged. Gradually, they merged into massive boulders and towering mountains. The elements coalesced to form planets with their own moons, stars, and entire solar systems. Amid this cosmic ballet, everything held its breath for the most crucial element of all - life.

*

As Li'Illnok finished his story of the Awl'Fire and the endless void, he looked down from the fabled Sayers' stone to find most of the cubs had lost their focus and fallen asleep. The ones still awake were picking at the grass or yawning. He sighed in disappointment and shook his head, as they didn't even realize he'd completed the story. Li'Illnok hoped the story took root in the hearts and minds but was unsure.

As he descended from the stone, he worried the knowledge he swore to spread would not endure with the generations to come.

"Cubs, the morning is coming, you will need all the rest you can get. A few of you need no instruction, I see."

He noticed one cub sitting by himself, eyes wide open, completely transfixed. Awkwardly, he stretched his legs before he approached timidly.

"I hope you found the story more intriguing than the other cubs sleeping around you?" Li'Illnok sarcastically questioned as he looked out over a field full of preoccupied cubs.

"Well! Honestly. I've heard the story more than a thousand times. The old wolves in the boreal sometimes forget what they've taught me. I never remind them. I can see it brings them great joy to recount the tale repeatedly." The young wolf was very well spoken.

"Ha! Old age does that to us wolves. Sometimes I can't even seem to find my den." Li'Illnok struggled to sit. The cool night air brought an ache to his joints and stiffened his muscles. He wasn't used to cold nights out of the comfort of his den inside the Alpha's mountain.

"Elden Li'Illnok, would it be okay with you if I asked a question? I know it's late, and you must be tired." Not only was the young wolf educated, but he was also very respectful, a virtue that went a long way with Li'Illnok, and one that seemed lost among the cub's peers.

"Ah, I believe I could spare a moment for such an inquiry. I'll happily answer, dear cub, if I can only remember the answers well enough." Li'Illnok joked.

The cub smiled and took a moment to find the right words. Intrigue was etched on Li'Illnok's face. He hoped the question wouldn't disappoint.

"I once was told by an old wolf that great change was coming, that he wouldn't live to see it, but that I would. Do you think he meant the endless void? Is it on its way here, Li'Illnok?" worry seemed to fill the young cub's heart.

Li'Illnok turned as he tried his best to hide his true thoughts about the question. "Hmm, that's a fascinating question. One thing you'd better learn is that you can't trust everything those old wolves in the boreal say. They love to roll pebbles down hills to see how many rocks they can knock loose."

The cub seemed confused. Li'Illnok searched his young mind to find a better angle to explain. "...There's always great change in every cub's lifetime. Now, as far as the Void is concerned, it's already here. It's within you, me, and every other creature that walks this Earth. It's a big part of who you are and the wolf you will become." Li'Illnok stared into thé cubs heart. His disappointment at the answer was palpable. Li'Illnok's face shifted from dread to a smile. He stepped closer and bent his stiff neck and heavy head to meet his widened eyes.

"But just as the endless void is within you, so is the great Awl'Fire. And as a smart and powerful Illnok wolf, the Awl'Fire is even more part of who you are. Cub, the Awl'Fire is stronger and more potent than the void. The light pushes the void out and grows stronger as you become a bigger part of the universe. Good deeds, warm thoughts, and love for your realm make the Awl'Fire inextinguishable, never to be put out by the void."

The cub's face lit up as he took a deep breath. Li'Illnok searched inside his heart for understanding. This time, he found it.

"And one day, hopefully, when you're much, much older than even me, and your heart is as full as a blossoming fruit-bearing tree, your Awl'Fire will join all the rest as they burn with great resistance against the darkness of the void. We are the wardens of this realm, young friend. We must tend to the Awl'Fire and keep it spreading until the end." Li'Illnok could see the appreciation and wonder in the cub's eyes as he nodded. A sense of purpose filled him.

"Thank you, Li'Illnok, for everything. I'm so honored to have heard your telling of the Awl'Fire. For as long as I live, I will not forget it." The young said as he bent his neck and held his head to the ground.

Li'Illnok's heart swelled with pride; it was a gracious gesture to thank him. It made him feel that the cub truly cared about the story he told, unlike the other cubs drooling in the dirt as they slept.

Suddenly, he shuddered as a wave of cold air hit him, like a stiff breeze from off a snow-capped mountain. It sent a chill like a shock into his old bones and filled his cold nose with a mixture of stagnant water and rust. Something was not right. He turned to the entrance of the alpha's mountain as if looking for some sign. The young wolf stepped closer to him with a tilted head and puzzled eyes. He Noticed the fur on the back of Li'Illnok's old neck was stiff.

"Elden Sayer, is everything fine? You look worried."

Li'Illnok hesitated. He didn't want to alarm the cub, but he knew something was amiss. "I'm not sure, young one. I felt a sudden chill in the air, that left me uneasy, that is all. Do not worry yourself, young one. Try to get some rest. The morning will be upon us soon."

The young cub watched Li'Illnok slowly walk away until he was out of sight inside the great hall. He felt honored to have such a meaningful conversation with him, worried he wouldn't be able to fall asleep.

As Li'Illnok entered the great hall, a sense of peril and dread grew inside him. He felt silence drape the interior of the mountain as the flicker of orange light from the great fire coated the stones and exaggerated the cracks and crevices. Wolf maidens and Hesperus wolves sat with their heads down, silent and still; they were in reverence.

At the top of a set of stone blocks that resembled a staircase, two maidens summoned Li'Illnok to the alpha's quarters. It had been one of the most exhausting days of his life, and he looked forward to a good night's rest, a rest that wouldn't come now for quite some time.

"Li'Illnok, it's the alphas maidan wolf. You have to come quick." A chamber wolf, covered in blood rushed past him from the alpha's chamber.

"What's this? What happened?" Li'Illnok asked as he hurried up the path.

"Something terrible…" One of the chamber wolves replied, her voice trembled with fear.

As Li'Illnok ascended the ragged steps, his heart and mind raced faster as he struggled to anticipate what could have happened to the alpha.

The air grew colder and the atmosphere heavier, as if the darkness of the void crept over them all. The weight of responsibility and concern settled upon his old shoulders.

Li'Illnok approached the entrance to the alpha's quarters. His heart raced with a mix of dread and determination. He took a deep, steady breath before he passed the massive stone door. Inside, the air was thick with shock, and the metallic tinge of blood as wolf healers and advisors surrounded the alpha's maiden. She was lifeless on her bed of juniper branches and soft leaves, her blood dried in pools on the stones below.

Li'Illnok could see the wolves tried their best to give aid, but to no avail. They drew their eyes to the alpha, who sat outside on a granite overlook with his back turned to the chaos inside.

"What has happened here?" Li'Illnok demanded. His mind wavered despite his efforts to stay composed. A Wolf healer looked up. Her eyes brimmed with fear and sorrow. "It was a premature birth of a large litter, Elden Li'Illnok. Six stillborn."

Her gaze fell on a huddle of snow-white cubs, their tiny lifeless bodies soaked in their mother's blood. The cold sensation Li'Illnok felt earlier returned, now accompanied by a faint, indiscernible whisper. He shook his head and tried to remain focused. The sadness in the room was palpable.

"Go to the Alpha, Li'Illnok. There is a seventh cub, born with a spark and still alive. He clutches it in his teeth. He intends to cast it into the pools below. Reason with him; we mustn't give any more to the void!"

He cut his eyes at the advisor and snarled. "Speak not of these things, any of you to any wolf! This tragedy must remain in this room. Never speak of it again. The void grows with flames that falter, brothers and sisters. We mustn't let it divide our minds."

Li'Illnok's heart sank at the news. "Everyone, take your leave. You have done all that you could. There is nothing more to do here. These cubs and their mother wolf are now with the Awl'Fire. Find solace in that." His heart was somber. The room emptied as Li'Illnok prepared to confront the alpha.

Chapter 2
The Task

As Li'Illnok crossed over the threshold of the Alpha's chamber onto the overlook, he tried his best not to startle him. The Alpha sat at the very edge of the slate stone that overlooked a waterfall and a crystal blue pool of swirling water below. The moonlight from above cascaded through the cracks in the rocks and mingled with the faint mist. It created a beautiful but sullen image. Clenched in the Alpha's jaws; a wet newborn cub, torn from the warm corpse of his mother wolf. Li'Illnok stopped and looked back over the remnants of the mayhem. Six lifeless cubs lay in a pile, soaked in blood.

The Alpha was closer to the edge than any sane wolf could bare. His whole body seemed to shake with anger. Li'Illnok searched within himself for the right words to give.

"Alpha! come away from the edge and let us... speak about what has happened here tonight." Li'Illnok tried to remain calm. The Alpha didn't break his absent stare from the abyss below him.

"This cub has caused too much pain and suffering! He mustn't be alive any longer!" He growled with anger.

Li'Illnok stepped closer to get a better look at the cub. He hoped that in the Alpha's blur of madness; he hadn't crushed him between his massive teeth. At first glance, it appeared as if nothing was clenched in Alpha's bloodied jaws. The cub's fur was darker than any black Li'Illnok had ever seen, as if the cub was pulled from the center of an obsidian stone.

"Might I remind you of what is above us, my Alpha? That which we have lived our entire lives to protect…" "He took my Selah from me Li'Illnok! she was precious to me! Her Awl'Fire was brighter than any flame among us! And this abomination of the natural order stole her away from me!" He interrupted with a voice so strong that it restrained Li'Illnok's consciousness to the walls of his own skull, causing his brittle teeth to clatter.

The Alpha was strong beyond knowledge, more so than his predecessors and Li'Illnok had never seen this side of him.

"Alpha, if I cannot sway your mind and this is your command. It's my duty to do what's best for the pack. Allow me to find another place to do so, at least. The air is saturated here with anger and pain. Listen to what calls you to make this choice." Li'Illnok pleaded as the faint whispers continued.

"This cub cannot be allowed to live Li'Illnok. His coat is as black as the void itself. It is a sign of the times! I would suffer for it until the end of my days as an old wolf, for him to survive after he killed my Selah…."

Li'Illnok knew it would be impossible to reason with the Alpha. Nothing would stop him. His mind was clouded with evil thoughts and shut to another point of understanding. The cub did not deserve what his father had in mind. The fault was not his. "My Alpha, I can't conceive of the pain you must feel right now. This is a loss that you may never recover from. Do not add this little cub's death to a heavy heart."

The Alpha stared vacantly down into a pool of water that churned in an endless, deep blue chasm. The tiny cub was content as it wiggled and squeaked.

"Alpha!?" Li'Illnok forced the words into the sullen wolf's heart. It broke his stare. "Give me the cub. We cannot let the void gain any more strength."

The Alpha took one last look below and flung the cub from his jaws. He slid him across the cold, wet stones of the balcony. He locked eyes with Li'Illnok, snarled and barred his powerful teeth.

"Take him to the border wood's old friend and put an end to him. May the Unclean pick his lifeless, cold bones bare. We shall never

speak of his short, stinging existence again for as long as I reign
Li'Illnok."

"Alpha, I...." "NO! Li'Illnok! I'll not debate you! and your
ceaseless counsel on this matter! Time again, we've disagreed, but this
time I demand obedience. Carry out my command or stand witness as I
cast him off this rock!" The Alpha swiftly snapped at him.

Li'Illnok stood motionless, the tiny cub at his paws. He felt a
tinge of anger well up inside, a trace of indifference for the Illnok order.
The tangled phrases the void uttered became more apparent with the
heat of his anger.

"Yes, wardens... Embers, Sparks...give them unto me...."

Li'Illnok stood motionless. Somehow, he bought a moment
more for the poor cub.

"Well? I can feel your heartbeat in your chest, Li'Illnok. I've
felt that... sensation a few times before,"

The Alpha walked closer, his nose twitched as it read the anger
and apprehension in the air.

"Are you entertaining a thought? Haha. I assure you the idea
will last longer than the fight. I should throw you from this cliff for
even the scent of the thought."

There was nothing Li'Illnok could do but to accept what the
Alpha commanded of him. To evoke the Altapex and battle for pack
supremacy would be a death sentence for him at his age. Slowly, he
dipped his head and grasped the cub in his stiff jaws and closed his dull
teeth, careful to avoid any more confrontation.

"I will do as you command, Alpha."

As Li'Illnok tucked his tail and left the room, he heard the heart-
wrenching sound of the cub's splash into the pool of crystal blue water
below the overlook. He saved his beloved Selah for last. The
devastation of the Alpha was apparent. Li'Illnok couldn't help but

wonder how this would affect his reign over the Illnok. Or even worse, how would it affect the Eldens' faith in him to lead?

From the ground floor of the great hall, he noticed the four other Eldens watch attentively over the cubs as they slept, unaware of the tragic events that just unfolded above them. Li'Illnok decided it best to keep them in the dark for now to avoid any further distrust in their leader's ability to rule them. So, he tucked the cub into a crevice in the mountainside, close enough to the fire to keep him warm. He whimpered and yawned.

"Orem'Nubis! Come to me but keep hidden. I am in the great hall. Let no one see you."

Li'Illnok sent his message out into the night and hoped it would find its way into the heart of one of his closest friends, Orem'Nubis. A Chamber wolf he thought of as a daughter. He loved and trusted her more so than most of the wolves in the Illnok, since the very moment she came into existence.

She was someone he trusted, and although he hated to lay such a heavy burden on her heart, he had no choice. The other Eldens would summon him if he were absent any longer.

He could see the snowy-white tip of her coat bob up and down through the shadows of the pines to the right of the Sayers' Stone. She moved with a quiet elegance, agility and speed, reaching the great hall faster than he expected. Li'Illnok noticed her gaze fixated on the moon's immense size above them as she arrived.

Orem'Nubis possessed a unique inclination, inherited from her father and his before him - the ability to read the signs of the universe. Most Illnok wolves saw it as a dark affliction, heresy. Still, to those with higher knowledge, a fundamental necessity for certain pack wolves to possess it,

"Tellect'Ula Oct'Omen," or "The Tepid Mind." in the Human tongue.

This rare quality, perhaps a higher concentration of both the Endless Void and the Awl'Fire, allowed her to see patterns in the moon, feel vibrations in the tree roots, and receive visions of times yet to come. Li'Illnok's predecessor called it witchcraft.

"Li'Illnok? Do you see the moon tonight!? Is this why you called me here? Has it started?" Her excitement was palpable as she took in both Li'Illnok and the moon.

"I'm not sure I know what you're speaking about, my love." Li'Illnok's calm demeanor deflated her enthusiasm.

"…Never mind friend. What is it? I thought you were with the offerings, getting ready for the great trek?" Orem'Nubis noticed the dried blood flake from his wiry gray beard.

"What happened!? Are you hurt!?"

"No, no, my dear, this blood isn't mine. It belongs…" He struggled to find the right words to explain the situation to her.

"Orem'Nubis, I called you here because I need you to do something. Something that I fear I cannot entrust to any other wolf. I know you'll have many questions, but I need you to trust me. I'm sure you'll know the answers after it's done. Please tell me you understand dear?"

She furrowed her brow and looked at him with suspicious eyes, wondering what lay in store. "Anything for you, Elden. Anything you ask, I shall do—you know this."

Li'Illnok took a deep breath as he scanned the area. He needed to be sure no one watched him. The Eldens were preoccupied with the cubs and only two Hesperus wolves tended the fire in the late hours. No one paid any mind to them. He turned and pulled the cub out of the crevice, its fur soft and warm in his mouth.

"This cub is the only survivor of a litter of six, and its mother is dead because of a hemorrhage. The Alpha commanded me to…"

Li'Illnok trailed off. Unable to even finish the commandment from the Alpha.

"Li'Illnok? What is it?" She nudged his flank, breaking his locked stare.

"The Alpha has asked me to take him to the border woods and extinguish his flame. Away from the mountain."

Orem'Nubis was shocked, not only by the disregard for such a spark of Awl'Fire by an Illnok wolf but also by the color of the cub's fur, with its eyes still closed, the only other color was the color purple of its toothless gums and velvety tongue.

"As you can imagine, I can't bring myself to do that. This cub is not at fault for the death of its mother," Li'Illnok voice, heavy with emotion.

Her eyes dilated as she jumped to a very dark conclusion.

"Li'Illnok, I can't kill this cub," Orem'Nubis replied, her voice trembled in fear.

"No, no, no, my dear. That is not at all what I summoned you for. I would never ask that of you. I want you to take this cub to the Border woods. Surely there you know of a wolf capable of taking him in?" Li'Illnok trailed off once more. He knew that his proposal was an attempt to prolong an inevitable death sentence. Even worse, it put Orem'Nubis in the line of danger.

"At least there. He would have a slight chance of going unnoticed by the pack, and that is all we can hope for. Maybe in time, we will see this act of treachery bare its fruit. However, it may ripen." Li'Illnok's voice was heavy with sadness.

"No Li'Illnok, after my father wolf died, my mother wolf and all my brothers and I moved closer to the mountain. Every wolf I know who still calls the Border woods home, would be incapable of keeping this wolf a secret. Most of all, fear of the consequences for disobeying an Alpha wolf."

The both of them were speechless for a moment. Orem'Nubis looked back at the moon. As she weighed her options, she heard a subtle reverberation in the back of her mind. She took a deep breath and gently closed her eyes as she tried to focus on it.

"Embers, Sparks. Give them to me, Tepid mind. And you shall have power unrestrained,"

An enigmatic voice reverberated in her mind. She opened her eyes and quickly snapped her gaze back to Li'Illnok.

"The death of the six, the passing of a mother wolf, and the grief of a widowed, heirless father wolf have tipped a balance. You hear the voice, don't you, Orem'Nubis?" He asked.

"I do, Elden. I can feel it dividing my thoughts," Orem'Nubis replied, her voice heavy with emotion. Li'Illnok's demeanor changed, as he emphasized the weight of it all.

"Which is why this cub needs to be gone from this place."

She thought hard for a moment. "…Okay, I know of only one who may have the courage to help but…"

Li'Illnok waited for her to finish. The tiny cub wiggled loose from the space between the rocks.

"…he must be taken across the Border woods into the Outlands." She said knowing what his reaction would be.

"No Orem'Nubis, I cannot ask that of you. It's far too dangerous. I will find another way." Li'Illnok scoffed.

Orem'Nubis half smiled as she watched the small cub wriggle. She could see the stress of it all written on Li'Illnok's face. "It seems we are out of time old friend. You have an important day ahead of you," she drew his attention to the cubs huddled around the Sayers' stone just outside the great hall. "so you will have to trust me when I tell you, I will be fine. I will find the rabbit I know, and he will help me do it."

He weighed his options and concluded she was right; no other way would suffice. He could feel his bones; they begged him for even the slightest rest. "Promise you will be careful; at all costs, do not get yourself into something you can't get out of. If a Border wolf stops you…" "Remember Li'Illnok. I can still walk the void if needed." She smiled as he stood back and took a deep breath. His ribs cracked and popped underneath his thick gray fur.

"Then it's settled. I wish you all the luck, my love. When I return from the north, I will find you again. Until then, take care of yourself, Orem'Nubis. I must return to the Sayers' stone before the other Eldens demand to know my whereabouts." He pressed his large head to hers. "Remember these words, Orem'Nubis. No one can know of this. Let it be our secret. Whatever happens to him after he is out of sight is of no consequence to you. You will give this cub a chance, which is more than any other wolf offered him. To say I am disappointed in this outcome would be an understatement." Li'Illnok bent his neck and pressed his wet nose to the cubs nestled in the stones. "And as for you, I will pray to the Awl'Fire for your spark. I hope to see you again someday."

Softly, Orem'Nubis gripped the cub and took to the cover of the forest as swiftly and silently as she arrived, slipping back into the tightly grouped pines and out of sight.

Li'Illnok, still shaken by what transpired, walked over to a small spring of water and used his paws to clean the blood from his fur, and even though the stains were washed clean, the one on his heart remained as a reminder of the events on that dreadful night.

As the hours passed and he found a comfortable cool spot in the grass next to the seasons offerings. His mind raced with conflicted thoughts and emotions. His responsibility as an Elden felt heavier than ever, and he knew that the next day would bring new challenges and struggles. Despite his weariness, he wrestled with his thoughts until the morning came.

Chapter 3
Clover

"Finnick, Finnick! Where are you, rabbit?"

Orem'Nubis trembled with urgency as she darted through the dense undergrowth of the mystical Illnok forest. Her heart raced as she called out for her trusted friend, the weight of the task given to her by Li'Illnok bearing down on her.

The midnight moon spilled its ethereal light over the hills, casting ghostly shadows on her fur.

As her thoughts raced about the mysterious cub's destiny, she remained committed to following Li'Illnok's guidance. The cub's unusual appearance hinted at the possibility of an affliction, and she couldn't help but wonder what it meant. Among the many options she considered, one was alarming—the cub belonged to the void. Born out of horrific circumstances. It was highly plausible. If this were indeed the true nature of the cub, she realized he might become something unspeakable.

"My goodness! What is all the fuss about, Orem'Nubis? I'm here! What is it?! What could be so important that you'd rouse an old rabbit this night?" Finnick's frustration filled the air, his giant ears and tiny head emerging from one of the many tunnels in the clover field.

"Ahh! There you are dear friend. Listen to me and keep quiet." Orem'Nubis stopped and ducked low beneath a patch of tall thistle weed. "Did anything see you arrive?" She questioned. Finnick chuckled as he stuffed his mouth with dew-covered clover.

"Don't you know who I am, dear wolf? I can go anywhere without the slightest blade of grass tearing." Finnick plopped down in the clover, his fat rear end popped a small twig, letting out a crisp crack.

"Okay… Just take a second, Orem'Nubis. You need to catch your breath before you pass out. I have all the time in the night to hear you out. Especially when I'm surrounded by these massive tufts of Illnok clover!" He plucked one from the ground.

"Look at this one; it's got four leaves! You know what that means, my lady Wolf? I'm getting lucky!"

Orem'Nubis sighed, grateful for Finnick's light-hearted demeanor. "Yes. Okay. Let me relax for a moment, and then I'll tell—" "by the feathers of a goose! What in the Mud is this, Orem'Nubis? Ha! There's a cub over here!" Finnick's excited exclamation interrupted her as he stumbled upon her secret.

"Oh my! Orem'Nubis, his fur is darker than a mole's hole. Look at this! It's magnificent!" Finnick's eyes sparkled with wonder, but then a realization washed over him, and his ears drooped. "Wait, a minute — This is why you summoned me here, isn't it?"

She was silent. Her eyes glistened with moonlight through the trees. "Yes, Finnick my old friend. This is why I have called you out here. This cub desperately needs our help; take him and—" "And what Orem'Nubis?" He interrupted, "What am I to do? Would you have me labeled as a cub thief again? I have spent a great deal of time changing the hearts and minds of the Illnok wolves since the last disruption I caused! Even worse, what if he gets hungry and tries to… you know… I could never live with myself if that were to happen…" Finnick's voice wavered, his concern evident in his trembling whiskers.

Orem'Nubis could feel the peril in the request she laid on his tiny back. Although a truce between the rabbits and the Illnok wolves had been established long ago, this cub would be of feral mind if not given a chance to learn the Illnok ways and traditions. Finnick's life and the reputation of not only him, but the warren in its entirety, would be in danger. She tried her best to break his line of thinking. "Stop jumping to conclusions Finnick. The cub doesn't even have teeth in his head yet. Just listen to me," Orem'Nubis implored, her eyes filled with desperation and urgency.

"Elden Sayer Li'Illnok summoned me to the great hall a few hours ago. He pulled this little cub from a hidden crevice and entrusted me with getting him out from the Illnok interior." She explained.

"Ha! Then this is not just a regular cub then! Probably illegitimate, that means we have something in common, but my fair wolf maiden, I am no smuggler! I can barely carry my weight around." Finnick dropped the tufts of clover he crammed into his mouth, his eyes wide with surprise. He hopped closer to get a better look at the cubs mouth just to make sure Orem'Nubis wasn't lying about the teeth.

"I didn't know my father either, little one." He said, captivated by the look of the cub's fur. "Alright then love, give it to me straight. Who's the father? One of the Eldens? Ha, Li'Illnok is too old. His old hips would lock up, leaving him in cramps and embarrassment—"

"Finnick." Orem'Nubis tried to interrupt.

"Oh, I see! Elden Seph'Ulinok, I hear he is a rather handsome wolf. Good bloodline, my boy—" Finnick nudged the cub's head.

"Finnick!" Orem'Nubis cut through his meddlesome thoughts with an intense voice. Her eyes burned with a white, iridescent glow. Finnick's ears fell downside his head. He could tell that she was serious. "My apologies love, It's Just my way of dealing with stress that's all."

Orem'Nubis's eyes regained their bluish color.

"I have known you for quite some time now wolf maiden, and I highly respect you and your abilities as a tepid mind. Whatever you ask of me, I will do it if you think it best." He stood back on his hind legs like a soldier awaiting his orders.

She smiled at him, "I'm sorry Finnick, but I feel in my heart that there's something more to this cub than even Li'Illnok or myself could know. I need you to take him away from the Illnok lands. Li'Illnok has asked me to do it, but my tepid mind tells me… that you must have a role to play. No matter how dangerous it may be for us." His heart sank with the inevitability of things to come. Orem'Nubis was often right about her predictions. Even more so than the others with the same affliction.

"Who does this cub belong to?" Finnick asked with a heightened sense of curiosity.

"…I didn't ask Finnick, but I didn't need to…and I don't think you need to, either." She said. Both of them stared blankly into the cubs black fur. It was like staring into the blackness of a moonless night sky.

As Finnick watched the cub wriggle and yawn, he couldn't help but blurt out, "The great bastard—"

Orem'Nubis shot him a piercing look, Finnick quickly corrected himself.

"Apologies, love. The cub has such an interesting look about him. I can't fathom how an Illnok wolf could banish him from such a place of safety and security." The more Finnick thought about it, the madder it made him.

"Yes, Finnick, I agree. But it's better for all of us if that secret remains hidden. I have my suspicions, just as assuredly you will have your own." Her voice trembled, the weight of the situation pressed down on her. Finnick remained silent. Deep down, he knew who the cub belonged to, but he chose not to say anything, granting Orem'Nubis the peace of mind she needed.

"Okay… But where should I take the runt?" Finnick asked, his brow furrowed in concern. "There aren't very many safe places to hide a wolf cub without something noticing."

Her expression grew anxious as she tried to think of a solution. Her mind raced to untangle the perilous web they found themselves caught in. The cub's fate and the fragile balance of the Illnok forest rested on their shoulders, and the stakes were never higher.

"What about the lands south? Past the Outlands. I'm sure there is a nice den of wolves that would take him in?" She questioned. He took a deep breath while he Searched for hope in the question.

"There hasn't been a forest safe enough for even a rabbit in quite some time. The humans used their metal machines to flatten the earth, so they could bury their dead by the bushel while burning as many in piles. And besides," He added, with a hint of exasperation, "How do you expect me, a plump rabbit with half as much muscle in my legs as there is clover in my gut, to carry this cub all the way through the Outlands to the south?"

Finnick rose and sat back on his haunches, exposing his massive round belly, stained green and brown from how it dragged along the ground as he moved.

"Listen to me now, Finnick! You listen well! She sternly interrupted him. Her eyes burned with an intense fire, and pointed to the full moon in the sky, the sign of a great turning.

Finnick's nervous laugh attempted to ease the tension, but the gravity of the situation was inescapable.

"Finnick, I beg you. I know I'm asking a lot, but I have faith that you'll figure it out…."

A rustling broke the silence of the night in the trees near to where they were.

"I have to go back."

As Orem'Nubis's words hung in the air, Finnick understood the magnitude of the task he was being asked to undertake. The fate of the cub and perhaps the delicate balance of their worlds rested on his shoulders, and he couldn't help but feel a mix of trepidation and determination.

"Keep the cub hidden; take him somewhere until you figure things out. I know you will find a way, Finnick. You must," Orem'Nubis implored, her eyes wide in the moonlight.

After a brief, heavy silence, she took a deep breath and cast one last lingering look at the young cub.

"Maybe I will meet you again someday, little friend. Until then."

Finnick watched as she disappeared into the shadowy embrace of the forest. He felt his life turn upside down; the freedom to roam anywhere, anytime, was now a distant memory. How to decide what to do with such precious contraband was a dilemma he would have to quickly solve. Soon, daylight would creep in, and the ravenous creatures that lived in the Border woods would awaken.

As the weight of responsibility settled on Finnick's shoulders, he realized that to carry the weight of the young cub would be considerably lighter than guilt if he left him behind on such a cold, unforgiving night.

So, he swallowed what he could of the sweetest clover within reach, and then, with determination and courage in his heart, he gently gripped the fur around the cub's neck in his tiny mouth and carried him down into his tunnel.

Finnick embarked on his treacherous journey, fueled by a fierce desire to protect the innocent life entrusted to him. The world outside the Illnok forests was full of unknown dangers, yet he knew of a wolf with strength and resilience to face whatever challenges lay ahead.

"Eurthrem!" Finnick exclaimed to himself, a glimmer of hope lighting up his eyes. "She's your best option, little cub. That's where I'm taking you, too sweet Eurthrem."

Chapter 4
Eurthrem

Finnick was no stranger to the treacherous terrain from the Border woods of the Illnok to the Outlands. Over the years, meticulously he dug tunnels connecting all his most cherished locations, making it easy for him to travel between them. And Eurthrem, an old mother wolf, held a special place on that list.

Many years ago, Eurthrem made her way into the Outlands through a small wildlife ranch beyond the Rimwoods. A portion of the Outlands that bordered the human cities. Man's world was feeling the total weight of the Rasping fever. Though showing signs of decline, big cities still pulsed with life, and quarantine measures were just beginning to take hold. It muted the once-bustling streets and buildings. The distant planes and the roar of traffic could still be heard. But Eurthrem saw the writing on the wall and freed herself from human oppression and fled the preserve with her pack.

When she slipped past the perimeter fence, Eurthrem allowed herself a fleeting moment of freedom. But the respite was short-lived, for although she was beyond the reach of human hands, she soon fell prey to the merciless grip of hunger, loneliness, and the malice of the Fracture.

She often wondered if staying on the preserve would have been a better choice—confined to a small, unkempt enclosure and torn from her family of cubs. At least there, she was fed, and although abused, paraded in front of humans and forced to give birth several times. She knew her life held value.

Eurthrem became weak and malnourished in the Outlands, her existence a mere shell of her former self. She heavily relied on the kindness of others for sustenance, her once-mighty frame reduced to a frail semblance of what she once was. The meaning of life vanished as her body withered away, a shadow of its former glory.

As Finnick arrived at her derelict den, he sent a greeting through the ether, hoping it would reach her still-beating heart. Whether he would feel the warmth in her reply was always a gamble.

"Eurthrem, wake up. I know it's early, but I need to speak with you. It's incredibly urgent," He called to her heart as he hopped out into the open.

The tunnel he dug for himself some time ago let him out under an old, decayed birch trunk. The further he stretched his tunnels underneath the Outlands, the denser dirt became. This was the reason Eurthrem's den was the final stop in his long and twisting tunnel.

Finally, she emerged from her shelter, stiff-legged and squinting as the sun's first light pricked and poked at her tired eyes.

"Hello there, Eurthrem. It's been a while. I'm sorry I haven't been to see you sooner. I hope you're doing well?" He greeted her.

"Oh, Finnick, you know how hard it is to get my old bones moving. Please tell me you have something of value for me, and I'm not just standing here half asleep for nothing." Her fur, choked with bits and pieces of old foam from a ripped car seat where she slept, fell from her like snow. She stared at him with such disdain that he almost left; only to return when she was in a better mood.

"…I will come back if you would like?" He reluctantly offered. She smiled and chuckled.

"I'm only joking with you. Lighten up. It's good to see you again. I have been so worried about you." Relief swept over him; he didn't want to carry the cub anymore, his jaw felt dislocated and sore as he laughed sarcastically.

"Come over here with me. I have something to show you. But before I do, I need you to stay calm. Don't make it a big deal. It's hard to tell if the Border wolves are watching; they must never know what I have for you." Finnick said excitedly.

She agreed and sauntered behind him. He moved quickly from side to side, as he scanned for watchers and sniffed at the air. His attempt at being covert made Eurthrem smile.

He stopped and stretched his head into a hole in the side of the old birch trunk. His little mouth tugged at something inside.

"Finnick, what do you have in there? Eurthrem eagerly awaited. Her ears perked up, and her eyes widened with anticipation. She sensed the gravity of the situation. Finnick turned and moved out of the way to reveal a black furry blob he dragged into the dirt. Eurthrem exclaimed,

"Finnick! You must bring him inside before he's seen! It's not safe for him. You know the outland animals are not as forgiving as those in your home territory!"

As Finnick attempted to pick up the cub, Eurthrem stepped back, her concern for the tiny creature clear. Finnick struggled under the cub's weight, and his small jaw and neck ached.

"Go inside, rabbit. I will carry him." Eurthrem's irritation was apparent.

As Finnick entered her shelter, Eurthrem followed, her expression disapproving. "Please tell me no one saw your fat rear end trundling through the forest with this cub in your mouth?" she asked incredulously. Finnick felt insulted that she questioned his abilities.

"Bite your spotted tongue, miss. You know me, don't you? Of course they did not see me! I'm a master at hiding in the bushes." He said.

"You would have to be with that fat end of yours." She interjected. Finnick playfully scowled as he continued. "Sneaking from tree to tree, lurking in the shadows, and anything else to do with not being seen…" he fell silent for a moment. "…I brought him through my tunnels all the way…"

Eurthrem smiled. "Finnick, I don't see how you by yourself, could fit in those tunnels, let alone carrying a cub. I'm very impressed by you rabbit."

"That's hilarious, Eurthrem," He looked down at his plump belly with pride.

"Don't take offense, rabbit. In this place, it's hard to imagine having enough food to have a belly like yours."

She leaned down to nudge the little cub with her nose to see if he was okay.

"It's hard to believe a little cub like this could make it so far away from his mother wolf without her noticing. Where did you find him, Finnick? And why would you bring him here?" Eurthrem asked as she curled him up close to her breast to see if he could nurse from her. She sensed there could be more to the story, but didn't press it.

"An old friend named Orem'Nubis gave me this cub. She is… she possesses a Tepid Mind" Finnick trembled as he revealed the emotional weight of the situation. His eyes glistened as he recounted the story.

She looked at him in confusion. Most of her life was spent in captivity with a group of animals. Many of them were too broken to speak. Most didn't even know how to speak with their heart and mind. When it came to wolf lore and lineage, she knew very little, aside from what she learned from the Outland wolves and Finnick. "What does it mean to have a Tepid Mind?" she questioned. Her voice was tinged with curiosity.

Finnick could tell he started her mind down a path that would take too long to venture if he allowed it. "It means she sees signs in nature that point to the future. The explanation is complex and beside the point; she brought this cub to me and told me I needed to take him away from the Alpha Mountain, out of the Illnok lands. She said that the one assigned to do it could not carry out the death sentence.

Eurthrem sighed as she tried to settle and let the cub nurse.

"I have my suspicions about who this little one belongs to, but it doesn't matter. What matters is what my friend Orem'Nubis read on the moon the night of this cub's birth; a full moon."

Her voice was heavy with emotion that betrayed her concern for the little one's future.

As Finnick explained to Eurthrem, the little cub latched on and nursed. Finnick was relieved.

"And What importance does that hold?" she asked.

"It's a sign of a significant turning point when things begin anew," He replied, her mind filled with his hope and apprehension.

The three sat in silence as the little cub took what he could from Eurthrem.

"I have little to offer you, little cub. But what little I have is yours," Eurthrem whispered softly.

Weeks passed. Finnick noticed more changes in her appearance. She lost more hair, and her ribs were even more visible. The conditions in the Outlands were harsh, like Eurthrem, they were rapidly deteriorating. Food was scarce, and what little was found was being fought over by the Fracture's most robust and most aggressive wolves.

"Finnick, what are we going to do with this young cub? I will do everything I can for as long as possible, but without food, I cannot nurse him for much longer." It filled her heart with worry, her maternal instincts taking over. He watched in awe as the cub drifted off to sleep.

"We will figure something out, Eurthrem. We will protect and care for this cub and together, we will ensure his survival." His voice was firm, fueled by the desire to safeguard.

"As soon as possible, I will go into the Illnok lands to find food for you. After that, I'll find somewhere north of here, somewhere safer to go. Somewhere far from the Outlands. I have a place in mind but haven't been there for some time. I'm unsure if it's still safe." Finnick thought hard, despite his newfound fear of endangering his new extended family. It was a challenge to reassure Eurthrem when he was equally terrified.

Months passed, and Eurthrem displayed further hints of malnutrition. Finnick still could not find a solution for a new place to stay or a stable food source to keep them all fed. It amazed them both that she lasted as long as she had, nursing the cub with barely any food. He did everything he could to help, but the nuts, herbs, vegetables, and mushrooms he gathered did not support a nursing mother. Her body needed fresh meat, which Finnick was not physically capable of providing.

They discussed seeking help from another wolf in the area but agreed it was too risky. Nobody could be trusted. Unlike the wolves in the Illnok territory, wolves in the Outlands lacked control over their hunger. With nothing else for them to consume, it consumed them, turning most of them ravenous and feral. A defenseless cub, a well-fed rabbit, and a dying wolf mother would make a feast for several feral.

Not only was the threat of being eaten looming over them, but The Fracture also wasn't prejudiced about recruitment. Finnick would be eaten, Eurthrem would reach a worse end, and as for the cub, if he wasn't made into a meal as well, his existence would surely take a dark turn.

Eurthrem held on by a thread, she ate as much as she could of the foraged items Finnick stockpiled in the shelter and tried to stay positive.

The cub had grown; he became stronger with every day. His eyes were open, the same obsidian black as his coat. Eurthrem explained to Finnick that a cub's eyes were often blue when they first opened but would change with age. She could not explain why he looked the way he did. Finnick had his assumptions just as Orem'Nubis did in the beginning.

*

Late one afternoon, when the cub was around three months old, Finnick arrived with a massive, sweet potato stuck on his large two front teeth. The sunlight filtered through the trees and illuminated the deep orange hue of the potato, casting a warm glow on the rabbit's face. His eyes twinkled with excitement; a stark contrast to the weariness that had been etched on his face for weeks.

"Look what I found, Eurthrem!" He exclaimed; his mind muffled by excitement. "I know it's not meat, but it's full of nutrients that could help you regain strength."

"Eurthrem!" Finnick called out, the excitement in his heart unmistakable.

"I found your favorite Eurthrem?" He didn't see her in the usual spot, only the cub lying on top of a bed of dried grass she bundled up inside the shelter. He turned and hopped around, searching for her, only to find her lying in the dirt about a reasonable distance away from him.

"Eurthrem!" concern gripped his heart. "What's wrong?! Are you hurt?" He tried his hardest to lift her head with his, but it was too heavy. Finally, after a few tense moments, she stirred.

"Ugh... I must've lost my balance on the way back in. I went to get a drink of water from the stream, and now I'm here. That's all I can remember." She expressed weakly.

Finnick worried, he didn't know how long she had been out there, but he knew it was long enough to draw the attention of the Unclean.

"I'm okay now," Eurthrem reassured him, though her body and mind wavered.

She got up and sluggishly walked back inside the shelter with Finnick's assistance. Above them, on the broken power pole, sat two of the Unclean that watched and waited. Eurthrem saw them, and her heart sank. She tried to ignore it, but she knew why they were there.

"Ahhh, I see you brought a sweet potato! That's my favorite!" she exclaimed as she tried to mask her unease. She took her time to savor every bit, chewing slowly with the few teeth she had left in her mouth. She could sense her time was close.

Finnick only witnessed this one instance of her losing consciousness, but it happened several times daily.

"Finnick, it's time to name this cub, I think. We have been so caught up in keeping him safe we forgot!"

"I wouldn't say we forgot. Maybe we've been scared to," Finnick confessed. "It would make it much more difficult to lose him if he had a name."

"That seems right, Finnick. I am terrified of losing him."

"Me too, lass, me too."

"Name him, Finnick. I won't get the chance to be his mother, but you, you will be his father."

Finnick looked at her, his ears gently fell. She said what they both knew. There was no way to hide from what was coming.

"You must pick something noble." She urged. Finnick thought briefly about the names he heard over the years, but something didn't feel right.

"The only names I can think of are names for rabbits, and rabbit names are not fitting for a wolf, Eurthrem," He expressed thoughtfully.

She understood the logic and nodded in agreement.

"Wait, I have an idea!" He exclaimed. Eurthrem looked at him with curiosity and concern.

"What were the names of your cubs you lost?"

She was taken aback by the question. Finnick had yet to learn loss on the scale she experienced. It opened a gate to a whirlwind of emotions, and Finnick could tell he crossed a line. But he could see the beauty in honoring her lost cubs by giving their names to this young one they were fighting to protect.

Eurthrem's eyes filled with tears as she remembered the names of her lost cubs, the memories flooding back, both painful and bittersweet. The sun split through the trees and cast shadows dancing on the dirt as she whimpered. Eurthrem sensed Finnick's distress and reassured him,

"I'm sorry, Finnick. I didn't mean to upset you." She smiled through her tears, her eyes glistened in the faded light.

"My love, you are not making me cry."

He moved closer beside her, offering warmth and comfort.

"There have been a few losses in life, Finnick. Great losses, difficult ones. But I know when my fire is gone on this earth, it will burn again when I'm with them. These last winters without them have been the hardest time of my life, but you, Finnick, are the greatest friend I have ever had. Selfless and sacrificing, two things I thought were impossible in a rabbit."

Finnick smiled through his tears, touched by her words.

"You didn't have to help this cub, or me either. We would both be dead if it weren't for you and your sacrifices for us."

He looked at the cub and felt a swell of pride. He knew everything he didn't go unnoticed, but feeling her thoughts about him was nice.

The three of them were silent, curled up next to each other as evening turned to night.

"His name is Morgrim," Finnick whispered, like it always belonged to the cub; he simply introduced him.

"To a rabbit, it means sacrifice."

Eurthrem was captivated by the name instantly but pretended to hate it. "To an old wolf, it's terrible…"

For a moment, Finnick didn't know how to react. He looked up at Eurthrem with furrowed brows, but she laughed, putting him at ease.

"It's perfect, Finnick."

*

As the night wore on, Finnick shared many colorful stories of his travels throughout the land, while Eurthrem fed Morgrim as best she could. The hour was late when the three of them finally succumbed to sleep, the cold air swirling around them, unable to penetrate their warm huddle. Curled closely together on top of a thick bedding of dry grass and leaves, they found solace in their makeshift family.

Finnick never had a family of his own. Of course, he had brothers and sisters, But different from this. A rabbit never stays too long in one place, always on the move. But being with Eurthrem and now Morgrim, he could see the appeal. The bond they shared was something he never experienced before - a connection built on love, trust, and the unwavering determination to protect one another. In their small, fragile world, they forged an unbreakable bond that would carry them through even the darkest times.

*

As the morning came and the sun rose. Light squeezed through the little cracks in the rusted metal, Finnick resolved to find something more substantial for Eurthrem to eat besides sweet potatoes. Morgrim was still not awake, so Finnick tried to leave without stirring him.

"Eurthrem, I'm leaving now, but I'll be back later in the afternoon," he whispered quietly, not wanting to startle her.

"Eurthrem?" Finnick nudged her with his nose. He noticed she felt very different from the night before.

"Oh, no, Eurthrem..." He cried as Morgrim stirred and tried to feed from her lifeless body.

"Stop it, Pup!" He forcefully batted at him. Sadness was quickly overtaken by Finnick's new responsibility for Morgrim. The cub was hungry and ready for meat.

Outside, the Unclean who'd been perched above on the wires of an old electrical pole was now joined by many others closer to the ground, signaling to other animals that something was dead. Finnick understood this was the natural order for scavengers in the Outlands, but it didn't sit right with him. Crippled with emotion, he tried to devise an escape plan, too small to carry Eurthrem out and not strong enough to break the soil below to bury her. The situation became dire.

Morgrim was now larger than Finnick, which presented a problem. To keep the cub safe, they ventured out only a few times, and Morgrim had never been inside the tunnel under the birch log. An escape under duress was never planned.

In a panic, Finnick grabbed a stick and broke it off to Morgrim's height; a crude measurement but it would have to do. He was too scared to take Morgrim with him, fearing the cub would run off after the Unclean and not return on his own. He took the stick to the tunnel and held it up to the entrance with his mouth. It was too long to fit. Finnick's stomach churned in knots.

How could we have been so stupid? He thought.

Finnick returned to the den and watched as more of the Unclean flocked to the area around the shelter. Inside, he found Morgrim bouncing around, toying with sticks.

What in the ages am I going to do? Suddenly, something in the air changed, thick with a heavy musk and a scent that invoked a healthy anxiousness within him.

The Unclean that perched above the den and on the pole flew away, squawking and beating their wings in fear.

Finnick saw a pack of massive wolves coming up the footpath to the den through the tattered metal flanking on the shelter's right side.

Finnick had never seen them before this close. Massive, brutish, and headed straight for him and Morgrim.

He grabbed a small metal scrap and wedged it between the side of the shelter's entrance and a door piece. Creating a makeshift barricade, he knew, wouldn't hold them back.

"Eurthrem, is it?" The largest one in the center of the pack bellowed. "We just met your neighbor down the path here. We don't get around to these parts often. Figured we'd come and pay our respects to an old wolf mother."

The four stood just feet from the shelter, where Finnick desperately tried to keep Morgrim quiet.

"Judging by the fanfare that just took flight, I may be a little late to meet you."

The hulk in the center joked. All four of the wolves laughed with a display of callous disregard for the solemnity of a flame being returned to the Awl'Fire.

"Ack'Reus, let's see what's inside, shall we? I doubt anything of importance, but the situation is far too dire here now to let anything go to waste."

Finnick's heart raced as he urged Morgrim to dig at the back of the shelter.

"Dig, Morgrim, dig!" He begged. To his surprise, the young cub imitated him, his sharp claws quickly tore through the dried dirt. They created an opening just large enough for them both to squeeze through before the giant wolves violently breached the shelter.

"Alpha, the mother wolf has passed," Ack'Reus reported.

"As if we didn't notice the stench?" One of the other wolves sarcastically retorted.

"Leave her for the Unclean. There's not enough meat here to feed even the smallest of wolves,"

The largest wolf conveyed dismissively as he walked away.

His name was Oct'Tulommon, A dire wolf who proclaimed himself the Alpha of the Outlands and the leader of the Fractured wolves. His taste for violence and malice was known throughout, with a massive neck adorned with a broken chain and a lock. He was the greatest evil any wolf had known in the Outlands.

"Wait!" One of the other wolves named Apollo halted them. "There's another scent here, one I'm all too familiar with. Rabbit!" His nose twitched as he drew in the scent from the den.

Ha'Kan appeared from the backside of the shelter. Oct'Tulommon stared at him expectantly and waited for him to speak.

"There's a hole in the back. Something dug its way out before we entered, Oct'Tulommon," He reported apprehensively, panting.

"I'd wager my hide. It's a fat rabbit, Alpha." Ack'Reus added. The thought of his teeth tensed, biting harder and harder into the flesh of a plump rabbit, unleashed Ack'Reus's feral side, followed by Apollo. They couldn't control the hungry wolf within themselves. It was impossible.

"Where are you, fat rabbit? Why don't you come and meet us?" Apollo's mind echoed in the Ether.

Underneath the birch trunk, Finnick pushed Morgrim deeper into the tunnel. By sheer luck, he coaxed the cub into the hole, and with even more luck, he realized he wasn't that great at measuring. Morgrim yapped at him playfully.

"There!" Oct'Tulommon spotted Finnick beneath the log. He watched as he sank ever so slowly into the darkness of the tight tunnel. Everyone except Oct'Tulommon charged for him. They tried to force their way far enough to reach their prey. But as all three wolves clamored for a better position to dig, they inadvertently made it even more of a challenge to catch their prey.

Oct'Tulommon stepped forward and urged them to dig faster, but it was useless. They lost their composure to the hungry wolf inside.

Finnick pushed Morgrim as hard as he could, forcing him further and further as the tunnel behind them opened up, filled with dust and sunlight from above.

"Please, Morgrim, run!" Finnick pleaded.

Further back in the tunnel, the only light source became blocked by another rabbit.

"Finnick! What's going on!?"

He tried to respond, but he was being pelted by clods of heavy dirt as he scrambled to put distance between himself and the flurry of sharp teeth and claws behind. He was wedged.

Morgrim barreled in from one of the meandering tunnels that led off in another direction. He playfully stopped, lowered his head to the dirt, and stalked the new rabbit.

"It's a wolf cub!" the other rabbit exclaimed. Fear swelled in both their hearts.

"Morgrim! No! Stay!" He tried to force the words into Morgrim's young mind, but he was still too new and had not yet learned to wield the power of the Awl'Fire.

"Finnick, what is this ugly beast doing in our tunnels?!" the other rabbit asked as it backed away slowly.

"Hahaha! I'm so sorry brother; I should have told you sooner about him!" Finnick replied as the claws inched closer and closer to him while he remained wedged between the roots and the dirt. "I don't think he will hurt you!?" Finnick guessed reluctantly; terrified something terrible was about to happen, either to him or his fellow rabbit further up the tunnel.

"Please, Morgrim!" He whispered into the cub's heart. Morgrim's head tilted as he looked back at Finnick. The other rabbit noticed the distraction and seized the opportunity to flee in the opposite direction, screeching for his life. In an instant, Morgrim snapped his head back and was gone.

"NO!" Finnick cried out as he finally freed himself from certain death. As he rounded turn after turn, all he could see were claw marks in the dirt and broken tree roots. In the distance, he heard barking, and a dying rabbit's screeching. Finnick's heart sank. His greatest fear came to fruition.

As he rounded the last turn leading into the Illnok Rabbits' central warren, he could hear the screeching of multiple rabbits and the sound of their tiny feet beating against the ground as they scattered.

"Morgrim! What have you done?" Finnick was terrified of what his decision caused. But as he made his way into the light, he found Morgrim had pinned the rabbit to the wall while he licked its fur and wagged his tail vigorously.

It overwhelmed Finnick with a sense of relief to see Morgrim's playful excitement.

"Chased by a wolf in my own tunnels! Ha never thought I'd see the day. Scared me almost to death." The rabbit laughed nervously.

*

It wasn't until a few hours after Finnick and Morgrim disappeared that Oct'Tulommon's battle wolves stopped digging. The worms in the fresh dirt they scattered about brought a parade of the Unclean. They pecked the ground and fought over even the skinniest of them.

"I heard a wolf cub bark from deep inside that tunnel, Oct'Tulommon." Ha'Kan panted. "What do you suppose Eurthrem was doing with a rabbit and a cub?"

Oct'Tulommon walked into the den where Eurthrem died. In the corner, there was a modest stash of sweet potatoes, clover and dried grass. He and the others were perplexed. In the distance, perched on the limb of a dead oak tree, Oct'Tulommon spotted a rather large falcon.

"I can't be too sure what she was doing here, but I'm sure he knows," Oct'Tulommon thought.

The other wolves turned to him, curious to see whom he was referring to. As the dust settled, the wolves climbed out of the crater they dug underneath the log in their failed attempt to catch Finnick.

They gathered beside Oct'Tulommon as he motioned for the falcon to come over.

"Peregrine! What brings you here today? I thought all the higher bloodlines left these parts long ago?" Oct'Tulommon asked.

"I've only come to see what all the fuss was about, same as the lot of you wolves, I suppose," the peregrine replied with a heavy condescension. He eyed the ragged body of Eurthrem, partially buried underneath the rubble the wolves carelessly piled on top of her.

"It is curious why a rabbit would burrow with a wolf, though."

The wolves stood behind Oct'Tulommon and tried to keep their teeth out of the bird's feathers. Of course, they were much larger than him, but couldn't kill anything unless Oct'Tulommon allowed them to.

The peregrine paused to place the stench that hit his beak. It was foul, much worse than the dead wolf and the rotting vegetables in the corner. It was Ha'Kan.

"Your leg wound is furious with you. I would be more worried than you seem to be, wolf. I could smell the foul sickness in your blood from those branches. It's disgusting," the peregrine poked haughtily. Ha'Kan tried his best to stay composed as Oct'Tulommon laughed.

"Yes, he is a little worse for wear; it's obvious. But he's going to pull through... we think... Can you shed some light on why a rabbit was visiting this wolf?" Oct'Tulommon impatiently waited for his reply.

The peregrine hopped down from the wood and stood atop Eurthrem's body. "The rabbit you almost caught fleeing was Finnick. I've watched him for quite some time, popping his fat head out of his tunnels around here and elsewhere, gathering food, and popping right back in. I wondered where he was going with all the foraged goods. Now I know he was coming here for her. Sweet mother Eurthrem." Oct'Tulommon looked at him and laughed.

"Ha! Peregrine, I think you may be mistaken. She was no mother; she was too old." He said as he nudged her lifeless corpse with his massive paw.

"Listen to me, you great fool! I know more about the happenings in your wasteland than you or these wolves you surround yourself with." The peregrine was annoyed.

"She only lost her cubs a short time ago. She was feeding a wolf cub! One from the Illnok lands, brought to her by that fat, mischievous rabbit, Finnick."

Oct'Tulommon snarled.

"Why am I hearing about this from a bird? All of you are useless feral hounds! All of you!"

The peregrine laughed as he picked through the cache of rotting vegetables. A tiny mouse poked its little head out just long enough for him to grab it and pull its head clean off, his talons gripped around its belly.

Oct'Tulommon and his wolves watched the mouse's headless body wriggle underneath the peregrine's foot.

"That's not all, Oct'Tulommon. That wolf pup your team of bumbling fools let best you. I watched as he was carried to the Border woods from the Alpha's Mountain." The peregrine smirked..

For the other wolves, the information meant nothing to them. But the significance of the cub's lineage was not lost on Oct'Tulommon, and his anger was barely concealed as he let out a bitter laugh.

"What difference does that make, Oct'Tulommon?" Ack'Reus inquired.

"Nothing to a dirty interloper like you, wolf," Oct'Tulommon retorted.

"You couldn't possibly comprehend the implications!"

He clarified that, for whatever reason, that wolf cub was his.

"If I were you, I would lose this lot. You may be better off in the long run," the peregrine advised as he flew away. The mouse gripped tightly in his talons.

*

In the weeks that followed Eurthrem's death, Morgrim's stomach matured, and he no longer needed her milk. He hunted grubs and other insects he discovered within the safe confines of the rabbit tunnels.

To keep Morgrim satiated, Finnick enlisted the help of his brothers to supply a steady stream of vegetables and fruits, as what he could gather on his own was never enough.

As time passed, Finnick regaled Morgrim with stories of the old ways and showed hunting techniques they observed being used by the Illnok wolves He was quick and displayed an impressive understanding of complex concepts for his age.

Finnick realized Morgrim was coming into his own when he was too large for the tunnels. With a heavy heart, he knew it wouldn't be long before it was time for Morgrim to venture out on his own. Over two winters, Finnick Took him above ground. He allowed him more freedom to venture further and further away. Never did he stay in one place for too long.

His sharp intellect allowed him to navigate the treacherous landscape and avoid confrontation with Oct'Tulommon. His life in the Outlands became a delicate balance of survival and adaptation, requiring cunning and agility.

The Fracture's reign of terror left a trail of destruction in their wake. They claimed the very essence of life from the creatures they encountered, leaving nothing but despair and desolation.

At the heart of the Fracture, Oct'Tulommon sat on his throne of brutality, a fearsome beast covered in scars and battle wounds. The rusted metal chain and padlock around his neck were a testament to his ferocity and dominance. His den, perched atop an abandoned oil derrick, housed a macabre collection of skulls belonging to the various creatures he hunted. Among these, the seven human skulls were his most prized possessions, a chilling reminder of the fate that awaited any human who dared to cross his path.

Outland creatures who were unfortunate enough to cross paths with humans, often traded their knowledge of their encounters for scraps of meat and favor with the ruthless Alpha Oct'Tulommon.

They told stories of their captivity in the clutches of humans and recounted stories of their cruelty. They described a world where animals suffered unspeakable horrors at the hands of their human tormentors. It fueled the anger that was already in his darkened heart.

Part II: The World of Man

Chapter 5
Fern Gully

"So, let me get this straight, Dad." Young Evan Grenlow exclaimed as he struggled to grasp the concept. "The whole time, he—" "Neo," his father Lennon interrupted.

"Okay, sorry, the whole time Neo was plugged into a computer simulation waiting to be picked like corn and used as a battery? By robots, they created themselves?" Evan questioned as he reached for a handhold on the peat moss-covered embankment, his father and their loyal Labrador, Tucker, waited at the top.

"That's insane!" He declared as he finally found a firm footing. Lennon wrapped an arm around him as they both laughed heartily.

"Not only that, but Morpheus, played by Laurence Fishburne, believed Neo was, "The One" whose destiny was to free humanity from the Matrix and defeat the machines." Lennon said, he waved a pointed finger in the air.

"That is…the stupidest thing I have ever heard!" Evan Laughed. Lennon pushed him and punched his arm at the same time.

"The movie was an experience Evan, I'm telling you! It was the greatest thing up until that point I had ever seen."

As they continued their hike; Lennon reveled in the opportunity to share the plot of one of his all-time favorite film trilogies with Evan. He described the memorable action sequences, such as the gravity-defying bullet-time effects and the iconic scene where Neo had to choose between the red and blue pills, symbolizing his decision to face the harsh reality or remain in blissful ignorance.

A week and a half had gone by since the trio departed from their home in New Ambridge, a provisional settlement at the southern fringe of Old Ambridge. Renowned as one of the most densely populated metropolitan areas in the United States.

When a wave of Rasping Fever began claiming lives once more in their area, Lennon had to decide; stay and risk illness while the community faced lockdown, meal rationing and mandatory wellness checks conducted by the remnants of the C.D.C. Or leave and employ his survivalist skills to safeguard his best befriend and his remaining son.

The trio fended for themselves since Anne; Evan's mother, and Corbin, his younger brother, fell victim to the Rasping Fever during the first quarantine five years earlier. It was a difficult period. Most of the people they knew became ill and died.

Tragically, the second and third waves claimed even more lives. Despite their immense loss, Lennon and Evan persevered. They managed to keep themselves alive and contributed to the New Ambridge community.

As circumstances declined. Lennon planned to abandon the urban areas and retreat with Evan to his childhood home. A sprawling 650-acre homesteader's paradise, nestled against the verdant expanse he and his brothers lovingly dubbed "Fern Gully."

"So, how much further before we get there? I feel like we're making good time?" Evan's curiosity was piqued as they stopped to make camp for the evening. It had been four long days since they left their temporary home in New Ambridge and headed east. He wasn't tired or sad about leaving. Instead, he felt a surge of excitement for the adventure and the opportunity to experience everything his father loved to do as a young boy, like camping, fishing, hunting, and hiking.

Lennon pulled a map from the backpack's side pocket; studied it for a moment, and then handed it over to Evan.

"Well, you tell me, son. Where are we, and how far are we from New Ambridge?" Lennon prompted.

"Wow! I can't believe we've come this far in a week!" Evan's eyes widened as he grasped the map in both hands.

The map was covered in penciled notes and markings that designated points of interest they discovered along the way. Among them were an abandoned quarantine zone littered with looted tents and vehicles, a CDC-operated burn site for bodies, and a military-erected medical center. A red line, drawn along the folded center, marked their path.

Lennon intentionally plotted a course that cut through the wilderness, in an effort to steer them clear of heavily populated areas while maintaining at least a miles distance from any town. They only crossed freeways and roads when necessary, so they traveled on foot.

Streets had become dangerous places, with looters and carjackings becoming all too common. Desperation only fueled the chaos as society continued its slow decline. Despite their careful measures, encounters with humans were unavoidable. Up to this point, their experiences were limited to only a few interactions; one of which was unpleasant.

Lennon's shoulder-slung rifle, the 9mm pistols tucked securely in their waistbands, and the steadfast presence of Tucker made up their safeguard during these unexpected confrontations.

"According to the map. If we push ourselves tomorrow, we could be there by nightfall."

Lennon estimated.

"That's great, Dad!" Evan enthusiastically replied. He was eager to reach their destination; Ready to embark on fresh adventures.

Evan folded the map and laid his head down on his sleeping bag. He didn't say it aloud, but Lennon knew what his son was thinking. He wished his mother and Corbin were with them. Evan missed them dearly.

Although two years had passed, the scars left by their deaths remained fresh in their minds, a pain that lingered and would never truly fade.

Lennon tried his best to help Evan cope; Tucker being one of his attempts, but he realized that this pain was necessary for their survival.

Lennon knew there was someone special Evan had to leave behind.

He watched him for months before they left, trying to build the confidence to tell her how he felt, pining over her from a distance. Lennon felt responsible for that, and the thought of stealing Evan away before he could truly express his feelings was almost painful enough to make him want to stay and risk their safety.

He noticed a somewhat fresh Polaroid picture of a young girl fall from a tattered Stephen King novel as Evan opened it. She was beautiful, with long black curly hair framing her face and a smile that reminded Lennon of Evan's mother—vibrant and full of life.

The Polaroid was taken the day before they left. Evan asked if he could snap it for a class study he was working on. A class that didn't exist, and she knew it. She was a volunteer at a provisions tent her father supervised; he was much older than Lennon, which led him to believe that his daughter was much older than Evan. Evan quickly tucked the Polaroid back between the pages. Lennon didn't ask questions. He figured if Evan was ever willing to talk about her, he would listen.

"Ahh! Well, I'm going to sleep, Evan. I love you. Don't stay up late reading." Lennon said. He turned his back to give Evan privacy to pull the photo out again.

"Okay, Dad. I love you."

"Love you too, son… Love you, Tucker!"

Tucker, their loyal Labrador, settled in close beside Evan. His watchful eyes lent a sense of protectiveness over the boy. As he lay there, his ears perked up at every sound, vigilant and ready to respond to any potential danger. His solid presence by Evan's side provided a sense of security and companionship that reassured Evan and his father that they were not alone in the vast wilderness.

During the night, Evan woke to find Tucker and his father's sleeping bag empty. At first, he wasn't alarmed. He just assumed they had gone for a late-night bathroom break. But after a few minutes, an uneasy feeling settled in as Evan realized something might be wrong.

"Dad? Dad?!" Evan called out. He tried not to panic. His calls were met with silence. "Where the hell are you, Dad?" He stood with his pistol at his side and slipped his feet into his boots. He tried to decide which direction to check first. From the left, the sound of breaking sticks and rustling leaves getting closer and closer. He raised the gun, unsure of what to expect as Tucker bounded back to his side, with Lennon right behind him.

"Evan! What are you doing?! Put that away!" Lennon said as he emerged into the firelight shirtless.

"I just went to pee, Evan. I'm sorry; I guess I stayed out too long."

"You scared me to death!" Evan shouted. Although he was 16 and becoming more independent, Lennon still worried about how Evan would handle himself alone if something happened to him. Evan still had some growing up to do.

"I'm sorry, son. Put the gun away and let's get some sleep."

After a few tense moments, Evan holstered the gun and snuggled back into his sleeping bag, with Tucker plopped beside him.

"Don't do that to me again, dad! Geez, I was terrified!"

They both laughed.

"Well, I could definitely tell Evan! You had a gun!"

*

Evan and his father broke camp quickly the following day while Tucker cleaned the oatmeal from the camping pot. Most houses they passed that day were barely visible from the decaying asphalt roads they walked on. It didn't take long for invasive weeds to take over the front yards, leaving only the rooftops visible from the road.

"It's incredible how quickly things changed after the first outbreak," Lennon said. "The forest will swallow these houses in a couple more seasons."

"Like the temples in the rainforest. I read jungles can grow so fast and thick that there could be entire civilizations yet to be discovered!" Lennon smiled and loved how his son was a bookworm just like him.

"In twenty years, it'll be a lot like that if things don't get any better. You think they'll ever find a cure, Dad?" Evan asked.

Lennon pondered the same question. "Well, they thought they had after the first outbreak, but the virus mutated and found new ways to invade our bodies. Kind of like this movie I used to love as a kid called—"

Evan popped his thumbs behind the straps of his pack and shifted the weight of it further on his back.

"Oh god, I hope it's not too much further," He interrupted his father. Evan loved to hear about the old movies and hoped that one day he would get to see them all, but listening to his father recite the entire plot was something he didn't love. Lennon laughed but continued anyway.

*

Just around dusk, Lennon pointed to a chained, rusted red cattle gate.

"That's it! That's the road to the house! Haha!" Lennon said with a smile. Evan could feel the excitement.

"It's not far now!" Lennon said with a renewed sense of accomplishment. It had been a long time since the last time he saw the dirt road. Everything seemed smaller than before.

It took a lot of effort to get over the fence with their packs, while Tucker had no problem squeezing through the bottom rungs. Lennon was right in his estimations; they had about another three miles before they reached the house and at least an hour of sunlight left.

"So, how far is the land from the house, Dad?" Evan asked. Lennon threw his hands up.

"It's here! Since we crossed the cattle gate, the forest on both sides is ours, buddy! All of it! Well, when my mother passes, it will be," Lennon said, crossing his chest after.

His relationship with his mother deteriorated a long time ago, but the land was set up in a trust for him and his deceased brothers, making him the sole owner upon her death.

"Grandma? She's not dead?" Evan asked.

"You told me she was dead!" Lennon smiled when he said it, but as far as he knew, she was.

"Close enough, Evan!" Lennon replied. Miss Evelyn Grenlow was not an ideal image of a mother. The disdain she brought upon herself from her family was no secret. He regretted saying it after he did. The look on Evan's face reinforced his embarrassment.

"Story for another day... Look, there it is!" He hoped to draw attention away from the subject of his mother. Lennon pointed to an old white house that looked even worse than most they saw on the way. It disappointed Evan to see the house in such a state of decay. The way his father described it, he envisioned a castle.

"Well, this will have to do for now," Lennon said. Tucker stayed by Evan's side as Lennon cut down the weeds with a machete just to get to the porch. They stumbled over broken boards and rusted patio furniture that had been scattered. He opened the door to reveal a twisted mess of weeds, furniture, and a collapsed ceiling. Animals found their way in and bedded inside the cushions and mattresses.

"We have a lot of work ahead of us, son. We should just camp until we can see what we're dealing with."

*

As days turned into weeks, Evan and his father spent half of their time doing repairs just to get the house in working order. Hidden behind some overgrown shrubs, Lennon found a metal shed built after he left. Inside were his father's tools, which he was worried he wouldn't see, thinking that his mother had it bulldozed before the outbreak just to spite his father's memory.

There was no running water or electricity, but that wasn't an issue. In fact, they both preferred it. Having utilities after everything came crashing down became a luxury in most parts of the United States. They spent the other half of their time planning for the future and hunting, which was their favorite part.

Even though the acre on which the house and storage sheds changed, Fern Gully was just as Lennon remembered. Streams and rivers stocked with fish and an overabundance of deer set their minds at ease; food sources and fresh drinkable water would never be an issue. After a few weeks, encountering other people wouldn't be a problem either.

Everything was going according to plan. Lennon was happy with just being there. He kept himself busy with the renovation of the house and fishing. It delighted Tucker just to be out in the wilderness. Evan, however, was a different story. Whether it was true love he felt, or just the idea of something he couldn't have, it didn't matter; he felt something. And the longer Evan went without seeing her, the worse it would become. The picture he kept in the book was tattered on the edges from holding it. Lennon could see it, and it still hurt him.

One night, as Evan sat at the picnic table with Tucker, cleaning two good-sized brims they caught earlier in the day, Lennon started a conversation about his emotional well-being.

"Evan, I've been meaning to talk to you about something, and I hope you don't think I'm trying to nose in on your business, but…." He paused for a second, wondering how to ask. Evan turned and smiled.

"Well, what is it?" Lennon nervously laughed; he wasn't good at this stuff. Anne was the one who had the conversations about love and sex while he just stood on the sidelines.

"Well… what's her name?"

Evan shook his head and smiled as he turned back around.

"Oh, uh, well, she—" "You don't have to tell me if you don't want to. I know you're a private kid, and that's just fine. I just figured you'd like to get it off your chest. I know when I was your—"

"Nah… It's fine Dad. I'll tell you."

Lennon felt a little pinch of relief. He felt silly for being worried about it now that he knew how open Evan was.

"Her name is Millie, Millie… Ross? I think? Could be, I guess."

"You think?! You sometimes stare at that picture all night and don't know her last name?"

Worried, he crossed the line with the comment. Lennon waited nervously for a reply.

"I know, Dad. I was too nervous to find out. But I'm telling you now, if I knew how much I would miss not seeing her every day, I probably would've asked… I just feel stupid."

His words resonated with Lennon. He regretted not spending more time with Anne and his youngest son before they died.

"...Honestly, I don't think she even knew I had a thing for her."

"...Did you tell her? Before you left?"

Evan didn't respond. He just turned his head and smiled at him.

"Evan! You didn't tell her?"

"I know, Dad, it's crazy, but it doesn't matter now. She is just a memory to hold on to, a picture in my favorite book, and that may be all she'll ever be now that I'm a five-day hike from her.

Evan saw the look on his father's face. He tried to turn away, but his smile faded too quickly to hide.

"Dad, I didn't mean… I mean, I just wish I had more time with her." He stood up and walked over to the fire pit, where the water was beginning to boil.

"You know, Dad, even if I had more time, I still would've been scared to tell her."

Lennon smiled and folded his arms.

"You know, you were a lot like me when I was young. It scared me to death to talk to your mother. I watched her date someone else in college for eight months before I worked up the nerve to say something. But you know, everything happens for a reason. If I had talked to her before that, we might not have even got married; you just never know."

Evan's smile faded as he stared into the fire. Tucker must have sensed his emotion change and walked over, putting his head on his thigh.

Lennon spent the rest of the night mulling over different scenarios. Asked himself a hundred questions, all the answers led back to one conclusion. So he decided. The following day, Evan woke up to his father and Tucker squatting next to him in his sleeping bag. Tucker's tail was wagging furiously.

"Fine!" Lennon said. Evan sat up in confusion—the smell of the coals smoldering in the doused flames of the campfire.

"It's settled!"

"Dad, what's settled?"

"Let's go tell her!"

Evans' face turned red, flushed with excitement and nervousness.

"Dad, don't be ridiculous."

Lennon stood up in front of him. "I'm being dead serious, Evan. I wanted this place to be our dream, a safe place where we don't have to worry about getting sick or going without food or water. Even though it took me this long to realize it, none of it matters if we leave loose ends. Our emotional well-being is just as important, if not more so, than our physical safety. We need to face our unresolved feelings and find closure. So, let's go tell her!"

Evan could see the sincerity in his father's eyes and felt a mix of emotions. He was touched by his father's support and overwhelmed by the idea of facing his feelings head-on. Lennon could see Evan's hesitation but knew this was an essential step for both of them.

"Son, I know it's scary, but facing our emotions and confronting our fears strengthens us. I don't want you to live with regret, wondering 'what if?' for the rest of your life. We'll do this together, as a team. And no matter the outcome, we'll have each other's backs."

Evan stood up and smirked. "You're seriously losing it, Dad!" he exclaimed, his voice, a mix of disbelief and amusement.

"We spent two weeks walking here, dealing with all those obstacles and rough weather. We can't just head back and retrace our steps and face all those challenges again, so I can confess my feelings to a girl who probably doesn't even know I'm gone."

Evan's eyes flickered with fear and hope as he imagined the long journey back, the exhaustion that would kick in, and the uncertainty of how Millie would react to his confession. He couldn't help but picture the moment he would finally see her face again, the surprise in her eyes.

"You! Don't! Know! That!" Lennon laughed as he brought his hands together and rubbed them like an evil doctor from an old horror film.

"Dad, what are you doing?" Evan said as he laughed awkwardly.

"Let me show you something, boy…" Lennon grabbed Evan's arm and led him to the old metal building where his dad's tools were. He went to the opposite end and stood in front of an old garage door.

"Allow me to introduce an old friend of my father's…."

Lennon slammed open the door, walked in, and jerked a dusty old car cover off a pristine orange Pontiac with a hand-painted Firebird on the hood. Not a scratch on it.

"Her name is Lola, and she's going to take us where we need to go."

"Dad! Jesus!"

Evan cringed.

"I'm sorry… I'm sorry, too much, I think. Let me dial it back."

Lennon started again with an even more theatrical expression.

"We're gonna ride this bitch into the sunset, you, me, and our boy Tucker here. And you, my friend, are gonna scoop that girl Billie up—" "Millie, Dad…" Evan interrupted him with a smile. He was in awe of the classic car.

"Sorry, scoop that girl Millie up and... say…"

Lennon gave Evan a chance to fill in the last words. He sensed Evan's heart was swollen with excitement. Evan stepped back and started doing an awkward dance.

"Hey, baby girl, you like my ride?"

They both paused before bursting into laughter.

"That's it, Evan?! That's your plan of attack? That's gonna work. I mean… look at this beast!"

Lennon and Evan danced wildly in front of the old firebird for a moment, forgetting everything else. Even Tucker joined in. He jumped and barked at them as they kicked dust up in the sunlight.

Evan slowed himself and watched his father while he danced with Tucker's front paws in his hands and the stunning car behind him. It almost didn't seem real. It looked straight out of a magazine or a comic book.

"What's wrong, Evan? It'll take us less than three hours to get there if we drive." Evan shook his head and teared up.

"Evan! What's wrong? Talk to me, son," Lennon said as he placed his hands on Evan's shoulders.

"You took all this time to plan our hike here, weeks of preparations. We avoided all the roads and all the people and hiked for two weeks through the woods and fields, and now you want to risk everything so that I can tell a girl I have feelings for her? That's insane! What if we get attacked? Or get sick? What if the roads are blocked, and we can't drive there? The car's incredible. What if…"

Lennon interrupted him. "Evan, this car has lived a sheltered existence. When I was a kid, it sat in a climate-controlled garage with the battery disconnected. My dad only drove it, maybe three times I can remember, and he never let me or my brothers ride in it, not once. I begged him to let me take my girlfriend to senior prom in it, he would've beat me for asking if my mom wasn't there. I admit, we are going to do this for you, but I'm going to do something I have always wanted to do. Trust me."

"Drive it?" Evan said. It broke Lennon's fixated attention.

"Hahaha!" Lennon laughed. "I'm not just going to drive this monster, no. Excuse my language Evan, but I'm going to shit whip this bitch while (THIS) is screaming from the tape deck."

He whipped out a cassette tape with a demon, whipping a chain over a churning sea. The band name "Dio" was written in old English towards the bottom side.

Evan was silent, but grinned.

"You serious, Dad?" Lennon hugged him and smiled.

"I'm dead serious."

For a while, they stood there and hugged. It was a special moment; they both needed it, even if they didn't know it.

“I guess I should see if it runs….”
“What!!!” Evan shouted out.

Chapter 6
Lola

Over the next week, Lennon assigned most of his time to tuning up Lola and teaching Evan how to drive. She was pristine, but Lennon could only guess how long she sat idle; At least 10 years. Thankfully, his father had enough sense to empty the gas from the tank before letting it sit.

Mice found their way into the engine compartment and chewed through the wiring harness. Everything else seemed in top shape.

"Well, Evan, there's one thing left to do. We have to get some gas." Evan snatched a green tennis ball from Tucker's mouth before he entered the garage and tossed it to keep him preoccupied while they talked.

"Yeah? And where do we find gas? the cars on the way here looked like they'd sat for a long time." Evan said.

"...Yeah, I noticed that too." Lennon used a red shop cloth to clean his hands and leaned against the car with his arms folded.

"There's a service station about twelve miles north. I'd have to get the map, but if we cut through Fern Gully. Maybe we shave three to four miles. What do you think? You wanna try? We ain't doing anything else, right?"

Evan shook his hand. "You got yourself a..."

Evan stopped short before he finished his sentence when he saw Tucker in the distance. It wasn't typical for him to bark at much; he was used to the wildlife and rarely paid much attention.

"Tucker!" Evan called out as he and his father walked out of the garage. In the distance, towards the tree line in the north, they watched Tucker leap over downed logs and high weeds. He was after something. It had been a long time since they'd seen him move that quickly.

"I'll get the rifle, Evan. wait for me to come back." Lennon said, his voice tinged with worry. Nothing could stop Tucker. No matter how hard he yelled for him to come back, whatever he was locked onto, had his full attention. *Stupid dog,* Evan thought.

As Lennon returned with a rifle, one of his go-bags packed for emergencies and a red 5-gallon gas can.

Tucker disappeared entirely from sight, likely half a mile away or more.

"What's all that, Dad?" Evan said. With his eyes glued to the tree line where Tucker disappeared.

"Which direction did Tucker run to?" Lennon often quizzed Evan to see if what he taught him was sticking. It took Evan a moment, but as soon as he got his bearings, he replied,

"North-Northeast?"

"Good job, Evan. We can keep going after we find him; he's headed in the right direction. It's early so we can still make it back before it gets too late." Lennon said. His go-bag contained all the tools they needed to make a rough camp, if they didn't.

Afternoon came and Tucker was still in hot pursuit. They heard his bark, but they were still no closer to him. Lennon and Evan were even more worried.

"Dad, I have a bad feeling. He's never run off like this."

Lennon became anxious as well but tried to hide it. He was right—even as a puppy, Tucker was well-behaved.

"It'll be fine, Evan. Let's just keep going. We're almost halfway to the service station." Lennon tried to divert his mind in a new direction, but things didn't look good. It had been fifteen minutes since they'd even heard Tucker bark.

Evan was deeper into Fern Gully than Lennon had ever taken him. They were closer to the abandoned oil drilling site. The air was different there. It carried a musty scent that clung to their clothes.

The forest sounds were dampened by the dense foliage. Lennon took point and used the machete to clear their path.

To the left was an ivy-covered fence. Downed trees created voids large enough to see through to the drilling site beyond. The barren wasteland stretched for miles. A stark contrast to the lush forest on their side of the fence.

Lennon and Evan pressed on despite how unsettled they were by the surroundings, determined to find Tucker and make it to the service station before nightfall.

"What is that place, Dad?"

"When I was growing up, we called it, "The Field." Honestly, I don't really know. I guess years of drilling and oil being spat out on the ground just killed everything. After the oil ran dry, they just left everything behind. The land is ruined. I guess no one ever wanted to move in. I think the land is twice the size of Fern Gully."

Evan was shocked. "It's such a shame, all that wasted land. You and your friends ever jump that fence?"

Lennon laughed. "Not no, but hell no! We were brave, but my dad scared us when we were kids. Told us about monsters that stole children and dragged them into oil pits."

"Wow! That's a terrible thought."

"Well, it kept us from even getting this close." As Lennon talked, Evan stopped. Something moved between the trees and caught his eye.

"What do you see, Evan? Is it Tucker?"

Evan didn't answer him. About three yards away, there was stone jutting out of the ground, covered in fresh blood. As Lennon stopped, he looked down to see the same blood-covered stone. He shifted the rifle from his back and chambered a round.

In the distance, they could hear Tucker's strained cries of pain, and it pierced their hearts. Evan, unable to contain his worry, broke out into a sprint.

"Damn it, Evan! Wait, a second! You don't know what's got him!" Lennon tried to keep his balance but slipped and landed on his backside. He wanted to stop himself but slid down the muddy embankment into a warm puddle of Tucker's blood. He let out a gut-wrenching scream, the horror of the situation consumed him. "NOOO!!!" Evan wailed as Lennon struggled to catch up with him. As he rounded a wide birch tree at the edge of the barren riverbed, Lennon found Evan on his knees. From behind, it looked like he was praying. Tucker's mutilated, lifeless body lay about ten yards before him. A wolf, twice the typical size of any wolf Evan or Lennon had ever seen; had Tucker torn open and scattered out in front of him.

He pushed Tucker's lifeless head into the mud with his massive paw. Around the wolf's enormous neck hung a rusty chain and lock that swayed with every movement. The beast hoisted its giant head and aimed his doom-filled eyes directly at Evan. Lennon's breath was knocked from his chest. The creature was an embodiment of cataclysm, a monstrosity ripped straight from the pages of an apocalyptic prophecy. His presence weakened their very souls.

Lennon knew they would find no value running; any attempt would be met with a chase that would surely end in death. He calmed himself and tried to think of something. As Evan's eyes filled with tears and his heart with hatred for the unnatural beast before him. He edged closer and closer to the only son he had left. The dire wolf stepped over Tucker, casually kicking him as it strode slowly forward, its claws dragging across Tucker's eviscerated abdomen.

"Evan... I'm begging you, please just don't move..." Lennon frantically whispered as he drew closer. His voice trembled with fear. The giant wolf stopped and tilted its head and sniffed the air that surrounded them. It then raised his eyes to focus on Lennon.

"Dad, what's going on?" Evan whimpered; terror seeped into every fiber of his being.

"Did you hear it too?"

The last bit of hope Lennon held onto to save his son vanished as so many things clamored for his attention. He thought it was his mind struggling to compensate for the stress of it all. Then the voice pounded against his head again.

"Ha! Apollo, Ack'Reus! Come quick!"

The words were muffled and faded inside of their minds but Oct'Tulommon's voice was deep. It resonated within their shook bodies and sent needles of fear down their spines. Lost within the confusion of it all, they felt like they had lost their sanity. They clutched their chests almost in unison to shield their hearts from the invasive force. The monstrous voice seemed to wrap around their insides, it enveloped them in an unsettling embrace. The sound was not audible, it was more like a feeling, or an emotional response called forth by the massive wolf before them. It intruded their minds, like a surge of electricity skittering over the surface, causing their heartbeats to race and falter. It was as if the creature's voice had the power to manipulate their emotions and cause a mix of dread and curiosity to well up inside them. Their breaths hitched, and their eyes widened in fear, unable to break free from the voice's grip.

"Can you understand me wolf?" Evan said out loud, but Oct'Tulommon didn't understand, His head tilted to the side with confusion. The air vibrated as it carried the weight of Oct'Tulommon's voice once more. "Say it with your heart boy…" The leaves on the trees appeared to tremble in response. The ground beneath their feet pulsed and mirrored the intensity of the sound waves that coursed through their bodies. It was an experience so visceral and powerful that it was impossible for Lennon and Evan to ignore. Evan tried again. This time when he spoke, he put his heart into it.

"Can you understand me?" His voice was clear both aloud and through his heart. Oct'Tulommon was still, his hair stood on his neck.

"…..**Yes**….."

At that moment, the boundaries between the physical world and their inner emotions blurred, and they found themselves precariously balanced on the edge of a total loss of control! But somehow, amidst the chaos, a shared determination took root within them, born from their love for each other and their will to survive.

Lennon stepped forward again to close the distance between himself and Evan. He raised the rifle, but before he could extend his finger and release the safety, another abomination of the natural world flanked them and forced Lennon's face to the mud. This one wasn't as sturdy but more angular and taller, with black-gray fur tight to the wolf's frame, almost like a Doberman Pinscher. As Lennon fell back against the rocks, yet another wolf emerged from behind. Now there were four wolves in total.

Even though Evan and his father both witnessed and confirmed the voice of the wolf permeated inside them, it wasn't enough to distract Evan from the tragedy that befell his best friend, Tucker.

"Why! Why did you do this to my dog!? There are plenty of other animals to eat out here!" Evan screamed at the top of his lungs directly into the giant wolf's muzzle, his face contorted with anger.

Oct'Tulommon laughed, a sinister and chilling sound that echoed through the forest. To Evan's surprise, the words that followed were crystal clear. The wolves' voices were pushed directly into his mind.

"Well, if you must know, the Druthe wouldn't have been my first choice. He was just slower and more eager to die, I'm afraid. He practically came to me wagging his pathetic tail," The monstrous wolf replied, cold and unfeeling.

Though his mouth remained still, the words fell sharply into Evan and Lennon's minds; they painted a vivid image of Tucker excited to meet the beast who stood still and watched as the happy dog wagged his tail on the way to his evisceration.
Ack'Reus, the tall, angular wolf, slinked around and stood beside the larger one, their combined presence casting an oppressive shadow over the scene.

"He can understand us?! How!?" Evan was still locked in a stare at Oct'Tulommon.

"Hey, asshole!" He shouted, his face inches away from Oct'Tulommon's snout.

"Look at me!"

Lennon was speechless, his heart aching as he watched his son, blinded by rage and unable to comprehend the danger before him.

"Evan, calm down. We have to get out of here," Lennon urged, his voice riddled with fear. Oct'Tulommon laughed again, his malicious amusement pulled knots into their throats.

"You know you're not going anywhere anymore Warden. I'm afraid the Void is all you have left…"

As the words sank in, a desperate determination ignited within Lennon and Evan. They knew they had to escape the clutches of these terrifying creatures or face a fate worse than death.

"Tell us, boy!" Apollo demanded as he sauntered over to Tucker's lifeless body. "Why do you feign sadness for this Druthe you call Tucker? Is he not your slave? Your plaything? Does he fetch your food for you? Does he lick your wounds when you're hurt?"

Apollo sneered as he lifted Tucker's limp head. It fell back onto the rocky ground with a dull thud. "…He doesn't look like much of a fighting Druthe."

Oct'Tulommon's eyes widened as if his mind was in a race through countless scenarios instantaneously. He nodded to let the wolves know that the time to take their offensive positions was at hand.

As Ha'Kan hobbled closer, Lennon caught a strong scent of infection and necrotic flesh. It was clear this creature Ha'Kan suffered an injury to his hind leg. It looked to be very old with blackened meat and maggots that clung to the rancid and matted fur. His eyes were sunken and his mouth was riddled with open sores and white, foamy drool.

Lennon felt a strange connection with the creature as their eyes locked. He sensed kindness, pain and a reluctancy for what events were sure to transpire. He whimpered and slowly backed away. Perplexed, Lennon clutched the gun behind him one more time.

"Evan RUNN!!!" He screamed as he raised the rifle and fired. The shot rang out, shattering the tense silence and echoed off the rocks that surrounded the riverbed. It was the first time they heard gunfire, except for Oct'Tulommon. Unfazed, he lunged over Evan and slammed Lennon to the ground. In one swift, brutal bite, Lennon's arm was severed. The force of the attack sent the two across the stones and stuck a solid ten feet. The rifle was knocked loose from Lennon's hands and within Evan's reach.

The air was tense as Evan's fingers grazed the rifle, his eyes flickered between the snarled mouth of Ack'Reus and the beast atop his injured father.

Time seemed to slow as he weighed his dwindling options, desperation fueled his determination. The wolves' menacing presence loomed over them, an oppressive reminder of the danger that threatened to consume them.

Pinned beneath the hulking wolf, a creature more akin to a hellish demon than any earthly beast, Lennon battled the urge to cry out in immense pain. But even on death's precipice, his foremost instinct was to safeguard his son from the deep-seated horror of their predicament. He gritted his teeth and braced against the torture and fear.

Apollo and Ack'Reus were still dazed by the sound of the gun and unsure of how to proceed with Oct'Tulommon preoccupied. Evan pulled the bolt and fired his own round, aimed at the back of Oct'Tulommon's brain. The bullet missed its mark as it sparked off the thick metal chain around the beast's neck. Ack'Reus and Apollo jolted with added panic. The sound of the gun caused more havoc than the bullet it fired.

Oct'Tulommon turned his head and revealed Lennon beneath him. His neck was ripped open, his chest caved in and his arm and half his face were torn to shreds and scattered around him like tatters of old bloody cloth.

Oct'Tulommon let out a low, sinister laugh as Lennon's blood dripped from his mouth. The fear for his son's life opened the door for the Void to sweep in. It allowed the three wolves to hear Lennon's subconscious pleas for mercy.

"We can hear your father's heart and mind boy." Oct'Tulommon Expressed.

*"Let him go. Take my life, but please let my son live. I beg you, kill me. Let **him live**!"*

"He is begging me to spare your life!"

The words received by the wolves unknowingly sent from Lennon's heart and mind, came through the void. They were broken and faded, faltering with the existential dread of his impending death. But the message was clear. "Take my life, but let my son go."

Oct'Tulommon's face changed when he realized what this meant. With his heavy paws still on Lennon's chest, he pressed down with ease. The pressure was immense. He turned his heavy head slowly to Evan once more.

"His heart is begging for your life. He is giving himself to me…."
Evan was in shock. Unable to move. Unable to breathe.

"Hear him boy!"
With one forceful direct push, Oct'Tulommon's paw flattened Lennon's chest to the ground.

Everything was quiet except for the laughter of the two wolves behind him. It seeped into his mind like venom from a snake. A Coagulant that slowed the pain and held it right where it hurts the most.

The third wolf, Ha'Kan, sat beside a tree with his back turned to the violence. His body shivered as he whimpered with remorse.
"He gave his Awl'Fire to save you? Such a weak boy? Just like a human, unable to comprehend the enormity of what he has lost."

Unexpectedly, Oct'Tulommon fell to the ground, his body contorted, his back arched, and his eyes rolled to the back of his skull. The other wolves watched in horror as their leader seemed to be rendered useless by some unseen force.

Evan Seized the opportunity and raised the rifle. He pulled the bolt and leveled the gun at Oct'Tulommon's face. But it jammed. Mud caked inside of the chamber wouldn't allow it to fire.

In the split-second Evan took to inspect the rifle, Oct'Tulommon recovered. He knocked the rifle from his trembling, blood-slick hands.
"Haha! It's done boy! It's too late for you."
As the beast prepared to lunge, he abruptly collapsed once more. Evan stretched his arm for the rifle but realized it broke into two pieces. He was out of options. The other wolves whimpered, worried for their Alpha.

Unable to bear the sight of his father's mangled body again, Evan clutched both sides of his head, ready to give up hope and fight the beast before him with his bare fists, even if it meant certain death.

Through his peripheral vision, he glimpsed his father's devastated face. One eye was out of its socket, the other buried beneath a pool of blood. It was impossible to tell if he could even see him, but his mouth repeated a single word. Oct'Tulommon's howls of pain were so loud and distracting that Evan couldn't make out the sound but knew exactly the message he willed to convey, like morse code.

"LO-LA... LO-LA..."

In a sudden surge of determination while the pack of wolves were distracted by Oct'Tulommon writhing in agony for what seemed to be no reason at all. Evan abandoned his resignation to defeat, left the rifle behind in the rocks, grabbed the gas and ran with more determination than he had in his entire life.

"Get him you bastards!" Oct'Tulommon commanded them through the Void.

Evan had more adrenaline in his veins than blood. He sprinted as fast as his legs could carry him, with no discernible direction. He just ran. For over an hour, his lungs burned and muscles atrophied but the wolves were nowhere to be heard or seen. He was lucky. It was the first time the ragged pack of Fractured wolves ever ventured from the Outlands to the other side of the fence. They were not accustomed to the foliage and the terrain. Their legs tripped up in vines and their fur bogged down with red clay and mud clots.

Evan refused to stop or to think; he just wanted to keep running, to put as much distance between him and the carnage-filled nightmare he just witnessed.

Chapter 7
Reanimated

"Get up, son. Get up and get moving…."

The voice of his father scraped at the bones inside his head. As he painfully unsealed his swollen eyes. He found himself on the ground in a stretch of Fern Gully. Leaves and small sticks stuck to the side of his face.

He did not know where he was or how long he ran through the forest. The sky was dark, and the air was thick with a wet haze that led him to believe the sun would rise soon.

His head pounded and his heart raced in his chest, undoubtedly he suffered from shock. Evan was in an altered state of consciousness, past the point of anger and tears.

"Keep going, son, Keep going." The voice of his father echoed again; it pulled him out of his dazed state and back into utter disbelief.

Evan tried to focus on his surroundings, but it was still too dark and dangerous to hike. He lay back in the dirt and shut his swollen eyes and called out for his father by name with a blistered throat and a sullen, broken voice.

"Dad!" He cried, as if by some supernatural will of the heart, he would speak to him through time and space. But all he got was silence and another tidal wave of sadness.

He took a deep breath to slow his heart long enough to stand. After a challenged climb to the top of a large embankment, he saw a different fence than the one that separated Fern Gully from the Fractured wolves' Outlands.

Resting his left hand on one of the nearby posts; he squinted as the morning sunbeams pierced his eyes from the right. After a moment of deep contemplation, he settled on a direction and decisively set forth.

After a few miles, he stumbled upon a road that led him directly to a small service station. The rusted sign at the end of the weedy parking lot had a few plastic numbers and letters still attached, but most of them were scattered around the cracked asphalt underneath.

[Bel i ger Servi e Stat on]

He tried to recall the name as he walked but couldn't.

To his surprise, it was still in operation despite the amount of junk piled everywhere and the disarray of the pumps.

He noticed people, both inside and out, which presented a few problems. The major one; his father was the one with the money. Evan opened a broken glass door that was held together by duct tape. He could smell something in the air, coffee and cigarette smoke. When he approached the counter, the old man behind it stood up, put his cigarette out, and pulled a cloth mask up from below his fatty chin.

"Son, you need to have a mask. Can't you read the damn sign?" The older man behind the counter said with a hint of attitude as he pointed to a piece of cardboard with words etched in red Sharpie.

"NO MASK, NO SERViS."

"I'm sorry, I... I don't have one," Evan stammered, overly conscious of his unkempt appearance. Tattered and soiled clothes clung to his frame, his eyes were bloodshot and injuries riddled his body. "I just need some gas, sir. I... I ran out... a few miles back." He lied, surprised at how quickly the falsehood came to him.

"If you ain't gonna wear a damn mask, I can't help you, son. And if you ain't got any money, you sure the hell ain't gettin' no gas."

The man retorted. The other patrons glared at him. As Evan turned to leave the store, he heard the old man mutter under his breath, "Fucking Meth head."

A surge of anger shot down Evan's spine. He locked eyes with the old man, his face laced with rage. Before he regained his composure, the old man yelled, "Get Out!"

As he sat on the curb outside, Evan tried to pull himself together. He heard voices inside the store—a man and women amid an argument. Moments later, the door burst open, and an older lady with sandy-colored frizzy hair and a black mask pulled down under her chin grabbed his gas can.

"Come on, son; I'll get you what you need. He's just a horse's ass, and he knows it. The worst part is, he doesn't care who else knows either." She said as she took a drag from her Marlboro between her chapped lips. She yanked the old-style gas pump from its hook, shoved it into Evan's mud-covered gas can, and asked, "Tough night last night, son? I've been there." She said as she rolled up her sweatshirt sleeve, her arms covered in old track marks. He wiped his eyes and dropped his shoulders.

"It's not what you think, ma'am," Evan said as he choked back more tears.

"It's okay; you don't have to tell me. But you don't need to take shit for it either. We all have our faults. You just gotta do better next time."

He decided it was best to let her think he was on drugs rather than tell her everything that happened—which he still couldn't believe himself.

After a final drag on her half-smoked Marlboro, the woman flipped the cigarette into the wet grass and released the handle on the pump. It shut off with a thud and only filled the 5-gallon can about halfway.

"Which way are you headed? Do you need a ride? I've been vaccinated if that makes a difference." She said as she lit another cigarette.

"I really appreciate your kindness, but it's not far, and I need to take my time to gather my thoughts," Evan responded. She smiled at him.

"Son, you don't have to call me 'ma'am'; I ain't no ma'am." She shook her head.

"I understand, though. I just want you to be safe, that's all."

With a sense of urgency, she walked back into the store. Her tiny waist and baggy jeans swayed back and forth. Evan saw the man scowl as she opened the door.

"Give me ten dollars on pump two, Bill, you fat asshole!"

She exclaimed. The two continued to bicker, their relationship unclear to Evan.

The woman's act of kindness ignited a tiny spark in his heart, soon smothered by a black cloud of dread, a savage wave of sadness in the back of his throat, and a tightly wound knot where his stomach used to be. He knew he had to return to the dense woods of Fern Gully—where his father lay dead, scattered among the dirt and leaves.

Intrusive thoughts tormented him. Thoughts of bugs and birds that slowly feast on him and carry his remains away into the farthest reaches of his childhood playground.

Determined to avoid another encounter with the wolves, Evan hugged the property line opposite the fence. Lennon taught him where the lines were, just in case he ever got lost in Fern Gully. Evan knew if he followed the line, he would make it back to the house.

The walk took all day, with no sign of the wolves. By sundown, he emerged from the tree line where he last saw Tucker alive.

When Evan saw the house again, it sent him into another emotional tailspin. Even if he was sure that the wolves would not return, it was impossible for him to stay there after everything. All their hard work over the last few weeks seemed so futile.

Evan took some time to gather his gear and prepared for the uncertainties ahead on the road.

He meticulously cleaned his 9mm handgun and placed it firmly in his belt behind his back. After he piled his camping gear in the trunk, Evan poured the gasoline into the tank and sat in the front seat and prayed the car would start. *Come on, Lola...* He twisted the key, and the engine turned over several times before she sputtered. *Come on, girl, please! I need this.* The engine growled again with another twist of the key as he vigorously pumped the gas pedal, careful not to flood the engine, just like his dad showed him. He could almost hear his father's voice guide him, as if he was right beside him. He forced the emotions down and focused on the task. The car sputtered out.

"Lola, please! Goddammit!" He punched the dashboard and screamed, then took a deep breath and tried again. The engine rumbled, and the hood vibrated with the power of the awakened beast inside. The tape deck lit up, and the speakers came alive with the vibrant sound of,

"Holy Diver" by Dio.

Adrenaline coursed through his veins as the music sent chills down his arms and legs.

"YES! Thank you, Lola! Thank you!" He was ecstatic.

Evan slammed the car into drive and carefully pulled onto the dirt road in front of the house. It suddenly dawned on him he almost forgotten one of the most important things—the Polaroid of Millie, his only cherished possession. He slammed the car back into park, pulled the emergency brake, and let it idle. The music blared from the tiny speakers while he dashed around the house to their makeshift campsite. After a few seconds, he returned to the car, positioned the Polaroid on the dashboard right in front of the steering wheel, gritted his teeth, and buckled his seatbelt.

"Okay, now I'm ready..." He said out loud.

It was hard to think with the intense electric guitar melody that rang through his ears. But it invigorated him, like fuel on a fire., he slammed the car back into drive. But right before he released the brakes, he spotted a figure about twenty-five yards ahead of the vehicle. It limped towards him.

The figure was half-naked, drenched in blood, and barely able to walk. Evan's initial shock at the sight of another person quickly turned to confusion. He squinted to get a better look as the figure approached.

"What in the hell?" Evan muttered; he gave the orange lit volume knob a slow turn.

As the figure straggled closer into the dim golden beams of the headlights, Evan hit the trigger on the floorboard and switched to high beams. The battered man threw his arm to shield his eyes from the light but continued to amble closer still. Evan rolled the window down midway with his right hand and yelled, "Hey! You need to leave. This is private property!" It didn't register with the figure at all.

The man lowered his arms. Evan realized the figure was wearing his father's ripped clothes. A rush of confusion and adrenaline caused him to reach for his seatbelt and the door handle simultaneously.

"Dad!?" He screamed at the top of his lungs. He knew it wasn't possible, he knew it couldn't be him. How could his father stand there when just a day earlier, the claws of a demonic wolf eviscerated and crushed him?

Evan glanced down at the loaded 9mm handgun in the seat beside him, pulled it from the holster, and gritted his teeth. He stepped out, ready to face whatever was to come.

"How can this be? How are you standing here?" Evan demanded. His voice trembled with fear and disbelief as the figure halted about ten feet away. "Answer me!" He screamed, every muscle in his throat and gut strained. "Answer me, please!"

He raised the gun and leveled it straight at the figure's head. The figure stopped to cough. Blood and bile sputtered from his hanging mouth. He laughed and twitched in pain.

"Evan, Evan, is it? Your father's likeness fits perfectly..." The figure reached out, studying his arms. "A little too tight in some places."

The voice Evan heard from the figure's broken and swollen face resembled his fathers to an extent, but it wasn't like he remembered, it was vile, dark and full of evil.

The figure pointed back at Evan, its bloody fingers in the shape of a gun.

Evan's brow furrowed in confusion. "Oct'Tulommon?"

The figure laughed as Evan's face melted into horror at the realization. It relished every drop of the hurt he caused. He stretched his hands to lunge, but the tight flesh that clung to his body ripped and tore with the tension applied. The sound of gunfire rang out as Evan fired the entire clip, landing only two shots.

The bullets struck Oct'Tulommon in the shoulder and caused the flesh that stretched taut around his monstrous frame to tear apart. As he rolled into the woods next to the road, the shredded remains of Lennon's flesh clung to the underbrush. It left a gruesome trail like torn, wet linen in the ditch.

Evan just stood there; disbelief etched on his face as he listened to Oct'Tulommon's massive frame crash through the underbrush. He gasped for breath and slammed the car door shut, floored the gas pedal and smashed through the red cattle gate.

He reached down and jerked the volume knob back the other direction. The music filled the interior of Lola; it muffled Evan's screams of anguish and frustration. The raw emotions surged within him and fueled a rage that threatened to engulf him entirely. The haunted melody seemed to echo his torment. It drove him further from the nightmare he just left behind.

He knew there was only a few miles in the tank, but he was determined to put as much distance as possible between him and Oct'Tulommon.

As the woods and the nightmare he left behind quickly disappeared, Evan clenched the steering wheel. The car careened from one end of the road to the other. Narrowly, he missed parked vacant vehicles and other items scattered about in the barely used roadway. Unsure of what lay ahead, but confident that he had to stay on the move.

Chapter 8
New Beginning

Lola finally ran out of gas about twenty miles into Evan's estimated a hundred and fifty-mile trip. He found himself on a long stretch of empty road as Lola's tires came to a stop. It still felt like he could have gotten farther.

Reluctantly, he realized that to find more gas and maintain a low profile in a bright orange Firebird would be difficult in the daylight. And so, with a full backpack and anything else he could manage, he took the Polaroid of Millie and the cassette he come to love from the stereo and bid Lola a heartfelt farewell after he stashed her under an overpass and a torn blue tarp; Evan set off on the next leg of his journey.

He hated the thought of his father's dream stashed beneath a random overpass, rusting and yearning for the open road. But there was no better option; it had served its purpose.

He felt somewhat safer with some distance between him and the demon wolf, Oct'Tulommon. Evan pitched his tent and tried to rest his weary eyes for a while. He hoped that if he slept, he might get a break from the relentless emotional whiplash.

However, it had only been a few hours before the sun rose and the morning birds belted their melodic spring songs. They woke Evan without consideration for his emotional turmoil.

He went through a mental inventory, as he always did, and tried to make decisions for the day. *The sun is up, I'm alive, the winds are cool, and the sky is blue.* The list continued with all the things in his immediate surroundings that brought him joy, followed by those that were not visible, *books, swimming, fishing...* Tears welled in his eyes as he named the same things his father loved. He took a deep breath, wiped his eyes and pressed on. *Birds, Tucker... Corbin, mom... dad...* He didn't think his heart could take any more pain, but now, with his entire family gone, the realization that he had nothing left to lose was staunch and freeing in some weird and twisted way. He had become a psychological ball of string, tangled and wound tight, intricate and distorted.

Most of the distance Evan covered was an uncomfortable guess. He had been lost on more than one occasion. Without a map, it took him much longer than he expected.

A few nights, he didn't even bother to set up his tent, instead he broke into abandoned houses and vehicles to rest. He rummaged for clean clothes and canned foods and read whatever books he could with his flashlight.

Evan knew he had become a hollow shell of himself, devoid of any genuine desire to go anywhere or see anyone—even Millie. This realization frightened him, so he forced himself to think about the future and what he looked forward to.

"Fake it till you make it." He told himself as he tried to keep hope.

After almost three weeks, Evan's pilgrimage was almost over. As he approached New Ambridge, the scent of fire grew more robust. He didn't need to consult his map; he could navigate by the smell alone. It was a scent he loved, and despite his exhaustion and emotional burnout. He couldn't help but feel a flicker of excitement. This small surge of emotion brought him a measure of comfort. He quickened his pace.

Rows upon rows of mailboxes, now obscured by rampant vines and weeds, stood at the end of driveways. Patches of vinyl siding and brick from the houses could be barely discerned through the dense, wild undergrowth. These homes had been forsaken when their inhabitants relocated closer to New Ambridge due to power grid failures. The land, once tamed by human hands, reverted to its primal, wild state. For many, the move was driven by the fundamental need for sustenance.

Traditional grocery stores, expensive department stores, and pharmacies became relics of the past with the advent of the second, significantly more devastating wave of the Rasping fever. In response, the government deemed such establishments too perilous, transitioning them into what were referred to as "Ration Centers'" or "RCs".

Initially, a digital ordering system was implemented to provide people access to necessities. However, as the labor force contracted, it became increasingly challenging to meet the skyrocketing demand. Eventually, the digital system was shuttered. The consequences of a faltering national supply chain, including looting, vandalism, and product shortages, led to the adoption of a rationing system. Despite its inherent drawbacks, the new system was seen as a step up in some respects. Evan had no memory of the time before the RC's.

Ahead, Evan saw the gravel road transition to a cracked, jagged blacktop, where water settled, frozen, and thawed. It caused it to separate and allowed weeds to grow sporadically. He felt a sense of unease as he walked between the abandoned, plundered cars, scanning them for valuable items. Occasionally, he was startled by a bleached human skeleton or on the ground. Although these grim reminders were few, they were never easy to see—signs of how quickly things worsened.

A little further up the road, Evan spotted smoke rise from the trees about a mile away. By his estimation, he walked about eight miles out of the woods, another two down the gravel road, and close to four more on the blacktop road.

As he neared the settlement, he encountered a group of travelers leaving New Ambridge. They stopped and asked if he had anything to barter, but Evan politely declined. Neither party had any reason to take advantage of the other humanity still held a semblance of decency, at least for now, when things weren't as dire as they could be during the harsh winter months.

When Evan reached the outskirts of New Ambridge, he passed under a sign that stretched from one side of the road to the other, suspended between two telephone poles. It read:

"New Ambridge."

The familiarity of the place provided Evan with a sense of comfort. Further down the street, rows of canvas tents were set up alongside a few well-maintained, older two-story buildings. They had power and running water, and an old-style trading post bustled with customers a little further up the road. Evan knew the area well, but a lot changed just in the brief span of time he was gone. The outdoor seating near the libraries, where people used to use the slow, unreliable internet, had been taken away, and the doors were shut. The cafe was boarded up with a small square hole cut into a sheet of OSB, where two beady eyes and a woman wearing a white mask could be seen taking orders. The people that queued the line were six feet apart and all wearing blue nitrile gloves and white N95 masks. The small park, where he remembered children on swings and a jungle gym, was now lined with caution tape and signs warning people to keep out.

The most significant change that Evan noticed was the absence of the food pantry where he volunteered with Millie was now gone.

He stopped a masked pedestrian who was walking a dog nearby.

"Excuse me, I'm sorry to bother you, but..." "where's your mask? Didn't you read the signs when you came in? There's a strict mask policy here." The pedestrian interrupted as she and her dog backed away.

Evan glanced back at the wall of an old building where she pointed. A sign listed five rules: outlines for quarantine guidelines, social distancing protocols, vaccine information, and C.D.C. updates on cases and deaths. The numbers appeared outdated, crossed out, and in need of maintenance. Evan turned.

"Ma'am, I'm sorry. I haven't been here for quite some time."

The woman interrupted him again before she turned and walked swiftly away. "Then you need to sign in with the health office and have them check you out before you can just…walk around like that. It's not safe. This is how things get out of hand, you know."

Evan didn't reply but simply turned to search for a sign that directed him to the health office.

After a lengthy search and several more looks of disapproval from locals, Evan finally spotted a place with a sign above it that read:

"Health Office."

He went to the door and was greeted by a woman fully masked with scrubs and gloves who squirted hand sanitizer into his hands and gave him a cloth mask. She blocked the door until he put it in the correct way.

Once inside, he met another fully masked and gloved lady who took his information and gave him a number. Only one other person in the office stared at Evan curiously as he sat down with his full camping backpack, complete with pots that clanked and a mud-caked sleeping bag.

"Sir, I'm going to have to ask you to leave that stuff outside, please," a woman at the front desk announced just after the pots stopped clanking. Evan sighed, stood back up, and set his things down outside.

On his second entrance, he was stopped by the same woman and given more hand sanitizer. No one showed any personality, but then again, neither did he. When he sat down again and finally got comfortable, a woman from behind a plastic shield desk came around and called his number. He was agitated beyond comparison. "I'm sorry, but I'm worried my stuff will get taken. Can I please just bring it in?" He asked politely as he met her in the doorway.

"Sir, if you go out and come back in, we have to give you another number, and you may lose your place in line." The woman replied. Evan chuckled a little and looked around at the empty room.

"Your choice, sir. You can't go anywhere in New Ambridge until we check you out."

"Fine., Evan grumbled hesitantly as the terse woman escorted him to a small room in the back. She pointed to an old recliner lined with butcher paper. He didn't know any different, but the health office needed more funds.

"Hang tight. Ms. Gentry will be in shortly to take your vitals." The nurse said as she left.

"Great, can't wait…." fake enthusiasm dripped from his voice.

It took forever for Ms. Gentry to come into the tiny room that was now filled with the stench of his soiled clothing. He pulled his book, "The Long Walk" by Stephen King, from his back pocket. He must have read it a hundred times until recently. He wasn't opening it to read the words anymore; only to look at her. The reason he was back in town. He smiled as tears welled in his eyes.

Once more, he found himself lost in thought. Waves of sorrow threatened to engulf him, but he took a deep breath and concentrated solely on her smile—the beauty of it, the one thing that still gave him hope. Just as he was immersed in this memory, two knocks on the door jolted him back to reality. It caused him to drop his cherished Polaroid on the floor. His stress level boiled over.

"Dammit!" He griped as the young nurse cut her head sharply.

"Good afternoon Mr... Grenlow?" She read it as she entered the door without seeing who she was speaking to. "Evan!?"

"Yes, it's Evan," He replied as he tried to bend down, careful not to rip the butcher paper on the chair with his dirty clothes.

"Oh... Evan? Is that you? Really?" He couldn't believe it. A familiar wave of Lilac and peppermint hit him like a ton of bricks. Her smell sent his heart straight to the floor along with the picture.

"...Millie?"

She looked down to see the photo on the floor. If she was smiling, Evan couldn't tell because of her floral-patterned mask.

"Yes, I, uh..." He stammered.

"Where have you been, Evan? I thought you and your dad got sick?" she asked.

He was surprised that she even thought about him after he left. '...My dad and I left to live at his old house... It's a long story,"

Her eyebrows furled slightly.

"Why didn't you tell us you were leaving?" She asked. It took Evan a second to calculate a response. He didn't realize that she even noticed him before.

"Well. It was kind of last-minute. My father was like that sometimes." He spoke. It became a challenge not to stutter. He underestimated how fast his heart could beat without an explosion.

"Was?"

Evan was confused.

"you said was. Where is your dad now?"

He gathered his thoughts. "He… died… a few days ago."

Millie teared up. "Oh my god Evan, I'm so sorry. You guys were super close."

He wiped the tears from his eyes. "My father died right after you left."

The room filled with a heavy silence as they both processed their emotions.

"I'm so sorry, Millie," Evan whispered.

"Everyone has lost so much, it's so hard to understand. It's just me, my little sister Steph, and my aunt Tulie. I wasn't in any shape to run the pantry after he passed, so someone else tried and got caught stealing. With the quarantine starting again, food is delivered to houses or drop-off points. It's absurd."

The sweetness of her voice captivated Evan even through the sorrow and felt mesmerized by it.

"Where are you staying, Evan? I noticed they gave the house to another family. I think your dad told them you weren't coming back?"

"Honestly, I don't have anywhere to go. Everything I own is sitting outside on the stoop if it's still there. I didn't think things through, but I'll figure something out."

As Millie checked his vitals, their conversation continued. She never mentioned the picture Evan picked up from the floor and shoved it into his pocket.

"I'm glad you're back, Evan. I know we never really talked." He clung to her every word, in awe of his luck in even having a conversation with her. Then she said it. "You know, before my father passed, we moved to a new house on Bay Ridge Road. It's pretty big and has a garage with a loft on top. You're welcome to stay there until you figure something out."

Evan felt like he'd struck gold, careful not to read too much into her words. "Yeah, of course. I would love to," He could barely contain his excitement. Millie grabbed a form attached to her clipboard, flipped it over, and drew a crude map.

"My shift here doesn't end for a couple of hours. Just head over there after your test results come back, and I'll meet you when my shift here is over." She said as she folded the map and handed it to him. He sensed her excitement and pushed the boundaries a little, remembering his dad's advice: "Take risks, be bold, and say something unexpected."

He stopped her shortly before she closed the door. "Oh, hey, Millie?"

She turned, and her gorgeous, wavy ponytail swung gracefully. "Are you smiling?"

She let go of the doorknob and placed her free hand on the clipboard. "...I am now" she shook her head. Her cheeks filled with blood.

He pulled the picture from his pocket. "Can you pull your mask down so I can see? I've been staring at this picture for so long. I want to see it in person."

Mortified and in disbelief that he dared to say it, Evan's heart raced. Whether it impacted, didn't matter; he was proud of himself for having the nerve. Her eyes sparkled like candles; it melted his heart even further. Slowly, she pulled down her mask and revealed a stunning smile framed by glossy, pink, full lips accentuated by dimples.

"Wow, Evan," she was still smiling even after she pulled the mask back up to hide her blushing cheeks. It had been a while since anyone made such a tactful advance and executed it so smoothly. It impressed her.

"You smell terrible..." She shut the door and left him alone with his thoughts. The map she'd drawn had a note written at the bottom, accompanied by a smiley face.

"Work-study, huh?"

He laughed out loud. The thrill of it all coursed through his veins. If Millie only knew the obstacles he overcame to get here. He felt indestructible as he made his way through the building like nothing in the world could stop him.

He exited through the front door where he came in, past the rigid masked bellhop. He yanked the mask off his face and threw his arms up, singing his favorite lyric from his new favorite song.

The woman at the door watched with her arms crossed. She stood silently. He looked over at her and without a thought; he smiled and threw up his middle finger, his test results and yelled.

"Still not as negative as you, bitch!"

She swung open the door and said some of her own choice words he couldn't make out with her mask obscuring the sound. He laughed at himself for a moment as the mad masked woman only pointed to the space on the stoop where he left his mud-caked belongings.

His hands dropped to his sides; disappointment was apparent on his face. "Damn it!"

He watched her pull down her mask from the other side of the door. She was laughing at him.

*

When he arrived at Millie's house, it surprised him to see how tidy and well-maintained it was; compared to the others in the cul-de-sac. He noticed a little girl swinging on a metal porch swing; she couldn't be over seven years old, and he guessed she was Steph, Millie's little sister. As Evan fiddled with the latch on the wooden gate out front, the girl spotted him, darted inside, and quickly returned with an older lady. She looked around sixty, maybe even older; Evan tried to recall her name—Julie, perhaps?

"Can I help you, son? Are you lost?" She asked as she stepped through the squeaking screen door. Though she didn't seem threatened, one hand hidden inside the door suggested he'd better stay outside the gate until they were more acquainted.

"My name is Evan. Millie from the Medical Center sent me here. We're old friends, …well, kinda old friends… more acquaintances, really." Evan stuttered. He didn't want to sound like a weirdo.

"…she said she had a place for me to stay for a few days." Evan said.

"I'm gonna need a little more than that to go by, son. I'm sorry, but you can't trust anyone these days," she replied cautiously. Evan stepped back from the fence.

"I completely understand. I'll sit on the sidewalk until she comes home, if you don't mind. She said her shift ends at five, so that's not much longer." Evan replied as he backed away from the fence.

"Are you Evan from the pantry?" Steph called out from beside the older woman.

"Yes, I am. I volunteered there with Millie and your dad, Steph." Steph grabbed Tulie's hand and smiled.

"That's the one, Aunt Tulie. That's the kid with the eyes."

The older lady hesitated for a moment before she sent the young girl to unlatch the gate from the inside.

As Steph approached, she beamed at him. Her small hand clutched around the left leg of a doll; she had to lay it on the hedge to work the metal latch.

"My name is Steph, and I'm six! How old are you? You could be my friend."

It had been a long time since Evan interacted with anyone younger than him. The sight of her smile warmed his heart.

"I'm 16, I think. It's very nice to meet you, Stephanie."

"Just Steph is okay." She said as they walked together inside the gate. The older woman came onto the porch to look him in the eyes. Evan knew she was giving him a silent warning; he could tell she wasn't to be crossed. Before she let him up the steps, her eyes went to Evan's waistband and back again. She wanted his gun.

"Oh yes, of course, I forgot about it, honestly."

It didn't matter what he said, he felt every word out of his mouth sounded like a lie. She half-smiled, removed the clip, slipped it between her white bra strap and leathery freckled skin and returned the empty gun to him.

"Take those nasty boots off, please. I don't want mud on the carpets." She sat down on the porch swing. Steph let go of his hand.

"I can untie them for you, Evan. I'm much closer."

Evan couldn't remember the last time he had taken them off. There was no telling what it would smell like. After a few tense moments as Steph fought with the wet, knotted shoelaces, Evan felt his emotions well up yet again. While he stood there on the porch in front of Tulie, unable to move with Steph at his feet. He cried. He was worried Steph would see him. Tulie caught on quickly.

"Steph, he can do the rest, honey. Why don't you run in and get some ice-cold glasses of lemonade and some cookies?"

Steph: without question jumped up and wiped her wet, muddy fingers on her overalls and rushed inside.

"I'm sorry, ma'am, but I'm embarrassed. I haven't taken my boots off in over two weeks, and I'm in no shape to be in anyone's home." She smiled sweetly at him.

"It's okay, son. I'll tell you what, go around to the back porch. There's a water pump you can use to wash your feet off. Once you do that, I'll turn the generator on, and you can take a hot shower."

She stood and walked closer and looked deep into his eyes with a smile.

"Take your time son, take all the time you need."

Tulie was wise, and she lived many lives. She could sense his trauma and see the signs on his face. She was very familiar with it.

Evan went around the house to the back and found the pump.

Once he finally got the knots out of the muddy laces, he could gradually slip the hiking boots off. He could smell the infected blisters on his feet. It was terrible, rancid even. The socks were so worn they unraveled as his feet came loose from the boots. He was so embarrassed.

Once he was dry, Evan knocked on the screen door and Steph led him inside as Tulie watched from the kitchen.

"Come on in, friend, make yourself cozy!"

"Steph, why don't you go play while Evan gets himself cleaned up?"

Tulie tried to keep Steph from smothering him. She was beyond excited to have another person around. Because of the quarantines, Steph's father decided it would be best to homeschool her and Millie. It was much easier for Steph, since she knew nothing about public schools. But it left her without a social network. Especially after the Rasping fever flared again, she spent most of her time in isolation with her family.

"Okay! You'll be surprised at how much better you feel when cleaned up." She said with a smile.

Evan could tell that Steph was very excited as she bounced down the hallway into her room. Tulie chuckled.

"I left you two towels and two brown grocery bags in the sink. Take your clothes off and put them in. I'll wash them for you."

"Thank you so much, Ma'am." He said as he started down the hall.

"Evan. Listen to me carefully." She stopped him. "I'm a little upset with Millie for putting me in a position like this with someone I don't know, so trust me when I say I'm going out on a limb with you here. Just know I'm watching you, and I have my gun in my waistband. It still has a full clip, and I won't hesitate to shoot you where you stand."

"Yes, ma'am." He didn't argue with her; he knew it would take time to build trust.

"Okay, go on now. The bathroom is that way." She said as she sipped a glass of lemonade.

Evan walked on his tiptoes so as not to drag his best the cuff of his wet, muddy pants on the carpet.

Making his way down the long hall, he found the bathroom himself. The walls were covered in portraits of the family that lived in the house before. The boys were big and strong like their father, and the daughter was just as pretty as the mother. They seemed like they would have been a fun-loving family. Evan wondered what happened to them. Did they get sick like everyone else? Did they try for one of the quarantine zones the government set up further in the city? He hoped they were all alive and together somewhere out there, with smiles painted on their faces just as they were in the pictures.

He could hear Steph in one of the bedrooms further down. He could see the light pink walls of her room through an open doorway. She was humming a song, and every so often, she would fill in with the words:

"Let it go! Let it go!"

He thought it sounded very familiar but couldn't place it. The only songs he could remember were the ones his dad would sing as they hiked through the woods. Something like "Here Come the Men in Black" and "Hakuna Matata." Songs from movies were always his favorite to sing.

The shower was warm, and the soap Tulie provided carried the same soothing scent as Millie's—a blend of Lilac and lavender. The smell brought a sense of relaxation and excitement. It enveloped him in a comforting embrace. The water from the showerhead was crystal clear and tasted almost metallic, starkly contrasting the filth it would soon wash away.

The water flowed through his hair and over his scraped and scarred skin. It transformed into an almost black hue, carrying the grime accumulated on his body. Dirt seemed to be embedded in every crack, crevice, and pore, making cleaning himself arduous but necessary.

Despite his best efforts to be quick, the process took longer than expected. Each stroke of the washcloth revealed an additional layer of filth, but with every passing minute, Evan felt his spirits lift as if the water were washing away not only the dirt but also the heavy burden he'd been carrying. Finally, emerging from the shower clean and refreshed, he couldn't help but feel a renewed sense of hope and determination.

It took Evan over an hour to get himself back to normal. The hot water lasted only for the first half of his shower. He worried that the well ran dry empty. After he toweled off, he used his hand to wipe the steam from the mirror. Steph was right; he felt incredible, but only on the outside. He knew it would take some time before the eternal pain would ease. Being in a house again with so much life was helping.

As Evan stepped into the kitchen, he heard Millie chatting with Steph.

"Has he been nice to you?" Millie asked Steph.

"Yes, Millie! He's very nice, and I like his smile; it makes me happy!" Steph laughed.

"That's great! Good boys are rare these days."

"Millie, he's sweet, but I think—" Tulie whispered to Sarah but noticed Evan round the corner, his wet hair hanging in his face.

"Enjoy the shower, Evan?" Tulie quickly changed the subject.

"Yes, ma'am, I did. Thank you very much." Evan wore a bright pink shirt with a game controller and the words, Eat. Play. Repeat; in black letters below.

"I see you've met my lovely family, Evan. They said you've been very nice. I hope you're ready to eat?" Evan hesitated, feeling awkward around all these new people.

"I... Don't think…" "Nonsense!" Tulie interrupted.

"I won't have someone in my house who doesn't share a meal with me. It wouldn't be right."

Evan silently ran his fingers through his long brown hair, trying to keep it out of his face.

"…Only if I can sit next to Steph."

He looked down at her beaming smile and it warmed his heart, as well as Millie's and Tulie's.

What was supposed to be a temporary stay turned into much more. Even though Evan was still emotionally withdrawn, struggling to process the tragedy of losing his father and witnessing dark magic that fateful night in Lola's headlights, he kept most of it to himself, despite Millie's incessant probing. He didn't know how to let it go and hoped it would get easier with time. But as long as the beast wearing his father's skin roamed free, he couldn't see how that was possible.

On a beautiful afternoon, as Evan and Steph tended to the garden behind the house, she posed a question he knew would inevitably arise.

"Do you Love Millie Evan?"

she gently asked, looking at him with curiosity and concern.

He laughed and welcomed the opportunity to talk about it. He secretly hoped to gain insight into Millie's feelings.

"Well, that's a big question, Steph. What makes you think that?" She shrugged her shoulders, still holding her little green watering can above a vine of ripening heirloom tomatoes.

"I see how you look at her. Kind of like how my dad used to look at my mom before she left." Evan felt his cheeks turn red as he tried to untangle the leaking water hose.

"Well, Steph, I care about her a lot, and I think she's the most beautiful girl I've ever seen besides you!" She smiled and shook her head. He wanted to tell her how he felt but knew Steph couldn't keep a secret.

"She's kind and smart. That may be a conversation I should have with her before I talk to you about it, though. Don't you think that's fair?"

"Hmmm, I guess so."

He hoped to learn more about Millie's feelings, but decided not to press it, primarily out of fear that she didn't feel the same way.

"Who's Oct'Tulommon, Evan?" The hose dropped to the ground.

"Where did you hear that name, Steph?!" Evan turned and asked sharply, his face sullen. Steph backed away slowly, uncomfortable with his sudden change in demeanor.

"Where, Steph? Tell me now!"

"I… I just…"

"Tell me, Steph, now!" He became more forceful.

"I'm sorry, Evan… I didn't mean to."

He realized he crossed a line when he saw tears in her blue eyes. When he snapped back, Steph was already running to find Tulie.

"Damn it, Evan," He thought to himself. A few moments later, Tulie emerged from the house with a glass of fresh lemonade for him. She sat down on the edge of the garden box and handed him the glass.

"Is she okay, Tulie? I feel terrible. I hope I didn't scare her too badly." Tulie smiled and straightened the fabric of her dress over her thighs.

"Ah, she'll be fine; she's tough. She's been through a lot, Evan—her mother leaving, her father passing. And on top of all that, she is trying to grow up during a pandemic. She's adjusted and made do with what she was given.

"When I moved in here after my brother passed—Steph's dad—she pulled almost all of her hair out. She bit her nails down to the quick. She cried throughout the night sometimes; it was terrible. She's much better now, and you being here has been a big part of that. Both Millie and I thank you for that."

Evan smiled at her as he sat down.

"But Evan, you're no good to us if you aren't willing to let us help you, too."

His posture changed.

"You need to talk about it Evan. It's the only way you're going to get through it. Sometimes we hear you screaming in your sleep in the house! Sometimes you say things that don't make any sense. We can tell you're hurting, which hurts us all."

He didn't look up from the ground, unsure how to respond. "Millie…"

As soon as she said her name, he looked up at her. She smiled and paused.

"Millie is why you're here, Evan. I know that. I'm very protective of her; I'll have you know. If I didn't think you were worth the boots you walked in here in, I would have told you to take a hike that day. You need to talk to her, Evan, and tell her your story. She needs that. You need that."

"I know, Tulie, I know." He said as he reached over and cradled her hand, a gesture that warmed her heart. Evan was an empathetic and perceptive individual with a caring nature.

"I will. I just don't think she's going to believe me, and I don't think you will either. It's so impossible. I still don't even believe it myself."

"Let us be the judge of that," Tulie responded softly, her eyes filled with understanding and reassurance. She knew that no matter how brutal the truth might be, it was important for Evan to share his story and allow them to support him on his healing journey.

Chapter 9
First Kiss

Millie was met with an eerie silence as she stepped through the front door one random evening. Silence was not something she was used to, especially with Steph's energetic presence usually filling the house.

"Hello? Where is everyone?" Her voice echoed through the empty rooms, unanswered. She caught the scent of hickory wood burning and sniffed her clothes, thinking it might have been residual from her bike ride home through the city. As she set her belongings down, Millie started searching the house. It was immaculate — every surface gleaming and not a speck of dust. It had been cleaned from top to bottom.

She found a note on the kitchen counter beside a massive magnolia blossom—her favorite. The handwriting on the front was unmistakably Steph's, with big, red letters spelling out "R.P.V.S." Though the acronym was out of order, Millie got the idea. Turning the note over, she found an invitation that read:

***

Good evening Lilliana Mae Gentry,
You have been cordially invited to a dinner engagement.

*

HOSTED BY: *Under the moonlight, in the backyard.*

*

WHERE: *Master Evan Grenlow*

*

*This is a formal event and requires your presence promptly at **8:00 PM**.*

P.S. *Please refrain from venturing outside until the designated time.*

***

With anticipation and curiosity, Millie prepared herself for the unexpected evening ahead.

Millie's excitement grew as she discovered the thoughtful gestures Evan prepared for her. Being older than Evan by five years made the possibility of a relationship slightly scandalous, but the world changed, and so did their priorities.

Evan was more mature, distinguished, and kinder than any man her age. He was intelligent, humorous, and undeniably attractive. His charm was irresistible, and Millie couldn't deny she entertained thoughts about him in a romantic light.

The most significant factor in their potential chemistry was how much Steph adored Evan and how much he reciprocated her affection. Millie and her younger sister Steph were a package deal; any romantic development would require her sister's blessing.

With Steph and Tulie's help, Evan meticulously planned the entire evening. He set the dinner reservation for later to allow Millie time to discover several surprises he'd arranged for her. In her bathroom, she found a bottle of her favorite bath soap and a tub filled with piping hot water.

"I hope you enjoy the hot water."

The attention to detail and thoughtfulness behind Evan's actions touched Millie's heart, making her eager to see what the rest of the evening held.

Millie marveled at Evan's effort to create a magical evening for her. After her bath, she found another note on her dresser, accompanied by a box.

"I think your favorite color is Emerald?"

She opened the box to discover a stunning silver necklace with an emerald pendant shaped like a heart. Millie fell in love with it instantly.

As she approached her mirror to put the necklace on, she noticed a tattered Polaroid of herself with yet another note attached.

"This picture got me through one of the worst times in my life. I'm so thankful to have you in my life now, not just in a picture. Love, Evan."

Tears welled up in her eyes and threatened to ruin her makeup. She glanced at her wristwatch, reading 7:50 PM. Millie had just ten minutes to fix her makeup. As she descended the staircase, she found Steph waiting for her, wearing a lovely pink dress, her hair styled in a fancy updo. On her feet were black closed-toed shoes with a slight heel and a gold buckle. Steph's smile stretched from ear to ear.

"Oh my god, Steph, you look amazing!" Millie exclaimed, almost tripping down the steps.

"Evan took me to town and traded some things he found in the shed outback for my dress! He even let me pick out the socks!" Steph proudly declared.

Millie glanced down to see one sock featuring Disney's Princess Belle, while the other resembled an ugly Christmas sweater.

"I couldn't decide which one I liked more, so I wore them both!" Steph announced, her excitement added to the enchantment of the evening.

Steph proudly displayed her mismatched socks, and Millie laughed and cried simultaneously.

"Right this way, my lady?" Steph offered as she extended her arm for Millie to hold on to.

Millie was wearing a blue, tight-fitting pencil skirt—the only one she owned—paired with black heels that were a bit too small. The heels clicked against the hardwoods as she walked through the kitchen toward the back door.

Evan draped the backyard with twinkling Christmas lights powered by a generator. Its hum was audible from the opposite end of the house—thick smoke billowed from the grill, where Tulie was working to prepare their dinner.

"This is incredible, isn't it, Millie? He worked hard, staying up almost half the night planning it with Tulie! Don't tell him I told you, though," Steph whispered conspiratorially. Millie smiled as Steph opened the door to the patio.

"It is Steph. It's beautiful."

Steph led Millie to a picnic table draped with a pristine white bedsheet. Tea light candles floated in glasses of water, surrounded by wildflowers Evan had collected earlier in the day. Tulie glanced over her shoulder, taking in Millie's reaction to the romantic setting.

"This is all so nice, Tulie. Thank you so much."

Tulie wiped her hands with a cloth and poured glasses of sweet tea.

"Don't thank me. Thank Evan. This was all his doing."

Millie saw Evan approach from the garage, dressed in a blue suit with pencil stripes. The sleeves were three inches short, and the pants cut off circulation to his crotch. Despite the ill-fitting suit, Millie couldn't help but smile, tears in her eyes. She raised a hand to cover her mouth, but Evan stopped her before he pulled her chair out for her.

"Don't you dare cover that up," He whispered.

"That smile is the reason for this."

She was stunned by Evan's thoughtfulness and ability to make her blush. His smile was infectious, stretching from ear to ear. He seemed more nervous than ever, but he did an impressive job of holding it together. After Tulie placed plates of fresh salmon and garden salads in front of them, she and Steph returned inside, giving Millie and Evan some privacy.

Following dinner, Evan led Millie to a porch swing he set up on the other side of the yard. He excused himself to shut off the noisy generator and returned with some firewood. Millie appreciated the silence and wrapped herself in a blanket that Evan thoughtfully placed on the swing earlier that day.

"I figured you might get cold out here," he said as he softly wrapped her with it.

"Thank you, Evan. Thank you for everything. You don't know how much this means to me."

He smiled as he started the fire.

"Millie, I've tried to find the right way to tell you how I feel for a long time now." She grinned and replied,

"Let me guess; the picture wasn't for a work-study, huh?"

"Ha, no, it wasn't. I knew I was leaving and wanted it so I could see you every day. I never thought I'd see you again."

His expression shifted as he started down the familiar path of painful memories.

"There's a lot that happened while I was away, Millie. A lot of bad things. Things I'm afraid to tell you. The night before my father died, he asked me about the picture of you I kept in my book. I told him who you were and that I never got to tell you how I felt." She smiled as he continued to add logs to the fire.

"The next day, he told me he would bring me back here to tell you how I feel, how I couldn't stop thinking about you. How I was afraid that...I would never get the chance to tell you."

Evan moved to sit next to her on the swing.

"Evan, I had no idea. I always thought you were nice and very handsome. I would've been flattered to know you had a crush." She reached for his hand.

"And after all this, Evan—this whole night and the entire time you've been here—I've been nervous about letting our relationship go further..."

Evan looked into her eyes. He understood her fears. She feared the anger in his heart.

"Evan, I need to know. If I'm going to trust you with my heart, Steph's heart, and Tulie's heart, I need you to trust me too. I need you to let yourself go with me. I can't love someone who is so guarded."

Evan took a deep breath and let his mind travel back to Fern Gully.

"My dog Tucker... he ran into the woods behind the house my father and I were fixing up. We planned to walk to a service station to get some gas for the car we were going to drive back in. So, we took a gas can and followed Tucker into the woods. He took off in the direction we needed to go. After about an hour of searching, we found him... He was..." Tears streamed down Evan's face. "...A wolf... an unusually large wolf with a chain and a lock around its neck."

Millie squeezed his hand. It was a very unexpected turn in his story, almost unbelievable. But she urged him to continue.

"...It was eating him. I yelled for it to get off, but when I did, three more wolves flanked us on all sides. All of them were extremely large, the size of... bears." Evan looked in shock. She placed her other hand on his to reassure him she was there. It broke his concentration, and he continued.

"...I heard my father pull the bolt back on the rifle but before he could get a shot, the wolf lunged over my head and landed on top of him. He tried to fight, but... the wolf was strong. I grabbed the gun and shot at it, but I missed. And then it turned to me... I saw my dad. He was... he was gone... I grabbed the rifle after my dad dropped it, but before I could shoot, the wolf knocked the rifle from my hand. Something happened… I think it had a seizure or something, so I grabbed the gas can and ran. I just kept running as fast as I could, for I don't know how long."

"My god, Evan, I'm so sorry. I didn't know."

He hesitated, reluctant to explain the second half of the story.

"…There was nothing I could do for him. I didn't want to just leave him there Millie…" His composure was faltering. " I knew though if didn't run, I would be dead too."

Both Evan and Millie sobbed uncontrollably for at least twenty minutes. Having heard Evan's story not only made her hurt for him, but also brought back the feelings about doing her own father.

"Millie, I know this sounds crazy, and I know you may think it was just the stress of it all, but... that's not the end."

She gripped his hands tightly. Her mascara stained the dinner napkin she wiped her face with.

"The night I left, I put the gas in the car and pulled it in front of the house. I stopped the car and got out because I left your picture inside my tent around the back of the house. I wanted to put it on the dash."

She smiled again as she dabbed her nose with her blanket.

"But when I started to pull away, my dad was standing in the headlights."

Evan could see her brow furrowed in confusion. He sensed she was becoming apprehensive.

"...Evan, what do you mean?"

He got nervous.

"Trust me Millie, I know I sound crazy. I watched my dad take his last breath in the forest the day before. He was bleeding from his neck, his chest… his arm was... there's no way it could have been him. But it was… At least, I thought so."

Millie could feel the chills rise up her neck.

"When I got out to get a better look, it wasn't him. The thing was…unfamiliar. And his skin looked stretched and torn." He paused as he wiped his eyes. "It tried to grab me, but I shot at it. I hit it twice, I think. It fell to the ground on all fours and took off into the woods. Laughing."

"What do you think it was, Evan?"

He didn't waste any time saying it. He figured it wouldn't make a difference if she had already written him off as crazy.

"It was the wolf that killed my father. I don't know how he did it, but the laugh. It was the same laugh I heard from him right after he crushed my father's chest and ripped his head almost clean off."

"... I know how this sounds, Millie. I'm not even sure what I saw was real; you don't think I could've imagined it all, do you? Like some kind of delusion from stress?"

She was silent, like she was searching her mind for an answer to the events that led Evan to her.

"…I will never forget his name for the rest of my life. It will forever be locked in my mind. Oct'Tulommon."

She slid off the porch swing, stood over him, and placed her hands on both sides of his cheeks.

"Wait a second,

"Millie? Are you okay?"

"Evan, you said the wolf that killed your father… Did he mention something?"

She paused in a fit of confusion, trying to remember.

"Oh my god, what was it… The Fire! The Owl… Awl fire! Did he mention the Awl'Fire?"

Evan stood up, completely perplexed.

"Did he mention—" "Evan, think! Did he mention the Awl'Fire?!... did he?"

Evan searched his memories over and over. "No, he didn't."

Millie's shoulders deflated.

"...But one of the others did. A taller, longer, sleeker wolf. He asked if the Awl'Fire allowed us to speak to one another. But the alpha wolf who killed my father said it wasn't. That it was the Void."

She put her hands over her mouth in shock.

"I will never forget his name for the rest of my life. It will forever be locked in my mind. Oct'Tulommon." Evan said.

"We need to talk to Tulie. You need to tell her this." Millie said as she pulled him up.

"What!? Why?"

"I need you to trust me. I think she may know what killed your father."

As they walked back to the house, hand in hand. The night wrapped them in an embrace of comfort. The soft glow of the moonlight bathed the surroundings in a gentle silver light, casting intricate patterns of shadows from the trees and plants that adorned the garden.

Their footsteps on the dewy grass were the only accompaniment to their shared silence, each lost in their thoughts about the night's revelations.

When they reached the back door, Millie took a deep breath and looked into Evan's eyes, her determination reflected in the depths of her gaze.

"Evan, everything you have done tonight for me, I loved. This was honestly one of the best nights of my life. I want us together but more importantly; I want us to be happy together. There is too much bringing us all down! I'm glad that you came back for me."

He smiled, and yet again, tears filled his eyes. But this time, they were happy tears.

She kissed his lips, and he held her close for a time. After she pulled back, he grabbed her again for another.

"Millie, that was my first kiss and second kiss."

She sank back down with a smile.

"Promise me, no matter what happens; we'll face it together."

Evan nodded, his expression resolute. With that, they stepped inside, ready to confront the mysteries of the past and the unknowns of the future, their hearts united in their love for each other and their unbreakable bond.

Part III: History

Chapter 10
Tulie's Past

The second time Evan recounted the events that led to him being there.
The more manageable it felt. He realized Tulie was right talking about
trauma helps to heal it, maybe better than anything else. He felt like
he'd been talking for hours, talking for so long that his throat was
scratchy. Millie stayed beside him the entire time.

Tulie was in tears. His father's death and the wolves, Tulie was
in tears. He spared her most of the graphic details for two reasons: one;
he didn't want to upset her any worse than she already was, and two, it
hurt his heart too much. Millie kept her eyes locked on Evan the whole
time, but she watched Tulie's reaction to what he was saying in her
peripheral vision. She was hiding something, trying not to seem like she
knew things.

After he finished, Evan and Millie sat silently to let Tulie take it
all in. But she didn't have the reaction Millie thought she would have.

"Tulie?" Millie said, "Does any of this sound familiar to you?"

Tulie was silent as she poured another shot from a Wild Turkey
bottle on the kitchen counter. They gave her a moment to respond.

"I'm sure Evan was just like he said, in shock. It couldn't be…."

"What? Tulie, couldn't be what?"

Millie snapped. Tulie appeared shocked.

"If you're talking about those stories, I told you when you were
a little girl, I was drunk. You know I had bad habits."

Millie bit her lip as she searched for the right words to say. The dim light from the kitchen window cast shadows across Tulie's face. It emphasized the wrinkles from a life of hardships.

"Tulie, you might have been drunk when you told me those stories, but they've always stuck with me. Now, with what Evan experienced, I can't help but feel there's more to them. You know something, and if we're going to face whatever it is, we need the truth. Please, Tulie. For all of us."

Tulie sighed and took a moment to gather her thoughts.

She looked into Millie's determined eyes and then at Evan, waiting with bated breath. Finally, she relented.

"Alright!" she said, her voice barely above a whisper. Suddenly, her posture changed, and she looked earnest.

"Evan, I need to know the truth. If this is some game you're playing, it's not funny and will end badly for you."

She stood on her side of the table and put her fists down. Evan could tell she was being sincere. She might've been older, but time with a motorcycle gang and even her few stints in prison made her tough.

"Aunt Tulie why are you–" Millie began, but Tulie's eyes didn't break from Evan's gaze.

"It's fine, Millie," Evan reassured her. He paused for a second.

"There were four wolves in total. They called the biggest Oct'Tolommon; he described himself as the ender of life. The others were Ack'Reus, Apollo, and Ha'Kan. Apollo was lean with short hair and pointed ears like a Doberman. Ack'Reus was smaller, more agile and red, like the color of clay. Ha'Kan was sickly and standoffish; I think he even gave my dad a window to escape. He was missing the bottom half of his hind leg and looked sick. They called my dog Tucker a...." "Druthe?" Tulie interrupted. Evan's brow crumpled in disbelief. He continued.

"They asked me why I was faking sadness over a slave—"

Millie was amazed; he omitted so much of this from his original telling. Tulie settled down and interrupted.

"Druthes... Wolves think of dogs as slaves to humans. The offspring of weak wolves that allowed themselves to be captured after the Dimming," Tulic explained, her voice full of sorrow.

"The dimming?" Evans' list of unanswered questions continued to grow.

Millie looked at Tulie, her eyes wide with shock.

"Tulie... the stories you told me as a child. Were they real?"

Tulie hesitated for a moment.

"Honestly, Millie, my love, I didn't think so then. I was with many people doing a lot of crazy drugs..." She backtracked.

"I was… with this guy. He was much older than me, a Vietnam vet. Sometimes, we would get high, he would tell me things—stories of wolves and what they believe. I always loved hearing him talk. I never thought what he said could be real! I just thought he was… fucking high, and his stories were incredible!"

Tulie chuckled as the memories of her past welled up inside.

"I mean… the man said he was a wolf for Christ's sake. You'll believe anything a boy tells you when you're twenty and in love."

"Tulie! You never told me this?! When did you see him last? Where is he now?" Millie demanded. Tulie hesitated, a faint smile playing on her lips as she recalled some fond memories.

"... Last week."

"WHAT!?" Millie exclaimed.

"What!? I'm not allowed to have fun anymore? He never comes to the house, and I never tell him anything about you. He doesn't even know Steph exists!" Tulie defended herself.

"This is the craziest thing I've heard and I'm currently living through a pandemic," Millie said as she scrunched her hair in her hands.

"Tulie, you need to call him. We must meet! If he knows any more about what happened—"

Evan insisted, his voice filled with determination.

"Why Evan?"

The look of curiosity faded to a scowl.

"What do you mean, why, Tulie? I watched that animal turn my father inside out! I'll find him and when I do, I'll make sure I don't miss."

The revelation mystified him and brought a new purpose to his life. Millie had a worried look.

Evan closed his eyes. Violence against all four wolves there that day took over every fiber of his being.

"I'm going to kill them all."

Millie and Tulie looked very disappointed in his thinking, but they could understand.

"Tulie, I think he is right. Revenge shouldn't motivate you, but it sounds like they need to be stopped."

Tulie fell silent again as if she was reluctant to reveal something.

"Tulie, what is it?" Millie asked, her voice laced with concern.

Evan and Millie exchanged glances as Tulie stood up and walked out the door. They followed her to the deck but stopped after she went out into the grass shy of the tree line. For five minutes, she stood in silence. Evan and Millie watched her from the porch, their curiosity piqued.

"What is she doing out there, Millie?"

"I don't know…" She replied. Then, as if she snapped back to reality, Tulie turned and walked past them. Her body settled into the porch swing as she lit a cigarette.

"He's coming..." she announced and exhaled a puff of smoke.

Evan and Millie turned to see a white wolf glide out of the woods. Its fur reflected the moon's silvery light. The wolf had one eye and looked ancient, its gait slow and deliberate. Millie's heart skipped a beat as if she just saw a ghost, while Evan's heart raced for a different reason - seeing the wolf emerge from the darkness brought back vivid memories of Fern Gully. He clasped Millie's hand and squeezed it as the mysterious wolf glided closer. Her pulse echoed his anxiety.

The wolf drifted around the back of the garage where Evan's room was and vanished. The air was thick with anticipation as they waited, nervous about what might approach from beyond.

Moments later, an elderly man emerged, his hair white as the wolf's fur moments before. He wore a black eye patch that concealed his right eye, which only added to his mystique. The metamorphosis from beast to man was astonishing, leaving Evan and Millie speechless.

Evan couldn't help but wonder what other secrets this enigmatic figure held and how his appearance might unravel the mysteries that haunted him since that fateful day in the forest.

"Hello there. My name is Atticus Atuawee, but you can call me Atohi. Tulie mentioned you had a run-in with some wolves." The older man gently spoke—his voice, deep and warm like the embers of a dying fire.

Evan still couldn't formulate a word to say.

"Please, tell me about that, son. I can be of some help."

Atohi waved at Tulie, who seemed pleasantly embarrassed now that Millie knew she was involved with an older, one-eyed, half-wolf; half-Native American who was also a decorated Vietnam war hero. After the pleasantries and introductions, Millie entered the kitchen to fix a few drinks and light snacks. She felt they would be talking well into the night. Evan and Atohi stayed outside, adding more wood to the fire.

"Evan, I'm sorry about your father and your dog, Tucker," Atohi said sympathetically.

"How do you know that? I didn't tell you anything!" Evan snapped back forcefully. Atohi remained calm.

"I know this seems strange, but I'm… in a way connected to Tulie, so what she knows, I know too; before she knows it herself even.." Atohi said as he chuckled a bit. Evan turned and continued to restart a fire.

He felt anxious and oddly familiar with Atohi, as if he were a favorite uncle he hadn't seen in a while.

"Millie, did you check on Steph? Is she okay?" Evan asked.

"Yes, I did," she replied and smiled at his concern for her sister. It made her feel like he would make a fantastic father.

"Well, let's not waste time—" Evan said, but Millie interrupted, "How'd you get here so quickly, and how'd you know Tulie wanted you here?"

Atohi chuckled.

"I'm a little embarrassed to say."

Tulie smiled. Her eyes glistened with unshed tears.

"Your aunt Tulie, she's imprinted. My "Familiar'' Our hearts connect with the Awl'Fire, what you may call the soul or spirit. A sacred bond that can't be broken. I love her, and she loves me. She doesn't have to tell me; I just know; I've always known. So when she needs me, she reaches through the distance with her heart and mind. I can feel her, and I don't hesitate when I do."

"So, you're not a man?" Evan asked as Tulie cried.

"No, Evan... I am not. This body is not my own. I am an Elden Void Wolf, serving the Alphas of an ancient wolf pack known as the Illnok - A banner of opposition to all Oct'Tulommon stands for. I traverse many realms and can only adopt the forms of those whose fires have been reclaimed by the great Awl'Fire; and have allowed me to do so—the man you see before you was once a cherished friend who faced a desperate situation. I would have sacrificed my life for his, but the Awl'Fire fanned my flame rather than douse it. There can only ever be one of my kind in this realm at a time, which explains the separation between myself and my beloved Tulie. A union between us would break a sacred law of nature. Risking pregnancy is too dangerous."

Everyone was silent.

"I never wanted to be a wife, anyway." Tulie made jokes to keep her emotions from overflowing. Millie puts her hand in hers.

"I can't stay in this form for long. The ability is powered by my Awl'Fire, which I have a finite amount of. Sort of how a man can only concentrate for a short time before it becomes exhausting. I must return to my original form to maintain my sanity."

"That's incredible!" Millie said in awe.

"And Tulie, I'm so sorry. I didn't know. I wish you would've told me this."

"Well, I've always been private about these things anyway," Tulie admitted, wiping away a tear.

"Evan, if you are to understand the reasons behind the horrors you've experienced, perhaps I should start from the beginning. However, to know everything, we would have to sit here for days - and days I'm afraid I do not have. With your permission, Evan. I can use this fire you've built to act as a conduit between us, a bridge connecting our minds. This way, I can show you rather than tell you, and it won't take as long."

Evan looked at Millie; her mind filled with questions and curiosity about this new world. He saw her deflated when he didn't invite her to come along on the journey.

"Okay, I'll allow it, but only if she can come too."

Her face lit up like the sun. Atohi put his hand on hers and Evan's shoulder and smiled as if he could feel the sparks between them.

"Of course I will allow it. Tulie, you know what this means. They won't be able to move for a while, and with the little one upstairs, I think it's safe if I leave you out here, just in case," Atohi said, concerned in his voice. Tulie nodded her understanding.

"Alright then, let's get started, shall we?" Atohi taught Millie and Evan a few techniques on breathing and spoke a few words to open their minds. He communicated through his heart. For Evan, the transition was smooth, as he already experienced something like Oct'Tulommon. Millie, however, took time to adjust. She jumped and squirmed in her chair as Atohi's voice tickled her mind, sending shivers down her spine.

"Okay Millie, focus!" Evan smiled.

"Like you're a professional already at this!? It tickles!"

"Just breathe, and I'll get started," Atohi encouraged.

After a few more tries, Millie could use the Conduit, and the three of them could pass feelings back and forth, then Words. She could fill the strength in Evans and the Anger, but most of all, she could feel the love growing for her, Steph and Tulie. Evan glimpsed Millie's as well; it washed over him. Refreshing, like a dream. But sadness was also abundant, still overshadowed by a blossoming love for him. Evan and Millie slipped into an altered mental state, like a shared dream. They saw each other and could interact but felt like they were floating above themselves. A vivid tapestry of colors weaved in and out, carrying them into another plane of existence. Everything went black, and they could only hear Atohi's voice:

Chapter 11
Wardens

"In the early ages of Earth, long before the dawn of modern man, a mysterious peak atop a great mountain called out to be discovered. Its summit remained hidden; veiled in the mist and clouds, untouched for centuries. This ethereal peak held secrets and powers beyond the comprehension of the natural world, and it whispered its mysteries to the winds as if waiting for those worthy enough to uncover them. Then, everything changed forever for an unlikely pair of weary souls."

The beginning of recorded history started with a solitary man, his features primal and rough-hewn. With a jutting forehead, deep-set eyes crowned by thick brows, and wide teeth resembling those of the grazing beasts in the fields, he looked every bit the primitive hunter. Scantily clothed in crude pelts harvested from long-extinct creatures, he was a roving brute, strong and brave, calloused on both hands and feet. His language was rudimentary and his intelligence was gained through trial and error. His skills were primitive, honed only for survival, throwing with great strength and accuracy, running and hiding, and crafting crude spears from stones for defense.

Wolves, too, were in their most basic of forms. They scavenged for food, wandering the wilds alone and hungry. Only by chance, the man heard the cries of a young wolf trying to rouse his mother's lifeless body below a cliff. Her injuries and location suggested she fell to her death. The cub seemed unharmed; the man saw an opportunity for a meal and resources.

He descended the cliff, keeping his distance from the agitated cub, who growled and barked at his approach. As the man saw the emaciated cub and his mother's decaying body, an unfamiliar emotion stirred within him — empathy. He lowered his spear and dug a grave for the mother wolf, and the cub, sensing his intent, allowed him to ease her body into the shallow resting place.

As he filled the grave, the man's heart ached for the cub, who whimpered and watched the entire process. Once finished, the man climbed back up the cliff, his stomach empty but his heart full. Looking down, he saw the cub curled up on the turned Earth, mourning his mother. Though saddened by the thought that the cub might die there too, he took solace, knowing he gave the young wolf a chance to grieve.

At this moment, the seeds of a bond between man and wolf were sown—a connection that would grow and evolve, transformative in ways both species could never have imagined.

After days of unsuccessful hunting and the ever-growing ache of gnawing hunger, the man found himself more desperate than ever before. His decision to spare the young wolf's life came with a steep price. Food was scarce, and his keen tracking skills failed him as the weather worsened. With each day, he felt the grip of starvation, a fate he swore never to suffer again.

Seeking refuge from the biting cold, the man nestled beneath a cypress tree, its fragrant needles creating a protective canopy against the snow. With his remaining energy reserves dwindling and the cold seeping into his bones, he succumbed to a night of restless sleep.

He awoke the following day to find a rabbit had sought shelter beneath the same cypress. The unsuspecting creature was a tantalizingly close meal, and the man's mouth watered at the thought of tearing into its warm, succulent flesh. As he reached for a rock to kill the rabbit, its searching eye and twitching nose caught his movement, and he felt his hope for a meal slipping away.

From the shadows beneath a nearby tree, a whirlwind of snow, wiry brown fur, and sharp teeth descended upon the disoriented rabbit. The orphaned wolf, now shaking the rabbit, its bones snapping in the wolf's mighty jaws. In mere moments, the rabbit was still, its lifeless body in the wolf's mouth.

The wolf approached the man, who remained still beneath the cypress and laid the limp rabbit on his chest. Confusion flickered in the man's eyes as the wolf nudged the rabbit toward him before settling down, pressing against his side. The warmth emanating from the wolf sent shivers up the man's spine.

The man brought the rabbit to his mouth and tore into the tender flesh, the warm blood revitalizing him. He ate, feeling his strength return with each bite. After consuming the rabbit's legs, he returned the rest to the wolf, who watched him eat.

In this shared moment, a bond formed between the man and the wolf, transcending their primal instincts and uniting them in a partnership built on trust, sacrifice, and mutual survival.

From that transformative moment beneath the cypress, the bond between the man and the wolf blossomed into a unique partnership never seen between their kind. The man chose compassion over brutality, while the wolf showed respect and gratitude in return, saving the man's life. Together, they roamed the lands, their complementary strengths forging a formidable alliance.

The union of the two sparked a remarkable leap in their collective intelligence. The man's cunning and resourcefulness combined with the wolf's keen senses and instinctive hunting prowess to create a synergy that allowed them to thrive, even in the harshest conditions. As the seasons changed and the lands grew cold and unforgiving, they faced the challenges together, overcoming scarcity and adversity with an unwavering spirit of cooperation.

Their shared experiences deepened their connection and transcended the basic needs of survival, an evolution into a profound friendship built on trust, empathy, and a mutual understanding of the world. This extraordinary partnership between the man and the wolf became a testament to the power of unity and the indomitable spirit of two beings, bound by a love that transcended the barriers between their species.

One afternoon, the man stumbled upon a set of elk tracks, which he hadn't seen since the colder months began. Ecstatic, he threw his hands in the air and yelled. The wolf was confused, but he understood the man's excitement upon sniffing the tracks. The wolf's keen sense of smell allowed him to follow the trail with the man in tow. They continued their pursuit until darkness fell and they could no longer see.

Seeking shelter beneath another cypress tree, the man and wolf reminisced about the first time they shared warmth under a similar tree. The man stroked the fur around the wolf's ears, and the wolf snuggled against him, offering comfort and warmth.

As they drifted off to sleep, they both had a shared dream, though they were unaware of the connection. In the dream, they saw themselves scaling the craggy rocks of a familiar mountain, an imposing peak that towered above the clouds, casting a vast shadow over the land below. The dream ended before they could reach the summit.

The following morning, the man awoke to find the wolf staring solemnly toward the mountain peak. He stood beside his companion, gazing at the summit and wondering what lay at the top. Despite the risks of venturing into the unknown, the man could not resist the call of the mysterious mountain. He motioned for the wolf to follow, and they set off on their journey.

It took them three days to reach the base of the mountain. The deep snow covered the man's feet, allowing frostbite to take hold of his toes. As they approached the mountain, the wind blew the snow away, revealing the extent of the damage caused by the cold. The man's feet were numb, but they pressed on regardless.

Their bodies were battered and weakened from the lack of food and water; their remaining fat stores were consumed for energy. The man's lips were blistered and cracked, and his face was raw and red from the windburn. As they neared the mountain's base, they found no signs of life—an ominous warning to those who dared venture further. The grim realization that they might die in the snow wore away their determination.

As they started their ascent, the slope of the land grew steeper, increasing gradually at first. Boulders dotted the incline, forming a labyrinth of stone islands in a gray, tilting ocean. They navigated the winding pathway between these massive rocks, which added to the length of their journey but also provided temporary relief from the relentless winds. In these brief moments of respite, their body temperatures rose just enough to restore sensation to their battered extremities, making them aware of the injuries they sustained.

The man's blackened toes were the worst of it. The path became steep, forcing the more agile wolf to scout ahead for the best route up the mountainside. They continued their arduous climb until the darkness swallowed the remaining footholds, forcing them to rest against the rocky mountainside, their bodies numb and their muscles tight. Despair gripped the man as he considered the possibility that this was the end, that he led them to a frozen wasteland from which there was no return.

As they slept, another shared dream enveloped them. This time, however, a mysterious voice from deep within the mountain spoke to them in an unspoken language that both man and wolf could comprehend:

"These rocks will not break you. Keep to the task, and you will be rewarded for your efforts."

The voice resonated within their minds, accompanied by a warm glow that soothed their battered bodies and granted them a peaceful slumber.

Upon awakening, they found that their proximity to the peak brought about a peculiar change. The cold no longer affected them, nor did the pain from their many cuts and scrapes caused by the sharp rocks. Their hunger and thirst were quenched, rejuvenating their spirits and motivating them to continue their ascent despite insurmountable odds.

So, with renewed determination, the man and the wolf pressed onward, driven by an unspoken promise of reward and the mysteries that awaited them at the summit.

Around midday, they were enveloped in a thick gray fog, visibility reduced to near nothingness. They cautiously continued their ascent, wary of the slippery, snow-covered rocks beneath their feet.

The winds picked up as the sun descended behind the mountainside again, clearing away the fog and revealing the landscape. By this point, the man and the wolf slowed, struggling against delirium and hallucinations. They did their best to stay focused, but ultimately decided to end the day early and seek respite in sleep, hoping to return to the warmth of the shared dream.

"Your steadfastness in the face of insurmountable odds is humbling. Do not give in to weakness. Rely on one another to see it through."

The voice encouraged them from within their minds, basking them in the comforting warmth once more. However, their rest was cut short by a rockslide that sent them scrambling for cover. Trapped in darkness and unable to see the oncoming barrage, they huddled behind the nearest boulder, praying to avoid being struck by the tumbling rocks.

As the sun rose, they remained pinned down by the relentless rockslide. Each time they believed it to be over and ventured out from behind the boulder, the sound of more rocks hurtling toward them forced them to retreat. It wasn't until midday that they deemed it safe to proceed, but they had only a few hours to climb before the sun disappeared again. Driven by urgency, they scrambled to make up for lost time, sensing that the mountain's peak was approaching.

They pushed their bodies beyond their limits over the past ten days without a proper meal, yet they somehow clung to life. The mysterious voice emanating from the mountain continued to call to them, an irresistible siren song that fueled their resolve. Exhausted, they collapsed in the darkness again, hoping to reach the summit the next day. However, the dream's warmth eluded them that night.

To their surprise, they awoke, already part way through their climb. Delirious, they believed they were still asleep, but they had been climbing for hours. Above them, the sun shone brightly, the oppressive clouds now far below them. The sight before them was awe-inspiring: a majestic peak, carved from the night sky itself, adorned with towering pillars of obsidian rock that captured and reflected the sunlight above.

Despite ascending beyond the cloud line, the summit remained an unfathomable distance away. Their breathing became rapid and shallow as the altitude threatened to suffocate them. Realizing that the summit was farther away than hoped weighed on their hearts. The obsidian rock face that loomed above them appeared insurmountable, even for a man in peak physical condition—and impossible for the wolf.

A sense of despair crept in as they stared at the daunting challenge. But the memory of the voice and the dreams that brought them this far stirred something profound within their spirits, a determination that refused to be extinguished. Together, they braced for the last leg of their incredible journey, driven by the unshakable belief that they could overcome any obstacle.

The voice within persisted, urging them to carry on. The man and the wolf resigned themselves to the possibility of dying on the cliffs, but they could not ignore the call to continue their ascent.

"Do not give in to defeat. Show strength when all seems lost."

The voice now echoed louder inside their minds, causing the man to bleed from his ear and cry out in pain. Despite the overwhelming odds, they pressed on, finding brief solace from the cold and pain each night.

As the man reached for a handhold above him, he mistakenly grabbed a loose rock, thinking it was secure. The rock gave way when he shifted his weight onto it, sending him tumbling backward. The wolf could only watch helplessly as the man fell twenty yards, his body violently bouncing off the jagged rocks below. He came to a stop on an outcropping, his broken femur protruding through his skin and his arm twisted unnaturally behind him.

The wolf carefully backtracked down to the man, skirting the cliff side to avoid causing a rockslide. He could hear the man's screams of pain and blood gurgling in his throat. Once the wolf reached the outcropping, the true extent of his companion's injuries became apparent. All the wolf could do was lie next to the man and wait for him to lose consciousness, hoping the mysterious light would relieve him from his agony one last time.

After more than two hours, the man passed out. The wolf stayed beside him, whining softly. Night fell, and the warm light enveloped them once more.

Beneath the stars on the mountainside, it seemed impossible for them to continue their journey. The man's broken body could not climb, and the wolf felt lost and weakened without his friend's strength. Resigned, they slept the entire day and into the night, remaining in the comforting embrace of the mysterious light.

On the third day, the wolf awoke with a sense of dread. Not wanting to face the reality of his companion's condition, he kept his eyes shut, gathering the courage to confront the sight. But something felt different—the warmth of the man's body was no longer pressed against his back.

When the wolf opened his eyes, he found himself in a room carved from the smooth obsidian stone of the mountain's summit. Behind him, a doorway led out to the open sky, a breathtaking view that left him perplexed, unsure of how they reached the top. He could see a large pool of red blood far below, marking the spot where the man's body rested. But the man was nowhere to be seen.

The wolf felt rejuvenated and full of energy. His coat was clean, and all the stiffness and aches in his bones vanished. But why? He surveyed the room. The floor, ceiling, and walls were all smooth and black. At the back of the cave, the floor seemed to descend further into he mountain. With nowhere else to go and unable to scale back down the mountainside, the wolf hesitantly ventured deeper into the cave.

"Wolf!"

A voice called out to him. At the entrance behind him stood the man, his faithful companion. The wolf couldn't contain his excitement, slipping and sliding on the polished black stone as he hurried to greet him, wagging his tail and yelping joyfully. He wasn't sure he would ever see the man again, yet he was, healed, just like the wolf.

As they embraced, happiness swelled in their hearts, causing the Awl'Fire to blaze.

"It's good to see you again, friend," the man said as he wrapped his arms around the wolf's neck.

"The voice in the mountain has given gifts upon us, brother. I'm speaking to you with my heart and mind. You can do the same, Wolf. Focus, and call out to me."

The wolf tilted his head. He realized that the voice he heard was indeed coming from his friend. He concentrated his thoughts and opened his heart, allowing a connection to form between them.

"Friend," the wolf whispered, surprised that it worked.

"Yes, friend," the man repeated, smiling.

"I thought I lost you down there before. My heart is overjoyed to see you here. But how are we here? Are we not alive anymore?"

The broken language from the wolf took some time for the man to decipher. It would improve as they used this newfound ability more and more.

"No, Wolf, we are very much alive. Something deep in this mountain called to us. We must go to it. Something within tells me that this is why we are here."

The wolf agreed with him.

"I will go with you, friend, anywhere, as long as we're together."

The man smiled and patted him on the head.

"We go forward then, see what comes."

*

So they set off. The further they walked, the more they noticed that the slanted floor was not slanted at all; it was flat for what seemed like forever. It only looked slanted because of the path's immense size, like an island on the ocean dipping behind the horizon line. There was no turning back. After an eternity of walking, the two saw something appear in the darkness ahead. It was a light source, too far away to discern what it was. They quickened their pace, eager to discover what beckoned them for so long.

The two of them spent a long time together before the voice called out to them. Hunting, exploring, and surviving, but they never spoke. They took the time to walk with each other to share their perspectives. All the things they wanted to say but never knew how. It was fulfilling to know what was in each other's hearts and minds all this time. It only solidified their bond even further.

As they approached, the surrounding walls widened, opening into a vast hollow space around the point of light in the center. Light from the entrance had long since disappeared, vanishing beneath the horizon behind them. The only light source was the orb ahead of them, illuminating the surrounding air with a glowing iridescent haze. It mesmerized them, staring at the many intricate details on its surface, like facets in a diamond, each one more brilliant than the next.

As they drew closer to the orb, they noticed the floor of the expansive room below. It did not reflect any of the light. If it weren't for the incredible sensation of the stone beneath their feet, it would have seemed like they were walking on nothing.

Time seemed to stop as they drew closer. They realized the orb's size was much larger than expected. With nothing to compare it to, they felt as if their minds were playing tricks. The orb seemed larger than the mountain that contained it—larger than anything they ever saw.

Finally, they reached it, close enough to touch the emanating glow from within—the same glow that enveloped them as they slept on the mountainside. They felt content and soothed in its presence. They sat beneath the great orb, resting their weary legs and feet.

"What is this brilliant light, friend?"

The wolf asked, staring wide-eyed.

"I'm not sure. I've never seen such a thing. It feels like warm water and sunlight."

The man reached out, and his hand passed through the surface, which was gelatinous and slightly pulled on him. He felt only warmth on the other side.

They noticed a shift in the center. A translucent outer shell opened in front of him. The comforting feeling they both shared was immediately replaced by fear.

The orb flexed and pulsed with light, creating a sonic boom that crushed the eardrums of both the man and the wolf, sending them tumbling and sliding away. Dazed and confused, they regained their balance. Blood trickled from their noses and ears as the open space of the orb filled with the silhouette of a giant celestial being. He stepped from the light, cracking the stone beneath his enormous feet. The two friends were dumbfounded, frightened, and awestruck as the creature from the orb stood upright.

He spoke in a language that did not register with the man or the wolf, but the words made perfect sense inside their minds.

"It is a magnificent thing to see you here together. I was beginning to lose hope, fearing weakness was an attribute all the creatures on this tiny rock shared."

"Weakness? My friend and I are far from weak," the wolf replied. The man turned to the wolf, amazed.

"I can hear you! I can understand you."

"Ha! Indeed! The Awl'Fire we share connects us all. It is a beautiful gift, the ability to express and understand what is in your heart. The others who were called attempted to make the journey to my mountain's summit but failed because of one thing the two of you possess: your unshakable bond with one another."

The entity lifted his hands as the surrounding atmosphere sizzled and vibrated.

"This light you see surrounding you both is the glow of the Awl'Fire. It brings life together. Every creature that lives on this planet and all other worlds has this fire burning within them, some more than others. When the bond between you formed, the Awl'Fire grew stronger. This saved you on your trek and sustained you both when the cold crept in."

He lowered his hands, and the light surrounding them dimmed.

"The fire is always there, even when you cannot see its warm glow. Life sustains its power with every experience you gather along your paths, ensuring that the fire will live on from one generation to the next."

"Is that what this is here in front of us? The Awl'Fire? Are you the Awl'Fire?" The man asked timidly.

"Ha! I am, just as all creatures are. I am merely a larger and much older amalgamation of the Awl'Fire, condensed. I settled here atop this peak long ago to protect what this orb contains. The power and knowledge locked away inside aid in bringing balance between all life in the universe."

The entity paused as he reached into the orb behind him and removed several light beams.

"These are the arrays of the Awl'Fire, meant to aid in maintaining balance throughout the Earth. This is the array of tongues I gave you the night you fell from the cliff, young man. It opened an unseen conduit allowing communication between the two of you."

He released the beam, and it levitated under its own power.

"The second is the array of knowledge. This will fill your minds with the great story of creation and the Awl'Fire so that you may know the reason for being."

The wolf slowly walked over to sniff it. It sent an arch of energy that swirled through the air and snapped him on the snout. I tickled and made him sneeze. The man giggled.

"This one is the array of ages. It will allow your internal time to slow, giving you a longer lifespan. Use it to build bonds across every land, between your kind and all the other life."

Once released from his massive hand, the white beam followed the other. It floated in midair only a few feet away.

"This one is the void array. It will allow you to see the spirits of the Earth who have come and gone and travel between the shadows of light and dark so that even in death, you will never be alone."

"This one I shall call the moon array." The yellow light was almost warm to them.

"First Wolf, this array will allow you to change into a human form, but only if a human's Awl'Fire is given freely.

He backed away, hoping he made his point.

"Wolf!" He called out.

"The day you watched as your friend lost his footing on the side of my mountain, I felt it in your heart. You would've done anything you could to help, to save him from his agony?"

The memory of the incident sent shocks of pain through both of them. The wolf felt sorrow in his heart, welling as tears fell.

"I would have given my life to stave off his pain."

The man looks at him and smiles.

"Yes! You would've. I watched as this man's fire slowly dimmed in the cold, blood puddling beneath him, air freezing in his lungs. You, Wolf, stopped death from creeping in; your Awl'Fire sustained him until nightfall. When mine could take over, you did not know it, but you freely gave yours to him to ensure his survival, just as I did when you entered my realm."

"Does that mean that I–" "It means you have a part of this wolf's heart inside you." The entity interrupts, "Never squander it."

His bellowing voice echoed through the cavern of darkness.

The entity returned to the orb of light as the pillars burned through the floor and permanently became part of the mountain.

"As I said, the arrays bring about balance so that life can flourish. But as I stand before you now, others like me wish to bring destruction and chaos. Not because of evil, but because evil, sadness, pain, and suffering are nothing more than the opposing natures of all that is good, balanced in all things. The purpose of your existence is not to overcome these things but to exist alongside them, no more, no less."

The man and the wolf looked at each other as if they were scared.

"Now, I will return you to the mountain base so that you may go out into the world and use the tools I have given you. There will come a time when I will be needed again, but until then, this mountain and the contents within will remain hidden."

"Before you go, what is your name?" The wolf asked.

"I am known by many on many worlds. You're far too primitive now to comprehend my name, and so you will know me as the Rock Prism, the emissary of the great Awl'Fire. Remember my words."

He turned and passed through the orb and disappeared into the light. As it collapsed, the air from around it pulled them close. Faster and faster, it dimmed. The wolf's claws screeched on the stone beneath him as he tried to keep his distance from the imploding light. The man quickly grabbed him around the neck but lost his footing. As they slid into it, it sucked the air from their lungs, rendering them unconscious.

The sound of the blast was still echoing in their heads as they found themselves back at the base of the mountain, the Rock Prism's message still filling their minds. Armed with the arrays and clear direction of their purpose, they set off into the wilderness to the south.

Chapter 12
The Dimming

For generations, humanity and animals coexisted harmoniously in a delicate balance. They shared lush forests, fertile fields, towering mountains and scorching deserts. The Earth was exquisitely untamed and pristine.

Over time, throughout the early ages. The sacred bond between man and wolf flourished. A partnership of two apex predators. The ancient man, with his ingenious mind and passion for innovation and the wolf, whose nobility was only surpassed by its exceptional hunting prowess and steadfast pack mentality. Both imbued with the radiant power of the Awl'Fire. Together, they are strong. Together, they were wardens of the realm.

They established a system of order to maintain equilibrium between all living things and the Earth itself. Simple rules, without the complexities of modern man, were easy to follow and easily upheld in every facet of life. Take only what you must. Use all that you take and spread the Awl'Fire.

For ages, it was good. The Awl'Fire blazed more brilliantly within them than ever before. They traversed the Earth together, tracking herds and the migrations of the grazing animals they hunted.

Along the way, they gained knowledge and uncovered ancient secrets hidden throughout the wild lands from a forgotten era—

knowledge that would lead humankind away from their unity with wolves.

It was subtle and slow, like a single grain of sand dropped into the ocean, the ripple inconsequential to the currents below but altered, nonetheless.

On a warm spring day, a man who searched for fish in the gentle waters of a familiar river; inadvertently catalyzed a profound shift in his species. One that led them from freedom onto a path of pride, greed, and discord.

As he caught a fleeting glint of sunlight that through the leaves above, the facet in a small stone lodged in the riverbank's silt shimmered with an emerald spark. The man had seen countless stones gleam in the sunlight before, but this was different.

Intrigued, he halted and waited for the ripples in the water to subside, then backtracked. He sought the precise position to allow his eyes to glimpse it again. Yet, it vanished. It sank further into the silt, its surface concealed and just out of sight. Or the sun dipped too low for the stone to reflect its light. Regardless of the reason, the enigmatic emerald spark was now embedded in only his mind, just as it was within the riverbank.

Later in the evening, the man sat among his gathered clan of huntsmen and wolves. He observed that the night sky was filled with the same spark as the one etched in his memory. He pondered whether the gleam of light in the riverbank was akin to the celestial bodies above.

Under the soft blue glow of the full moon and stars, the man captured the attention of the others. He narrated the tale of the mysterious green refraction. He was using words and expressions that they never heard before. He drew parallels and similarities between the mysterious stone and the heavenly orbs that hung from above. Excitement and curiosity spread as swiftly as a fever. What started as something insignificant grew into a grand tale. One weaved with intrigue, with imagination. They speculated on what might lie beneath the embankment if they excavated the dirt and removed the stones.

Did the light from the bank fall from the night sky? Or had it been there ages before he stumbled upon it? Their conjectures and theories led them to a common resolution when morning came, and the sun rose high enough to provide sufficient light. They would go to the river and unearth whatever it might be.

The men and the wolves slept little that night. They stayed awake into the early morning in the thralls of an exchange of imaginative ideas and stories. The anticipation and excitement whipped them into a frenzy that left them too exhilarated for sleep.

As the sun broke over the trees and the morning fog lifted, a large group set out for the river to find the elusive light. As they journeyed, they gathered more men from the surrounding area. They recounted the tale of the glinting stone, and with each new iteration, it became too large to control. The man noticed the crowd behind him but only knew the spark's location. He realized that with so many eyes scouring the tiny riverbank, another might claim his prize for themselves. The thought stirred an emotional response he never experienced before. Sweat beaded on his forehead and a tightness gripped his stomach as he imagined how he would feel if someone else retrieved his treasure from the river. His mind raced; trying to find a solution. Then, like a bolt of lightning out of the sky. An idea struck him. Instead of directing the crowd to the exact location, he would lead them further down river.

Once the crowd was close enough to hear the river, they took off without hesitation. His simple yet effective plan worked, and they were none the wiser.

As he watched the others scour the banks, He slipped away unnoticed. Further north of them. To the same spot as the day before.

Once he reached the actual Riverbend, he eased himself into the water, taking care to keep the water still. He paced the same stretch of the river, back and forth, back and forth, but to no avail.

He rummaged through his memory and attempted to identify the minute difference that allowed him to see it. As far as he could tell, everything appeared identical. Then he realized—his shadow shifted; it was longer now. As he strolled, his elongated shadow blocked the sunlight from the bank, the stone concealed in the dark without a light source to reveal it! He raised his eyes to the sky, and instead of the sun being to his right, it now shone from the left, higher than eye level.

There was nothing he could do but wait for the afternoon and then resume the search.

He felt a new sense of accomplishment in his selfish plan to lie and deceive, two relatively new concepts for his kind.

He assumed everyone would give up before the evening and return to the camp frustrated and empty-handed, while he alone would arrive with the precious stone.

The man found a large fruit tree to rest under until the day was nearly over. He drifted in and out as he caught up on the sleep he lost the night before. He felt confident he could locate the stone once he deciphered the last crucial piece of the puzzle.

As he awoke from a long sleep, he saw the sun staring at him in the face. He knew it was close to the time it was the day before when he had seen the stone, so he set off, running toward the riverbank. He was so excited that he nearly broke his legs when he jumped down from the high bank. He gathered his thoughts, breathed deeply to calm his racing heart, and trudged through the knee-deep water.

After a while, the man felt he was losing hope. He walked the same stretch of river repeatedly once more. His stomach tightened as he tried to accept that the stone may have just been something he imagined. Or had he just missed his chance? Was his sense of security misplaced in his plan? Then, out of nowhere, like a flash of lightning, it hit him right in the eye from the left side of the river. Set back under a bundle of loose tree roots, a green shimmer of light reflected from beneath the water. He gasped in shock and propelled himself in the light's direction.

As he neared the bank, he moved more cautiously, trying not to dislodge the stone from the mud. The man slowly found his footing on the rocks as the rippled water calmed and the silt below settled. He could still see the flashing of the last remaining beams of sunlight bouncing a reflection from the stone's smooth, green surface. He reached into the mud of the bank and scooped out the surrounding Earth, using his hands to loosen the mud and the roots that cradled it. An emerald around the size of his fingernail, weathered naturally by the flowing river. He was speechless. Never had he seen anything so beautiful. He held it up like a newborn baby, like a beacon of clarity in the faded sunlight. The light that passed through it was greener than the grass in the open fields and bright, just like the lights in the night sky, just as he described it to his fellow man.

As excited as he was to find it, he was even more eager to show it to everyone who already returned to camp.

As the sun retreated below the horizon, the man triumphantly marched home. He clasped his prize in one hand. The other waved to get the attention of everyone as he entered the camp. But they were too busy to pay him any attention. They were all set in clusters, running back and forth and shouting at one another in a frenzy of excitement. The man was confused. He envisioned his return to the camp differently than how it unfolded. He expected to be met with fascination as they first laid eyes on the famed stone he alone pulled from the riverbank. But they ignored him.

As he walked closer to the flurry of moving bodies, he was furious and sadly disappointed to see what caused such commotion. Everyone with hands to carry had fists full of the same stones, some much bigger and some much brighter than his. He learned from the others that the entire river was flush with stones that flickered a broad spectrum of colors, emerald, ruby, sapphire, and even some that reflected them all. So many colors they didn't even have names for them all.

The man's stone was rendered almost worthless immediately compared to all the others. The grins and smiles on their faces enraged him, and he was embarrassed that he made such a big deal out of his own, which was so small in comparison. He was envious of the others whose stones were more of a prize than his own.

The wolves, who watched from a short distance away, were not built by the universe to glorify such a tiny facet of its entirety. They could not see the colors that emanated from them, nor did they have the hands to carry them out of the rivers; to them, they were like all the other stones in the river. Perplexed by man's excitement over such a thing, they thought it best to stay back as they became excited.

They could see a look in their eyes as they compared sizes and argued over whose stones were superior—a frenzied craze look, like that of a rabid animal.

On this night, a tiny crack splintered the extraordinary bond between the Earth's first wardens.

As the ages passed, men devoted more of their Awl'Fire to seek knowledge and amass a wealth of inconsequential items that did nothing to aid in the realm's protection. They lost touch with the importance of their bond with the wolves and the natural world.

Even as they grew weaker and their stomachs cried out for nourishment, they continued to turn a deaf ear to the wolves' pleas.

The wolves tried to remind them of the value of unity and balance, but their words went unheard. Men persisted in their pursuit of material wealth and power at the expense of their once-strong connection with the wolves and the Earth itself.

Men adorned themselves with the jewels that shimmered. They weaved their precious gems into their clothing and fashioned crude jewelry from sticks, cordage, and sparkling stones.

They measured their worth by the size and beauty of their gem collections, turning their backs on the wisdom and teachings of their wolf brethren.

The wolves, who saw no value in such treasures, were relegated to a lower class in a man's eyes. Never to be thought of as equals again.

Men developed more advanced tools to extract gems from the Earth. They also created more destructive weapons to protect their hoarded wealth.

Elaborate dwellings replaced simple structures that once housed men and wolves, Symbols of status and power built solely for man's use. They abandoned their nomadic lifestyles and settled in temperate climates better suited to their weakened bodies. No longer were they hunters. Instead, they relied on the preservation process so their food would last through the seasons when the migratory animals were gone.

The wolves, unable to see the value in such a sedentary life, continued living as they always had, close to nature and bound by the traditions of the pack.

Some wolves remained with men, either by choice or circumstance, but they were treated as slaves rather than companions. They were made to perform tasks such as pulling sleds, guarding homesteads, and tracking animals, enduring abuse and neglect when no longer needed.

Humankind wholly severed the bond they shared with wolves as the years passed. Men lost the last remnants of the Awl'Fire within them and became entirely dependent on external sources of warmth and light. They delved deeper into the Earth, extracting metals like iron, copper, gold, and silver, using these resources to create more destructive technologies. Entire forests were leveled, rivers polluted, and the sky blackened with the smoke of industry as they prioritized progress and wealth over the sanctity of the Earth and the life within it. They lost their ability to communicate with wolves as they created new languages that excluded them forever.

The wolves, ever the Earth's Wardens, upheld the pack's age-old traditions and maintained their close connection to nature. As humankind spread across the Earth, leaving pollution and destruction in their wake. The wolves retreated to the places where men feared to tread—inhospitable regions like the Illnok Mountains and the dense, untamed forests of northern wildlands. The wolves found sanctuary, living in harmony with the Earth, far from the destructive reach of man.

Chapter 13
The Loft

After experiencing what seemed like days' worth of events in Atohi's narration, Evan and Millie found themselves back in their own bodies, astounded to find that only about thirty minutes had passed in their actual timeline. Having concluded his tale, Atohi rose and gestured for Tulie to rejoin them.

"All creatures, great and small, can alter the balance between the void and the Awl'Fire. A man's choice affects the balance even more than all the other creatures combined. Why that is, we may never understand. With everything you witnessed, know that Oct'Tulommon is only a pawn in a much larger game. His path is certainly dark; His disregard for the natural order and life within this realm has made him strong with the void. Now that he has been given a man's Awl'Fire, he has unlocked the power of the moon array. The ability to shift. It makes him even that much more dangerous." Atohi said, visibly worried.

As the two of them came out of the catatonic state, their eyes faded from white back to normal. Evan came to with a violent jerk, while Millie gracefully sat up and stretched.

"Evan, you must listen to me. You are a catalyst. Occasionally, I cross paths with one, an usher of significant change in the world. I can't tell you why. Perhaps it's what humans call fate. But you must understand, the part you will play is more significant than your quarrel with the wolf, Oct'Tulommon. I can see the void in you young Evan, and it is growing."

They were silent as they pulled their minds back inside the confines of their skulls.

"I think the only reason it hasn't completely swallowed you whole by now is what you feel for her and what she feels for you. Love is the great equalizer. It can mend even the most tormented of spirits. You need to embrace it and fan the flames of the Awl'Fire within you both."

They wrapped their arms around each other.

"You mustn't let it take hold," Atohi warned.

"Evan, I feel it too. The pain from what he did is genuine pain. I'm afraid if you let it, it will consume you." Millie said, her hand gripped inside his. He didn't reply, just stared at Atohi.

"I'm sorry to speak the words you hide in your heart so bluntly, but you must understand, the great balance is teetering on the edge.

The Dimming was only the beginning. World wars, genocides, neglect for the environment and now a pandemic on a global scale which humans have only experienced during the black death. All these things have diminished the light of the Awl'Fire here on this Earth.

If you were to engage in a battle with an emissary of the void, it could potentially be the beginning of the end for humans."

"What should I do then, sit here while he is loose, terrorizing what little life we have left? As if living through rasping fever wasn't enough, now they have to worry about being eaten by wolves the size of grizzly bears? He could kill us all! What's stopping him from crossing over and finding some other skin, one that I wouldn't recognize?"

Evan started to think it would be better to walk away from what he had with Millie. At least, it would mean they were all safe.

"Stop thinking like that, Evan!" She knocked him out of a trance, still in his mind.

Tulie walked over and placed her hand on Millie's shoulder. Atohi wiped the tears from Evan's eyes.

"As much as I hate to say it Evan, your father's violent end was not premeditated, you two were simply in the wrong place at the wrong time. He will not single you out, but that doesn't make him any less dangerous to you on a larger scale. Take comfort in that."

It infuriated Evan to be told that his father's death was meaningless, even though he knew he was right.

"I cannot tell you what to do, Evan. I can only tell you I will be on my way to find him within the coming days. To offer him a way out of whatever it is he is planning. If he does not accept, his pack of battle wolves and their limited understanding of the void will be no match for the full power of the Illnok."

Evan felt no different about the idea of tracking the wolf down. He had no confidence in this "Illnok" he knew nothing about.

"I'll make a deal with you, Evan. When I have word that Oct'Tulommon has been dealt with, I'll return here to give you the news myself. If I don't, then assume the worst and know that if the Illnok fall, the world of men will see the Rasping fever as a small plight compared to the reign of the void's harbinger. And then you might not have a choice but to face him."

The seriousness of the situation weighed on the three of them.

"Wait for me to return, Evan. Please, for everyone's sake…I must go now."

Tulie and Atohi walked to the edge of the property and exchanged goodbyes. Her dress billowed in the breeze as tears streamed.

"Evan?" Millie called. He looked over to see her. She reached for his hand. He grasped it and pulled her up to meet him.

"I do love you. I want you to be here with us. I cannot lose you. We cannot lose you."

Evan sunk into her. The smell of her hair and the warmth of her body next to his in her blue dress was an excitement like he never felt.

Millie spent the night in the loft above the garage with Evan, while Tulie stayed with Steph inside the house. Even after all that happened and all that they had learned about the true past of man.

It was still the best night of his life.

Part IV: Death and Savior

Chapter 14
The Vanishing Man

It had been almost three years since the day Morgrim left the comfort of his father's burrow. He returned several times to visit, but the older he got, the further away he traveled, much like Finnick would. Even though they were not blood or the same species, they were more alike than both knew.

On a warm spring day, Morgrim reached the edge of the Rimwoods. He heard many tales of forgotten human antiquities that littered the earth between the human cities and the Outlands. The place was unsafe for animals, but he couldn't restrain himself.
Huge metal antennas, linked by cables, reached out as far as the eye could see in both directions. They made a constant humming and buzzing noise, much like bees around their hive. The nearby blacktop paths were filled with trash and ruined cars. Inside these cars, though not many, were the skeletons of men - hanging from car doors, bent over steering wheels, or lying together in the back seats.
The sight of it all confused him. There was no sound, no movement. There was nothing to be scared of. Yet, the eerie silence suggested that everything around him was dead and been so for a very long time. The scene was a haunting reminder of life that once was, now eerily frozen in time.

Morgrim weaved in and out of the ancient relics of human life, he happened upon a giant, red squirrel gathering acorns and stuffing them inside a glove box of a rusty old truck. His mouth watered at the sight of it. It had been quite some time since he had any meat to feed the hungry wolf inside of him. He ducked down as quietly as he could and hid behind an old suitcase; it spilled over with wet, tattered clothing. he crept up behind it, careful not to alert it of his presence, when a loud crash of glass breaking against a rock startled both him and the squirrel. Before he could grab it, it scurried away out of his reach, it bounced from one hood to the next.

Morgrim was furious but curious about what could have made such a noise. His paws left the blacktop's heat back into the soft soil's coolness.

Set off the road in the distance about thirty yards, he stumbled upon an old man in the ruins of a makeshift campsite. Morgrim never encountered a human in his six winters of exploring the Outlands and Rimwoods until now. The hungry wolf inside of him filled his head with violent ideas and curiosity about how the meat clinging to the old man's bones would taste. Was it dark and greasy, like the meat of an opossum, saturated with greasy fat? Or was it lean like the meat of a young deer, tough and full of energy? Morgrim's favorite meal had always been fresh salmon out of the stream. He imagined it tasting like that.

He learned many years ago from Finnick that a human was never to be hunted. A wolf who eats the flesh of man is unclean, likely to eat his own brother given the chance. Finnick also taught him that man used their mind to rise to the top of the animal kingdom. Out of their weakness and inability to survive in the wild, they made weapons to protect themselves from it. Bows initiated the progression, then metal blades, and finally rifles.

He explained the latter in great detail so he would know to steer clear if he ever came across one. He made it clear that rifles could kill from distances farther than a wolf's eyes could see.

Driven by curiosity, Morgrim crept closer. Using his innate ability to stay silent, he descended a muddy embankment and circled around the man from behind.

How ironic he thought. *Even the weakest creatures could stand at the top of the food chain by being weak enough.* He observed the old man and studied the items scattered about the campsite. Nothing

Finnick described as dangerous was there, at least not in plain sight. He inched even closer. The man, hunched over a mossy tree stump, was oblivious to Morgrim's looming presence. He was close enough to see the blood pulse through a thin neck vein. The sight of the man's pale flesh caused Morgrim's mouth to water and his stomach to tighten, a reaction he learned to control at a young age when he lived among rabbits. The man's skin appeared soft and paper-thin, so easy to tear with his sharp teeth.

Morgrim was so hungry and close that if the man tried to flee, it wouldn't save him. If it had been a Feral wolf, death would have been imminent. Morgrim stretched his neck out to sniff when a sharp, pungent odor emanated beneath the old man's skin. It turned his stomach into a heavy stone that sunk to the bottom of his gut. He backed away to reach the fresh air just a few feet away. The foul smell caught him off guard and caused him to snap a stick under his paw as he retreated.

The sound alerted the old man to his presence. In shock, the man stumbled down from the mossy tree stump and shrieked in terror, digging and clawing to escape as quickly as possible. He stopped flailing as he clamored around the opposite side of the stump as if it could shield him from such a wolf tearing his weak limbs from his body.

After a few moments, the man's breathing calmed. Morgrim sat still in the same spot, perplexed and amused by the old man's frantic reaction to him. After the display of cowardice, Morgrim was confident the human was no threat. He was weak and sick with yellow skin and eyes. Morgrim sensed he had little life ahead of him, the foul-smelling odor a mixture of infection, alcohol and death.

Behind the stump, the man peeked to see if the wolf's black, limitless eyes were still fixed on him, panic rose again, he feared for his life, uttering words in a language Morgrim never heard.

"AHHH!! Just do it already, you devil! I knew it was a matter of time before something came for me." The old man yelled from behind the stump.

"I'm sick of these woods, anyway! I never wanted to be here!"

He shouted, his voice strained with fear and anger. He envisioned the wolf lunging over the mossy stump, snarling, ripping into the skin of his face, tearing it off, and consuming it as he writhed in pain. Along with terror, the man grew impatient. Irritated by the wolf's lack of commitment to do what he thought he was there to do.

"Why are you toying with me like this, wolf?! Do you hear me, demon?!" He yelled with a tremble in his voice. Morgrim's head tilted, concentrated on the man's words.

"Alright then, you dirty mutt! If you're not gonna come for me, then I guess it's time for me to come to you, you old bastard!" He declared as he struggled to get to his feet.

He intended to vault over the stump, but his frail body only collapsed on top of it.

Morgrim vanished.

The man searched but found no trace of wolf anywhere—no tracks, no rustling leaves, only the broken stick that had given Morgrim away. The only piece of evidence that reassured the man what he saw wasn't his imagination.

As intrigued as Morgrim was by the man, he couldn't wait any longer. He was famished and decided to find the squirrel before the trail went cold. Near the man's campsite, Morgrim found another squirrel foraging for acorns in an oak tree to add to its horde. He waited for the right moment when the unsuspecting squirrel came down low enough on the trunk for him to grab.

The light seemed to fade quicker now when he didn't need it to. It wouldn't be long until the darkness provided the squirrel enough cover to escape. In the distance, he spotted an orange glow, growing brighter, illuminating the dense forest around it.

A fire? Morgrim thought to himself; a rare site to see where humans didn't venture often. He could only remember one other time he had, during a lightning storm, when a tree was struck and its trunk splintered, sending shards of wood in every direction. The fire had drawn quite a crowd from the Outlands, watching the flames dance over the carcass of the old oak tree for days. This fire was different—it belonged to the man. The crackling of the moisture as it evaporated in the wet logs as they burned distracted Morgrim from his hunt just long enough for another squirrel to vault into the same tree as the first.

He steadied his breath and waited for the right moment, careful not to alarm them. Morgrim was too tired and hungry and in no mood to give these plump little squirrels any chance to flee. He snatched the first one up, breaking its neck before the second even realized its companion was gone. He set the lifeless squirrel down in the grass, hoping the other did not see, then lunged with tact and skill.

The squirrel had no chance to flee from the swift attack. Morgrim twisted its neck so violently that the creature's head was almost detached, killing it instantly.

The two squirrels were so plump that Morgrim had difficulty fitting them into his mouth, showing restraint to keep from devouring them whole. He carried them back to the campsite, one for himself and the other meant for the man. Morgrim hoped that offering the squirrel would establish trust between them. It seemed the man hadn't eaten in quite some time.

Morgrim found his way back to the campsite, guided by the smell of the fire and the sound of the man's voice, which carried through the trees on the night's calm, stagnant air. As he got closer to the man and the light of the fire, something peculiar happened. The man's words became more familiar as if Morgrim had always known the language but somehow forgotten.

With every step, the man's speech became more precise. Earlier that day, when Morgrim first encountered the man, nothing he said made any sense; the old man's voice sounded muffled and broken, not like it did now. His voice was crisp, like fish swimming in a fast-moving stream, invisible from above but clear when seen from below. Morgrim felt amazed, perplexed, and frightened all at once.

"Ladies and gentlemen! Please welcome Sir Ivan Prewitt: The Vanishing Man!" He proclaimed as if addressing a crowd of people, yet there was no one there but him. Morgrim sat down a few yards back, just out of the old man's peripheral vision. He didn't want to cause any more fear than he already had and wished to sit and observe for a while.

The old man tried his best to stand up, stumbling a few times before standing upright. He raised his arms in the air and took a bow.

Reaching into the pockets of his tattered coat as if searching for something, he pulled a small glass bottle out of an inner pocket close to his chest.

"Ta-Daa!" He exclaimed, taking another bow.

"Ohhhh! Ahhh!" Pretending to be a person in the imaginary crowd.

"And now! Ladies and gentlemen! I will… regretfully, make the contents of this lovely glass bottle... Disappear!" He announced, his voice full of theatrics and flair, despite the lack of an audience.

The man took the bottle cap off and threw it into the fire. Once he emptied the bottle of every last drop, he tossed it in Morgrim's direction, not realizing he was there. Rolling over tree roots and grass, the bottle came to a halt just short of Morgrim's paws. The smell from the bottle stung his nose; the scent kept Morgrim from biting the old man earlier. "Old English" was printed on the paper label wrapped around the bottle. The old man was drunk. He stumbled backward and fell to the ground and hit his head on a rock, knocking himself unconscious.

Morgrim didn't move from where he was for a while, waiting to see if the man he'd come to know as Ivan would wake up again. Still in shock at what transpired, he remembered the squirrels he'd brought to eat. Not knowing how long Ivan would be out, he ate both squirrels to prevent the meat from spoiling. After filling his belly, he explored Ivan's belongings.

The man's canvas tent, where he slept, was in ruins, torn by falling branches and damp from the moisture in the forest air. The campsite was old, with the ground around the campfire rutted out and the surrounding trees stripped of all low-hanging limbs and bark. It wasn't a very comfortable space to dwell in.

Hanging from a support post inside the tent were two ragged wallet-sized pictures. One showed a young boy wearing a black shirt, holding what looked like a fishing pole. The name "Logan" was written in black ink below the image. The second picture was more worn than the first, featuring the same little boy, a beautiful older woman, and Ivan. Ivan's face was clean-shaven in the photo, and his jet-black hair was groomed. He wore almost the same clothes now: a button-down shirt and khaki cargo pants. Now, however, they were mere rags, with stains around the collar and frayed bottoms on his slacks that clung to his emaciated frame. His hair had grown into a nest of gray tangles, and his beard was thick and uneven.

Feeling the intense heat from the fire blazing in front of the mossy stump, Morgrim stepped away for a moment to cool down. As he exited the tent and passed the stump where the old man still lay, he noticed a tree to the left of the man's campfire. Below it, scattered around its massive roots, lay many glass bottles identical to the one Ivan had thrown at him.

As the fire continued to burn, Ivan showed no signs of stirring. He was still alive and no longer bleeding from his head. Morgrim decided that the best thing to do was to let him sleep it off and hope that he would wake up in the morning.

So, Morgrim found a soft bed of grass to lie in on the opposite side of the fire, far enough away that he wouldn't be the first thing Ivan saw in the morning. The heat from the fire and the flames dancing atop the burning logs gave a surreal, primal feeling.

It made Morgrim feel at peace with the man lying in the dirt. He heard the story of the great Awl'Fire from Finnick. This was Ivan's fire. He made it for warmth, as he couldn't survive the cold without it. He made it for protection against the animals that hunted him, as he had become easy prey, blind at night. He had made it to cook his food because his gut was too soft now for raw meat. He made it because he was alone now without it. The only creature that walks the earth that tends a fire to stay alive.

Chapter 15
The Death of a Brother

As the sun turned the morning dew to fog, Morgrim rose from the soft bed of grass to check on the old man. He could see the moisture in the old man's breath condensing in the beams of sunlight breaking through the trees, feeling relieved that he had not died during the night.

The air carried a slight chill, hardly noticeable to Morgrim with his thick fur coat, but to the old man, it was a shock to his senses when he came to. Disoriented and in pain from how his twisted body had laid the entire night, he winced and gasped as he unfurled his kinked limbs and stretched out in the cold dirt. After readjusting his sore muscles and aching bones, his eyes opened, meeting Morgrim's gaze as he stared across the campfire's smoldering embers.

No flames remained and the faint orange glow in the coal and ash dwindled, extinguishing the old man's sole source of heat. He held his breath, trying to decide if what he saw was real. Morgrim's appearance; now that he was sober, was jarring. A wolf of his size was, most definitely, something to fear.

"I guess if you were here to eat me, wolf, you would have already done so while I was unconscious," He said.

Morgrim's ears stood straight up. Once again, he could not understand the words from the man's mouth. Confused and eager to solve the puzzle, he searched his mind for an answer. What was different the night before? Could it be something in the dark that allowed him to understand? Was it because the old man had been drunk and didn't realize he spoke the ancient language? Morgrim took inventory of all the variables that could have caused such a thing, but nothing added up.

The old man gave up on feeling threatened by Morgrim. He was too tired, sore, and cold to care about being breakfast for a wolf. With a sigh of resignation, he dragged himself up from the ground, wincing as he did so.

"Look, can we talk about this after I get this fire going, please? I'm freezing out here," He said as he rubbed his arms for warmth. He waited for Morgrim's response, expecting the wolf to speak. Again, Morgrim could not comprehend the old man's words but watched as he gathered a handful of small twigs and dried grass around him. Throwing them one by one on top of the remaining embers, the old man got down on his knees and bent over the rock retainer he built to keep the fire in the pit. He took a breath and blew into the smoldering embers. Morgrim was surprised; it was as if the old man had a fire in his lungs.

As the tinder caught, the old man grabbed larger sticks and stacked them around the growing flames, grunting as his old stiff body fought back with every movement. He took another deep breath and blew a few more times, causing tiny orange specks of embers to swirl up into the morning sky. The flames grew more prominent and the surrounding air warmed.

"There! Much better, don't you think, wolf?" He said with a hint of pride.

Morgrim was astounded! The words were crystal clear, just as they were the night before. He realized that the fire acted as a primitive conduit for them to communicate. Like a switch had been flipped inside of his head, he remembered the story of the dimming and how in the time before, man had the Awl'Fire within them just as a wolf did. It connected them, allowing them to communicate through heart and mind, as wolves still do with each other. Now raged between them, this fire restored a bond that hadn't been present for ages.

As the old man sat down on his stump, he rubbed his hands together in the heat of the fire. Morgrim was unsure how he would react if he answered his question, but he figured that now, when he was sober, was the best time to do it.

"This is only the second fire that I have ever witnessed with my own eyes, friend,"

Morgrim took the chance, the words flowed to the old man's mind from his. It was the first time Morgrim ever spoke with a human so it was a little strained and muffled at first but still able to be translated through the fire that connected them.

His mouth did not move and his voice was not carried through the air but propagated from within, as the old man's language.

"Hmph...!" The old man exclaimed, startled yet intrigued by the sudden connection with the wolf.

He had been alone so long that hearing voices in the forest wasn't odd. He shrugged off Morgrim's communication as a figment of his imagination. He smiled as he stoked the fire with a long stick.

"Old man? Can you hear my voice in your mind?" Morgrim asked as he got up and walked around the fire. The old man dropped the stick; he realized Morgrim was on the approach. His words sunk in a little deeper than before.

"If you can understand me, please know I am not here to harm you. If I wanted, I would have done so long before now."

Morgrim sat down, about six feet away from him. It was the first time the old man got a good look at him.

"My god! I must've truly lost my mind out here." He said as his body collapsed on the stump, heavy with the realization of his slipping reality.

"No, my friend," Morgrim replied in a very calm tone. "I don't believe you have. It is your Awl'Fire you've built. It's acting as a conduit for our words to travel back and forth, like a bridge connecting us, like it used to be before. I speak only in my heart and mind with my kind old man. You hear my thoughts, translated by the great Awl'Fire and given to you in your tongue."

The old man took a moment to process this.

"Well then, this is just par for the course in these woods. Nothing has felt real since I've been here." He leaned back and pulled another bottle from his pocket, opening it. Morgrim was confused; he realized that the day before, when he rifled through the old man's belongings, he never came across any full bottles of liquor, just piles and piles of empty ones.

"What is your name? If you say we are friends, I feel you will be less likely to eat me if we know each other's names." Morgrim grinned.

"My name is Morgrim. I have only one, given to me by my father who is a rabbit. I never knew my Wolf father."

Morgrims' internal voice was very calm, collected and soothing like a warmer fire. He had no reason to be any other way. Even though his surroundings were dark and miserable, most of his life was full of love and laughter in the burrow with his family.

"Morgrim. That is a very fitting name for such a wolf as yourself. I admit, you are the first I have ever seen in real life, and you are a very beautiful and frightening creature to me, so I am glad you call me a friend."

The two laughed together. As they stared at the fire, content for the time being in each other's company, they realized it had been a long time since they enjoyed any type of conversation.

"And your name is Sir Ivan Prewitt?" Morgrim asked.

The old man turned to Morgrim with his brow furrowed.

"How did you come to know that Morgrim?"

"Last night, before you fell and hit your head for the second time, I must've come close enough to your fire for your words to reach me. I hunted up two squirrels and planned to bring you one as a peace offering. You introduced yourself to a crowd of humans who were not present."

"Huh." It surprised the old man to know that Morgrim, despite being an animal, was intellectual, empathetic, and thoughtful.

"Wow! Squirrel. It has been so long since I had anything like that to eat. But as sick as I am, I don't think I could have enjoyed it, Morgrim. My body is too far gone now for that. However, I appreciate the gesture; it was very kind."

Morgrim remembered how the old man smelled like a sickness when he first found him. The old man took a minute to stand up. He walked away from Morgrim a few steps, adjusted his coat and slacks, turned around, and faced Morgrim.

"Sir Ivan Prewitt! The Vanishing Man!" He announced before bowing to Morgrim. "I always wanted to be a magician, a trickster. I guess whenever I've had too much to drink, I get a little carried away, I must admit."

"Magician?" Morgrims head tilted. "You have the Tepid mind?"

Ivan was flush with intrigue. "Hmmm my mind is definitely something, maybe not tepid."

Morgrim felt pity for Ivan. He could tell that he was despondent and lonely, on top of being very sick.

"I wonder, Ivan, this place, this forest that surrounds you, is no place for a human. Why are you here?"

Ivan deflated his chest and hung his head.

"I assure you, Morgrim, I did not choose this place for myself. However, it is my fault that I am here."

Morgrim could see the emotion welling up in him.

"A story for another day, perhaps."

Morgrim was curious about the old man, but it frustrated him to know that he didn't want to tell him more. He left it alone, not wanting to be rude, hoping they would revisit it later.

"...Well, since I told you I wanted to be a magician, I might as well show you a trick!" Ivan laughed hysterically.

"I never thought in a million years I would perform a trick for a talking wolf in the forest!"

Ivan got up and gathered a blanket from inside his tent. He went to an embankment that ran the length behind him, positioning himself in the foreground like a stage.

"Ok, are you ready Morgrim? Don't look away!"

Morgrim stood up and fixed his eyes on the blanket that blocked Ivan from sight. A few moments passed, and Morgrim grew curious. He could see Ivan's feet under the blanket. The excitement was palpable. He had no clue what would happen behind the wet blanket. He waited with his ears perked and his mouth clenched.

"Just one sec!"

Ivan yelled out from behind the blanket as if more time would be the solution.

As Morgrim sat on his haunches and watched the sheet wriggle, he spotted two pointed ears slowly rise up over the embankment behind Ivan. Before Morgrim could react, Oct'Tulommon already committed to a full-scale assault on the sick and unsteady body of the old dying man. The earth shook under the weight of his massive frame as it pummeled the ground.

Ivan screamed, but only for a second, and then nothing but the sound of agonal breaths, saturated with blood gurgling in the back of his throat. Morgrim turned his head as blood and dirt flew from the makeshift stage where Ivan was now being shaken and torn apart. The smell that turned Morgrim's stomach to a stone was now in his fur, the mud, the trees and in the fire, sizzling as it burned. Oct'Tulommon took his time to feed on the lifeless body of Ivan.

"This man's flesh is rancid! I know the taste all too well."

Morgrim stood in shock at the mangled mess of blood, flesh, and broken bone that Oct'Tulommon left his new friend in. his ears straight up and eyes wide. He heaved and vomited.

"Haha! What's the matter, wolf? We are all the same on the inside." Oct'Tulommon nodded back at his kill, rummaged and gone through.

"Look at me when I call to you, Wolf!"

Morgrim turned to see Oct'Tulommon now mere inches away, his massive head blocked everything from sight.

"Tell me, do you know me, Obsidian Wolf? Have you heard the stories?"

Finnick told him of the day his mother wolf died, how Oct'Tulommon tried to eat him, and how they narrowly escaped through the tunnels. Morgrim could do nothing but sink into the dirt and back away.

"I didn't know what your importance was then. I do now… Haha… do you know your importance? Bastard wolf? Bastard obsidian Wolf?" Oct'Tulommon taunted.

"Tell me, what did that fat rabbit tell you of your lineage?"

Morgrim was silent still, stricken with fear.

"Answer me at once!" Oct'Tulommon's massive voice pressed him.

"He told me I am from the Illnok lands, but I had fallen out of my mother's mouth when she carried me into her den after I was born. I was lost in the darkness because of my fur."

Oct'Tulommon stopped.

"That is the most ridiculous attempt at a cover-up I have ever heard! and you are too stupid to ask questions? Haha, Finnick is a liar, wolf!"

Morgrim shuttered, Oct'Tulommon's voice splintered in his head.

"Your mind is too small to understand the complexity of your own existence, Morgrim. You have that in common with the lot I surround myself with. I swear it will be my downfall if I'm not more careful. Trusting wolves who swear their fealty to me…Unless you aren't as you seem. You've eluded my fractured wolves for over three winters, bested the droves of the Unclean I have sent in service to find you. You may be of use in my ranks."

Out of the Rimwoods behind him, the same three battle wolves emerged from Eurthrem's day of passing. Apollo and Ack'Reus hurried to feed on the remnants of Ivan. They filled themselves so quickly they couldn't hold it in and vomited, then continued to feed. The assortment of rusted metal objects that hung from their necks clanked as they vigorously tore and chewed.

Ha'Kan stood to the side, watching with disgust. Morgrim felt his anger slip under his instinct for survival.

"What do you say, Morgrim? Will you swear your fealty to him? Alpha Oct'Tulommon will spare your life. No more running hungry and scared." Ack'Reus asks mockingly.

Morgrim furled his snout and growled, showing his sharp teeth, watching for an opportunity to strike at Oct'Tulommon's neck. He could feel the anger swelling inside, his muscles tight, and his legs gearing up for a lunge. Suddenly, his attention was taken by the sound of massive paws sloshing through the mud of the forest floor.

"If you choose to run, bastard wolf now is your chance. You won't get far, but it will make this more fun for us!" Apollo taunted. The Four wolves flanked Morgrim, circling around the perimeter of the camp.

Backing away from Oct'Tulommon, Morgrim waited for the right moment to move, his options dwindling as the wolves closed in on him. The battle wolf Ha'Kan was to his right. He appeared to be the weakest, missing one of his hind paws. He could still walk but painfully. His wound was old, and it was still open and infected. It permeated the air with the stench of maggots and rotting flesh as he got closer.

"We have waited a long time for this Morgrim, even longer than you can remember. The last time we were this close was when you escaped Eurthrem's' den with Finnick," Apollo taunted as he closed in on Morgrim.

With no warning, Morgrim unleashed the force in his muscular hind legs. He buried his claws forcefully into the earth for traction and raced towards the Ha'Kan. He was running as fast as he could.

At the last viable second, he cut to the right and used the flank of a boulder to launch himself, flying over him, he could not bounce to meet him quick enough. Morgrim was shocked to find himself on the outside of the circle. His plan worked. He didn't waste any time sprinting at full gait into the forest, knowing that there were still three very capable wolves to seize him.

Morgrim faintly picked up on Oct'Tulommon cursing the sick wolf Ha'Kan, scolding him for his deficit as the stretch widened between them. Looking back, he could see Oct'Tulommon's most robust battle wolves, Apollo and Ack'Reus, leading the hunting party and gaining ground. While Oct'Tulommon and Ha'Kan brought up the rear. Apollo was gaining ground faster. Not as agile as his brother wolf Ack'Reus, but His legs were longer. Morgrim knew at the pace he ran; he had no chance to outrun them. He needed another plan.

The Rim Wood forest that separated most of the Outlands from the human cities deviated little in terrain, color, and plant life. The trees were tall and bare, with limbs and leaves that began as high as ten feet from the ground, which made it a tough place for a wolf with a black coat to hide. Just as he was giving up on any chance of survival, he heard the distant sound of a river coming from the left. He took a chance to see if the river could be helpful.

"Morgrim! I can tell you're weakening. Your pace is faltering!" Apollo taunted him, trying to shake his confidence.

"I'm gaining on you, bastard wolf!"

In the distance, Morgrim could see a break in the Rimwoods, the forest split in two. The river carved its way through the earth a great distance below. With nowhere else to go, Morgrim stopped at the edge and turned to face the three wolves, ready to take his life.

"Morgrim, I thought we might lose you, Haha!" Oct'Tulommon tried to catch his breath. He was too big and out of shape, a gluttonous tyrant who cared for no one but himself.

"If you're expecting me to beg for my life, brother wolves, I will not give you that satisfaction," Morgrim declared as he stood with his back paws almost off the cliff's edge.

The two wolves laughed. When Oct'Tulommon made it to the edge alongside the others. He circled behind them. "We don't expect you to beg, bastard wolf. We only expect you to die! Tell me, Bastard wolf, did that fat rabbit ever tell you why no one ever came looking for you? Did he mention it while you were ducking your head from hitting those... Loose jutting stones in the smelly warrens you grew up in?"

Oct'Tulommon had a sinister talent for invading one's mind and manipulating their emotions. His words cut like hot steel, penetrating even the most resolute hearts. Finnick, in fact, never divulged the reason for his fragmented youth. It was swiftly dismissed if anyone dared to bring up the topic, a silent understanding that it should never be spoken of outright until a time of he chose to be right.

"I never wanted to know. I never had a reason to. As a cub, I was loved, treated fairly, fed, groomed, and taught the ways of balance and kindness. I didn't have to imagine what yours was like Oct'Tulommon, starving in the canyons to the east as your father made land deals with the Illnok? Finnick may have kept my past hidden, but his way of caring for me was based on how poorly your father raised you."

Oct'Tulommon was stunned by the retort.

"If there's anything to hold dear from your time as a cub Alpha, let it be the excruciating knowledge that your father's legacy is a masterclass in the sheer incompetence of raising a wolf."

Ha'Kan, Apollo, and Ack'Reus were staggered by Morgrim's words and how well they were placed. The air surrounding all of them became humid and stale. Oct'Tulommon's muzzle pulled so tightly that his nose bled.

"Anger makes you weak, and weakness will be the death of all of you. It doesn't have to be like this."

Oct'Tulommon laughs as the other three seem more curious about what Morgrim was saying.

Ack'Reus, the most eager to show his fealty to his Alpha wolf, lunged without a warning or command, making a grave mistake. Having no recourse, Morgrim latched his powerful jaws, sinking his teeth into the front shoulder of Ack'Reus, sending them both tumbling from the cliff side. Morgrim made a quick last-minute decision; it was better to die, dashed against the rocks below, than to feed the bellies of the soulless beasts watching him and their friend from the cliffs above. Apollo howled at the sight of his brother descending into the plumes of white mist swirling around the rapids and sharp rocks below. They were both gone.

With no quick way to descend the cliff side, Oct'Tulommon and his remaining wolves could do nothing.

"Damn you, Ack'Reus!" Oct'Tulommon cursed, not realizing that Apollo was distraught over his brother. He seethed with anger, his insides burning. He could think of nothing else but the thought of his brother lying twisted and mangled on the rocks below. Apollo turned with a stare that cut straight through him.

"That wolf is of the Alpha's blood. He has power! Untapped power that I need! Apollo, bring HIM TO ME!" Oct'Tulommon demanded.

"You selfish, fat wolf, Oct'Tulommon. This is your fault! Ack'Reus's blood is on your hands! I will find that wolf, but not for you. I will find him to avenge my brother," Apollo retorted.

"Apollo, watching your step around me would serve you well. I know your aspirations, but if my death comes prematurely, your seat as Alpha will be dashed against the rocks, just like your brother's skull, right down there." Oct'Tulommon warned.

Apollo became so blinded by rage that the only thing he could do was run. Oct'Tulommon laughed, "That's it, Apollo! Run! Just like you always do!"

He shuddered and felt a pinch of relief as Apollo ran away, skirting the cliff's edge, looking for access and disappearing into the distance.

Staring down into the churning mist, Ha'Kan secretly wished he possessed the nerve to toss himself off the rocks. His life was nothing but senseless violence and sickness he seemed to constantly battle. He watched Oct'Tulommon scan the area.

"... I could push him, but I don't think I could hard enough to send him on his way." Ha'Kan uttered in his own mind.

"What!?" Oct'Tulommon whipped his head, his metal chain clanging together.

"Nothing, Alpha." Ha'Kan put his aching head to the dirt in submission.

Oct'Tulommon cautiously backed away, feeling the tension between him and Apollo gradually dissipate. Apollo was much stronger than any wolf, and if he challenged Oct'Tulommon to a fight, he would surely emerge victorious.

Oct'Tulommon was acutely aware of the simmering resentment in Apollo's heart and his aspirations to become the Alpha of the Fracture. To safeguard his own life and prevent a confrontation with Apollo, Oct'Tulommon struck a deal with all the wolves in the Fracture's ranks, ensuring they would kill Apollo if he were to take Oct'Tulommon's life prematurely.

"Ha'Kan, pull your wretched self together, go back to the den and hunt an offering for the peregrine. Tell him to find that wolf before Apollo does." Oct'Tulommon commanded.

"I thought you said…" "I know what I said, you fool! Do it, or I will throw you from this cliff side myself!"

With his ears pinned back and wincing in pain with every step, Ha'Kan hurried away to fulfill the command.

As Oct'Tulommon stood at the edge of the cliff, he strained to see through the thick mist below, but to no avail. It gnawed at him, leaving the cliff's edge without claiming the power of the pure blood's

Awl'Fire. This failure intensified the situation's urgency, it fueled his determination to find Morgrim no matter the cost.

Chapter 16
River's Edge

Beneath the mist churned by the white river, Morgrim's pursuer, Ack Reus, lay dead, his head smashed against a sizeable moss-covered stone. Regaining consciousness, Morgrim discovered a pair of vultures already feasting on the scattered bits of flesh torn by the impact of Ack'Reus against the riverbank. By sheer luck, Morgrim survived the fall from the cliff side unscathed, barely. He landed in a small shallow pool, just a foot from where Ack'Reus met his end.

Morgrim laid still for a time, gathering his thoughts and planning his next move, trying not to act out of panic. The river's icy waters masked the pain of a broken leg he didn't feel until he tried to stand up. His front leg buckled under his weight, causing him to shriek in pain. He couldn't wait for Oct'Tulommon and the others to flank the cliffs and go downriver. It would only be a matter of time before they found him alive, and running was not an option with a broken leg.

He clawed out of the shallow pool and onto the crushed shale rock lining the river. Once he found his strength, he dragged himself into the cool water. There, he let the current carry him away, not knowing where it would lead but sure it had to be safer than where he had been.

He lay motionless for more than an hour as the slow-moving water carried him downriver, taking him further away than he ever ventured before bringing him back to the upper Border woods of the

Illnok Forest. He watched as the cliffs descended around the river, and the banks transformed into beaches of river rock and pebbles. The water calmed as the river widened. To his left, he could see towering buildings rising above the tree line, their glass windows flickering like diamonds as sunlight reflected off them from a distance. To his right lay the edge of the Illnok territory. He made his way over. It wasn't ideal, but it was certainly the lesser of the two evils. Even though the Illnok didn't take kindly to Outsiders, he was more likely to run into a human on the other side of the river than a Borderwolf.

As he got close enough to feel the silt of the riverbed beneath him, he used his hind legs to shift his direction toward the bank. A little further downstream, he spotted a giant oak tree that fell across several large boulders. It was the perfect place to tuck himself in, rest and warm up without being seen by anything.

Once he made landfall, Morgrim found he could no longer rely on the buoyancy of the water to help him along. The energy it took to cover a short distance was taxing on his weakened body. He passed out from exhaustion by the time he made it underneath the oak.

As the sun rose high above, the warmth gathering in the surrounding stones soothed his aching body. Wishing he could have slept longer if it wasn't for the gnawing sensation in his leg.

"Okay, What are you going to do, Morgrim? You can't stay under this log forever. you need a plan, a way forward." \

He tried to rouse himself into motion. He used his hind legs to turn and scan the forest's edge in hopes of finding something useful. "There!" He spotted a hill with several rabbit holes a reasonable distance away from him. "If I can make it over there, maybe I could squeeze in." In theory, the plan was simple, if he could fit.

It wouldn't be long before the sun would be gone, and he would shiver in the dark with Apollo standing over him. Just before he popped his nose out from under the long, there was a rustle in the bushes behind him. The sound came from something too small to be Oct'Tulommon o Apollo, but hopefully large enough and naive enough to venture closer so he could sink his teeth in. He waited until the right moment as the tiny creature made its way around the oak log. Barely able to see through the cracks, he could make out the silhouette of a plump rabbit with a very familiar scent. He paused and tried to place it.

"...Finnick?" He called out. The rabbit stopped and sniffed the surrounding air.

"Morgrim? My boy, is that you underneath this log?" He hopped down to look. "And waiting to eat me?!"

He exclaimed, excited and perplexed.

Morgrim was so excited to see Finnick. It had been a few months since they crossed paths in the Outlands.

"Nonsense, I could never finish such a fat rabbit."

Finnick made his way around the bushes and the boulders to the opening of the makeshift hideaway.

"Wow… I'm speechless. Haven't seen you in over winter, and you're just casually hanging out underneath a log? On the side of a river? This close to Illnok land? At dinnertime?" Finnick noticed Morgrim nursing his front leg.

"It's a long story, but I need you to get me out of here. My leg is broken, and I need a place to lie low while it heals. Oct'Tulommon and his battle wolves are after me. Just like old times, they said."

Finnick laughed as he hopped out into the open to look for a path to retreat.

" I did manage to kill one of them, though." Morgrims tone took a severe turn.

Finnick stood on his hind legs. "Huh! You don't say? Which one, the sick one? The one with the funny name? Appaloosa? Alpaca?" Finnick chortled again, trying to make Morgrim feel better while hopping around the log.

"Apollo is his name. No, it wasn't that one. It was his brother Ack'Reus—the red one with beady eyes, like a stretched fox or an angry mud-covered fawn."

"Wow… the imagery of that son is impeccable. Well done. I can't say I'm not relieved. One less of that lot running around, wreaking havoc, and killing hounds is a win. Don't worry too much my boy."

Finnick fell silent momentarily as he tried to work the problem out in his head. "Well, I certainly can't carry you out of here. I'm going to have to enlist some helpers. You'll have to trust me when I say this: I'll be back as soon as possible."

"But Finnick, I—" "hush now, boy, that's just the way it is. I'm going to have to get help, and you'll have to sit this one out, I'm afraid. Just wait here."

Morgrim could sense the sarcasm in Finnick's words. There was no way he could leave, even if he tried. The river was too far, and the tree line was even further. If any of them were to spot him going in either direction, it would all be over for him.

"Where am I gonna go? I can hardly walk."

"Okay, hold on. Before I go, let me see if I can find some wild lettuce for you to eat. It will help with the pain."

Finnick darted into the woods so fast that Morgrim chuckled. He couldn't believe that Finnick could still move like that. He was at least twenty winters old when Morgrim found him in the woods three winters ago. He remembered the stories that Finnick and his brothers would tell him about rabbits outliving most of the creatures in the forest, seeing entire generations of wolves come and go. Morgrim regretted not spending more time with Finnick over the years. Finnick was the closest thing to a father he had.

"Okay, Morgrim, eat this." Finnick came back with several leaves of green, wild lettuce in his mouth. "We have been using this as pain relief for a long time. Although I'm unsure how much you need, I've never given it to a wolf."

Morgrim hacked as he tried to swallow the wild lettuce. It was bitter and had fur on the stems that pricked and tickled his throat as it went down.

"Okay, I'm going to go now. You need to stay in the shadows. Your fur makes it almost impossible to see if you do, and I can almost guarantee that if Oct'Tulommon is searching for you, he will make an offer to the peregrine to find you from above. If he does, it won't be long before they come for you." Morgrim settled in.

"Finnick!" Morgrim stopped him before he retreated into the woods.

"... I'm scared." Innocently, he admitted to feeling vulnerable and it hit Finnick hard. To think of his cub in such a state made him sad.

"I love you, Morgrim. I'll be back, I promise. Just sit tight."

Chapter 17
The Peregrine

Under the direction of Oct'Tulommon, Ha'Kan traveled as fast as his broken body would allow back to the interior of the Outlands and the abandoned oil derrick, hoping to spot anything that could pass for an offering. His body was feverish and doing its best to fight the effects of the septic shock spreading from the infection in his leg, but it was failing to do so rapidly.

The pain he felt was more intense than ever. His heart pumping the poisoned blood throughout his body, was doing more damage as it worked harder to carry him through the bogs and the dead fields of damp grass. After three hours of frantically trying to find a substantial offering for the peregrine, he spotted a decent size mole pop his head out of his tunnel. He knew the peregrine preferred rabbit, but it wasn't a secret; the food was becoming scarce in the Outlands. He snatched it as quickly as he could, maiming it. The mole squealed and hissed, trying to escape his teeth, but it was useless. Even though he was sickly, his instinct to kill was still intact.

When he returned to the oil derrick, he climbed all the way to the top, trying to make the offering before the sun dipped behind the trees and the last light of the day was gone.

He laid the mole on the top rusted platform and waited. He could see the falcon floating on the warm air high above the derrick in the distance through the low-hanging gray clouds sporadically covering the blue sky above. Once he spotted the mole, he folded his wings back and dove.

He was covering an extreme distance in no time, slowing just in time to perch on the rail above the platform. He was beautiful, sleek, and very large, almost the size of Ha'Kan. The scratching of his razor-sharp talons against the rusted metal railing sent chills down Ha'Kan's spine, beginning at his gritting teeth.

It wasn't common for a bird to take a chance interacting with the animals of the earth. It was a risk that was easily avoidable for them. This bird, however, found an ingenious way to keep his belly full with minimal effort. Oct'Tulommon convinced the wolves in the Outlands that the peregrine was some sort of god-like creature. Able to see the future. Possessing knowledge of things that only existed in fables and stories of old. Fearful of him, they presented costly sacrifices they could hardly afford to secure his protection from the beasts that lurked within the haze and obscurity of the Outlands. For this, the peregrine agreed to be Oct'Tulommon's eyes from above any time he needed it. Ha'Kan, however, was more intelligent than he let on. He could see right through the lies they convinced everyone else of. He could see the peregrine for what he was: a gluttonous, egotistical fat liar with only one priority - himself.

"Ha'Kan, it's been a long while since we've spoken. I'm a little surprised you're still alive, to be honest. What is this you have brought me?"

The peregrine hopped down from the rusted railing to the broken platform, using his sharp beak to peck at the mole.

"It's the only thing that I could find." Ha'Kan sighs, anticipating the falcon's reaction to his hastily prepared offering.

"You know just as well as I do that food is becoming scarce out here." The peregrine clutches the mole with his beak and tosses it over the side of the derrick without even sampling the meat. The mole's lifeless body plummets toward the ground, a mere speck in the vast expanse below.

"I can't stand the taste of dirty moles. I have told you this many times, you fool!"

Ha'Kan fought the urge to pounce on him, fury burned like a smoldering ember inside him. *What I wouldn't give to snap your tiny, feathered head clean off!* He thought. But he knew that if anything were to happen to this so-called divine creature from above, he would surely be put out of his misery once and for all.

"Oct'Tulommon wants to speak with you. He is to the north, just beyond the Rimwoods."

Ha'Kan slumped back down, overexerted from standing too long.

"You mean he wants me to find the wolf you and the other fools let escape? Why Oct'Tulommon would be so careless as to use a dying wolf as you perplexes me. He is smart enough to know better than I would think." The peregrine says sarcastically.

"I'm not dying, you arrogant bird. It's just taking longer than normal for my leg to heal; this air, the dirt here is full of sickness, it's hard to keep a wound clean," Ha'Kan says as he lays down, wincing with every move. The pain shoots from the blunt bone showing through his skin. The peregrine laughs as he watches him struggle to stay conscious.

"Ha'Kan, death is a scent I know all too well," The peregrine remarks, his voice cold and mocking.

Ha'Kan is silent as the peregrine's words sink in.

"And I could smell your foul stench of decay from up in the sky. It won't be long now. It's a shame, though. The only part I will eat is your eyes. The rest of your carcass is rotten."

The peregrine flies back to the rail, overlooking the desolate land below. "If you see him before I do, you can tell Oct'Tulommon I will find the wolf you let get away. I'm certain he will pay my asking price. Next time you expect me to fly through your stench, the least you can do is bring me a rabbit, or I won't even bother coming down from the sky."

The peregrine flies away into the gray sky above, his laughter echoing through the emptiness. When he is out of sight, Ha'Kan collapses, the weight of his pain and despair dragging him into the stiff embrace of unconsciousness.

Chapter 18
Arbiter

Morgrim couldn't shake the image of the poor man who became entangled in the wolves' conflict. He wished he could turn back time and save what little life the man had left to live, no matter how miserable or sick he was. The guilt weighed heavily on Morgrim's heart, adding to his already enduring physical pain.

"How could I let myself be ambushed like that? After going unnoticed for so long? I ran circles around those bumbling fools." He chastised himself, mentally replaying the events that led to his current predicament. The memory of the attack was vivid, from when he realized he was surrounded to the desperate struggle that ensued. He could still feel the adrenaline pumping through his veins. As he wrestled with the bitter pain and stiffness in his front leg, he kept hidden underneath the logs, shielding himself from seeking eyes. However, being unable to stretch out only exacerbated the pain in his fractured bones.

The wild lettuce and its analgesic properties had worn off, and the deep teeth gritting ache settled back in. He tried to focus on the positive aspects of his situation. At least he escaped Oct'Tulommon's grasp, and Finnick had come to his aid, offering support and guidance. But as the hours dragged on, Morgrim found himself tormented by his memories, each replaying the events that unfolded and his inability to change them.

His thoughts were interrupted by a faint rustling near the shelter. Morgrim's ears perked up, alert and ready for whatever might come next. He knew he needed to stay solid and focused to survive the dangers lurking in the shadows. But it turned out to be nothing but a squirrel, too far away to try to catch.

As the afternoon light gradually gave way to night, Morgrim's hope that Finnick would return before the dark dwindled. The prospect of spending the night crammed inside his makeshift hideout filled him with dread. He watched the moon rise over the water, captivated by its beauty. Such enchanting sights were rare in the Outlands, but nature's splendor abounded here on the edge of the Illnok lands. The crisp, clean air and the rich scent of the forest and its inhabitants filled his nostrils, intensifying his desire to run freely through the woods.

Just as he drifted off to sleep, lulled by the soothing sounds of nature, a sudden noise jolted him awake. His heart raced as he spotted a shadowy figure in the darkness, its stench of despair hanging heavy in the air. It was Apollo, panting and sniffing the ground as he trotted along the riverside. The relentless predator locked onto Morgrim's scent.

Before Apollo could come any closer, Morgrim quickly grabbed several pieces of loose wood from around him and placed them in front of his hiding spot. Apollo circled the area several times, searching intently.

"Where are you? Bastard wolf, I can smell you. Come out and face me!" Apollo growled, inching closer to the pile of logs. Peering out from his hideout, Morgrim watched anxiously as Apollo passed by, scanning every direction. The imposing figure stopped ten feet from Morgrim, who silently prayed to the Awl'Fire that Apollo would continue down the river.

To his astonishment, Apollo turned and looked straight into Morgrim's eyes, holding his gaze for an agonizingly long moment. Morgrim braced himself for the worst, thinking Apollo was merely toying with him. But then, as if by some miracle, Apollo turned away and continued on his path. It was as if Morgrim was invisible, his black coat and eyes blending seamlessly into the darkness of the night—a walking void undetectable even by the most fearsome predators.

Relief washed over Morgrim as he watched Apollo round the bend and vanish into the night beyond the trees. If Apollo discovered him under the logs, there would have been no escape.

After some time, Morgrim regained his composure and removed the pieces of wood from the entrance, allowing the cool night air to flow in. For a while, he was on edge, expecting Apollo to return, but he never did.

An hour or so later, Morgrim's mind filled with a faint voice that called him from the Illnok tree line. "Morgrim! Are you still alive in there? It's Finnick, and I have brought friends!"

His body tensed with anticipation, eager to escape his cramped confines and stretch his legs.

"Barely! Apollo came through here earlier but couldn't find me. I don't know if he's going to come back this way; maybe it's not safe to do this," Morgrim worried, looking out to see Finnick standing at the tree line with three other rabbits.

"I think you should go back; it's not safe."

He didn't receive a reply from them.

"Hello? HELLO!" He called out, shifting his weight to look towards the tree line. But Finnick was already in front of him.

"You scared me half to death, Finnick! Why are you panting like a dry beaver!?"

Finnick's belly bounced up and down with laughter.

"Funny wolf you are, you try digging a tunnel on an empty stomach when you are as fat as me and not end up wheezing like a goat in heat." He retorted in his usual manner.

"Finnick, I don't think this is safe. Apollo could return any moment now. He couldn't have gone that far." Morgrim sunk back down into a vulnerable little cub. It broke Finnick's little heart to see him scared.

"Where's your backbone at? Funny, I don't remember raising a coward. You are a wolf, right?" Finnick teased, trying to lighten the situation while he furiously dug out the shelter around the front so Morgrim could get out easier. He tried to not show it, but he was also terrified.

Morgrim could smell it emanating from him. The adrenaline in his veins turned his stomach, The same smell that comes from dying prey after a hunt. The overwhelming feeling that something evil was in the air. The idea of Finnick in the midst of gnashing teeth made him choke back on tears.

"Wow, I'm completely out of breath. I have to stay away from those damned clover fields."

Morgrim sighed as he tried to get up.

"Hold on now, big fella, don't move! You need to listen to me carefully. On my way to fetch my brothers, I spotted the peregrine in the skies above us. Knowing what I know of Oct'Tulommon, I'm sure he has asked him to find you. If Oct'Tulommon wants to find something, he usually does with that bird's help. So, we three did what we do best."

Finnick paused and waited for Morgrim to respond. "...You... du—" "Aye, we dug! That's right wolf!" Finnick interrupted with enthusiasm.

"Finnick, I can't fit in those tunnels; you know that," Morgrim said, ready for the challenge ahead.

"What, you think I don't know that Wolf?! That's when young Nilian over there came up with the greatest idea of all. I'm so proud of him!"

Morgrim looked over to see Nilian and another rabbit he wasn't familiar with, standing just inside the mouth of a tunnel.

"We found the biggest tunnel that led us here and made it big enough for you to fit!"

Morgrim was silent, waiting to hear what the greatest idea ever, was.

"That's what took us half the night, you ingrate! It leads from this tree line to our burrow in Illnok territory, deep underground, safe. It might take a while, and you'll only be able to fit on your belly." Finnick explained, his voice laced with pride and determination.

Morgrim's uncertainty subsided, and he asked, "Okay then, so what do I need to do?"

"Well, Nilian is going to create a diversion downriver. If the peregrine is close, he won't waste any time trying to catch him. Rabbit is his favorite meal, after all."

"Wait a second, Finnick. I can't ask him to do that. It sounds like certain death, and I can't let him sacrifice himself for me. And what if Apollo is still around the bend? Then what?"

"Then I will bring him back to you so you can tell him how you feel about him!" Nilian popped up out of nowhere and interjected, grinning as the other rabbits at the tree line snickered. They had been listening the whole time.

"Don't be so serious, Morgrim! I've been dodging that bird for as long as I can remember. And as for that wolf you speak of, if you can outrun him, well, Haha," Nilian chuckled.

"He's right, Morgrim! I'm not scared of a wolf that couldn't catch you! You're slower than a slug on a hot rock!" Finnick teased.

"And as for the bird, he might be a pigeon that just looks like a falcon; it's questionable. honestly."

"Good one, Finnick," Nilian agreed, as he finished up his leg stretches.

"Alright then, it's settled. Here I go. I'll see you both back in the burrow." Nilian's words faded as he disappeared into the night. Morgrim watched astounded "Wow! You weren't kidding, Finnick. He is undoubtedly fast."

"Faster than any rabbit I have ever known," Finnick gleamed with pride.

After a quick sprint, Nilian slowed down. He waited in the open, pretending to search for clover among the rocks while secretly checking the skies above. It didn't take long for him to spot the black silhouette of the peregrine passing underneath the moonlight with its wings outstretched, floating like a specter in the night sky. Nilian squealed as if he were wounded.

"Okay, Morgrim, that's the sign. Let's go. Try to make it as quick as you can. We have little time," Finnick urged as they prepared to embark on their daring escape.

Morgrim fought the cramps in his hind legs and the stiffness that crept into his crooked spine. As he climbed out into the open, his back popped and his hind legs buckled.

"Run! Now!" Finnick shouted, leading the way. Nilian shrieked, but the peregrine continued to hover about thirty yards up, making no change in altitude.

Why aren't you diving, you old chicken? Nilian thought to himself. Something didn't feel right. He caught a powerful scent floating past his nose on the cool evening breeze.

"What's all the fuss for, rabbit? You seem fine to me, for now," Apollo taunted as he charged toward Nilian.

The peregrine had watched the rescue attempt play out the whole time with no intention of attacking. Nilian raced back in the direction he came, trying to make it to the new tunnel they dug. As he rounded the bend in the river, Apollo was right on top of him.

Morgrim only made it five or six yards into the tunnel while Finnick stood just outside, waiting for Nilian to return, when he saw Apollo hot on his brother's heels.

"Nilian, faster!" Finnick shouted, but Apollo was gaining too. Just moments before Nilian could dive in, Apollo pounced with all the power he had left in his legs, grabbing Nilian by the fur on his back mid-air. He shook the rabbit violently as Finnick helplessly watched.

"Please, Apollo, no! I beg you, take me and let him go. He has done nothing to you," Finnick pleaded. Apollo released Nilian, sending his tiny body flying against the rocks, knocking him unconscious. Apollo approached the tunnel entrance.

"This reminds me of the last time we met, only I'm not leaving with an empty stomach this time. I'll make a deal with you. Tell me where to find that bastard wolf, and maybe you can save your little brother from my belly," Apollo threatened.

Morgrim was in a state of Panic. He could hear the commotion at the tunnel entrance, but the narrow tunnel didn't allow him to turn. Trying to back out was not an option with his broken leg. "Finnick!" He called. Growling as frustration consumed him. Finnick turned his eyes to the darkness inside of the tunnel. "Morgrim, go as fast as you can. And get the others." Finnick attempted to rouse him with a false sense of hope. Even though he knew there wasn't. Morgrim was immobilized by the dirt and roots around him.

"Please, we must keep going. There is nothing we can do here and the faster we make it to the warren the quicker we can send help." The rabbit in front of him tried to be a voice of reason. Tears of frustration filled Morgrim's eyes, without any other option he pressed ahead. "Show me the way ahead then."

Outside, Finnick was shaking, trying to restrain his anger. His heart was pounding inside of his chest. "I do not know where he is, Apollo, but even if I did, I wouldn't tell you..."

Apollo sniffed the air from the tunnel around Finnick's hulking frame. "He is in there. I can smell the desperation."

The sleek black fur around Apollo's slender neck bristled and his snout curled, barring his jagged teeth.

"If he is trust me, he is long gone by now, Apollo. You could never catch him. You're too big for that tunnel." Finnick hoped that Apollo would take his word for it. He had been wrong at judging size before. Furiously Apollo turned to grab Nilian.

"Then you can watch, and when I'm done, I'll tell you how delicious he tasted" "Wait, I'll tell you where to find him!" Finnick pleaded, Nilian's little body dropped from Apollo's mouth. Apollo's demeanor calmed as Nilian regained consciousness, confused as he came to.

"Well, that took little, Finnick. I thought you were a little tougher than that?" Apollo sneered. In a split-second decision, Finnick spun around and kicked dirt into Apollo's eyes. He then sprang towards Nilian and slung him by his neck into the safety of one of the other tunnels.

"Run, Nilian, and don't look back!" Finnick shouted before breaking into a slow burdened sprint in the opposite direction. They didn't get far when the peregrine swooped down from the sky faster than a bolt of lightning, he clenched Finnick by the fat on his back. The peregrine's talons pierced his flesh Pinning him to the earth. Finnick shrieked in pain as the falcon snapped the vertebrae in his neck, causing his lower half to go limp.

Nilian, still in shock, stood frozen in his own urine at the mouth of a different, much smaller tunnel, unable to move. He watched as the peregrine stood on Finnick's back, pulling bits of his fur out, trying to get to the meat underneath. Despite the intense pain of his pierced skin and the falcon's weight on top of him, Finnick delivered one last blow to the peregrine's pride.

"Is it true?" Finnick gasped.

"Focus and articulate. I can't hear your mind over your flesh tearing. Is what true, rabbit?" The peregrine stopped and turned his head to investigate Finnick's fading eyes, somewhat amazed that he could still move.

"I was in this field not too long ago... and I overheard two guinea hens…" Finnick's voice trailed off as he started to lose control of his diaphragm.

"What? Speak up, rabbit!" The peregrine commanded, hopping down from Finnick's back to allow him more air.

Finnick continued, "Two… no… three guinea hens… ugly as mud, you know the type… you have to agree they're ugly… it's sad…"

The peregrine became more frustrated, he placed his claws on Finnick's back and shook him to keep him from fading out again.

"Say it! Hurry before it's too late and you're dead."

"The guineas said... you're a half chicken, and not the better half either. Is it true? Is your mother a chicken?"

Finnick lifted his head and looked down the peregrine's chest, then to his stomach and a little further.

"I guess it's good you have feathers down there… aye half chicken?"

Nilian laughed through his breaking tears. The peregrine's feathers were sticking up all over his neck and head.

"No matter where you go or how high you fly up there, there will always be two guineas and now a battle wolf who thinks you're half chicken. Take that to the clouds with you… half chicken… I'm ready now." Finnick poked with resignation and a deep breath. The peregrine hesitated, then placed his talons around Finnick's throat and twisted, the force of the motion broke his neck and killed him instantly.

Apollo, who watched the act of malice out of morbid curiosity, realized how far Nilian retreated in the tunnel before it was done.

"Damn rabbits," The peregrine was not amused. Barely able to get any lift as he carried Finnick's lifeless fat corpse into the nearest tree.

Apollo watched as the peregrine took the massive feast too high to share.

"Damn, selfish bird." He bent and shoved his head into the hole as far as he could before his broad shoulders impeded, bringing him face to face with the tiny rabbit. Nilian realized he could swallow him whole if he wanted to.

"I know that was hard for you. To watch as your brother is torn apart. It will stay with you for as long as you live."

Nilian couldn't move. Paralyzed with trauma.

"I lost my brother today, too. I watched him get pulled from a cliff by that Wolf you're saving."

His voice tinged with madness. Nilian's gaze remained fixed on the peregrine high in a cedar tree, Finnick clutched in his claws, bloody and fireless.

"Hey! Look at me, rabbit!" Apollo demanded. Nilian turned and locked eyes with Apollo, tears soaking the fur around his eyes.

"You know, this was all because of him, your adopted "Nephew" He's why your brother is dead. He's also why my brother is dead, too." Apollo feigned a careful inflection, his voice growing darker. Nilian broke down and cried.

"Shhh... Hush now, little rabbit. It will all be over soon. Go back and give a message to that wolf in your burrow for me. Tell him I will find him, and when I do, I will kill him for both of us, for me and you."

Apollo's fake attempt to console the young rabbit was laced with the seeds of hatred. He was bating him. Nilian's brow furrowed into a scowl, anger swelled inside him just as it had with Apollo.

"Go before you find yourself inside my empty stomach," Apollo warned.

As Nilian prepared to leave, he called out, "Apollo! I'll only give your message to Morgrim if you deliver one for me."

Apollo, curious, turned back around and walked to Nilian.

"Oh, but of course, this should be good. What is it, tiny rabbit?"

"You tell that bird that I will spend the rest of my life figuring out a way to make him pay for what he did here,"

Nilian voice filled with determination.

Apollo was shocked at Nilian's audacity to say such a thing to a creature that could eat him without consequence.

"I will most definitely deliver that message to him. Goodbye for now, Nilian."

Apollo watched as the young rabbit disappeared into the darkness of the burrow. Deep down, he felt a scrap of sadness for what happened. Finnick may have annoyed the Fracture occasionally, but he was an innocent creature who didn't deserve what happened to him.

The peregrine, however, was detached from any feelings for any of the creatures of the land. He was cold, murderous, and lacked any type of emotion.

Apollo trotted a little quicker to get within distance of the peregrine.

"I must go find my brother's body. I need to know for certain that he is dead. I'm sure Oct'Tulommon is waiting for your report," Apollo walked beneath the peregrine overhead in the trees.

"No need to find him, wolf. I flew beneath the river's spray where he fell." The peregrine replied with amusement.

Apollo stopped. His hope of ever seeing Ack'Reus again dissipated. "You saw him there?"

The peregrine laughed. "Oh yes, Apollo, I'm afraid Ack'Reus wasn't as lucky as Morgrim. Would you like me to describe in detail the carnage? Or will you take my word that he is very much... dead?"

Apollo hung his head and turned away so the peregrine wouldn't see him cry. "No need for that, bird."

Chapter 19
The Burrow

The journey to the old burrow in the Illnok territory through the haphazard, poorly dug-out tunnel took over three hours. Morgrim thought the pain he felt stuck inside the hole in the riverbank was unbearable, but the pain he felt when he made it to the den was much worse.

The skin on his belly was worn down, bleeding and irritated by the rocks and dirt he had to force himself to drag it over. He couldn't lie down without wincing in pain. His leg was throbbing with such force he could've sworn it had its own heart.

All his physical pain was overshadowed by the tension he felt as he waited for Finnick and Nilian to arrive. As he breached the last bend, he could see the welcoming moonlight shining downward inside the main chamber of the burrow. Long ago, the rabbits expanded the walls to accommodate Morgrim as a growing young pup.

"Help!" The rabbit who assisted Morgrim called out, hopping head.

"Finnick and Nilian are in trouble at the other end of this tunnel! Go!"

A large, muscular and stoic rabbit came into view. Morgrims heart caved as soon as he saw him, Mulgris Awl'Ginna, the warren ruler.

It had been a long time since they saw each other.

"Morgrim? Is that you in the darkness?"

He stopped a few yards from the end of the tunnel. His fur hid him and his emotional break.

"Yes, it is me, Mulgris. I'm afraid something terrible has happened." The Emotion in Morgrims heart spilled out into the small chamber. Mulgris was silent, he searched Morgrim's heart and mind for what he felt and shuttered as he stumbled upon it. "Ar'Lewin, send the tepid minds to the end of the tunnel. Find Finnick. Bring him to me." Mulgris turned back to Morgrim. "We will go back as well to see what's keeping them. You…" "I will go with them," Morgrim interjected, as he attempted to return to his feet. His used body was visibly shaking under his own body weight, but he was ready to go.

"No, Morgrim. You are in no shape to crawl through that tunnel," Mulgris insisted. Morgrim sank back down, he knew he had no choice; Mulgris would not let him go.

"Burren and Unis will be here with you. If you need anything, ask either of them," Mulgris's voice was firm.

Rabbits were like wolves in that they needed to apply order to the population for it to endure. This was a little harder, considering their packs grew almost exponentially. There were seven rabbits to every wolf in the Illnok territories alone. A sprawling system of interconnecting tunnels laced the earth underneath the land, ensuring their travel was safe inside the territory's borders and further out in every direction. Here, Morgrim spent his days as a cub when he was small enough to fit.

"Morgrim, I'm going to see if I can find the ingredients for a healing salve. Those wounds on your belly will heal much faster if I do," Unis jumped into a tunnel above her.

"Try to sleep while I'm gone." She pressed her tiny little nose against the side of his face.

"It's good to see you again."

"It's good to see you again too Unis, although I wish it were under different circumstances," Morgrim replied as she smiled at him.

"Get some rest. I'll be back soon." She hopped out into another tunnel that led off into the darkness.

It had been several winters since Morgrim saw Unis. He could remember how he used to watch her teach the younger rabbits about different plants in the forest and how some could be useful for different things while others could be deadly. She was brilliant and just as caring. In her absence, Morgrim couldn't help but feel comfortable knowing she was there to help him heal.

Once Unis was gone, Morgrim realized the only rabbit left with him was Burren, the only brother older than Finnick. Burren was a handsome rabbit, missing an ear and with eyes glazed white from blindness. He spent most of his days in the burrow beneath the Alpha's mountain, communicating with the Alpha's Elden wolves. He saw the goodness in the hearts of the wolves. Even though he almost died in the clutches of an Illnok pack wolf. He was wise enough to know his place in the natural order of things. But it didn't stop him from being bitter about it.

"Hmm, this brings back fond memories, doesn't it, wolf? I remember the first time I saw you. I thought Finnick lost his mind by bringing a wolf into our burrow," Burren said.

Morgrim raised his head to see the old rabbit. He was glad to see him but also terrified of what news was coming and how it would affect Burren.

"Wow! Burren! I never thought I would see you again!"

The old rabbit smiled. "Well, I hate to say it, but I don't get to go outside as much as I would like to anymore, so if you hadn't made your way down here, I don't think you would have old friend." Burren chuckled as he made his way to Morgrim. Being almost blind, he used the burrow's wall to guide him closer.

"Ahhh, there you are," Burren said as he

Morgrim bent his head down and pressed his snout into his fur, tears falling from both their eyes. After a few moments, Burren stepped away.

"Morgrim, the warmth has cooled inside of you," Burren trembled. Morgrim knew something changed in him after he escaped Apollo, but he couldn't quite figure it out.

"It was a tough day, to say the least. I have never seen a human before." "A human?" Burren interrupted Morgrim.

"Yes, I was stalking a squirrel beneath the Rimwoods and noticed the smoke from his camp. I was curious about him. It was the first time I had ever seen a human. I could speak with him. It was his fire, I believe; I could feel his Awl'Fire and his heartfelt… kind and gentle," Morgrim explained. Burren stayed silent, waiting to learn more.

"As I got closer, his words made sense to me, so I stayed in the light of his fire for a time. He was sick and sad. I felt emotional towards him. It was… bizarre," Morgrim continued.

"Well, old friend, the world of men is blighted with sickness as of late. They are weakened, and I'm surprised that there are any out there still with the least bit of a flicker in their hearts," Burren was solemn.

"I've been around for a long time, Morgrim, Longer than even I expected…."

As Burren spoke, the sound of several rabbits interrupted him. They were going through the large tunnel Morgrim used to enter the burrow. Mulgris came walking in. followed by young Nilian. Morgrim knew immediately that something wasn't right. At that exact moment, Unis went from the tunnel above, dropping various flowers and roots.

"Nilian, where is your brother?" Burren asked but was answered with silence.

"Where is Finnick, Nilian?!" Morgrim asked, with ragged breath. Nilian stopped and turned to Morgrim with a look of disdain and anger.

"This is your fault, Morgrim. You don't even belong here among us... I overheard your stories when I was younger, how he said you were so special." Nilian's voice shook with emotion; Mulgris could barely stand, weakened by his feelings. The hurt inside of Nilian became more visible on his face with each passing second. Mulgris stepped forward and put himself between Morgrim and Nilian.

"I think we just need to calm down, Nilian."

"No!" Nilian shouted, tears streaming down his face. "You're just like the rest of the wolves in the forest, Morgrim. You're selfish and you only care about what benefits you! He is dead now because you couldn't handle yourself out there!"

"That's enough! Unis, take him out of here. We will speak again when you have had the chance to cool off, Nilian." Unis was in shock, unable to move. It broke her heart into pieces. Mulgris commanded again. "Unis, take him away. "

It devastated Morgrim. He hated himself for what happened to Finnick and didn't know how to improve it.

"Morgrim, he doesn't realize how big a part of your life he was. He cannot see past his anger right now... give the rabbit some time; he will come around." Burren's voice was gentle and understanding but did little to soothe Morgrim's heart.

He cried out in despair. Drawing the peaked ears of several pack rabbits, filling the tunnels in every direction with wet eyes. "No! He is right, Burren. It is my fault. I should've known. Tomorrow I will leave this place. I don't want Nilian to be reminded anymore of the pain I caused."

Burren came close to Morgrim and used his head to wipe the tears from Morgrim's eyes. "This is your decision to make Morgrim, but eventually, your past will call on you." Mulgris cast a worried glance at Burren.

"Burren, I still don't understand! Why me? Why are the hearts of some so bent on sniffing the flame from others! Why!? He was good to me! He was good!"

Burren and Mulgris stepped back towards him. "It was never any of our places to tell you before when Finnick was alive..." "Burren! Still your heart and mind! This is not the time!" Mulgris interjected, his voice firm.

"He needs to know, Mulgris! He needs to know!" Burren insisted, his voice filled with urgency.

Morgrim was speechless. "Know what, Mulgris!? Tell me!"

Mulgris rolled his eyes and stamped his little foot down in the dirt. "Stop! Everyone, just stop…."

The den went silent with his command.

"Morgrim, you will stay here and rest. I will talk with Nilian and see if I can soothe the pain in his heart, but you need to understand you are in no shape to travel. When your leg has had ample time to heal, we will take you to Alpha's mountain. You will meet an old friend, one of the oldest and most gifted of the Alpha's Elden wolves.

"Mulgris... Burren was-"Morgrim began, but Mulgris cut him off.

"Burren has no right to reveal such heavy affirmations at a time like this. He knows better. Trust that we will tell you all we know if it is what the Wolf Sayer commands."

Morgrim knew he was right; as much as he wanted to know everything about his past, he needed to get through all the day's events first.

"I'm sorry, Morgrim, for your loss." Mulgris' words were gentle, allowing the tension in the room to dissipate and allowing the sadness of loss to gently fall back into their hearts.

"Burren let's go to Nilian and see if we can help him. He is in a bad way." Mulgris urged.

Morgrim heard Unis in the adjacent chamber as the two left, sobbing. Burren turned to Morgrim and stopped for a moment.

"I'm sorry, Morgrim. Give it time." With that, Burren followed Mulgris, leaving him to his thoughts.

For the rest of the evening and well into the night, Morgrim thought about all that happened and wept. A storm of emotions - anger, sadness, guilt and regret- swirled together, weighing on his heart. He knew the days ahead would bring new challenges, but he also knew he couldn't face them without the support and wisdom of his friends. Through loss and pain, he needed strength to keep moving forward, to uncover the truth about his past and his role in the world.

Part V: Decisions and Deceptions

Chapter 20
Power

"What is this? Ha'Kan, wake up!" Oct'Tulommon tried to rouse Ha'Kan, he was unconscious on the rusted metal scaffolding and had been since his conversation with the peregrine.

"I guess the bloody bird was right about you cripple." He returned his bloodshot eyes below.

"That bird is nothing but a liar, Oct'Tulommon. I swear it's getting better." Ha'Kan argued, raised his head and stood up. Once on his remaining three paws, his peripheral vision narrowed and dimmed. He shook his head, his consciousness waned.

"Lying to yourself is not doing us any good. I swear, most days I fear the only one I can trust is the damn bird. The only one who hasn't failed me yet." Oct'Tulommon turned his head away from the air that rose around Ha'Kan. It was swollen with an odd wet heat.

"How long have I been asleep?" Ha'Kan inquired.

Oct'Tulommon laughed. "Close to a full day. I received word from The peregrine last night as to the whereabouts of that wolf. He is with the Illnok rabbits now. All of them except one, to be exact. He gave me a trophy to add to the collection."

Ha'Kan's eyes journey to a metal scaffold in an old control room of the Derrick. An assortment of items littered it: tools, batteries, and human skulls. Near the edge of a table was a flat slate stone with a severed rabbit's head. The violence Oct'Tulommon was capable of, never ceased to disgust Ha'Kan.

"After you left me by the cliff side more than a day ago. I made a few stops on the way back from the Rimwoods; it seems I have a few more allies on the outer edges than I thought."

Ha'Kan looked at him with puzzled eyes. "I'm not sure what you mean."

Oct'Tulommon walked to the platform's edge and looked down at a pack of twenty wolves scattered around the various storage containers and burned-out vehicles. "Come and look for yourself."

He hobbled over to the edge to stand by him. He looked down at the wolves below, his chest tightened. He stood in awe of the turnout, familiar wolves he hadn't seen in several winters and some he never met. Interlopers, with no allegiance to the Fracture before, now, as the Outlands were becoming inhabitable and food scarcer, They were forced into allegiance to Oct'Tulommon.

"They have grown tiresome having to rummage through garbage and dodge bullets in the cities of men. Would you believe there are Druthes down there as well?"

Ha'Kan scanned the gathering below and found several larger dogs in the mix. They weren't as large as the ferals, but just every bit as menacing.

"Tired of their pitiful existences, their disdain for the humans is something I admire." Oct'Tulommon was proud of his work.

He laughed as Ha'Kan backed away from the ledge.

"You know Ha'Kan, you are from the lands to the west. You aren't privy to the more storied history of our plight here in the Outlands. So I don't expect you to share the same hatred for those entitled fools in the Illnok lands…"

Ha'Kan stopped just shy of the end of the platform and let Oct'Tulommon take the lead down the steps.

"…Bred with the most important purpose of them all: to protect the fire in the Alpha's mountain!" Oct'Tulommon declared as he scoffed. "They have no right to hoard the fertile lands all for a pack of fewer than one hundred wolves! While the greater collection suffers!"

Oct'Tulommon passed through the broken door of the oil rig. "That's about to change."

He turned and walked into the center of the wolves. Ha'Kan watched as every wolf turned to give him their complete and undivided attention.

"Most of you standing here have never heard the great story of the Awl'Fire. If you have, I can only assume it was a diluted version from an unhinged mystic passing through, containing only a portion of the truth. The truth is much more terrifying. Fortunately for us, I am privy to the knowledge that has been kept from all of us."

Oct'Tulommon turned toward the Alpha's mountain, rising high into the sky, its peak shimmering like a beacon of hope in the afternoon sun.

"I don't expect any of you to know this story, nor do I look down on you for your ignorance. The past is where it should be, in the past. The future is much more important to me as it should be to you, and if we do nothing, our future here in this desolate wasteland will fade while the wolves beneath that peak prosper." Oct'Tulommon paused and turned his head in the other direction, towards the cities of men.

He didn't want to reveal his entire plan to them. They were not ready. His crusade to end the reign of the Illnok was not the only victory he sought. It was only just a warm-up. The void was calling to him, telling him to strike now while humans were in a weakened state of decay. The Rasping fever opened a window of opportunity.

Ha'Kan entered the crowd as he watched Oct'Tulommon rouse them into a frenzy. Even though he held the title of battle wolf, Ha'Kan and Oct'Tulommon rarely saw eye to eye on the decisions he made. Several winters prior, Ha'Kan tried to escape after he watched Oct'Tulommon kill another wolf simply for disagreeing with him. The other wolf fought hard but only scratched Oct'Tulommon's hide. When he found out Ha'Kan tried to leave, he sent Apollo and Ack'Reus after him. He was sure they were going to kill him, but Oct'Tulommon was satisfied to keep him alive. He told him his existence was punishment enough.

Ha'Kan had given up hope his wounds would heal; Too sick to escape and too weak to stand up for himself; his approaching death was to be his only way out.

"I want to make a promise to all of you here before me," Oct'Tulommon bellowed, "but before I do, I ask for something in return. Some of you here do not know of me, you will, some of you do not fear me, trust me when I say, you will, and if there is one here; of either Wolf or Druthe that feel their abilities to rule and provide for the pack can be more effective then step forward and call the Altapex, I will gladly give my life to them."

As he spoke, all the ferals in attendance drew closer to see who would take the ultimatum. The pack was silent until.

"And what of the lives you've taken with impunity, Oct'Tulommon? Their brothers and sisters. Mother wolves and father wolves. Do they know what you have done to gain favor with the void?" A strong and confident presence within the crowd rose above them; it filled every single one of their minds, thick with a challenge. The air grew tense as the crowd of wolves stirred.

"Why does this band of jilted wolves mean so much to you now when you've offered so many of them to the void? This place could be great, but fear chokes the air; sewn by you and your band of misguided thugs."

"And who is it that calls my integrity into question? Please come forth and show yourself to all of us, brave wolf."

Oct'Tulommon scans the crowd, his heart raced, afraid that the challenger might be a larger, more fearsome wolf than himself.

Behind a rusted metal cable spool, an older, gray wolf with a jagged scar over an empty eye socket emerged.

Oct'Tulommon laughed as his accuser stepped out of the group and moved forward.

"Ahhh! I have seen you around these parts before. I have never had the pleasure of meeting you face to face. You seemed harmless, so I left you well enough alone. I see that was a mistake. Please, old wolf, I think it is only fair to know the name of someone who makes such alarming accusations against me—accusations that are conjecture, if not proven, friends. Remember that."

The wolf stops in front of Oct'Tulommon and calmly sits. "Yes, I pass through the Outlands; this is true, but I have been here long enough to see the malice you and your pack of fractured wolves unleash on these undeserving wolves. I have also learned something more sinister about you."

Oct'Tulommon was not expecting any rebuttal to his plans. But seeing such an opportunity to show his strength bolstered his sense of reputation. "Is that so?"

The mysterious wolf seemed very familiar—the color of his fur, his size, and the odd scar that ran over his empty right eye socket.

"I fear they will soon witness the horrors with their own eyes, Oct'Tulommon. My path has brought me here to offer them the truth about your plans. To open their hearts and see the anger in yours. Do they know of your transformation? the countless husks of dead wolves and humans you leave to rot in the ditches and bogs?"

Oct'Tulommon could see the resolve in the wolf's eye. He had values and purpose, and he knew those qualities were something to fear. "Haha! That's very noble of you."

He planned to reveal his transformation to them in time, for fear that seeing it up close might cause them to run. Most of them never seen a human, let alone a seven-foot-tall half man half wolf hybrid, that he was still trying to control.

The mysterious wolf stands, knowing what's to come. He came to the Outlands to see if Oct'Tulommon could be reasoned with, but the tiny flicker of the Awl'Fire left in his heart was gone. The void sunk in and turned his heart to black stone.

"Hear me! This wolf that stands before you possesses a power that will destroy every one of you. He took lives—your brothers and your sister wolves with impunity, trying to harness its power. He will need much more to sustain it."

As the mysterious wolf continued his pleas to the crowd of seething feral wolves, he noticed their attention shifted from him to Oct'Tulommon. They watched as he fell to the ground and convulsed. His bones snapped and bent in unnatural ways. His face contorted and blood ran from every orifice on his head. He howled and writhed in pain as his skin and fur sloughed off. He was in the thralls of an unholy change. The wolves in the crowd whimpered as they watched a massive human rise from a pile of meat and bones. He became a distorted copy of Lennon Grenlow. Still incapable of full control over the human likeness he gained through aggression. The transformation was easier, the skin looked fresh, and the wounds he caused while killing Lennon were all but gone. The new version of Lennon was around seven feet tall with muscles that bulged with wolfs blood.

The mysterious wolf, still lamenting, was now doing so while packing away. He back peddled amongst the crowd of wolves witnessing the change, Ha'Kan was disgusted with Oct'Tulommon's display of power, just as he was when he watched him toy with Evan and Morgrim. He felt ashamed as he watched the other wolves quiver in fear of what they were witnessing. The power to use a human's Awl'Fire was sacred, given to them by the rock prism during the time of the first man. Oct'Tulommon was powering the array with the growing void in his heart, which meant that no matter how easy the change became for him, the new version of Lennon Grenlow would always be distorted and disfigured.

"I guess the secret is out now, wolf," Lennon spoke using his mouth and not his heart, his voice deep and bitter. The words he said were not human but somehow understood by the wolves. It sent fear spikes into the hearts of every wolf in the area.

"I know what you have done to get this likeness, Oct'Tulommon. The pain you caused in that young boy's heart. He is very strong and has a way about him. His Awl'Fire burns brighter than any man I have ever encountered. He has sworn to himself to avenge his father. The Tepid minds of the Illnok have seen the signs in the forest for some time. A great change is looming over us all."

Oct'Tulommon had almost forgotten about Evan, distracted by his plans. He snapped and flexed his massive arms. "Ill-fated plans set in motion by a grieving heart rarely make their mark; he is of no consequence to me; let him come and test his mettle. He will never even get close to success.

Oct'Tulommon scowled at him.

"You speak from a tepid mind, Wolf! Your insight and vague predictions offer little help to me now, so why bother speaking to them!"

Oct'Tulommon reached into the cab of a burned-out truck beside the oil derrick. As he walked over, the wolf noticed how awkward he was on his feet. The wolves parted and stayed a safe distance from him. He pulled out a dirty old rifle, the one he had taken from Evan's hands, brushed the dust and dirt from the barrel, and aimed at the wolf.

"I caution you, Oct'Tulommon. Do not meddle with sacred things. The void is poisoning you! The Illnok—"

"I'm tired of hearing about the Illnok. They have yet to do anything to reach out to us here in the Outlands. We are the same as them, and they leave us here to suffer! No more! I will use the void to take what they owe us."

He pulled the bolt back on the rifle and took aim at Atohi's glowing head. "You're going to make one hell of an example."

The wolf closed his eyes and took a deep breath and vanished. Then appeared right beside Lennon as Atticus. He slammed his fist into the side of his head, the gun thudded as it hit the hood of the truck before ending up in the dirt. Lennon flashed with anger as he tasted the human blood in his mouth. He charged but Atticus moved to the side and let him slide across the ground, His flesh peeled, and sloughed off on his chest. They came together again in an exchange of heavy strikes to the face and the stomach. Lennon was much more powerful but clumsy, Atticus was nimble with more stamina, able to dodge Lennon's attacks with ease.

"Hear me wolf, this can all be over, atone for what you have done. And maybe the Awl'Fire will have mercy when you go to me it today." Atticus tried to reason. There was no way he was going to let him survive. He climbed to Lennon's back and could get him in a full choke hold. Lennon fell to the ground and crushed Atticus but still he didn't let go of him. He was winning. Just before he lost consciousness, he pulled with all his might and slipped out from under Atticus's grip, the flesh around his neck split and stayed in place, while he slipped away.

A look of shock swept over Atticus as he noticed the skin of Lennon's head resting on his own chest.

"Today is not the day I meet the Awl'Fire," he declared.

He raised his gaze; Atticus was met with the unnerving sight of Oct'Tulommon's head grafted onto Lennon Grenlow's body. The horrifying spectacle was too much to comprehend. Blood seeped from the torn skin and mingled with the damp fur around Oct'Tulommon's snarl. His massive teeth and glowing white eyes stared back at Atticus. Swiftly, he shifted his attention to a nearby group of feral creatures huddled together.

"Sink your teeth into his flesh," he commanded them. They were reluctant but were more afraid not to. As Atohi scrambled to get to his feet before the fray was on him, but it was too late, two wolves sunk their jaws into his thighs and one his right arm. Oct'Tulommon ran to the truck to grab the gun as Atticus flashed from the flurry, leaving the ferals dumbfounded. He flashed into the void and returned to the gun by the truck.

Oct'Tulommon pulled the bolt and raised the rifle, *Show yourself to me you dog. Show me where you go.* He focused the void array, trying to do something he didn't think possible, but the growing darkness, fueled by the void; was giving more power than ever. He watched the shadow figure of Atticus walking in the void. Almost like he was behind a waterfall, distorted and out of place, but there. He kept the rifle leveled waiting for the right moment when Atticus crossed back over.

On the other side Atohi tried to come up with a plan but he was at a loss. He took a deep breath and cleared his mind before he crossed back over.

Oct'Tulommon pulled the trigger. It released a delayed blast. The bullet ripped through the front of Atticus's chest and exited through his back and sprayed the wolves behind him with a warm mixture of bone fragments, blood and fur. Blood pumped from his open wound into the mud. Not one wolf moved, petrified and shocked by what just happened. Lennon dropped the rifle from his shoulder to his chest and watched as Atticus changed back into a wolf. The bullet wound was still fresh in his chest.

"I am Elden Void Wolf Atohi, and now I know who you are… Oct'Tulommon. Your choice has been made."

He pulled back the bolt action again, releasing an empty shell. He jammed it back in as quickly as he could and raised it again. The shot rang out, causing the wolves around the circle to flinch. Atohi's gleaming eye flashed white before the bullet made contact. He was gone.

Oct'Tulommon was dumbfounded; the crowd was silent, looking to him for an explanation of what happened. This was the first time any of them, except his closest wolves, had seen the void being used.

Learning he just shot an Elden Wolf of the Illnok pack, Oct'Tulommon's black heart felt like it dropped from his chest into his stomach.

"There is no going back now." He threw the rifle against the truck, smashing it into several pieces. The time had come, there was no going back now.

"Yes! I have killed! Yes! I have murdered! But I have only done what I've had to do to survive! Just like all of you! Not one of you can stand here and say you're innocent! It isn't in our nature to be violent, maim or murder! But we must do what we have to because of them! The selfish Illnok, safeguarding us from man, ha! Once we all have taken that mountain, we will take the fight to the world of man and bring back the balance for us! Not them!"

Ha'Kan could tell Oct'Tulommon won them over. His violent actions only proved that he was what Atohi said he was.

He knew he had to do something; this crack in Oct'Tulommon's resolve was enough for him to slip out. It wasn't hard to do since the wolves in the crowd were so fixated on the stolen form Oct'Tulommon was inhabiting. They were in a frenzy of excitement and mob mentality, fearless and ready to do whatever Oct'Tulommon commanded. The Illnok were made to protect the arrays from man, but they were just as dangerous in the hands of bloodthirsty wolves and the power of the void.

He knew that he couldn't let Oct'Tulommon's vicious plan come to fruition.

Chapter 21
The Evil Draws Near

For over three weeks, Morgrim battled the boredom that accompanied his bed rest and the anticipation of learning about his past. Finnick's death still weighed on the hearts of all who knew him, but Morgrim decided he had to accept that the pain would ease rather than trying to push it away.

He fought with himself every day not to pry Burren about the conversation he was so desperate to have, fearing that if he did, Burren might be banished for going against Mulgris's wishes. He had to take comfort in knowing that the answers were coming.

Unis was very strict about limiting the time Morgrim moved around inside the burrow and even enlisted the help of a few pack rabbits to keep watchful eyes on him. The time he spent waiting for his Fracture to heal was only exacerbated by the burden of Finnick's death, which he felt Nilian placed on his shoulders.

Since the incident, Burren, Mulgris and Unis tried many times to make Nilian see that Finnick's death was the fault of only the demons who carried out the act. He died a protector, doing what any older brother and father would do—saving the ones he loved the most from harm. Burren did not reveal to Morgrim that Nilian was still adamant about blaming him. Instead, he reminded Morgrim that wounds to the heart take the longest to mend and that his own heart also needed healing.

"Unis, it's been almost three weeks since I've seen more than that beam of sunlight teasing me at the other end of this chamber. don't you think I would benefit from some time outside?" Morgrim asks as he works the stiffness out of his cramped hind legs.

Weeks of watching that sunbeam come and go made him long for the warmth of a spring day, even more so now that he was deep in the heart of Illnok territory—uncharted lands he never dreamed of seeing that were just feet away from where he lay, encapsulated in the earth beneath. Unis giggled.

"You're more like Finnick than I think you could even imagine, Morgrim." She said of fondness in her voice.

"He longed for the warmth of the sunlight too. Being in the burrow only made him feel trapped. He would stay out in the clover all night, naming the fires in the sky and dreaming of distant lands far away."

The memory brought a small, bittersweet smile to Unis's face as she recalled those tender moments with her late mate.

Unis smiled as memories of Finnick flooded her mind - the sight of his smile and the smell of his windblown fur after a long trip. It dawned on Morgrim that Unis was more than just a friend to Finnick, but he didn't venture to know any details of their relationship. Instead, he just listened.

"Well… I suppose a little sun couldn't do you any more harm than wasting away down here with us. Why don't you get one more good night's sleep, and in the morning, I'll give Mulgris and Burren permission to take you to meet the Illnok's wolf Sayer."

Morgrim's tail dropped, hearing she was keeping him from the rest of the midday sun again. He thought about saying please but knew it wouldn't do him any good.

"Letting you out of your prison, aye Morgrim? My word, Unis! You've become less of a dungeon master than when I broke my leg all those winters ago. Had me climbing the walls trying to get out of this wretched tomb of a burrow, Morgrim,"

Burren entered the room, just as he had every evening over the past three weeks. Morgrim was growing tired of his visits but dared not say. Burren was old, deaf, and often told the same story multiple times with just as much enthusiasm as he did the first. But he was wiser than most creatures walking the earth. Nonetheless, Morgrim gave him satisfaction because he cared for him and saw the wealth of knowledge inside his head.

"I say, Unis, you, of all rabbits, should know that the sun has incredible healing powers. No need to worry; we will take good care of him topside."

As Unis left the room, she pressed her head against Morgrim's and wished him a good night.

"I'll be back in an hour or so to ensure he goes," Unis whispered to Morgrim.

He laughed a little as she disappeared around a wall of tree roots. As soon as she was out of sight, Mulgris filled the doorway with his giant body. It had been almost two weeks since he visited him. This time, he had a particular look on his face.

"So! Unis is giving your freedom back, aye Morgrim? I think it's time to meet the Elden Sayer." Burren nodded his head in agreement.

Morgrim's heart pounded with anticipation.

Mulgris sat down next to Burren.

"Finnick was a rabbit like no other, Morgrim. I want to say that foremost. His memory will be forever present in many hearts, above and below. His love for you, his family and his friends was immeasurable. Burren can attest to that just as much as I can; we have been good friends for most of our lives. Never once did I question his ability to make the right decisions when it involved the safety of our burrow... Until the day you came down that tunnel so long ago."

Burren interrupted him as he snickered and Mulgris turned to him, agitated. "I apologize, Mulgris. The memory of Finnick's fat hind end struck me, trailing a wolf pup in that tunnel from the Outlands. I thought, my god, his fat rear end will get wedged, and that wolf will have all of us for supper!"

Mulgris' stoic face broke into a smile, a rare sight.

"That's something I miss, Burren. He was no stranger in the clover fields; all knew it."

Burren picked up the conversation. "That was the first time we had seen you when you were much smaller."

Mulgris sighed. "Yes, Morgrim, as Burren told you before, we never understood why Finnick wasn't honest with you about your past. In fact, he had a way of stretching the truth about many things, so we are just as curious about the truth."

Morgrim chuckled.

"One thing we know for sure, Morgrim, is that you were loved. Eurthrem loved you, Finnick loved you, and we all love you still. Rabbits have just as big of hearts as wolves do."

"That's where our knowledge of your past gets a little…Foggy," Burren finished his thought.

"We know you were brought to the forest's edge by a wolf maiden. We know you were given to Finnick; we know Eurthrem nursed you in the Outlands until she passed and you fled capture by the Fractured wolves. Since then, Oct'Tulommon has been hunting you."

"But why, Mulgris? Why me?" Morgrim Asked.

"That is where what we know is clouded with conjecture. We don't know why for sure."

The air was silent.

"He told me you were dropped from the sky, carried from the Illnok lands and dropped by one of the higher bloodlines," Burren interjected again. Mulgris seemed agitated. "...Yes, yes. Morgrim it's true we heard many versions of your origin story. That's why we need to visit the Elden Sayer. I fear your path may be... predetermined."

Silence fell over both Mulgris and Burren, reluctant to speak their minds. So far, Morgrim felt his life was more or less mundane, spending most of his energy trying to survive.

"I… don't know what to say. I don't know what I'm supposed to do."

Burren stepped forward and sat down next to him. "Don't worry Morgrim. We are here for you and will be here every step of the way. You are family to us."

As Mulgris crossed the den to sit beside the two of them, Nilian and Unis walked into the room. Nilian came in second with tears staining his cheeks. I shocked Morgrim to see him. It had been almost three weeks. He walked over to the group and collapsed right into Morgrim's side.

"I'm with you too Morgrim, forever, and I'm so sorry... I shouldn't have blamed you; I was just angry."

Morgrim's heart swelled with happiness, having so much love surrounding him. Seeing Nilian and hearing his heartfelt words made everyone cry a little more.

"I love you, young uncle. Never forget it."

Late into the evening, the five spent hours telling stories and reminiscing about their best times with Finnick. It was a perfect way to spend the last night in the burrow. Even though they were still managing their grief, Morgrim couldn't remember when he felt this close to family. It hurt his heart to know that he hadn't spent more time with them over the years. Things may have turned out a little different for him. After the night settled in and the others ventured off into separate parts of the burrow, Morgrim laid awake in his bed of dried grass and thought about what Burren had told him when he first arrived. *What is past is past; the future is much more important.* He slept soundly for the first time since Finnick's death.

Chapter 22
Last Name

Morgrim looked across the den, the tunnels and chambers filled with shadows and memories of Finnick. The once comforting darkness seemed to be colder now, the echoes of laughter, replaced with a silence. He promised Unis and Nilian that he would return to spend time with them in the future, but he was unsure of when that day might be now that he was on the way to Alpha's mountain. They smiled when he said it nonetheless. Mulgris decided for Burren to stay with Unis and Nilian. Even though the Illnok wolves granted sanctuary to the rabbits within their territory, danger was still prevalent. Burren's poor eyesight and tendency to tire made the journey too risky. The last thing Mulgris wanted was for Burren to get hurt. Of course, Burren pouted, but deep down, he understood why.

"Are you ready to go, Morgrim? We should leave now if we are to make it to the mountain while there is still light in the sky."

He finished his goodbyes and stretched out his legs, excitement filling his body. It had been three weeks since he had been topside, even though his leg was still in pain and healing. He refused to let it stop him from the truth.

"Okay, Mulgris, I'm ready." Morgrim allowed Unis to help him up before he set off to climb the tunnel's walls to the surface. As he got closer to the top, he felt the temperature rise.

The soil nearer to the surface kept the sun's warmth far more effectively than the layers situated deeper below. The adjustment for his eyes was a challenge. It took him a few moments to keep them open for more than a second.

"What does that feel like, Morgrim? Did you miss it?"

Mulgris smiled. Morgrim took a deep breath, stretched his back and legs and stood tall.

"This is the best I have felt in a long time! It's amazing."

"Haha, that's excellent, young wolf. Enjoy it while you can. I know your nose works just as good as mine."

Mulgris laughed as he nodded his head up. Morgrims nose twitched as he looked up to the sky to see heavy rain clouds swarm in from the east.

"The first day out of that hole, and it's going to rain?!"

Morgrim pouted.

"Well, think of it this way: at least it's still shining for someone. It may not be you, but someone somewhere is enjoying it." Mulgris couldn't help but laugh at Morgrim's lousy luck.

As they started their journey, Morgrim noticed several striking differences from where he grew up. It appeared life was thriving everywhere he looked - birds singing, deer and rabbits alongside each other, and squirrels leaping from tree to tree, all without fear of being prey for their natural predators.

Animals grouped as if they were laughing and sharing pleasantries. The grass and the leaves of the trees felt alive. There was no fear.

"Mulgris, all this life; it's beautiful. Where I grew up, it's the exact opposite: death and decay everywhere."

"I know. These lands and all the life in them exist in a deliberate balance. The wolves only take what they need to survive and enforce the same standards on all the other creatures. They keep their hunting grounds beyond the borderlines in the northern lands. Those lands are wild and belong to no one."

It had been quite a while since Morgrim had anything substantial to eat. Morgrim's hungry wolf was enticed by everything he never hunted before. Mulgris could see that he was distracted.

"Morgrim! You mustn't get any ideas in your head. I don't think it would bode well for you to hunt and kill a protected animal on your way to meet an Illnok Elden wolf."

He stayed silent as he forced himself to maintain control over the hungry wolf inside.

"Finnick taught me long ago the importance of control over his hungry wolf, especially around the burrows."

"Hmm, it makes sense that the first lesson he taught you was not to eat all of us. If he was good at anything, it was self-preservation."

They both chuckled a little.

*

As the day went on, Mulgris and Morgrim continued on their journey. The rains fell, and they trudged through the wet grass and mud. Once the rain subsided, Morgrim basked in the sunlight's warmth. He felt the tension in his chest melt away again. Mulgris could tell how much it lifted his spirits.

They encountered two pack wolves returning from a hunt as they approached the mountain. As they drew closer, Morgrim noticed the leg of a deer dangle from one wolf's mouth. He struggled to keep his hungry wolf quiet while the two wolves conversed with Mulgris.

"It's been a while, Mulgris. It's good to see you again," they exchanged pleasantries. One of the Illnok wolves laid the deer leg down so he could press his forehead to Mulgris's.

Morgrim sniffed at the leg, prompting the other wolf to reclaim it.

"Morgrim!" Mulgris redirected him, "That's not for you. I suggest you back away."

The two wolves were astonished when they encountered Morgrim. Not only because of his stark contrast in appearance. But also because an old tale stirred their memories. One that bordered on myth and legend, propagated by gossipers and rumormongers all over the Illnok territory. They stood back, taking with them the deer leg. Morgrim was so fixated on it he failed to see their reaction to him.

"...This meat is for the elderly wolves in the alder forest friend. If you want something to eat, might I suggest the feast tonight? Elden Dire Wolf Volcrim Sul'Ilinok will present his hunt to the pack. I'm sure they would offer you a share, outsider."

Morgrim's heart pounded at the prospect of feasting on the fresh meat of animals that he never tasted. Mulgris nudged Morgrim once more to gain his attention.

"Ugh, yes, thank you, I'm glad to have met you too... as well. Also." Morgrim was not faring well. Mulgris felt they might have been too hasty with the trip to the Alpha's Mountain.

"Pull it together, Morgrim. First impressions are important with his lot." Mulgris hoped he would heed his instructions.

As they parted ways and continued, Mulgris explained that when a hunting pack returns from the north, they bring back as much as they can carry for the pack to feast on.

"Morgrim, if Li'Illnok invites you to partake in the feast, you must go. However, I will caution you, living amongst these lands, we rabbits must come to terms with certain... truths. The wolves are our great protectors, but their nature dictates the hunger for fresh meat and the need to hunt. Though they're forbidden from hunting rabbits here in the territory, in the north, it's a different story."

It was Morgrim's first thought about that facet of regular life for wolf.

"So, with that being known, I will not be attending and won't be able to advise you on what you should or shouldn't reveal about yourself. You must navigate that challenge on your own. The Illnok wolves differ from the ones you know. They are loving and caring but also committed to preserving the sanctity of the pack and their roles within it."

"Will you wait for me?" Morgrim asked, attempting to mask his nervousness.

"No, my friend, I'm afraid I will take my leave after the introduction is made with the Elden Sayer."

As they rounded the last hill, Morgrim caught sight of the imposing pillars chiseled out around the entrance of a vast cave that led into the mountain's interior. Intricate symbols and drawings adorned the rock faces, and a flickering flame danced in the distance inside, casting a mysterious glow on the surrounding darkness. The sheer enormity of it all captivated Morgrim. The darkness seemed to stretch endlessly, as if the entire mountain were hollow. Along paths to the left and right of the cave entrance, Morgrim noticed wolves poking their heads out of dens, with many more emerging from the cave and approaching from behind.

"Halt, wolf! You are unfamiliar to us! State your name and your purpose here!"

A wolf emerged from the cave. His head dusted with white ash. He wore a circle of entwined roots and sticks around his neck like an ancient talisman. Like his head, his paws were coated in the same white ash, and a bold, crimson line traced a path from the tip of his nose to the top of his head, centered between his perked and attentive ears. The wolf's eyes held a depth of wisdom and mystery, reflecting the experiences of a life lived in the borders of the Illnok. He was an Illnok battle wolf, sworn by the Alpha to protect the sanctity of the great hall and the flame inside.

Fear seized Morgrim, rendering him speechless. Terror took hold, leaving him unable to utter a single word. Mulgris waited patiently, expecting Morgrim to break his silence, but he remained petrified. Meanwhile, Morgrim's unusual looks attracted attention. An increasing number of curious wolves encircled them, their numbers swelling with each passing moment.

"I apologize. My dear friend, he is shy, is all. I am Mulgris Awl'Ginna, Warden of the Illnok Burrows, and this is—"

The white-faced wolf stepped forward into the sunlight, revealing his immense size, rivaling even the fracture wolves.

"Mulgris! Good friend!" The battle wolf interrupted before Mulgris could finish.

"I hardly recognized you. It's been so long since I last saw you and Finnick. How is that old, plump rabbit doing?"

Mulgris was speechless, recognizing the wolf addressing them as Rex'Onok, one of the Alpha's mightiest battle wolves. Finnick had a lengthy list of acquaintances he enjoyed spending time with, and Rex'Onok was among them. Mulgris tried his best not to stir Morgrim too much with an in-depth reply. But it seemed to be unavoidable.

"Well, friend, I'm sad to say we lost Finnick recently. It's still fresh in our hearts, so please forgive our somber demeanor. We're doing the best we can."

Mulgris and Morgrim watched as sadness washed over the faces of several wolves in the crowd. Finnick left a lasting impression on many of them. Rex stepped back and looked around at the wolves who gathered. They were also aware of the stories about an obsidian cub, banished by the Alpha and raised secretly by a rabbit.

"Wolves! Let us take a moment to remember a great example of strength, love, and compassion for not only his kind but every kind of creature in the realm. A true Warden when Wardens are scarce." Rex'Onok said, his voice full of emotion. He paused for a moment.

"What was his full name Mulgris, so we may honor him."

"His full name was Finn Orem'Exula..." Mulgris hadn't spoken the name in quite some time, and it felt unnatural. Finnick preferred the nickname his father gave him as a child, "Finnick," because he was always in motion. Morgrim turned to Mulgris with surprise.

"I never knew his full name. I always just called him Finnick." The realization left him stunned and saddened that he never took the time to ask.

"Finn Orem'Exula," Rex'Onok announced. The surrounding wolves bowed out of respect. Tears welled up in Morgrim's eyes, touched by the outpouring of love for his father. He wished that Nilian, Burren, and Unis could witness this moment.

As the wolves raised their heads, Rex'Onok addressed Morgrim. "And you, friend, what is your name?"

Morgrim looked at Mulgris for a moment and took a deep breath.

"My name is Morgrim, Morgrim Orem'Exula."

The wolves gasped and chattered among themselves. Puzzled, they pieced together that the outlier standing before them was the truth of all the rumors. A fabled, almost ghostly figure. Morgrim Orem'Exula, Alpha Ult'Ilinok's bastard child.

Chapter 23
The Wavering Heart

"Elden Sayer Li'Illnok, you have a rabbit here to see you. He has a wolf in tow, and they—"

Rex'Onok introduced Mulgris Awl'Ginna to the Elden Sayer, perched on the edge of a colossal stone in the hall of Awl'Fire. This hall, reminiscent of a grand cathedral, was above the great hall where Alpha Ult'Ilinok held court, listening to the counsel of his advisors and most trusted pack members. The room, cold and simple by nature, was warmed by the flickering light of the roaring fire below while sunlight streamed through openings in the cavernous ceiling and walls, casting an ethereal glow.

"Does he vouch for the temperament of the outlier wolf accompanying him, Rex? Do I need to be worried?"

Rex stood at attention as the Elden spoke. Behind Li'Illnok, on a bed of fresh juniper branches flanked by two beautiful young, snow-white wolves with glowing iridescent eyes. Alpha Awl Ult'Ilinok lay adorned with a crown made from deer antlers. His blackish-gray speckled coat was splashed with ash from the fire below, and his face bore not one but two thin lines of red from his forehead to the end of his snout. Around his neck, a twisted circle of roots and ivy created a stunning effect. The Alpha was a sight to behold. Majestic and regal. But also terrifying. Almost as much as Oct'Tulommon.

"He vouches for him, Elden. Shall I send them in?"

"Yes. I was quite bored today; not much else going on!" The Alpha did not speak, appearing unenthused about the entire situation.

Li'Illnok winced as he stood, his bones cracking and popping with every move.

"I will return with them at once, Elden Sayer."

Li'Illnok moved over to a slab of stone that held a cornucopia of fresh fruits, vegetables and a massive spread of fresh meat. He glanced over with disdain,

"Is living without wanting, living?" he thought to himself. The disappointment was evident in his voice. Rex re-entered the great hall.

"Sir Mulgris Awl'Ginna of the Illnok rabbits and Morgrim Orem'Exula of...the Outlands, for you, Elden."

Before Li'Illnok could turn around, he stopped chewing. The name Orem'Exula sounded familiar, but he couldn't place why. "Orem'Exula? That name is…." He turned to see Morgrim standing beside Mulgris. His obsidian fur coat seemed to soak up the surrounding light in the room. He remembered the rabbit that Orem'Nubis loved to spend time with—the rabbit she convinced to smuggle an obsidian-coated Wolf into the Outlands. Finnick. The hair on the back of his neck stood up.

Alpha Ult'Ilinok sprang to his feet, his fur bristling and his ears standing straight up.

"Rex, who else saw this wolf come to my chambers!?" he answered with fear in his heart, fear that he did something wrong.

"...Everyone, Elden... Every wolf in the Illnok seemed to be there."

"I want you to go now and stand guard at the steps to the hall. I think it's better if no one enters."

"Yes, Elden. Should I make way for the other Eldens?"

"No need, Rex. I will tend to this matter."

Li'Illnok felt the weight of his choices from all that time ago crashing down upon him.

Mulgris and Morgrim grew nervous; their presence was unexpected. The two wolf maidens stepped away, their eyes losing their white luster. Ult'Ilinok descended from his bed of juniper and approached Morgrim. Unsure of what to do, Morgrim looked to Mulgris for guidance.

"Don't look him in the eyes and keep your head down Morgrim. Address him as Alpha Ult'Ilinok... And don't put your voice in his mind until he is in yours."

Morgrim did his best to remember everything, but his nerves got the better of him, causing his body to tremble.

"How old are you, Outlier?"

"Five winters, Alpha Ult'Ilinok."

Ult'Ilinok circled Morgrim. He examined his fur and muscles, and he shifted his gaze to Li'Illnok before halting in front of the young wolf. He remained silent, an intense look on his face. Mulgris and Morgrim did not know what was going to happen. They tried to stay calm.

"I hold a high station that binds me to an unrelenting duty. The fire that burns below is my sovereign responsibility. It must never alter... I must stay strong! For protecting the balance between the Void and the Awl'Fire." He paused and glided over to stand in front of Morgrim.

"Look at me, Outlier."

Morgrim glanced at Mulgris, who gave him a nod of approval. He then raised his eyes to meet Ult'Ilinok's. They were deep, like wet river stones, and full of pain.

At first, Morgrim didn't understand. The weight of it all was so heavy. The words that emanated from Ult'Ilinok were mysterious and rhythmic, like a song.

"My son. You're alive?"

"You're my father, wolf?" Morgrim was in shock.

Li'Illnok stood up in response, surprised by the unfolding events. "...Alpha, I believe we should have council on the matter before—" "Li'Illnok. Is his presence not affirmation enough for you!?" Ult'Ilinok interrupted.

"You knew this day would come. Do not feign surprise, old wolf. You know better! I know better."

"I don't understand, Alpha Ult'Ilinok—" "Be quiet..." Mulgris cut his eyes at him. He grew more frustrated with his lack of competence to remain silent. Ult'Ilinok looked at Mulgris.

"It is fine, Alpha Mulgris. Are you not my equal? Please stand. Your station does not require you to submit to me."

The room fell silent as Mulgris stood up.

"Morgrim, I'm sure you must have a multitude of questions about why I decided to—" "I only have just two," Morgrim interjected. In the whirlwind of emotions, he didn't have time to wait for long-winded ramblings by old wolves.

"...by all means."

"My mother wolf? Where is she?" Morgrim Asked. Ult'Ilinok took a deep breath.

"I can only guess what your second question might be, but I suspect the answer to the first will suffice for both,"
Ult'Ilinok began.

Morgrim swallowed hard, as he braced himself as his heart pounded.

"Your mother was Selah'Rah, the love of my life. She brought me immeasurable joy. Her beauty was incomparable. She gave birth to you but suffered a hemorrhage afterward. This led to the stillbirth of your five siblings."

Morgrim felt a wave of profound sadness wash over him. "Was it my fault? Did I cause their deaths?"

Ult'Ilinok brooded. The memory of that night stirred up deep-seated pain. Li'Illnok could sense it; the temperature in the surrounding air dropped perceptibly.

"My Alpha, I don't th—" Li'Illnok began, but was interrupted. "Li'Illnok, please, I need to do this for myself," Ult'Ilinok insisted, taking a deep breath as he watched Morgrim quiver with sorrow.

"No, Morgrim. Nothing that happened that night was your fault However, I let anger cloud my judgment. My inability to control my rage ultimately led to the decision to banish you from this mountain."

Mulgris shook his head in disbelief, wanting to comfort Morgrim but too shocked to move. The truth was as surprising to him a to everyone else. The shift in the atmosphere was palpable as a chilling voice filled the room.

"Embers, sparks… Feed them to me…"

The Endless Void made its pleas again, drawn to the weight of Morgrim's and Ult'Ilinok's grief. It threatened to tip the already precarious balance.

"That night, I blamed you and your birth for the tragedy of what happened. I was blinded. To... taken by the Void. to see the error in my judgment.

"Morgrim! Do not give in to the pain. It will only feed the Void. I know it's difficult, but you must hear the truth." Li'Illnok watched, seeing the pain take hold of Morgrims heart.

"Morgrim, I once sought to extinguish your life upon this hallowed mountain. Desperate to cast blame, I nearly succumbed to a dark and twisted path," Ult'Ilinok confessed, his voice laden with remorse.

"Yet, Li'Illnok, courageous, defied me that fateful night. He spirited you away and concealed you from my wrath—or so he believed. Just days after your exile; when my anger was still raw, I considered sending my Battle Wolves to the Outlands to rectify what Li'Illnok had done."

Ult'Ilinok's voice softened. His eyes took on a distant look. "I was told an elderly she-wolf in the Outlands took you in. Earthwin—"
"Eurthrem," Morgrim vehemently interrupted.

"I stand corrected. When I discovered you were flourishing under her care, I decided to let her continue raising you."

Confusion etched into Morgrim's brow. "You watched us...flourish? Finnick told me of the struggle to even keep Eurthrem alive! She starved to death trying to keep me alive, is that what you call flourishing?!"

"...The flame falters..."

The voice strengthens. Ult'Ilinok continued, his voice grew unsteadied. "...I was torn about whether to retrieve you from Eurthrem and the rabbits. The day I decided to send the Battle Wolves to bring you back, they came upon a horrific sight. Then den had been raided, Eurthrem was..." He stumbled over the words. "The tunnel where Finnick led you into the Outlands was destroyed. We assumed you and Finnick had been killed. It wasn't until a full season later that my Battle Wolves spotted you and Finnick emerge from the tunnels once more in the Outlands. I was overjoyed to know you were alive. But by then, you had found a new home and a loving family underground. I couldn't take that away from you." He looked over to Mulgris.

"Instead, I received updates about your life in the burrows with Finnick. The rabbits of Illnok are our cherished allies — gentle, caring creatures. I couldn't bear to separate you from them, knowing they provided the nurturing environment you needed."

Morgrim stayed silent, wavering back and forth from anger to gratefulness.

"I believed that fate would bring us together again, that the moonlight on the night of your birth and exile hinted at our inevitable reunion." Ult'Ilinok said.

Li'Illnok was shocked. He always respected his Alpha but never saw him as wise. Until this point.

"Now, you stand before me, ready to reclaim your place in these ancient halls," Ult'Ilinok declared, his voice grand and resonant.

"Li'Illnok's wisdom and foresight saved you from my misguided wrath. He was your guardian, guiding you towards a gentler fate."

As the Alpha concluded his explanation, Morgrim remained silent and shocked. The cold voice subsided and the air warmed slightly.

"Do you have any idea what I have endured because of you? Do you know what life is like beyond the borders of your kingdom, Alpha?" Morgrim interrupted, his voice shook with bitterness as he approached Ult'Ilinok.

"Have you ever had to survive in a place where even the Unclean starve to death?"

Before he could continue, Mulgris rose with a commanding presence. "MORGRIM OREM'EXULA!!!" His voice cracked in the minds of everyone with such force that it made the stone room shudder. "You would do well to remember who you are speaking to!"

Ult'Ilinok lowered his head and averted his eyes from Morgrim's as he approached.

"My father was not a wolf. My father never abandoned me; you are an old, lonely wolf on a mountain. My family is underground, and my lands lie barren and fruitless to the east of here. I am not your heir Ult'Ilinok, nor would I ever want to be seated next to you in this tomb of comfort and stability, blind to the rest of the world. I know my purpose now and will acknowledge you for revealing that to me, here today. My home and the lives of those who fight to survive there require aid. Aid that you should've rendered long ago... I will take my leave, Alpha Ult'Ilinok of the heirless mountain."

The entire room was taken aback, no one ever spoken to him in such a manner.

The tale of the outcast exile circulated throughout the territory for five winters and now, every last creature within the Border woods would know the truth of that night.

As Morgrim and Mulgris prepared to depart the great hall, every Hesperus wolf, wolf maiden and chamber wolf averted their eyes from him. He was real.

"Mulgris, did I just make a mistake?" Morgrim asked, as he noticed the show of respect from all the alphas wolves.

"No, my boy, you found yourself… and your father would be so damn proud of you, So damn proud." Mulgris replied with tears in his eyes. As they were about to step into the woods, Li'Illnok trotted up from the rear and stopped them.

"My boy, I need—" "I'm so sorry to leave without speaking to you, Elden Sayer. Thank you for saving my life that night. I wouldn't be alive now if it weren't for you. And your courage, I'm grateful," Morgrim interrupted him.

"Doing the right thing was essential, dear boy, but I must inform you, I have been acquainted with that wolf, Alpha Ult'Ilinok, for many years. He is good. It does not excuse his negligence for you and anything else you have accused him of; I fear he will have to come to terms with that. Might I impart a piece of wisdom I learned long ago from my wise predecessor?" Li'Illnok replied,

"Of course, Elden." Morgrim said with a smile.

"Holding onto feelings of resentment, anger, and hatred does not alter the perceptions or feelings of those around you; it only transforms your own heart."

Morgrim fell silent, and Li'Illnok could tell that his words struck a chord deep within him.

After a moment, Mulgris tried to break the silence.

"...Well, Elden Li'Illnok, as always, it was very good to see you. I wish things would have happened much differently, but here we are.

"I wish you both would stay. If for nothing else, I would love to learn more about your time in the Outlands Morgrim. You have built a name and a purpose for yourself here. In all my years, I have never heard a tale as vivid and captivating as yours."

Morgrim pondered the option of staying. Morgrim was intrigued by the option of learning more about the Illnok and the fire in the great hall.

"I cannot stay; I have too much business to attend to in the burrows." Mulgris sighed. "But Morgrim, I think staying with The Elden Sayer would benefit you. I can return to the burrows and let everyone know you are safe. They will love the story I return with I assure you." The confidence pumping through Morgrim was palpable.

"Then I will stay for the night at least. I guess I owe Elden Li'Illnok that much."

Li'Illnok's old and ragged tail gave a very short-lived wag of excitement.

"Fantastic, Morgrim!"

Before Mulgris left, Morgrim bent his head down and pressed it against his. Mulgris looked deep into his eyes.

"I love you with all my heart Morgrim. I am so proud of you; Finnick would be so proud too."

"Mulgris, I love you too. And I will never forget what you and the others have done for me. When I return to the burrow, we will have a lot of work ahead of us."

"…I'm not sure what you mean, Morgrim?"

"We are going to unite the Outlands, and I will kill Oct'Tulommon and anyone loyal to him. It's time for a change."

Morgrim meant every word he spoke as he walked away. Mulgris felt a fire inside of him like never before. Watching Morgrim walk with purpose was an entire experience altogether. As the two wolves walked back into the great hall, Li'Illnok spoke.

"I have one question that's been plaguing my mind regarding your late father… Sir Finn Orem'Exula, is it?"

"Yes Elden but everyone that knew him well called him 'Finnick.'"

Li'Illnok looks down his nose at Morgrim. "My question is… and please don't take offense. Was he really as fat as they say?"

For a moment, Morgrim stopped and stood silent. "Yes! He was so very fat…" Both of them laughed.

"Then I will call him Finnick as well because, if nothing else, we at least have that in common!" Li'Illnok laughed as he hobbled up a rock ledge.

*

Over the next few hours, Elden Li'Illnok instructed the Hesperus wolves to fill his room with a lavish spread of raw meat and wild vegetables. It was more food than Morgrim had ever seen in one place.

"This display seems to trouble you, Morgrim. I find it very intriguing that you could control the hungry wolf inside you while living amongst the creatures we consume."

Morgrim took a small portion of raw meat and carried it over to Li'Illnok, sitting with it between his legs. "Well, have you ever felt inclined to tear into the flesh of the ones you love because you are starving?"

"I understand your perspective, Morgrim." Li'Illnok did not elaborate further, because he never experienced the effects of starvation in his entire life.

After devouring his modest portion of deer, Morgrim observed several Hesperus wolves standing motionless around the room, waiting to fulfill any request, their mouths salivating as the scent of blood filled the chamber.

"Are they not going to share this meal with us, Elden?" Morgrim inquired.

"I'm afraid not. These wolves serve the Alpha and only eat at the end of the day, with the others in service."

Morgrim noticed that most of them were emaciated and showing signs of malnourishment, with drooping faces and shaking legs. Li'Illnok could see that this was bothering Morgrim, which made Li'Illnok uncomfortable. It seemed as if Morgrim's presence alone led him to question everything. Of course, it was wrong to let meat spoil while starving wolves watched you eat it fresh. He struggled to justify it.

"The traditions that are carried out here in the Alpha's mountain have remained the same, unchanged for ages," Li'Illnok attempted to explain.

Morgrim stood up, his voice firm but respectful. "Traditions? Elden Sayer, I do not wish to overstep my bounds, but while traditions are meant to be honored, starving is not a tradition any creature should be forced to uphold."

"I see your point, Morgrim. You speak the truth; there is no justification for accepting this."

With every turn, Morgrim saw his path more clearly. He felt strong and empowered. For the rest of the day, Li'Illnok invited the other Elders to meet Morgrim. They shared stories and feasted while sharing their food with the Hesperus wolves and Wolf maidens in the den. It was a different experience than the average day inside the Alpha's mountain.

As the day winded into the evening, Li'Illnok decided it was time for everyone to take their leave, summoning wolf maidens to escort the sorted party from his den.

"I have prepared a place for you to stay tonight, Morgrim. It's a fair distance from here, but if you need anything, you let a Hesperus know."

Through the entrance of Li'Illnok's den, a beautiful, snow-white wolf gracefully strode in. Her body was long and slender, with a thin waist, and her tail flowed through the air like wisps of cloud. Morgrim could feel his throat tighten, he never knew such beauty existed.

"Morgrim, this is El'Wren, the daughter of one of my dear friends, Orem'Nubis, the Tepid mind who escorted you to the Border woods the night of your birth."

He turned and bowed his head in admiration. Almost stunned by her beauty.

"I owe your mother wolf my life. I'm so sorry she is no longer here for me to thank her."

Li'Illnok spent the better part of the evening before the other Elden wolves arrived, explaining to Morgrim the details of his first night on Earth.

"Thank you, Morgrim. I will tell her when I speak to her later tonight."

He tilted her head in confusion.

"I'm not sure what you mean, El'Wren.

"Oh…"

Li'Illnok intercepted their conversation and tried to avert it.

"El'Wren, let us not meddle in supernatural matters just yet. Morgrim has been through a lot, and he needs to relax. Please, take him to the far North chamber. That is where he will spend the rest of his night."

Before he exited the room following El'Wren, all the Elden wolves stood to wish him a good evening.

"Please come with me,"

As she led him out, he was intoxicated by her scent, like fresh flowers and the smell of the Earth after the rain.

He shook his head, trying to regain his composure. "Ye… yes, 'm sorry I was just…"

The chamber wolf laughed. "Right this way, please. I'll show you to your den."

As the two of them walked, El'Wren could see the amazement in Morgrim's eyes as he gazed at the vast size of the great hall underneath the mountain. The height of the cavern's ceiling was so far away that the quartz and mica in the rocks above sparkled like stars in the night sky. In the center of the great room, a large fire burned brightly, tended to by several of the Alpha's Hesperus wolves, all with white ash on their feet and collars of tree roots and sticks. The chamber wolf could tell it amazed him.

"The fire has seemed to diminish in size and intensity over the past few winters, yet the Hesperus wolves never cease their devoted task of stoking its flames,"

El'Wren explained as they gazed at the hypnotic dance of the fire. The flickering light cast a warm, golden glow across the cavern, illuminating the intricate patterns of the rocks and casting long, dramatic shadows.

The Hesperus wolves moved with determination, their eyes gleamed in the fire's light as they piled more logs and stirred the embers. It filled the air with warmth and a comforting scent of burning wood, mingling with the earthy aroma of the cave. As the flames licked the air, they breathed life into the cavern, casting a magical, mesmerizing spell on all who watched.

"Morgrim?... Morgrim!" She had to stop and go back to get his attention.

"It's impressive isn't it?" she asked.

"Why, though? It's not our way as wolves to tend a fire. The Awl'Fire is what keeps us warm."

She sighed. "Well, Morgrim, some believe it is ceremonial, started in the early centuries of the Illnok by a native man named Nah'Hele. Others say it holds more significance than that. I believe the actual truth was lost over the ages, swallowed by the waves of time.

"That seems strange to me, to toil over something that carries no meaning. It seems like a waste of time," Morgrim pondered aloud.

"Ahhh, but just because something seems to hold no value, does it mean it's useless?" El'Wren countered, her eyes twinkling with wisdom. Morgrim thought it was a silly way of thinking about it but didn't want to offend her.

"Well, what do you think it's true purpose is, El'Wren? Why are those wolves still stoking the flames of a fire built by a man?"

"Hmmm, I know what my mother taught me." She remembered; her voice took on a somber tone. "She said that since the night the rumors started about you, the fire has seemed to lose its robustness as if it has faded. And since that night, wolves around the Great Hall and throughout the Alpha's mountain have been said to hear a faint chattering of words so insignificant that you have to hold your breath to hear it. I think it's the Endless Void, and I think it's growing in strength."

"That still doesn't answer the question. What do you think the purpose of the fire is if not to keep us warm?" Morgrim pressed further, intrigued by her insight.

"…I think it's fear—fear of the Void. Adopted by us from humans before. We tend the fire because it reminds us of man's mistakes. To remind us not to make the same ones." El'Wren admitted.

Morgrim couldn't help but notice the Hesperus wolves again as they continued walking.

"I'm sorry, El'Wren, but why do they cover their legs in ash? And what are the collars of roots around their necks for?"

Morgrim felt like he was being a bother to her for asking so many questions, but El'Wren also enjoyed them and his company.

"Don't apologize, Morgrim. I'm happy to answer. The ash is from the great fire they tend to. It is a tradition for the Alpha's Hesperus wolves to cover their paws with ash to symbolize their duty to the Awl'Fire. Those same wolves are tainted and have been given a new purpose in servitude; rather than face banishment or worse, the Alpha allows them to stay in the mountain." El'Wren said as she came to a stop overlooking the fire.

From the surrounding walls hung an array of objects that made no sense to Morgrim. Large deer antlers, flanked by wooden spears and the skins of the grazing animals, were among the many relics left by the early man.

Down below, he also noticed collars made of roots around the Hesperus wolves' necks symbolize their servitude to their pack.

"Further up the mountain are the Eldens' dens, the Alpha's cabinet of trusted advisors who counsel him on matters in the Illnok territories. You met them tonight, all but one—Volcrim Sul'Ilinok, the Alpha's Master of Hunt. He is out with his Border Wolves, hunting for our feast tomorrow. Along with the battle wolves, they dye their coats red to show fealty to the Illnok banner."

"That is incredible," Morgrim marveled as he took in the depth of it all.

"Will you be joining us tomorrow for the great feast?" El'Wren inquired, a hopeful glint in her eyes.

"…I don't believe so… It makes me very uncomfortable to watch all these starving wolves watch as I eat. It feels wrong.

They stopped just before the den's entry, where Morgrim was to rest for the night. The anticipation of parting ways made his heart race.

"Maybe I will see you tomorrow before I go El'Wren?" Morgrim asked, trying not to sound too desperate.

"…I know where you are, Morgrim. Until we meet again?" El'Wren replied, her eyes softening.

"Until we meet again, El'Wren." Morgrim echoed her words, feeling a warmth spread through his chest.

Throughout the night, she consumed Morgrim's thoughts. It amused him, every time there had been a chance to rest, his mind only swirled with chaos, sadness, anger, fear, and now, love.

"I don't think I'll ever be able to rest again." He smiled at the realization.

The stones of the Alpha's mountain cooled his aching leg, and the den had the perfect amount of air circulating between the rocks and the corridors. The space was lit with small fires tended to by the Hesperus wolves. The smooth stones that made up the floor had trails of white ash scattered everywhere. Morgrim could sense the mountain's ancient history; how many wolves slept in the same den over time? How many Alpha wolves ruled over the packs that protected the fire in the Great Hall? He was grateful that his questions were being answered, but with each answer, he discovered more questions in need of asking.

In the middle of the night, while Morgrim lay asleep, the Sullen Ult'Ilinok stood in the shadows of the doorway, watching him. The darkness enveloped him but his eyes, glowing with a dim light, revealed his presence. He studied Morgrim's slow, rhythmic breathing, the rise and fall of his chest, and how his fur glistened in the flickering light of the small fires scattered around the den.

He considered the sleeping wolf before him. The stories and whispers about Morgrim reached his ears, and he could not help but feel a mixture of curiosity and unease. The Alpha wondered what wolf Morgrim was and what his presence might mean for the future of the Illnok pack.

As he watched Morgrim sleep, Ult'Ilinok's mind wandered to the recent challenges that plagued his pack. Would Morgrim prove to be an ally or an adversary? Could he be the key to overcoming the obstacles they faced, or would his presence only create more?

*

It wasn't until Rex'Onok came to check on him that Morgrim stirred from his sleep. It was midday, but he didn't mind; it had been the best sleep of his life. Eager to explore more of the Illnok lands, learn about his past, and, of course, see more of El'Wren before he left for the burrow. He rose from the soft bed of juniper, much like the one Ult'Ilinok laid upon in the Alpha's Hall. As he clicked his claws against the cold stone floor, two chamber wolves appeared, ready to adorn him with ash and red dyes from crushed berries. He declined, clarifying that he did not bend a knee to the Illnok Alpha. As they left the room, Rex'Onok laughed.

"Morgrim, I think you scared those Chamber Wolves half to death. They'll never try to dye a wolf again without consent," he teased.

Morgrim chuckled at the thought.

"Let's leave now. We have to meet Li'Illnok at the Sayers Stone. He requested our help to prepare for this evening. It's Li'Illnok's favorite season, when he gets to gather up a bunch of cubs, bore them to death with his long-winded story about the Awl Fire, and then complain when he finds them all asleep with their faces in the dirt."

As they approached the Sayers Stone, they found Li'Illnok perched atop a massive boulder, surrounded by towering oaks and cedar trees. He appeared to be rehearsing a speech, his voice echoing through the woods.

"In the beginning, there was a great...." Li'Illnok's words trailed off as he noticed Morgrim and Rex approaching from behind. Startled, he regained his composure. "Good morning, Morgrim! I trust you slept well?"

"Yes, thank you, Li'Illnok," Morgrim replied, his mind wandered back to the soft bed of juniper that cradled him through the night.

A glint of realization flashed in Li'Illnok's eyes. "I recalled this morning, as I was preparing my commencement speech for the rites of passage, that today marks the sixth winter since the night you came into this world. It's your birthday, Morgrim."

Morgrim was astounded, Finnick only picked a random time each year for a celebration since he couldn't remember the exact date. Rex nudged Morgrim's flank and exclaimed, "Ohhhh! Happy birthday, Morgrim!"

Li'Illnok continued,

"So, you must stay for tonight's ceremony and the following feast. It would mean a great deal if you heard my story."

Morgrim caught sight of El'Wren walking along the path into the Great Hall, his heart pounding at the mere sight of her. "Well... A birthday is just as good of a reason to stay as any, but I do not think I can be a part of..."

"...I also wanted to let you know I sensed a lot of apprehension about some of the way we do things here, so I have taken it upon myself to request a few changes for tonight's feast. I spoke with the Alpha, and I will invite all the wolves in service to attend. By the morning light, there will be only full bellies."

Li'Illnok interjected with a prideful inflection.

"That's great Li'Illnok, but—" "also, there will be no rabbit, no tonight and never again, in remembrance of Finnick."

Rex'Onok looked disappointed and then realized the reason for such a change. As El'Wren made her way back into his line of sight, his heart picked up the pace again.

"Well, I guess I could stay one more night. That is very thoughtful of you Li'Illnok."

As Li'Illnok continued to speak, Rex'Onok's attention was drawn to two battle wolves on the approach from the west, they flanked a severely malnourished wolf missing a back leg. As they drew nearer, Morgrim recognized the emaciated wolf as Ha'Kan.

Enraged, Morgrim charged with unprecedented speed, slamming into Ha'Kan and sending them both tumbling to the ground. Morgrim's speed surprised the battle wolves, leaving them unable to react in time.

"Your friends almost killed me! and then they killed my father!" Ha'Kan wheezed, his body frail. His leg wound showed no signs of healing since their last encounter.

"I know, Morgrim, I know," Ha'Kan panted, he struggled to remain conscious as he wobbled on his remaining legs. "No amount of apologies will take that back. I deserve every bit of what's coming to me."

Morgrim's fury surged, and he lunged again, knocking Ha'Kan to the ground. Standing over him, the stench of infection from Ha'Kan's leg made Morgrim's stomach churn. Through gritted teeth, he growled, "Tell me why I shouldn't kill you right here, right now, for all the wolves you've helped Oct'Tulommon kill!"

"Morgrim! Stop!"

The wolves that escorted Ha'Kan tried their hardest to pull Morgrim off, but their efforts were futile. As Rex got close enough, he tackled Morgrim and pinned him to the ground to calm him down.

"Morgrim, listen to me! Listen!" Rex pleaded; his eyes locked onto Morgrim's.

Morgrim growled and struggled, baring his white teeth at Rex. "Get off me! This wolf is part of the Fracture!"

"Wolf!" Rex barked, Morgrim still pinned in the dirt. "What do you have to say? Why have you come? Speak now, or I will release this wolf on you!"

"Oct'Tulommon needs to be stopped," Ha'Kan rasped, his voice weak and strained. "He has stolen the blood of the first man and taken his form. I watched him do it with my own eyes."

Li'Illnok chimed in, concern etched on his face. "This wolf is suffering, Morgrim. The infection coursing through his veins is causing him immense pain. It's only a testament to the power of the Awl'Fire within him." As he sniffed the air around Ha'Kan, he gagged.

Morgrim reeled back his anger, his gaze softened as he looked at the injured Ha'Kan.

"Morgrim, I'm not trying to make excuses for my actions, and I'm not looking for forgiveness from anyone that I have ever helped to hurt." Ha'Kan took a labored breath and continued. "The choice to fall in line with Oct'Tulommon was my own. I take full responsibility for it. I watched him commit atrocities and tried to distance myself from them, but I've always been too sick and weak to fight him."

Rex stood and allowed Morgrim to get up.

"Then you should have taken your own life and let the Awl'Fire judge your actions." Morgrim said with a well of anger behind his words.

Ha'Kan was barely conscious on his feet. "I tried… but I was even too weak to do that."

Everyone present could fill the sadness in his heart and mind. It radiated outward, just as pungent as his septic body.

"The situation with Oct'Tulommon has gained the attention of Elden Seph'Ulinok. Rex said. He broke the silence that hung over their heads. "We know he possesses the Array of the Void; we saw it the day of the Altapex he called against Alpha Alt'Ilink. If he does possess the Moon Array, and he has in fact aligned himself with the void. He must be stopped."

Morgrim ambled away from Ha'Kan, the smell of infection had become too much for him to bear.

"Rex, go with me to the Outlands, and we will stop this before it gets started," Morgrim implored, his eyes filled with determination.

"As much as I would love to, The Alpha will never sanction an attack. And Morgrim, you're still too young to know the true power of the Void. Let us go; This decision is for the Eldens and the Alpha. We must be smart with this information." Rex'Onok turned to Morgrim, his expression resolute.

"I will not try to talk you out of anger, but I will tell you anger makes you weak and only strengthens the Void. This wolf is sick and dying, and he has trekked miles to come here and warn us. I will let you decide his fate," Li'Illnok was calm, his eyes full of wisdom.

As Morgrim watched the life ebb and flow within Ha'Kan's eyes, he turned his back and walked away, his decision clear. Li'Illnok observed Morgrim, his expression conveyed that he wasn't surprised by his choice. It was almost as if he knew what Morgrim would do.

"Rex, guide Ha'Kan to the river and find Elden Vog'Morlinok. He will see to his recovery." Li'Illnok commanded. "It may take some time, wolf, but he will heal you if that is what fate allows." Li'Illnok instructed, his voice steady.

Li'Illnok watched as Ha'Kan hobbled out in front of Rex. He turned and looked at Morgrim for a moment, "If I survive this Morgrim. whatever you ask of me, I will do."

Morgrim stopped but did not look back. It was the first time in a long time that Ha'Kan was shown respect.

"You're such a colorful wolf, Morgrim, even with a fur coat black as night. I never doubted that you would spare his life. You have gained so much more than his Awl'Fire in doing so. You breathe life back into your own while fanning the flames of his. The sign of a true Alpha is a reinforcement of solid values and virtues. Finnick was a good father and teacher to you, wolf; he raised you right," Li'Illnok praised.

Morgrim felt different about himself, even more so, his chest swelling with pride. Hearing Li'Illnok speak highly of his values boosted his confidence in ways he never thought possible, especially after such a significant loss.

"Now, I think it best that in light of the news brought to us by Ha'Kan, this season's rites of Passage ceremony will have to take place at a later time. The Eldens and I need to hold council with the Alpha." Li'Illnok continued, his eyes locked onto Morgrim's. "There is much we need to discuss." The surrounding air seemed to grow heavy with intrigue and anticipation, as if the trees were leaning in to hear their conversation.

Chapter 24
Apollo

Several days passed after Oct'Tulommon's run in with Atohi. Even though his human likeness took the brunt of the abuse, The pain and stiffness from the melee somehow telegraphed through to his wolf form.

The feral wolves who were still around and hadn't died from starvation were prepared for a war—a war that Oct'Tulommon decided had to come before the first snow of the winter months, or else the meager food sources available to them in the Outlands would be utterly depleted.

The Fracture had grown in numbers but was still only half the size of the Illnok. Most of the ferals present on the day of Oct'Tulommon's show of power still lingered nearby, even though they were sick and emaciated. Oct'Tulommon's resolve to attack remained unchanged as the Outlands grew more restless with each passing day.

"Oct'Tulommon!" A familiar voice called for him from the ground. He stepped onto the balcony and spotted Apollo below, the sun casting a golden glow on his fur.

"Well, well, old friend, it's been some time since I've seen you. I thought you were dead, along with your brother," Oct'Tulommon remarked, his voice dripped with disdain as he descended from the balcony.

Apollo stood tall his eyes blazed with determination.

"Our friend in the sky told me about your failed attempt to capture the obsidian wolf, how he and a group of little rabbits got the better of you and escaped. I can't even trust you to kill a defenseless rabbit? Haha! I'm surprised you showed your face here after failing me again."

Apollo noticed several wolves surrounded him, all moving with no energy, ready to do whatever Oct'Tulommon commanded.

"It doesn't matter. I've put up with you for too long. After Ack'Reus died, I realized you are the problem. We gave you everything, and for what?! Nothing but death, decay, and hollow promises by a wolf who tucked his tail and ran to the void during his only Altapex."

Oct'Tulommon stopped, his eyes narrowed. Apollo's words struck a nerve. His fur bristled along the length of his spine.

"Speak up, Apollo. If you claim superiority, declare your intentions loud for all these wolves to hear."

Apollo looked around at the sick and half dead wolves—about thirty. Before he made his choice, he watched as the peregrine landed atop the scaffolding. The sight of the bird brought back memories of that fateful day and it filled his heart with hatred for both of them.

"Hear me, wolves! We can do better than this! He is nothing but liar who will stop at nothing to get what he wants, even if that means sacrificing you to do it," Apollo proclaimed, his voice echoing through the barren landscape.

Apollo's words fell on deaf ears; the crowd surrounding him remained silent. The peregrine swooped down from above and landed on a rail next to Oct'Tulommon, whispering something in his ear. Oct'Tulommon smirked, revealing his sharp teeth. "Haha! Things have changed a little in your absence." The air was heavy with tension, the wolves' breaths visible in the chilly air, their eyes reflecting the dying light of the setting sun.

From behind Apollo, an elderly wolf with a coat of silver and gray limped toward Oct'Tulommon. As he passed, Apollo looked into his eyes and saw nothing but emptiness and pain. The old wolf sat before Oct'Tulommon, his head hung low and his ears pinned back. his sorrowful gaze returned to Apollo, filled with weary resignation.

"Call it out old friend. And we shall see what fate will decide for us." Oct'Tulommon commanded.

Blinded by rage and the thirst for retribution, Apollo ignored the truths about how the altercation was going to end.

"...I challenge you to an Altapex, Oct'Tulommon."

As soon as the words seeped into the empty hearts and clouded minds of all the wolves present, Oct'Tulommon sank his brittle teeth into the neck of the old wolf. The old wolf didn't struggle or fight back but let out a blood-curdling shriek, it made all the wolves around him flinch.

As the blood and life flowed from the wound in his neck, his coat faded from silver and gray to an inky black.

Oct'Tulommon released the lifeless body and took a deep breath as the last remaining flames of the stolen Awl'Fire spread into his heart, his eyes turned from brown to a glowing, piercing white.

"I accept, Apollo."

Oct'Tulommon vanished into the void, leaving only a chilled breeze swirling the air in his wake. Apollo: in disbelief, braced himself and tensed his rippling muscles. He dug his claws into the dried and cracked dirt. Time seemed to stop. Surrounded by whimpering feral wolves, he stood in the silent stillness. Waiting to see where Oct'Tulommon would strike from.

"I can see inside your heart, Apollo. Your resolve is faltering; your confidence is fading. Everyone here will watch me snuff you out of existence..."

Apollo tried his best to calm himself. Oct'Tulommon's mastery over the Void array improved. It scared him.

"...You're meddling in things you shouldn't, Oct'Tulommon! We have all done terrible things, but this is too far..." Apollo growled as he backed away from the center of the circle. The wolves behind him blocked his exit and forced him back in. His ego had trapped him.

"Haha! Apollo! There is no place you can go where I will not find you!"

Oct'Tulommon reappeared from the void above Apollo and knocked him down. His eyes white, his fur rippled as if he were underwater.

Apollo landed a powerful bite on Oct'Tulommon's neck and tried his hardest to hold on as Oct'Tulommon shook violently to get him off. For a moment, Apollo's bite was too strong for him to overcome until Oct'Tulommon disappeared once more, his mouth left open, full of blood and fur.

"You coward! You retreat to the void in fear, fear that I will best you."

Once again, Apollo waited for his rival to return from the void.

"Apollo?" A familiar voice called to him from outside of the circle.

"Brother! you must keep him from the void. He will destroy everything if you don't. We shouldn't have allowed this to go this far!"

"Ack'Reus?!"

The voice that called to him from beyond was that of his dead brother. Oct'Tulommon's careless use of the Void Array left a thin corridor open between the physical realm and the void. He could hear his brother, but he could not see him.

"Stop him, Apollo, at all costs! Too much is at stake!"

The emotion of hearing his brother's voice once more overwhelmed him. Tears welled in his eyes as he gritted his teeth, determination surged throughout his tense body.

"I will do what I can, brother."

Once more, Oct'Tulommon flickered in and out of the void, dancing between dimensions within the circle. Apollo waited, his muscles tensed and poised to strike before Oct'Tulommon could vanish again. With precise timing, he lunged at Oct'Tulommon and slammed into his chest with a rugged force. He clawed at his face and ripped through his lip and ear. Apollo stood over him, pressed his head into the dirt, and recited the tome of the Altapex.

"Oct'Tulommon, I renounce your authority of the Awl'Fire to wield the arrays as Alpha. I, Apol—"

Oct'Tulommon laughed, blood from his torn ear and lip stained the fur on his face, his eyes still bright white. Before Apollo could finish the tome and seal the fate of the Outlands, Oct'Tulommon's front leg twisted as it transformed into a grotesque misshapen human arm. The hand reached out, grasped a length of jagged metal rebar, and with a vicious thrust, he shoved it between Apollo's ribs, tearing a hole right through his heart. His last breath came almost immediately after. Oct'Tulommon slowly slid the rusted length of rebar further in.

"Still a disappointment, Apollo, even in death. I hoped to watch you struggle more."

Apollo's life was over. His coat seemed to fade to black as Oct'Tulommon stole the void he cultivated inside his heart and added it to an already overflowing vat of it, darkness inside of his own.

Oct'Tulommon rose to his feet and shook the mud from his matted coat, his white eyes filled with a fierce determination.

"I am done fooling around! It is time."

Chapter 25
Obsidian Desert

"It's time to wake up…WAKE UP!" The voice that reverberated within the confines of Ha'Kan's fevered mind was familiar and enigmatic. The arduous journey from the Outlands to the Alpha's mountain and then from there to the riverside in the north drained the last vestiges of life from him as he slipped in and out of consciousness. With a broken spirit, a heart pumping infection throughout his decayed body, and his will to carry on extinguished,

Ha'Kan was on the verge of collapse. Rex'Onok and a group of Border Wolves helped get him to his destination. Still, under the strict instructions of Elden wolf Li'Illok, they offered no shoulder to lean on or encouragement to keep him moving. Ha'Kan's penance would have to be secured by his own will. What should have taken only a few hours stretched into an exhausting day, leaving Ha'Kan's life hanging by a thread.

Upon arrival, Vog stood by the riverside, observing the fish as they swam. Rex called out to him, "Elden Vog'Morlinok! Under the direction of Elden Li'Illnok, we have brought this wolf to you. He said you could help, but I fear he may not last."

Vog ambled up the riverbank, his coat stained red with berries and his face painted white with ash. His wiry, grayish-blue fur resembled the needles on a hedgehog's back, though far more unkempt. Narrow shoulders and long legs lent him a sleek, enigmatic appearance.

"Ahh, I know precisely what this wolf needs. Leave us. We have a lot of work ahead and little time to do it. Thank you for seeing him here, Rex."

"I hope, Elden Vog'Morlinok, for his sake, I hope very much." As Rex and his wolves departed, Ha'Kan crumpled to the ground.

"You stay here…" Vog remarked as he took mental notes of the ailments that afflicted the sick wolf.

He then vanished into a small opening beside the roots of a birch tree hidden beneath the riverbank.

Inside the opening lay a vast chamber illuminated by crystals embedded in the soil above. Earthen vessels and wooden boxes lined the cave walls, filled with tools, medicine bottles, liquid in jars that shimmered, and other artifacts discovered in the ruined human cities across the river. Seated in the center of the room, Vog inhaled and closed his eyes. His body quivered and contorted as his fur sloughed off like snow sliding off a smooth rock face. Standing tall in human form, naked and bloodied, he reached for a pair of pants and a shirt, buttoning them up before a grimy mirror in the corner.

"He was right. It gets easier." He gathered two bottles of medicine and a syringe from a shelf. His hands trembled, but he knew what to do. He pulled the solution into the needle and strode back to the riverside in his new human form, leaving his shed fur on the chamber floor. After he administered the injection of antibiotics to Ha'Kan, he used his human strength to pick him up and carry him back to the room. Ha'Kan's eyes remained closed throughout.

Inside, Vog laid Ha'Kan in a corner and started a fire in an old, rusted wood stove that vented the smoke through the Earth above. He grabbed a rag and a bottle of sterilizing alcohol and cleaned the broken bone and torn flesh where Ha'Kan's foot had been ripped off. The rot was severe, maggots were the only thing that kept the infection manageable enough for Ha'Kan's body to survive.

"I'm not a doctor, but I know this is bad. I'm surprised you're not dead," Vog commented, although Ha'Kan was too far gone to hear him. He poured some water into Ha'Kan's mouth; his tongue barely moved, but he swallowed. "Very good, Ha'Kan, very good. You just rest, and I will see to your recovery."

Ha'Kan slipped deeper into a catatonic state, further and further away from the physical realm.

*

"WAKE UP!"

Ha'Kan's body jolted awake, and he stood alone beneath an infinite expanse of space, surrounded by spiral galaxies and an infathomable number of stars. The sight was awe-inspiring. Below him, his paws felt the coolness of the black sand in the obsidian desert. Each grain reflected the celestial wonders above. Stretching out around him, in every direction, lay flat, empty land—no trees, no mountains, no life. Just a horizon line where the light from billions of stars met the black sand beneath.

"I know this place. I've heard the stories. The obsidian desert."

He lowered his head and sniffed the sand, detecting no scent. He tasted it, but it had no flavor. There was no wind, no sound.

"Hello?!" He sent his words out like a signal flare, but no one answered—not even an echo resonated in his mind. As he gained his bearings, he realized that his foot had returned. He felt no pain, no sickness.

"I must have died," He thought, fearing that this desolate place was his punishment for the evil deeds he committed on Earth. In the distance, he spotted a flicker of light that hovered above the sand. With nothing else to draw his attention, he investigated. As he approached, the light seemed to move, still it hovered but veered to the left as if it sensed his presence. Ha'Kan, feeling a newfound strength in his body, picked up the pace, transitioning from a trot to a full-out sprint. He was faster than he ever was on Earth.

"This is amazing!" He exclaimed as his feet contacted the sand below, propelling his body forward. The light was there, but it matched his speed, continuing in the opposite direction. Time felt different here, and it was as though he'd been running forever, yet the light remained just as distant. The same bleak flatness lay below, and the same expanse of the cosmos stretched above. His body didn't tire, but he seemed to get no closer than when he started. Frustrated, he stopped running and sat down, watching as the light ceased moving.

"There's only one way to reach it, and running is not the way." He thought. Now there were two voices inside his head, one beginning the sentence and one finishing it.

"Who are you? Where are you? How come I can't see you?" Ha'Kan had a million questions and the number kept growing.

"Must you see us to know us? Has it been that long? Time passes differently for us here than it does on Earth." A mix of two separate voices passed over him.

"I'm very sorry. I can't place your voices. They are very familiar, but I don't know why."

Silence returned, and he sat and waited for more, but only found further solitude.

The light in the distance moved again. Ha'Kan smiled as a memory flooded his mind, a memory of when his cubs were alive. No matter how hard he tried to keep them close, they would take off running as fast as they could whenever they had the chance to escape the den and enter the open fields. They were so fast that Ha'Kan could never catch them. Frustration would consume him, and he would resign to sit in the open field next to his den, watching as they burned off their boundless energy. Only then would he be able to grab them and carry them home.

So, Ha'Kan cleared his mind of all his questions and resentment about being trapped in this place. He took a deep breath and watched. The slow-moving light picked up speed and split into two separate entities. Now, moving in two directions, the lights sped up, coming together and splitting apart, covering impossible distances. After what felt like an hour, they slowed down. Ha'Kan started walking towards them. This time, he could see them growing larger; he was drawing closer.

"What are you doing here?" The voices called out to him. Ha'Kan laughed.

"I guess that would depend on where 'here' is."

"This is the Obsidian Desert, the plane beneath everything. This is where the dead come to scavenge for a spark of the Awl'Fire. It's sad. We were all born with fire in our hearts, but over time, some fade out, some are stolen, and some don't care enough to tend to it. But once we die and are left with nothing, mere husks in the cold sand of the desert, we learn the importance of it all." The two wolves stood silent.

"I feel that regret now." Ha'Kan admitted as he cried, still he walked towards the lights. He was met with more silence as the lights sped up again. He felt disappointment flood his heart. As he cried, he sat again, to watch the lights skim over the top of the sand. His mind went back to when he first felt the Awl'Fire slip from his broken heart. It was just after he crossed the southernmost borderline into the Outlands.

A trapper's snare caught his hind leg. He struggled for days on end to free it, but the wire was made from a steel cable shielded in a rigid plastic sleeve that was too strong to bite through, and struggling only caused it to tighten more, cutting off the circulation to his paw. After many attempts, he resigned to die from starvation or by the hand of the man who set the snare.

Ha'Kan traveled north from a forest close to a city, where he lived in peace for many winters. He was the proud father of two cubs, full of the Awl'Fire, and a companion he loved since he was young. Together, they made a den set back into a ridge overlooking a field of marigolds.

One evening as he returned home from scouting the area to the east of his den, he watched as a diesel-powered bulldozer flattened the fields and crushed his home into the dirt, his cubs and companion fleeing for their lives, only to be shot as they ran away. He was broken. Another truck unloaded a heap of white, human-shaped sacks in the dirt while another with a torch set them on fire. He stayed in the shadows until nightfall, the fire still burning bright as they drove away, leaving the bodies of his cubs and companion in the grass and dirt pushed into piles from the fields.

The smell of the fire was settling close to the ground in the cool night air and filled his lungs with the stench of burning plastic and flesh.

He had no choice but to head north into the Outlands, a place known for its disparity and injustice. That's when Oct'Tulommon, Apollo, and Ack'Reus found him. His foot had gone black from lack of circulation and his heart had been destroyed by the wickedness and carelessness of man. In and out of consciousness, unable to discern what Oct'Tulommon was saying when he spoke. He could only remember the metallic taste in his bloody mouth and the intense hunger that pushed against the walls of his barren stomach.

"This wolf is too far gone, Oct'Tulommon. Best to leave him in this snare and wait for the hunter to return. He will make much better bait than a Fractured wolf," Apollo looked down at Ha'Kan with pity. He sniffed the mangled foot, his eyes and his stomach both clenched tight. "The flesh of this paw is already rotted; even if he could make it out, he would lose it for sure, maybe even more." "nonsense, Apollo, have some heart. What if I shared that same sentiment about you and your brother in those cages all those winters ago? I could have used you as bait to kill that fat, ugly man who was to watch over you!" Oct'Tulommon interrupted. "Every broken and downtrodden wolf deserves a chance," Oct'Tulommon counters, his voice firm.

The once fierce gaze in the wolf's eyes had dimmed. Its proud stance was replaced by a listless slouch, the spirit that once sparked like wildfire was now only a wisp of smoke.

"How do you know this wolf has been broken? What if he is… just unlucky?" Ack'Reus questions Oct'Tulommon.

"I know because only broken wolves come here to the Outlands. That's why we are the Fracture," Oct'Tulommon replied. He steps closer as the other two step back.

"Wolf! If I set you free, you belong to me, forever…" He waited for a response. Ha'Kan's eyes move to meet Oct'Tulommon's, his mind too cloudy to give a simple answer.

"I'll take that as a yes. This may hurt, but it'll all be over soon, my new friend."

Oct'Tulommon leaned back, licked his lips and bit down on Ha'Kan's leg just above the wire. Ha'Kan jolted back to life as the pain spiraled throughout his body. It burned every inch.

Oct'Tulommon's jaws were powerful enough to break through rock. Severing Ha'Kan's thin leg should have taken no time, but he ensured it did, just to see the pain on his face. It gave him enjoyment to see. The metallic taste of Ha'Kan's blood spurting in his mouth caused his pupils to dilate and his jaws to clamp down even harder. He savored every second.

After what seemed like a lifetime, Oct'Tulommon pulled as Ha'Kan dug his front claws into the dirt and tried to stay still. The skin and muscle that wrapped his leg snapped and popped as it separated. He was free of the snare but now missing a leg. A leg that was now inside Oct'Tulommon.

Apollo and Ack'Reus were mortified at what they witnessed, disgusted that Oct'Tulommon could be so sadistic as to eat another wolf's infected, rotted leg right in front of him.

The moon cast a ghostly pallor on the scene and made the grotesque act even more chilling. Ha'Kan's ragged breath echoed through the cold night air, a testament to his ordeal.

"Get him to his feet! See that he makes it back to the derrick. I have some more business to attend to out here. and try to get him something to eat and drink on the way; he deserves it, I think. Haha!" Oct'Tulommon ordered with a sinister laugh.

Ack'Reus and Apollo did as they were told, but they both felt it was pointless; Ha'Kan was so sick that it seemed impossible for him to make it any further.

As they continued into the Outlands, Ha'Kan gained more awareness. He walked without his escorts' aid and drank a little from the inside of an old rubber tire. Apollo took it upon himself to explain his new role as a fractured wolf as they traveled across the desolate landscape.

"From now on, Oct'Tulommon decides when you eat, drink, and sleep. If he calls on you for anything, you must do it or die. There is only one way to leave this pack now: through death. Whatever life you had before is over; this is your life now. Just be thankful you didn't die in that snare or worse."

"My life was over before I crossed into the Outlands; nothing matters anymore," Ha'Kan responds, his voice heavy with despair.

Oct'Tulommon was right; Ha'Kan was broken. His good memories of his cubs running through the fields were overtaken by the images of their legs sticking out from underneath the dirt.

*

When Ha'Kan emerged from his memories, he noticed the lights were even closer. So close, in fact, that he could see they were not just orbs of light but wolves; glowing and shimmering as if their fur was made from pure light. He was so close to them that he could feel the heat from their luminescence. They panted with mouths wide open, gasping for air, lying in the cool sand, watching Ha'Kan come closer.

"Do you recognize us now, Father Wolf?" one wolf asked.

He couldn't believe what he saw: his cubs from so long ago were now grown. Ha'Kan was speechless. The two wolves stood up, almost twice his size. They bent their heads and rubbed them against his. His heart shattered. He had so many things he wanted to tell them and so many more that he wanted to apologize for.

"I… I am so—" "Father Wolf, we know what is in your heart; we have no boundaries now, not here. We love you, and we forgive you. Your actions afterward were marred by a heart filled with sorrow. It does not excuse your behavior, which is why you suffered and will continue to. Time is a never-ending circle. Your past pays penance for your future, and your future is penance for your past. Let go of it here, and let your heart mend," One of the cubs consoled him, his voice just as soothing and wise as the other.

Ha'Kan cried as his cubs cradled him, their love flowed into him like a warm, gentle stream.

"Run with us, Father. We have something to show you," the other cub beckons.

As Ha'Kan stood, the two wolves took off. They started slow to let him catch up and then gradually picked up the pace. It was as if he had unlimited speed within him. When he matched the pace of his cubs, they only went faster and faster until he they were going so fast that his feet were no longer needed.

The three became pure light! They soared through the expanse above, past planets and suns, nebula clouds, and the remnants of dead solar systems. they broke through the very fabric of the universe.

Swallowed by white light, Ha'Kan shielded his eyes until they adjusted and his vision returned. He stood in the middle of the field in front of his den, the breeze carried the smell of marigolds and the warmth of the summer sun.

He laughed from the excitement of seeing that special place again, so many wonderful memories in such a short time.

"Ha'Kan, my love," A new voice behind him whispered. It sent shivers down his spine and straight into his heart. He was frozen, a lump swelled inside his throat as her soft fur brushed his flank as she walked beside him.

"...I miss you so much, my love," Ha'Kan whispered, his voice trembling with emotion.

"Ha'Kan, my love," She nestled her head underneath his chin. The smell of the marigolds weaved in her golden fur. He couldn't move, yes squeezed shut in fear that if he were to open them, he would realize her presence was just a figment of his imagination and vanish like water in the desert.

"I'm sorry, I don't know if I can take this; this is too much. I'm afraid to even look at you." He stuttered and struggled to maintain his composure.

"It's okay, love. I'm here with you whether you see me. I have always been and always will be," she lovingly reassured him.

"I... I don't deserve to see you again. It's my fault you... you..." she stopped him to stave off an emotional tidal wave he would be unable to control.

"No, what happened that day was of no fault of yours Ha'Kan. You always did your best for us and the cubs and that's all a mother wolf wants." She pressed harder into him, He could feel the blood pumping through her neck and the warmth in her chest. "You still have more to do down there, more to endure. Why the universe has chosen you for so much suffering is beyond understanding my love. but it's almost over now. When your time is up and you take your last breath, just know that you will return to me, to us. Here. My love... Look at me." She backed away.

Ha'Kan took a deep breath and opened slowly opened his wet eyes. His love stood in the field facing the sun, her fur caught the wind as the two cubs ran free around her.

"All the things I wish I would've done differently, all the things I can't change." The weight of emotion finally overwhelmed him.

"Nothing matters now; it's coming and you must ready yourself." Her voice echoed in his mind.

The clouds in the distance turned gray as lightning spread out from massive thunderheads. The wind picked up, and the grass wilted. He turned to see his family run into the old den where they spent their time together. They motioned for him to follow.

"It's coming; you must be ready!" her voice repeated as he entered the dark den. He glanced back to see the wind carry limbs and trees across the field. Boulders beneath the surface were pulled out until nothing was left—just a void of emptiness and the sound of wind that lashed the rocks of the den's entrance.

His companion's voice slammed into his mind through the noise of it all "Oct'Tulommon is coming!"

It jolted him awake. Vog'Morlinok busted into the den from the outside, still in his human form. Ha'Kan was hampered by confusion. In fear, he bolted to the other end of the room and growled at Vog.

"Ha'Kan! My name is Vog'Morlinok. I'm the Elden of Tongues for Ult'Ilinok, the Alpha. Li'Illnok sent you here for me to heal you!" He Exclaimed in a voice and language Ha'Kan only heard a few times before. His growl intensified as his fur bristled.

"You can't understand me…" Vog realized. "Okay. Okay. Give me a moment."

Vog removed his shirt and transformed back into a wolf as Ha'Kan watched; unsettled by the process. It reminded him of the last time he saw Oct'Tulommon undergo the same change.

"There. My name is Vog'Morlinok. I'm the—"

Ha'Kan interrupted him. "…I know who you are. I'm sorry, I just didn't know that it was you inside of that human skin…." Ha'Kan slowly sat on his back leg, wrapped in a white gauze. He looked down and noticed a cut along the underside of his belly.

"…I watched a wolf named Oct'Tulommon steal the likeness of a man. Now, He's going to use it against the Illnok. That's why I'm here—I left to warn you all of the coming storm. That's when Elden Li'Illnok sent me to you. I'm afraid we have little time…"

"Yes, I am aware, Li'Illnok instructed me to bring you to him as soon as you were capable of communicating, I assume that is the reason."

Ha'Kan watched him drag the discarded flesh into a hole and attempted to change the subject to avoid the awkwardness of it.

"Why does my stomach and chest hurt so bad?" Ha'Kan asked as he grimaced in pain.

"Well…your body was choked with infection… I had to open you to… let it heal." Vog said "you're lucky to be alive friend, you were sicker than I have ever witnessed. Any more time out there in the wilderness and I don't think I could've saved you. I had to remove some of the rotting flesh around your leg wound. Your bandages should stay on for a while, but it's going to itch. Try your best not to bite at them."

Ha'Kan ambled around the room the best he could with the pain, examining the various items as Vog spoke.

"What is this place, Vog? Where did all these strange items come from?"

"Well, these are items I've collected from the human cities on the other side of the river during my visits. I've learned so much there and intend to use this knowledge to aid my brothers here in the Illnok territory. I haven't found the right moment to reveal it all to them. Lately, things have become scarcer in the human cities, but I procured the medicine needed to save you. Without it, I fear you might have been beyond help. You're not out of the woods yet, but you'll improve soon."

Ha'Kan was mesmerized by all of it. "Is that where you found the man you transformed into? In the cities?" He asked. Curious.

Vog hesitated and sighed nervously. "No, it's not. There was... a wolf a long time ago. But that's a story I keep close to my heart, I'm afraid. No offense to you. Anyway, I'm under strict orders to bring you back to Alpha's mountain as soon as possible. So, today is a good day to showcase my abilities in a human's body."

Ha'Kan found it odd and sensed Vog's reluctance to explain the origin of his power and decided not to press the issue further.

As they exit the cramped den, Ha'Kan takes a deep breath, savoring the fresh air. It had been ages since he could appreciate the simple pleasure of inhaling the forest's scent. However, the aroma he cherished from a long past was absent. Vog's den had a repugnant odor, because of the pile of discarded fishbones by the riverbank or the array of chemical-filled jars outside the entrance. Ha'Kan couldn't pinpoint the source, but something was tainting the once-refreshing air.

As they began their journey back to the Alpha's mountain, they couldn't help but notice something else. A faint wisp of smoke, perceptible, yet enough to raise concern.

"Vog, can you smell that? Or is it just me?" Ha'Kan asked, sniffing the air.

Vog follows suit, he lifted his nose to determine the direction of the scent. "Yes, I smell it too. I believe it's coming from the West, like Hickory. There are hickory trees near a clover field near the border, where the rabbits dwell."

"Let's climb that hill over there and see if we can spot anything," Ha'Kan suggested, feeling a renewed vigor course through his veins, thanks to Vog and his medicines. Once they reached the hill's peak, they saw a column of smoke rise above the trees to the northwest.

"You're right; it's close to the Outlands border."

Ha'Kan scrutinized the landscape and tried to pinpoint the exact location.

"I'm afraid it's the clover fields near the rabbit burrows. We must hurry to the mountain. I fear the invasion has already begun." Ha'Kan said.

"What invasion, Ha'Kan?" Vog's lengthy brow furrowed in confusion.

"Oct'Tulommon's invasion." Ha'Kan sensed a shift in Vog's demeanor, as if he were withholding something deep within a guarded heart.

"We must hurry and warn them; there may not be any Borderwolves nearby. They're all getting ready for the feast tonight."

Vog said as he started down a trail towards the mountain.

They attempted to cover as much ground as quickly as possible, but Ha'Kan's weakened state hampered their progress. He lagged further behind Vog, who appeared to widen the gap between them. It aroused even more suspicion. He stopped to catch his breath, Ha'Kan realized Vog vanished from sight.

"Vog?" Ha'Kan called out, he was met with only silence. The smoke from the West thickened and enveloped the trees, it urged him to press on.

After what felt like twenty miles, Ha'Kan found himself amid the cedar trees below the Great Hall. His belly and chest seemed bloated and heavy and his legs ached he vomited several times whimpering through the pain of his muscles tightening around his ribs. The peak loomed high above the treetops, an impressive sight. He spotted a patch of disturbed Earth to his left as if something had been hastily buried. He cleared the leaves and sticks with labored swipes to reveal a hidden chest below.

Ha'Kan couldn't comprehend what he found, but he was certain it was out of place. Despite never spending time in the Illnok lands, he knew their territory was guarded against outsiders. These mysterious items only heightened his sense of urgency and unease.

His heart pounded in his chest; adrenaline surged through his veins. Ha'Kan knew he had to reach the mountain as quickly as possible. With the discovery of the buried boxes, the looming threat felt even closer and more dangerous. He couldn't shake the feeling that something sinister was about to unfold, and time was running out.

Part VI: A Turn for the Worst

Chapter 26
Scattered

"Mulgris! Is that you, old friend?!" Burren called out from one of the chambers deep in the Illnok Burrow. It had been nearly two days since he set off with Morgrim to the Alpha's mountain.

"I didn't expect you back so soon Mulgris, How'd everything go? Did Morgrim get the answers he was looking for?" Burren asked, he started his question with curiosity but it quickly turned to concern. He wasn't getting any answers in return, just the sound of Mulgris panting as he tried to catch his breath. And the smell of fear that emanated from his tensed body.

"Mulgris? Is everything alright?" He waited for a reply.

"They're coming over the hill. I saw them just as I rounded the bushes on the east side," Mulgris gasped.

"Who did Mulgris?"

By the time, he caught his breath. Unis and a few other rabbits gathered to see how Morgrim had fared with the Elden Sayer.

"Unis! They're here. Take the younglings and head to the southern cliffs. You need to get as far away as you can. Use the tunnels on the south side. They will be watching every entrance from here to the Alpha's mountain before long. Whatever you do, do not go topside. I'm sure the peregrine is in the skies."

"Is it him Mulgris? Is it Oct'Tulommon?" Burren asked as the rabbits hustled and hopped from one tunnel to the next to prepare for a mass exodus.

"Yes, but he appeared as a man, Burren. It seems the tales were true. He stood naked amidst a flood of feral wolves, pouring into the fields beyond our borders. I've never witnessed such a sight. We must evacuate everyone immediately." Fear trembled in Mulgris' voice.

Burren's ears drooped with concern. The rabbits always thought the story of the moon array was a myth, too fantastical to believe. Why would a man need to become a wolf, or vice versa? It made little sense to them. Mulgris directed the rabbits to safety.

"We must find a rabbit fast enough to make the trip back to the Alpha's mountain. We must warn them before it's too late."

"I'll do it! I can go faster than any rabbit here. Remember, I have my brother's blood?" a determined voice piped up, ready to take on the responsibility.

Burren and Mulgris exchanged glances as they considered Nilian for the task. They hesitated and hoped for a more experienced rabbit to present himself. But as the silence stretched, it became apparent that Nilian was their best hope.

"He's right, Mulgris, he can do it. Let the rabbit go," Burren finally said, with a mix of determination and worry.

Mulgris was reluctant to dispatch such a young rabbit on such a risky mission, yet he knew there was no better option.

"Fine. Then go now, Nilian, and don't look back, no matter what. Countless lives are at stake here; these lands are counting on you. Make us proud, young one."

At Mulgris's heartfelt send-off, Nilian felt like a hero, his confidence soaring. "Yes, sir!" he exclaimed, and he was gone in the blink of an eye.

"I hate to say it, but I fear that we may never see that little rabbi again," Burren lamented.

"Me too," Mulgris agreed. He knew the gravity of the situation and the battle they were about to face. They could feel the threat closin in. It surrounded them.

"Burren, I don't know about you, but I don't want to die in this tiny, suffocating burrow. Let's make sure all the rabbits are out and go to that clover field where Finnick knocked down that hornet's nest on his head."

They both burst into laughter at the memory, determined to make the best of the little time they had left.

"My heavens, I'd forgotten all about that! I didn't think his ass could get any bigger until it got stung!" Burren cackled, tears in his swollen eyes.

Their laughter carried them through their rounds, ensuring all the rabbits were on their way to safer places. Finally, they made their way north to a fertile clover field Finnick used to frequent when he was alive—a place filled with memories and camaraderie, where they would face whatever fate had in store for them.

"Oh my, I have seen nothing like this in all my days, Mulgris," Burren whispered, eyes wide as they observed Oct'Tulommon, still as a man. He piled limbs and branches in the center of the field, the stack almost as tall as he was.

"What exactly is he doing with all those limbs, do you think, Mulgris?"

"I think he's going to start a fire, perhaps to smoke the rabbits from the tunnels." Oct'Tulommon chose the Illnok burrow as his first stop on the way to the Alpha's mountain, most likely to feed the hungry wolves in his ranks.

"Don't worry, Burren, by the time that fire is ready to use, our brothers and sisters will be long gone. We will be the only ones left." Mulgris tried to reassure him. "Do you think you can climb that tree over there, old rabbit?"

Burren looked over to see a tree with two massive hornets' nests hanging right over the clover. They both laughed again. "I think I may have it in me." He said, his heart burned with determination, it had been a long-time sense he felt so much enthusiasm.

"Okay, this is what we'll do: I will get their attention and run them around the field until they tire. Then I'll bring them back by the tree so you can drop the nests. They won't know what hit them until it's too late." Before Mulgris could finish his sentence, Burren disappeared.

It occurred so swiftly that Mulgris's brain couldn't comprehend what happened. He looked all around, but Burren was nowhere to be seen. Suddenly, Mulgris watched Burren's headless body fall from the sky in front of the pack of feral. They greedily devoured him. The peregrine dropped Burren's head back down in front of Mulgris. Right in the exact spot where it snatched him up from the clover.

Mulgris tried to move, but he was in a state of shock. The wolves spotted him, and he knew he didn't have the speed to get to the tunnel before they caught him. Even if he had, smoke was already billowing out of the earth. He took a deep breath and looked at the peregrine in the tree above him.

"Hey! Is it true your mother was a chicken?" He shouted, just before the peregrine swooped down at him. Mulgris rolled just in time, leaving the peregrine clutching clover instead of him. He seized his opportunity and vaulted himself over tall shrubs and logs, gliding up the length of the tree to the hornets' nest. As he scaled the long branch, the peregrine landed just behind him, shaking it just enough for him to tighten his little body against the bark, worried he was going to fall before he made it.

"One thing I've learned about rabbits here lately is that they find lamenting jokes before their deaths somewhat amusing." The peregrine snarled.

Mulgris stood and backed up to the nest.

"Peregrine, I wasn't joking. It's a question I think needs to be answered; it would explain a lot if it were true. An identity crisis is not a laughing matter." He chuckled.

"Never mind it now, Chicken. Do what you want with me," he taunted as he felt the branch narrow above the buzzing nest.

He could see it in the peregrine's eyes; the anger blinded him so much that he overlooked what was beneath. Mulgris fell, and on the way down, the peregrine followed. It wasn't until he was close enough to contact Mulgris that he noticed the nest falling beside them. It burst open as it hit the ground, sending hornets everywhere. Even Oct'Tulommon wasn't spared from at least three stings.

"Rabbits..." the peregrine muttered as he flew away, unable to capture Mulgris before the swath of Hornets choked the air. Laying underneath a cloud of hornets, Mulgris stared at the darkening blue sky. Resigning himself to death. But as he heard the feral wolves yelp and shuffle through the clover, he noticed he created a window of opportunity. The path to the east was mostly clear, barring the two distracted ferals digging their paws into their flesh, trying to dig out the stingers. Mulgris anchored his head low to the ground and took off. Narrowly escaping the swarm.

Oct'Tulommon changed back into his wolf form. The sting from the hornets was much worse on him as a human than he could remember as a wolf. Trundling into a swathe of billowing smoke, the hornets dispersed from around him. The skin he left discarded by the fire was pulled away and devoured amidst the chaos. "You said we would feast on rabbits for an entire day before they came to stop us? There were only two and a nest full of angry hornets!" One wolf growled, frustrated and hungry.

Scattered throughout the field, the fractured wolves yelped in pain and scratched at the dirt, trying to find traces of the rabbits they were promised. Their agitation grew as their plan to smoke the tunnels and their hopes of a fresh meal died. Oct'Tulommon tried his best to remain stern as he became surrounded by the disappointed wolves.

"Do I need to remind you of who you are talking to? Look around you; do you even know where you are?" He snapped. The fractured wolves stopped and listened.

"This is the Illnok territory. The wolves here have guarded these lands for more than a thousand winters. The animals here are comfortable, fat, and lazy. If you want to eat, go hunt! There are plenty of opportunities here; use your skills as wolves and find them! The rabbits were merely meant to be an appetizer, anyway. Go! Find your main course! Return here when you've fed yourselves. We need to prepare for the next part."

The wolves howled and barked in agreement as they dispersed in all directions to hunt. Oct'Tulommon looked east, where the mountain's summit reflected the morning sun.

"I'm coming for you, Ult'Ilinok." He vowed.

Reaching the Alpha's mountain from the Illnok burrow was at least a five-hour walk. Nilian made it in less than two. As he arrived, smoke had become visible in the distance. Several pack wolves tried to stop him on his way, but he promised Mulgris that he wouldn't let anything stand between him and the Alpha. They tried to chase him down, but there was no way of keeping up with his swift pace. As he climbed the last stretch of trail to the great hall, Rex'Onok and a regiment of battle wolves met him.

"Stop right there, rabbit! Why are you in such a hurry?" Rex barked as his wolves stepped closer to one another. Nilian showed no sign of slowing and blazed right past Rex and underneath the legs of the battle wolves.

"Stop that rabbit!" Rex commanded. He aimed to enlist help, but no one could match the pace.

Once inside, Nilian did not know where to go. It was the first time he had ever seen the great hall. He darted around the fire in the center and raced down hallways and corridors, causing chaos. As he rounded the stones and headed back inside the great hall from a meeting room, he found himself trapped between the claws of a giant, dire wolf.

"Well, so much speed! I can feel your heart beating; it's like a hummingbird!" Volcrim observed.

"I'm here to see the Alpha. I have a message for him from Mulgris! Let me go! It's very urgent!" Nilian pleaded.

"Hmm, I know Mulgris; he is a dear friend, but I cannot allow you entry to the Alpha. State your business here, and I will pass it along to him, little one," Volcrim was stern but curious.

When Nilian gathered his breath and to speak, a group of wolves who tried to chase him down came trudging up the hill into the great hall. They were exhausted from sprinting as fast as they could. Volcrim looked at them in amazement and laughed.

"It's the Fracture! They have breached the border to the west, and they're headed this way. Mulgris sent me here to warn the Alpha. He said there were more wolves than he could count," Nilian gasped.

Volcrim, sensed the urgency in Nilian's voice. He lifted his paw and let the rabbit go.

"Well, that is news worth spreading."

"Rex, go tell Seph'Ulinok to get his wolves ready. We need to prepare ourselves for a fight," Volcrim ordered.

"Yes, Elden Volcrim!" Rex replied before he took off to deliver the message.

"And you, Little Nilian, you stay with me. I have never seen such fire in such a small creature as you," Volcrim was impressed by the rabbit's determination. He bent down and allowed Nilian to climb onto his back.

"We will tell the Alpha, but we must find Li'Illnok first."

Volcrim and Nilian headed out of the great hall and down the path along the mountain's base. The sound of Volcrim's giant feet pummeling the earth beneath him brought the pack wolves from their dens as they sped past. Seph'Ulinok could be heard from the side of the mountain, howling and calling all his battle wolves to the great hall. Volcrim stopped at the edge of a great cliff, looking down on a valley to the west. He could see the smoke rising from the clover near the Illnok Burrow.

"Those are the clover fields to the north of the Illnok Burrow. Why are they burning?" Volcrim wondered aloud. After a moment of thought, he continued, "They must be using the smoke to drive the rabbits from the tunnels."

Nilian laughed. "Haha, they are wasting their time. They were leaving when I left; I'm sure every rabbit was gone before they even came close."

"I hope so, little one, I hope so," Volcrim's voice was heavy with emotion.

"Li'Illnok! They are in the clover fields just past the border. You must come quickly," Volcrim called out to Li'Illnok, using the ability they developed to call out over long distances.

"We aren't too far from you; we will be there shortly," Li'Illnok responded.

"Volcrim, I have also seen the smoke rising from the west. I am coming to you," Vog'Morlinok announced, having overheard the conversation.

"Good. Very good! I'm going to summon the Alpha. It's time he knows. Do we all agree?" Volcrim asked.

"Agreed," Li'Illnok responded.

"I agree," Vog'Morlinok added.

"I too agree." Seph'Ulinok concurred.

*

Back at the great hall, Seph'Ulinok had twenty hardened battle wolves lined up at the fire. The Hesperus wolves led them through a pit full of ash, covering their legs with it. The battle wolves were always the first to see conflict. If their lines broke, the Hesperus wolves would be next in line to protect the mountain. If the Hesperus wolves failed to maintain the great hall, the fight would be with the Elden wolves. Neve in the history of the Illnok pack had an army made it past the battle wolves.

"Volcrim is in the Alpha's chambers," Seph informed.

"He would be in the wolf maiden's den any other time. The one time I need him, and he's all the way at the top of those bloody steps? That's my luck," Volcrim grumbled.

He and all the other Elden wolves had an understanding; they a felt the same way about the current Alpha. He was not ideal, but Li'Illnok urged them to bear with it.

"Orem'Nubis was right. The turning started with the birth of the obsidian wolf," Seph mentioned..

"He is part of it, whether he knows it. Trust me, brothers. We must see this through. Our lands, our packs, and the great balance depend on it," Li'Illnok insisted.

Volcrim made it to the top of the steps, with Nilian still on his back. He called out to Ult'Ilinok, but the Alpha was nowhere inside. He had never seen the inside of the Alpha's chambers until now; the walls were chiseled with ancient text and drawings. Artifacts from past civilizations were scattered from one end of the room to the other. Further back, he saw the chambers opened to a balcony. Ult'Ilinok was sitting at the edge, staring into a giant waterfall across the expanse. A rainbow framed him, created by the mist rising from the pools of blue water below. The sight was breathtaking and mesmerizing, adding an air of intrigue to the situation.

"Alpha Ult'Ilinok, it is your master of the hunt, dire wolf Volcrim Sul'Ilinok. I'm here to inform you that our lands have been breached. Oct'Tulommon and his Fractured wolves are setting fire to the clover fields in the west. As we speak, they are hunting the wildlife and making their way here," Volcrim announced.

For a moment, Volcrim thought the Alpha may not have heard him, as there was no response.

"Alpha?" He probed.

Ult'Ilinok didn't move. He merely turned his head to the side and said, "Then why are you here in my chambers and not with the others below?"

Volcrim restrained himself from speaking the words he truly wanted to say. "My apologies, Alpha. I will return to them."

As he turned around to leave, Nilian spoke out, "Coward!"

Volcrim smiled and grimaced simultaneously. He braced for the fallout. But nothing came. He sighed with relief and started to walk again.

"Did you hear me, Ult'Ilinok? You're nothing but a coward!" Nilian exclaimed.

Volcrim turned in surprise at the little rabbit. "Friend, do not speak again." He said sharply.

"I heard you, rabbit. And you're not wrong. I am scared," Ult'Ilinok admitted, as he got up and walked toward them. "And you should be too, all of you. Now leave; we all have our parts to play. Let's play them, shall we?"

Volcrim was sure he was about to witness his new little friend lose his life. But he came out of it with a realization. Maybe there was more to this than what was obvious. "Brothers, he knows and is ready, but something doesn't seem right."

As the two of them made their way back down, Li'Illnok and Vog'Morlinok stood beside Seph'Ulinok. Morgrim was speaking to Rex when Nilian spotted him from above.

"Morgrim?!" Nilian called out, jumping off Volcrim's back and speeding down the steps to him. "I'm so glad to see you!" He said as they pressed their heads to one another. "They said you made the journey from the burrow to here in record time! I'm so proud of you, little uncle. Where are Mulgris and the others?"

Nilian's expression shifted to anger. "Mulgris told me to leave after he sent Unis to the south with the little ones. He saw the Fracture come over the hills past the western border. He sent everyone away before they got there. He knew what they were going to do," Nilian explained.

Morgrim sighed. "I hope they got out safely."

"Me too," Nilian replied.

"Morgrim! What's going on?" From across the great hall, El'Wren called to him.

"Oct'Tulommon and the Fractured wolves have breached the border; they are headed this way," Morgrim informed her.

"Wow…" Nilian said as he looked at El'Wren. "Nilian Stop it." Morgrim replied. He knew what he insinuated.

"…Okay sorry." Nilian didn't want to say it because he became bashful. He thought she was ethereal, so beautiful, like she stepped out from the Awl'Fire.

"It's a long story, El'Wren. I promise I will tell you, but now is not the time. Listen to me, El'Wren. I think you need to leave here. And I want you to take my little uncle with you."

"What?! I don't think so, Morgrim! I'm staying with you, and that's the end of it!" Nilian declared angrily.

"Nilian! This is serious. Oct'Tulommon has the void array and the moon array. He will stop at nothing to get to the top of this mountain. You don't know the whole truth about this place as I do. You need to trust me."

"What do you mean, 'the whole truth,' Morgrim?" El'Wren's worry was written all over her face. Throughout the last couple of days, she'd grown very fond of Morgrim, and so had he.

"El'Wren, I know you can feel my heart. I can't let anything bad happen to you, and if that means we can't be together for a while, then so be it." She cried as she reached into his heart, feeling the love growing for her and the worry surrounding it.

"Okay, Morgrim, I will," she agreed, tears streamed down her fur..

Nilian, obviously upset by Morgrim's decision to send him away, listened as Morgrim tried to console him. "Nilian, I heard you are the strongest and fastest rabbit in all the Illnok territory? Is that true?"

Nilian emerged from behind Morgrim's leg.

"Well, I don't know about the strongest, but I know I hold the record for the fastest trip from the Illnok burrow to here."

Morgrim smiled, tears filled his eyes.

"Nilian, please do me a favor and take care of her? She is very important to me, and I know she will be much safer with you by her side."

Nilian looked at Morgrim and then at El'Wren. "I guess I can do that!"

Morgrim was relieved that he agreed. "Ah! Thank you so much, uncle. I knew I could count on you."

"Stay safe, Morgrim. If you think it's best, I will go to the cliffs. Only if you promise to meet me there when this is done."

"I promise," Morgrim assured her. El'Wren cried as she led Nilian away.

"I love you, Morgrim!" Nilian called out.

"I love you too, Nilian," Morgrim replied, watching them leave through the front of the great hall.

As Ha'Kan entered the hall, he looked distressed, as if he saw a ghost. His walk looked better, but he seemed to be in just as much pain as before. He spotted Morgrim from below and started making his way through when Vog stopped him. "I see he is doing much better." Morgrim mentioned to Li'Illnok,

"he looks to be in even more pain though." He wanted so badly to hate Ha'Kan, but it was difficult after he learned all that he'd been through.

"It will take time. Vog is very good at what he does. Maybe in time, he will become a trusted ally to you."

As Morgrim watched Ha'Kan from above, he noticed Vog instructed him to go sit and wait by the fire. He seemed weary of Vog, like he was trying to figure something out. Morgrim tried to hear their minds, but they were too far away. He looked tense. It was the first time he had seen all four Elden wolves together. They all looked strong, well-fed, and healthy, with full coats that shimmered. In contrast, Vog'Morlinok's coat seemed unkempt, and his presence seemed restrained and hesitant. Perhaps he was sick? Or just not as sociable as the others. He was undoubtedly intelligent, far more than the others. Maybe his coarseness was because of a separation in knowledge?

"Where is he going?" Morgrim said. He watched Vog leave the great hall in a hurry, down into the pines below. Ha'Kan looked up at Morgrim with a look of worry.

"Something isn't right Li'Illnok."

In an instant, several things occurred:

The wolves gathered in the great hall fell silent as they all turned to look at Ha'Kan, almost in unison; every ear stood straight up, every head turned in confusion. Something from inside Ha'Kan had all their attention.

Beep…Beep….Beep…beep..beep.beep.

A flash of searing light pulsed from Ha'Kan with unprecedented speed and intensity; before they pulled their eyes shut, the searing light was gone. As was Ha'Kan.

A percussive sound wave dislodged bones and tried to knock their hearts clean from their rib cages.

A blast viciously ripped limbs from bodies, tore skin from meat and pulverized flesh against the splitting rocks of the great hall.

The great fire, nurtured and kept alive for thousands of years, was reduced to embers and hot coals, that rained down over the bloodied masses.

Chapter 27
The Bargain

In the early morning hours, a month after Oct'Tulommon stole the form of Lennon Grenlow, he searched the Outlands for the biggest piece of meat he could find, hoping to entice the Peregrine from the air for a conversation. He'd seen the bird's presence looming over a dilapidated barn several times before and assumed that this was where it roosted, most likely in the rafters of the collapsing roof. Oct'Tulommon could sense the Peregrine's jealousy and disdain for him and his wolves. The bird loved meat and had a propensity for evil but lacked the anatomy to carry out those thoughts and actions. The Peregrine was a loner; any winged creature that wasn't of the Unclean had been smart enough to leave the Outlands long ago, but this bird was too afraid to. Oct'Tulommon saw an opportunity to use the Peregrine to his advantage. He had a message to send and couldn't trust any of his closest wolves with the task.

The old barn, full of mold and decay, was where Oct'Tulommon found a giant wharf rat. The rat was feeding on old grain, spilling from ripped bags stacked in the corner. It was massive and slow-moving. Oct'Tulommon was surprised that it took so little effort to catch the rat and after a brief chase, the wharf rat seemed to give up altogether, like most of the animals in the Outlands. Oct'Tulommon climbed as high as he could atop the old barn and on a collapsed overhang that covered the rotting straw. He laid the rat's broken body down, found a hidden spot underneath the soffit, and waited for the bird to land.

The morning sun rose overhead and cleared out the dense gray fog, Oct'Tulommon watched the heat waves rise from the tin roof in front of his cool hiding spot. He fell asleep as he listened to the wind blow through the loft behind him. Time passed as the afternoon sun carried on into the west. Oct'Tulommon woke and looked at the cloudless sky above. His throat was dry and the smell of the wharf rat baking in the heat was enticing the hungry wolf inside him. He thought about eating it all himself and finding something smaller to coax the bird from the sky.

"The rat is too big for him anyway," he thought while licking his wind-blistered lips. *Maybe I can just take a chunk from the side, convince him I had to get a little more aggressive to catch it.* He got up, feeling the hot, rusted tin under his cooled pads. But it was already too late. A shadow crossed over the top of him.

"Damn." Oct'Tulommon shuffled back under the shade of the soffit. A black speck high above him crossed underneath the noonday sun. For a moment, it was almost as if the bird wasn't moving at all, hovering in the warm jet stream without effort, viewing all the many things occurring throughout the area. Then, with a sudden tilt in his wing, the bird plunged from above, dropping faster than a stone, without a sound and with little effort. At the last moment, he fanned his wings out and turned them down, his talons outstretched, landing with a thud on top of the dead wharf rat, the rusted tin below bending underneath his added weight.

"I thought that you couldn't see that giant rat from way up here," Oct'Tulommon said, startling the bird. It took him a moment to see where Oct'Tulommon was, a little surprised that he made it up to the roof without it caving in.

"I see all," the Peregrine replied with confidence. Oct'Tulommon scoffed. "Right, even a giant wolf climbing atop a metal roof?"

The Peregrine didn't respond. He turned to inspect the bait that Oct'Tulommon laid out for him. Fat underneath the short, wiry hair of the rat had broken down, releasing oils and a distinct odor, like copper.

"This is a disgusting piece of flesh. I prefer rabbits; you know this from the last time we met, Oct'Tulommon." He stuttered to reply,

"I searched for the better part of the morning and covered the lower part of the Outlands; there are no rabbits to be had here, not anymore. This is the only thing I could find for you."

The Peregrine looked at Oct'Tulommon with disdain. "There are plenty of rabbits in Illnok land. I suggest you look past your own wasteland next time you mean to catch me."

As he turned to fly away, leaving the dead rat where it lay, Oct'Tulommon stopped him.

"Wait! I can offer more than just rabbit, Peregrine."

He stopped and folded his wings back against his breast. The Peregrine turns to see Oct'Tulommon begin to break and fold, bursting out of himself into a man. Seeing such a horrific occurrence drew him in, transfixed by curiosity. The sight of the blood as the flesh tore enticed him.

"My, my, Oct'Tulommon, I've heard the story of this… they call it the moon array? How did you do it? Where did—"

"I killed this man you see before you some time ago on the other side of the fence. His son watched as I tore him apart. Now I can turn my body into his. It is excruciating, and his flesh is tight and ill-fitting." Oct'Tulommon explained as he walked closer into the sunlight. The Peregrine flew to the corner of the roof above him to look closer.

"Pay attention. Since we first met, I could feel what you desired in your heart. As much as you try to feign this persona of intimidation and status above all other creatures beneath you, I know in your heart your lust for the Earth, the urge to run through the wild, tearing flesh with teeth you don't possess, cracking bones with a strong jaw and the power of muscle. All the things your little frail body cannot do for you now. Tell me I am wrong, Peregrine? Tell me I am wrong, and I will leave you alone."

He stayed silent.

Oct'Tulommon scoffed. He stood tall and flexed his muscles, running his bloody hand through his long, wet hair.

"I will have all the creatures in this disgusting place convinced you are a god in the sky. I get you are useful; your ability to see the Earth from above is a significant advantage over us. Even if you cannot see that."

His exactness of the truth appalled the Peregrine. "What do you ask of me then, wolf?"

Oct'Tulommon changed back into a wolf. Again, the Peregrine watched with amazement as skin ripped and muscles tore again as he shed the coat of flesh.

"You will only answer to me. You will be my eyes in the sky whenever I ask for it. For this, I will make you a true god, your mind and your heart... inside a wolf."

The Peregrine's mind flooded with excitement. He tried his best to hold it all in.

"That's quite a respectable offering, Oct'Tulommon. But how do you plan to do so? I'm sure that magic in your body is not given or taken?"

Oct'Tulommon grabbed the discarded flesh with his mouth and flung it over the side of the roof, leaving a bloody smear on the weathered tin and wood. It hit the ground below with a squishy thud.

"Well, I have a brother whom I haven't spoken with in quite some time. We were never on good terms, but I aim to remedy our relationship with my newfound talents. Once I do, he will unlock the secrets to this... array I have stumbled upon, and then I will see that you get your reward."

The Peregrine stayed silent.

"I realize that there are a lot of unknowns here, but what do you have to lose?" Oct'Tulommon asked.

"Fine, I agree to your terms, Oct'Tulommon. If I spend my time doing your bidding and find out that this is all a ruse, I will make you pay for my time, wolf."

Oct'Tulommon smiled, he knew that there was nothing the bird could do to hurt him but he didn't say so; he just agreed.

"So, what will you have me do first? Spot you a good meal from the sky? Find out what your precious fractured wolves are doing in your absence?"

"First, I need you to go to the river's edge. Find my brother Vog'Morlinok and tell him I wish to speak to him."

Chapter 28
Smoke and Mirrors

Lying among the tattered remains of the Alpha's Hesperus wolves, Seph'Ulinok's battle wolves, and the cracked stones from the walls of the great hall, the Eldens call out to one another. The conduit between the four of them has been reduced to a tangle of confusion that only connected three. Li'Illnok was knocked unconscious by a stone that fractured his skull and tore his left ear. Seph'Ulinok suffered minimal damage, aside from two ruptured eardrums and several cuts that would heal given enough time. Volcrim Sul'Ilinok's fur was singed on his right flank, and cuts to his neck and back left exposed flesh that bled profusely. All of them were clamoring to find each other, except one.

Oct'Tulommon had successfully executed a surprise attack on the Illnok, utilizing his secret accomplice. Together they managed to plant explosives gathered in secret from the human cities across the river. Vog exited the great hall through the front entrance, without question or regard from anyone inside. From his hiding place in the trees below, he watched as his plan unfolded with no resistance. As the initial shock wore off, the remaining wolves gathered themselves back together while Vog'Morlinok made his way to a small cave by the riverside, where his brother and the Fractured wolves waited for him to arrive. The second wave of the attack was to begin soon.

"Li'Illnok! Li'Illnok! Where are you?!" Morgrim called out, his ears were caked with blood and still ringing from the force of the blast.

Everyone is dead… Everyone he thought as his eyes widened; he tried to process all the death and chaos around him.

"Pull it together; we aren't." Li'Illnok broke through the terror.

"I'm here with Seph, we're alive!" Volcrim whaled. "We cannot hear Vog though is he with you Li'Illnok?" that began to search frantically through the violence.

The sound of wolves yelping and whimpering in pain was momentarily muted by the message that permeated the air around the chaos. Everyone who still had a beating heart heard it.

"…EMBERS AND FLAMES THE TIME IS AT HAND."

"The fire must remain lit!" Elden Li'Illnok started to fumble his way closer to the remnants of the great fire. The firewood collection that had been stacked against the rock wall was strewn about, covered in blood. He grabbed what he could in his mouth and watched as several battered Hesperus wolves did the same, they flung them as fast as they could onto the fire.

"Where is Vog!?" He cried out again.

"I do not see him among the dead! I think he got out before the blast, Li'Illnok," Volcrim replied as he lifted stones off the dead and continued to help the wounded to safety.

"Eldens! Can all of you hear me?!" Morgrim called out to the three. They all respond with surprise. "Yes!"

"Li'Illnok! How is he able to raise all of us? He is no Elden wolf?" Volcrim asked.

"…I'm not sure! There will be time later for questions and answers. Listen to him now. Go on, Morgrim, speak to us!" Li'Illnok commanded.

"I don't know how but Ha'Kan he—" "His belly made a strange sound before it happened, I heard it, like the others around him." Seph stated.

"Yes, and I watched Vog leave his side quickly just before. It was like he almost knew what was going to happen."

Morgrim said. There was a tense silence.

"What do you speak of, Morgrim? Speak plainly; we do not have time to mince words now," Seph'Ulinok urged.

Morgrim could sense the mounting tension as the intensity in their hearts and minds surged. Like a smoldering fire that threatened to burst into uncontrollable flames, their emotions fed off one another and fueled their determination and resolve. Their thoughts raced, each one more intense than the last. It created a palpable energy that crackled in the surrounding air.

"I think he is responsible for this. I think he used Ha'Kan."

*

Vog'Morlinok had never run so fast in his life. His heart pounded from the adrenaline that coursed through his veins. As he arrived at a cave somewhere between the river's edge and the mountain, his brother was already there waiting for him.

"Vog! It's good to see you're still alive; what an awful sound that was!" Oct'Tulommon called out to him.

"Quick! We have to change to open the door. It won't be long until they send out the Border Wolves to find me. My actions have severed my connection between the Eldens and my mind. They can no longer sense my location. Once they realize I'm not dead, they will figure it the rest out."

The urgency in Vog'Morlinok's voice was palpable, and the tension between the brothers thickened the air. The cave, surrounded by gnarled trees and moss-covered rocks, seemed to swallow them as they entered, its shadows casting eerie patterns on the ground. The sound of the rushing river nearby underscored their need for haste.

As he transformed, Vog screamed in pain and vomited on himself as he dropped to the dirt in a violent convulsion. Once he finished, he worked hard to steady his breathing.

"Vog? Why is your human form different now? You look nothing like me?"

Oct'Tulommon questioned him, the face of his new body is that of a young man, clean-cut with stark blue eyes and a chiseled jaw. His muscles are strong, and he has tattoos covering his arms and legs.

"I will explain, give me a moment to pull myself together."

Once composed, he looked over to see Oct'Tulommon already changed and laughed at him.

"Shut your mouth Oct'Tulommon, you know it's extremely painful."

Vog was so nervous that he fumbled the keys to the padlock and dropped them in the dirt.

"Ha! Slow down, Vog! Let them come! It is already too late! I have an army of Fractured wolves lusting for blood, coming over that ridge any moment. They will be here long before the Illnok. And let me tell you, they're ravenous! Nothing will stand in our way."

Vog steadied his hand just long enough to feed the key into the padlock. The metal door clanked and creaked as it slowly opened.

"What is that wretched smell?" Oct'Tulommon said as the heavy metal door cracked open. "I will never get used to the human nose."

Vog stopped just inside the doorway of the room and turned to Oct'Tulommon.

"I assume you know that you have to have Awl'Fire to power the arrays?" Vog explained.

"Yes, but the more I change, the less I feel I need. It doesn't hurt as bad, and it's quicker."

"That's in part because you have aligned yourself with the void now…"

Oct'Tulommon seemed to be confused. As the Fractured wolves crested the hill and piled up in front of the cave entrance, the peregrine landed in a tree just above them.

"Oct'Tulommon!" He called out. "They have found Vog missing; they know he is not among the dead in the cave. The explosion drew the creatures and the pack wolves from the forests. They are all gathering around the Alphas Mountain to help with the wounded."

"That's a good bird, very good! Now, Vog, what are we doing here? What is the answer to this riddle?"

Oct'Tulommon's eyes gleamed with anticipation, and the tension in the air grew thicker as the Fractured wolves eagerly awaited their next move.

"When you told me that you changed after killing that man across the fence, what was it he said to you?"

Oct'Tulommon took a deep breath and closed his eyes, almost as if he was savoring the last pieces of a meal. "He begged me to spare his boy and take him instead, to end his life and stop the pain I caused. It was an emotional situation for him; he offered his life to me in order to save his offspring," Oct'Tulommon explained, his voice void of remorse.

"Therein lies the key, brother. The moon array is within us all, each wolf possesses the ancient power, but in order to wield it, a fire must be given! Freely given, or so I thought," Vog mused.

Oct'Tulommon laughed. "Ha, Vog. His life was not freely given; I took it from him in every respect of the word, I assure you."

"Yes, which brings me to my conclusion," Vog said, as he looked at the ground, trying to calculate an explanation.

"Perhaps we are different, our allegiance is to the void—"

"I despise that word, brother, 'Allegiance.' I swear no fealty to neither the void nor the Awl'Fire. Those are fantasies told to the affluent fat cubs of the Illnok!" Oct'Tulommon snapped, his voice dripped with scorn.

Vog stepped back, apprehensively. "Even so, you can't deny the fact that what we are engaging in is violence, a disruption of the natural order. I think the act of killing him in the manner you chose gave you tepid blood, and when you shared your blood with mine and I chose in my heart to align it with yours, my blood now runs tepid as well. It's getting easier for us to change because we are getting further from redemption."

Vog's demeanor changed as if he realized the weight of his decisions for the first time.

"These arrays were meant to be tools to build unity between humans and wolves, we are—" "spare me the history, Vog, I don't give a damn. Man has made a choice, that's evident by the ruins of their cities they once lived in. There is no hope for unity with such a useless species. We are the rightful wardens of this earth! We alone could've ascended the summit long ago and taken the arrays ourselves, but our ancestors were weak, We! are not!"

Vog fell silent, his eyes heavy with the burden of the choices he made.

The silence hung heavily between them for a moment, as the tension dissipated once more. The Fractured wolves outside the cave couldn't understand what they were saying since Vog and Oct'Tulommon were speaking with their human tongues. Determined to move forward, Vog struck a flint and lit a torch, illuminating the dim interior of the cave. He motioned for Oct'Tulommon to follow him deeper into the shadows.

"Watch your head, the rocks are hanging low in here." Vog warned as they ventured further into the darkness.

As the flickering light of the torch reached the back of the cave, it revealed a disturbing sight. Four men were chained to the rough stone walls, their faces gaunt and hollow from the extended time spent in darkness. Though they appeared well-fed, their eyes betrayed a deep fatigue, and their pale skin was a testament to their prolonged deprivation of sunlight.

Oct'Tulommon's eyes widened at the sight, his initial shock giving way to a twisted smile. " What have you been up to brother?"

Vog hesitated for a moment, the full weight of his actions now evident.

"Since I learned of your plans to infiltrate the alphas mountain, I've been gathering these... resources."

Oct'Tulommon edged closer to the nearest captive, his stark blue eyes taking in every detail of the man's weak and malnourished frame. He leaned in and sniffed the nape of the man's neck, inhaling the scent of fear and desperation that hung heavy in the air. He already knew the answer to the question that formed in his mind, but he posed it anyway, his voice dripping with anticipation.

"And what do you suppose we do with them, Vog?"

Vog switched to speaking through the void to Oct'Tulommon to ensure the prisoners could not hear their conversation. "We will let the Fractured wolves torture and feed on their flesh, just as you did with your likeness. They, too, will assume human form. Once they become stable on their new legs, we will march to the Great Hall. I've managed to bury a wooden crate stocked with various items we can use to aid us in the assault. Rifles, explosives, and canisters of smoke. We will prepare them and allow them to get used to their new bodies as we make our way there."

As Vog's plan unfolded, the torchlight cast ominous shadows on the cave walls, reflecting the darkness that now enveloped their hearts. Both brothers knew that there would be no turning back from the path they chose. The fate of the wolves and humans hung in the balance, and the darkness in their hearts threatened to consume everything in its path.

"I'm very impressed, Vog. You've been keeping yourself busy!" Oct'Tulommon remarked, his twisted grin only hinted at the twisted depths of his ambition. The air in the cave grew colder, and the flickering torchlight seemed to grow dimmer as the full extent of their treachery and cruelty to take shape.

Back outside Oct'Tulommon addressed the gathering of wolves that seemed to grow larger since they crossed through the border woods.

"I assume you all have had your fill of fresh meat since you are here now, are you ready for more?" The wolves howled in agreement.

"We are getting closer to the end, and full lives where every day will be exactly the experience you had today. Never again will your bellies be empty."

Oct'Tulommon didn't hesitate for a moment to consider the repercussions of their actions. The only thing he could see was the impending slaughter and the thrill of what would come after. He turns to Vog and gives the order.

"Bring them out on their chains and tie them to that old stump in the center."

he commanded, his voice cold and unfeeling.

Vog disappeared into the darkness of the cave, and the pitiful pleas of the weakened men echoed through the chamber, reaching the ears of all the Fractured wolves. Their hearts pounded in their chests as the naked, pale flesh of the captives was paraded before them. Vog looped the chain over a stump and walked back to stand beside his brother.

The naked men were very weak and could barely muster the strength to sob, desperately they tried to free the chain from the stump but their efforts were futile; they had no strength and being confined in a dark cave sapped them of what little energy they had left.

The wolves watched as the men struggled to keep their composure, shielding their faces from the burning sun, wincing in pain. It had been a long time since any of them had seen the light of day.

The chilling scene evoked a mixture of terror and sorrow, Vog couldn't help but empathize with the plight of the chained men, their eyes brimming with tears, and the mercilessness of Oct'Tulommon's actions. The air grew heavy with the weight of the impending bloodshed, a chilling reminder of the darkness that had taken hold of all the wolves' hearts.

Oct'Tulommon used both the human tongue and the void to speak, so the men clung to the stump and the Fractured wolves circled round them could both understand. He didn't need to speak out loud, but he did just to let the men inside the circle know what was about to happen to them.

"Understand me, wolves. The world of men does not care about you, your land, or what they have done to the kingdom they swore to protect long ago. They hunt us for sport, take our fur to make coats to warm their frail bodies, and destroy the land we once roamed freely in. They even stole our ancestors as cubs and bred them into the Druthe." Oct'Tulommon's voice was filled with contempt and anger.

The wolves were seething, foaming at the mouth as their eyes glazed over with rage. "Remember that and please, do your worst," Oct'Tulommon broke out in a sadistic laughter.

As the men huddled together for safety, the vicious onslaught commenced. First with a single bite to one man's leg, then another. As one man fell to the ground, clutching his torn calf muscle, the man beside him dropped both his elbows as fast and hard as he could, striking a wolf in the middle of his spine, breaking it in two. That same man lost his throat to another wolf. A few strikes landed from the men, but even more wolves were now entering the fray, eager to taste the blood pouring from the wounds.

Eventually their screams and their pleas for mercy faded into muffled moans of agony until they were completely drowned out by the sound of bones snapping and flesh tearing as the wolves ate their fill of the ragged men. They were no match for the wolves. The entire melee lasted only minutes, from the first attempt at defense to the last. Vog and Oct'Tulommon stood side by side as the blood from the blood from the violent clash reached their bare human feet.

"Now is your moment of truth. Be forewarned, the transformation will be excruciating at first; you will come close to your death. I won't lie to you; you will wish for it by the time it is done. But it will get easier. For those of you who don't make it through, I wish you luck when the Awl'Fire calls you home. He will not be happy with what we have done here," Oct'Tulommon said with a sardonic smile.

"Now, the next part is simple. All you must do is call forth the man you have locked inside of you now. Treat that poor soul as if it were... a pet, a slave living within you, only there for your use.

The chilling words hung in the air, casting a shadow of darkness and foreboding over the gruesome scene. The wolves' eyes were filled with determination and hunger, ready to embrace their twisted destiny, while the lifeless bodies of the men lay strewn across the ground, a stark reminder of the horrors that unfolded.

"Be forceful; he is scared, he is afraid of you. You need to show him your strength with violence," Oct'Tulommon commanded the trembling wolves.

At the end of the line, the last wolf whimpered and writhe in pain. He fell to the ground and violently shook, biting his tongue as his legs broke and his body split into two halves. The wolves were shocked that it worked. It was just how it was the first time they saw Oct'Tulommon change, only this time the wolf couldn't finish. He laid on the ground in a pool of blood, half shifted, his heart still beating but not for long.

"Damn you!" Oct'Tulommon cursed. "We can't afford to lose any of the rest of you. Hold yourselves together like wolves! Don't be weak like him."

He could tell they were all frightened now, given what they just witnessed.

"Do it! All of you! Do it now! Or I will adorn these woods with your insides myself!" Oct'Tulommon threatened, his voice filled with rage and impatience.

One by one, the wolves took deep breaths and closed their eyes. They ripped and tore at their own bodies, breaking bones and vomiting all over themselves. It sounded like torture, but it was working. After they shed their coats, the Fractured wolves, now enveloped in warm, bloody flesh, stood as tall as they could, twitching and crying, in awe of their new human forms.

"Very good! Look at us! You will not have a lot of time to get used to this new form, but you must by the time we get to the base of the mountain.

Not all the Fractured wolves were able to eat enough of the flesh to be rewarded with the ability to change, but enough did. As they staggered to their feet, their new human forms awkward and unfamiliar, they knew they were crossing a line from which there was no return. They had become the very monsters they despised, and together, they were a force to be reckoned with.

As the group of transformed wolves moved further away, a half wolf, half man amalgamation was left behind to die alone in a puddle of urine and blood. He tried to call to them, hoping one would have the decency to put him out of his misery before they left.

"Looks like no one is left to heed your calls, wolf? What a shame," a voice said from above.

"Please Falcon… take my Awl'Fire with you, see that it is put to good use against the wretched Illnok."

The Peregrine laughed sarcastically, "Did you not listen to anything your masochistic leader said? You're not aligned with the Awl'Fire any longer wolf, Your heart is full of the void."

The peregrine descended from his perch in the pines, looking around to ensure Oct'Tulommon and his wolves were out of sight. "And you are a fool if you think the Illnok is where he will stop.

"Please Falcon… I'm begging you!"

He hopped closer, surveying the grisly scene. "Will you give your likeness to me? Say it! You need to say it!"

"Yes! Yes! Anything you ask!"

With a determined look, the peregrine climbed into the wolf's rib cage through a split in his gut. The wolf's eyes practically popped out of his skull as he widened them in pain. The peregrine dug around inside, finding the weak heart beating against the gravel underneath. He used his beak to tear through the soft tissue until blood poured out vigorously killing the wolf within seconds. The cavity filled up faster than the peregrine expected, making his exit quite precarious. Once he made it out, he shook his feathers, spraying blood all over the wolf's lifeless face.

"You're welcome, friend. Good luck in the void." He said as he adjusted his feathers and swallowed a small chunk of the Wolves heart.

"I hope this works."

*

As the Elden wolves and Morgrim approached the Alpha's den at the top of the stone steps, they stopped, frozen in shock at the scene below, overwhelmed by the devastation below. Crimson pools of blood spilled over rocks and down corridors, while the sounds of pain and sadness echoed high in the stone arches above.

Further away, they saw alpha Ult'Ilinok catch his first glimpse of the bloodbath below. In shock, he tucked his tail and retreated once more into his den. Ult'Ilinok was in the same spot as before when Volcrim entered, his front paws just inches away from the edge.

"It wasn't supposed to happen this way, nothing like this was supposed to happen," Ult'Ilinok repeated, wide-eyed and staring into the chasm below the crystal blue falls.

"You! Bastard! Ult'Ilinok! There are countless dead below. Please tell me you didn't know!" Seph shouted, as Li'Illnok held him back.

"I had a border wolf tell me they were tracking a man, across a land bridge over the river north," Ult'Ilinok stammered, his voice trembled, laden with fear.

"He said they would always lose him in the darkness until just a few days ago, when he witnessed the man transform into a wolf. That wolf then traveled here, and now I see it clearly—that wolf was Vog."

As he spoke, the once-confident king seemed to shrink before the eyes of his pack, the weight of the revelation pressing down on him. His gaze darted nervously, in a desperate search for answers that would not come easily. The pack could see the fear and uncertainty in their leader, and they knew they were up against a dire threat, one that could unravel the very fabric of their existence.

The other Eldens were mortified. Even Li'Illnok, the most intellectual among them, had no idea.

"Did you not think to tell us about this?" Li'Illnok asked, his voice strained with disbelief and frustration. The weight of the situation settled heavily on their shoulders, as they tried to make sense of the carnage below and the potential danger that now loomed over their pack.

"He told me he was using the array to better the Illnok pack, to keep us healthy and safe. I was… going to tell you, but I didn't know how it would be received." Ult'Ilinok's voice wavered, reflecting the burden of his guilt and the enormity of his mistake.

"The Illnok trusted you to keep them safe, out of harm's way. This is your charge as alpha; you are no stronger a wolf than I or any of the other wolves in this room," Volcrim said, his voice filled with disappointment.

"...I should've known. He was just like his brother..." Ult'Ilinok whispered, turning back to the falls.

Li'Illnok's head snapped around. "His brother? Who is his brother, Ult'Ilinok!?" Silence filled the room.

"WHO IS HIS BROTHER!?" Volcrim's voice boomed against the walls.

"…He promised to show us the same mercy At'Linok showed his father." Ult'Ilinok turned to Li'Illnok, tears streamed from his wild eyes.

"I dare say to you, Alpha, I have lived longer than you, seen the reigns of Alphas more worthy than you come and go. The very tapestry of our lineage is woven in my heart, pa–" Li'Illnok's passionate speech was interrupted by Ult'ilinok.

"Passed down from your father and his father and his father, and so on and so forth… Li'Illnok, you're so long-winded, and you repeat the same verbose verses. Repeatedly. Honestly, I don't have the patience for it any longer." Ult'Ilinok's words shocked them all.

"I'm weak! I know! I have always been weak! The Alpha who sits on the Seat of Power, ha! I see that now, more than ever." His voice trembled with emotion. I had to do something; The void is close! I tried to be diplomatic, I tried to do it softly to not disturb the balance!"

"IT WASN'T SUPPOSED TO BE THIS WAY!"

He snapped, caught in an emotional whirlwind as he realized what he had done.

"I apologize. You all swore your fealty to me long ago, and that much is greatly appreciated. Your service is paramount to the survival of our home here and the safety of all. But I've squandered all of it. I don't deserve it anymore."

Morgrim stepped forward. Ult'Ilinok stopped speaking and teared up even more. "And you, Morgrim Orem'Exula: the Obsidian wolf, raised by a rabbit under the extreme conditions of the wretched outlands... Abandoned by his father wolf… Me..."

Morgrim remained silent.

"Well, that's why you are here, isn't it? To claim your rightful seat as my predecessor? Ha! You can have it! There is not a day that goes by that I wish I hadn't cast you out of my home. Even now, as you eyes are black, I can see my Selah. Trust me, Morgrim, the father you had was much more than I could have ever been to you."

Everyone was shocked by Ult'Ilinok's openness. He single-handedly made everyone in the room to question their existence and the value of the Illnok lands.

"If I have only one thing in this life that brings value to my name, let it be the truth. And the truth is… I caused all this."

Everyone remained silent as the sound of the falls behind Ult'Ilinok filled the void in their minds. It had been a tough day so far, and it was only going to get worse. Each one of them knew it.

"…Then you need to buy us time, Ult'Ilinok. If they are coming here, it's because he wants his Altapex with you. Fight him and win... or die. Either way, you have the power of the First Wolf and the arrays; you are the only one who can," Ha'Kan mentioned.

Ult'Ilinok remained silent.

"Instead of throwing yourself down into the depths of the cavern below, fight him.… Protect the Fire by killing him," Li'Illnok urged as he walked over to him.

"He is right, Ult'Ilinok, you need to make this right. Fight him, give us a chance to rebuild the fire." Volcrim said.

"It will be inconsequential; the fear in your heart is growing, the coal grows underneath cold flames..."

The voice that emanated from the walls is only heard by the alpha but it was bigger and much louder now. He Struggled to focus through the booming words that filled up his heart and mind.

"…I will do what I can..."

"Let's go, everyone; he needs some time to prepare," Li'Illnok ushers them all out of the room.

"Li'Illnok! Come here to me," Ult'Ilinok commands as they all leave the room.

"All of you, go; I will catch up."

"Li'Illnok, you must understand, he does not plan to keep any of us alive. He wants what's above us. And what's above wants him."

Li'Illnok's heart thudded with nervousness and fear. As he tried to listen for the void, the sounds of the carnage below and his beating heart filled the room. Amidst the chaos, the words came to him.

"He is coming to release me from my prison; there is nothing left for you to do but die and feed my power."

"Focus Li'Illnok! He has gained the power; all he needs is one final push. We cannot let it happen." The Alpha barks.

"I will fight with every fiber in my body, but I am weak and he is obviously very strong. He will kill me, and when he does, you need to be far away from here. Li'Illnok. There will be no end to the suffering he will unleash when he does. Not just for us wolves, but the entire world."

The air felt heavy with dread, and the shadows seemed to dance with sinister intent. The impending doom cast a pall over the entire room. Li'Illnok knew that the fate of their world rested on their shoulders, and he couldn't afford to let fear consume him. Determination filled his heart as he prepared for the battle ahead, knowing that every moment was precious.

As the group of wolves broke from the Alpha chamber, they were left with an emptiness. Morgrim never knew the difference an apology could make coming from his blood father. The thought of calling an Altapex against him never crossed his mind. But after he heard his name spoken with the adornment of such an illustrious title, it was now forever engraved in his thoughts. As they descended into the great hall once more, Rex'Onok lined up another regiment of battle wolves, and what little Hesperus that remained were readying themselves for another attack. The Great Flame seemed to be holding steady, but it was half the size of what it was the first time Morgrim saw it.

"We have to see as many of these wolves out of the lands as possible, and we must do it quickly. If Ult'Ilinok is right about Vog returning with Oct'Tulommon, then they will eradicate anyone left standing in the great hall," Volcrim said.

Seph called out to Rex. "Gather a few wolves, Rex, and send them to the southern cliff, let us make that the rallying point if all goes wrong. We need to ensure the survival of the Illnok wolves now. Tell them to take shelter there until we come to see them home."

"Where will you go?" Seph asked Volcrim. Someone needs to see Li'Illnok to safety, if he dies, the array of knowledge dies with him. It must remain.

Seph stood to the right of the entrance to the great hall. After Rex moved his wolves out, he was explaining the escape plan to the Hesperus wolves when a sharp crack could be heard from the trees outside the entrance.

A bullet struck him on the right side, just below his shoulder. Li'Illnok and Volcrim immediately winced in pain. They didn't see him get hit, but they felt it, just as he did. As they turned to look and see what happened, they saw several battle wolves get hit by a spray of bullets. Two men, with assault rifles, laid waste to all the wolves that stood below the steps. Behind the two men were at least ten more with machetes and handguns and about twenty more Fractured wolves. It was a complete bloodbath; they showed no mercy, the execution of one wolf right after another. Seph was one of them.

The two men in front were Vog'Morlinok and Oct'Tulommon.

"Li'Illnok, we have to leave; we cannot save them!" Morgrim shouted. Li'Illnok sobbed as he hid behind the rock ledge at the top of the staircase.

As the two of them took aim at the wolves inside the great hall, Oct'Tulommon called for him.

"Ult'Ilinok!" His voice echoed alongside the cracking of gunfire.

Volcrim growled, it caught Oct'Tulommon's attention. It reverberated through the hall, a mixture of anger, pain, and defiance, as the wolves that remained tried to shield themselves from the onslaught. The air was thick with tension, as the smell of blood and the sound of gunfire filled the once-sacred space.

"Look at all the familiar faces!" Oct'Tulommon had an ego about him that was sickening. "My brother did a fantastic job rearranging this place." Oct'Tulommon walked in their direction but stopped short of the first step, he stood still as he watched Ult'Ilinok descend the stairs behind Li'Illnok, Volcrim and Morgrim. They hadn't noticed until he passed them by. Oct'Tulommon laughed at the first sight of him.

"So, this is the great Alpha Ult'Ilinok! I don't think we ever cordially met, you and I left these lands before you annexed my inheritances."

"If you want your Altapex, Oct'Tulommon, then your fight is with me, not them."

"Haha! That's not so, Alpha. My fight is with all of you, the ones that are left anyway."

Morgrim seized the opportunity while Oct'Tulommon was distracted to gather the Eldens together behind a pillar of granite, out of the way of stray bullets and shrapnel.

"I see you, Morgrim! He smiled as he looked back at Vog.

"Send word to the Fractured down the path. if they see them leave, follow; don't let them get out of the border woods."

Volcrim and Li'Illnok were absolutely devastated emotionally, but they did their best to fight off the random Fractured wolves that found them hiding behind the stone. Their faces were a mix of anguish and determination as they battled to protect their comrades. Morgrim was still present, but he was silent as he tried to hold himself together the best he could. He took satisfaction in watching the large, fearsome Elden wolf Volcrim obliterate the fractured wolves. Each powerful bite from Volcrim seemed to echo the pain and anger he felt inside.

Morgrim held his own as well, strong and full of the Awl'Fire. He fought for the right cause and it gave him an intense sense of purpose. His movements were swift and precise, cutting down any Fractured wolves that dared to approach. His eyes shone with determination, unwilling to let his newfound family be harmed any further.

Down below on the ground floor of the great hall, the intensity of the attack was relentless. The clash of teeth and snaps of gunfire filled the air as the Illnok wolves fought bravely against the onslaught. Fresh blood added a second coat to the once-pristine stone floors, a stark reminder of the price they were paying for their survival. With each fallen wolf, the resolve of those who remained only grew stronger, but as each fire was taken, the void grew in strength.

Part VII: Cataclysms

Chapter 29
The Altapex

(Oct'Tulommon Vs. Awl Alpha Ult'Ilinok)

Oct'Tulommon broke away from his brother. He transformed into his wolf form and discarded the used flesh of Lennon Grenlow in front of the great fire. His massive tongue licked his lips as he stretched out his neck muscles, his eyes filled with a dark hunger for violence and victory.

"Let all who are present in this great hall of death hear me. I, ire wolf Alpha Oct'Tulommon of the Outlands, invoke the sacred Altapex and challenge Alpha Ult'Ilinok of the Illnok wolf pack."

The Fractured wolves created a barrier circled around Oct'Tulommon and Ult'Ilinok. It ensured that no one could stop him once he started the invocation. The few Hesperus wolves left in the great hall were soaked in blood, injured and pleading with the Awl'Fire and the army of twisted human-like husks for mercy. Desperately they tried to stoke the flames but were executed one by one. The constant rumble of the stones seemed to grow louder under the weight of the impending battle.

Ult'Ilinok sighed, gritted his teeth and listened as Oct'Tulommon's men put bullets in the heads of the wolves. The ones that cried the loudest were the first.

It had been years since another challenged Alpha Ult'Ilinok, but never on a scale as large and brutal as this. He had become old, fat, and out of shape. A life of laziness and leisure took away his youthful vigor and left his muscles stiff and his bones brittle. Though that didn't matter in this fight. He knew he would not walk away from Oct'Tulommon as the victor. He made peace with it.

"Well?" Oct'Tulommon's eyes burned. "What is your answer, old wolf? Do you except?"

"Oh, I'm sorry, Oct'Tulommon. In all your rambling, I missed the question. I heard you decorate your name with the embellishment of Alpha, though. That's quite a jump in standing for a band of misfits in a wasteland. I take it they didn't have a choice in the matter?"

Oct'Tulommon scoffed at him. "The arrogance in your words is apparent. Do you accept my challenge? Or will I just kill you without a fight?"

"I don't really think it matters much what I say now. You're going to kill me, regardless."

Ult'Ilinok twisted his head from side to side and tried to work the stiffness out. It popped and cracked like dead limbs being snapped from a tree. His fur stood straight out and made him appear larger and more ferocious than he already was. He planted his claws into the cracked stones of the great hall's blood-soaked floor and prepared.

"I accept."

As soon as the words left Ult'Ilinok's mind, Oct'Tulommon's eyes sank into his massive skull and returned as two haunting, iridescei white orbs. In an instant, he evaporated into the void. The great hall fel silent. The only sounds left were the crackling of the fire and the rumbling of the stones. Ult'Ilinok watched as a crowd of terrified pack wolves around the territory formed at the great hall's entrance.

"Come! Every wolf here is in the balance now; there are no sides until the Altapex is complete, and the new alpha is crowned. The circumstances that contributed to this matter not!" Oct'Tulommon called from the void. Ult'Ilinok felt the weight of his own helplessness as the pack wolves came to the circle. They stepped over the bodies of their brothers and sisters, their fur saturated with blood.

"I'm... I'm so sorry I couldn't protect you all..." Ult'Ilinok lamented, staring into the frightened eyes of his pack.

"everyone! you need to run!" Ult'Ilinok's mind pulsed as he felt the air shift. But it was too late. More fractured and human-like abominations already started up the hill to swarm the great hall's entrance. Forcing all those in attendance to stay until the Altapex is over and the new alpha takes his place.

Oct'Tulommon reappeared behind him and sank his fangs deep into his neck. Ult'Ilinok's eyes shut tight as bolts of flashing agony ripped through his body. He took another deep breath and centered his mind.

The fire in the center of the room grew higher and higher. As if fanned by an invisible wind. His eyes turned white just like Oct'Tulommon's and he disappeared, leaving Oct'Tulommon's mouth hinged wide open and empty. He could hear him laugh from the void.

"I guess we all have our tricks to play."

Ult'Ilinok reappeared on the opposite side of the circle amid a full sprint. He slammed into Oct'Tulommon's right flank with a thunderous boom. Together, they slid across the bloody stones into the pit of white ash. Oct'Tulommon struggled to get to his feet. He clamored to get his head higher than the thick cloud of ash that suffocated him. He was in a panic. Ult'Ilinok reappeared on top of him, landing a heavy, critical bite to the neck, breaking his black rusted chain, and sent it deep into the ash pit. He forced Oct'Tulommon's face down as hard as possible in an attempt to suffocate him in the white ash. But Oct'Tulommon slid into the void again, to escape asphyxiation. His reserve of the void was depleted. It allowed him only as far as the side of the pit before it expelled him. Back into the living plane. Ult'Ilinok grabbed his hip as he tried to run. He pulled his lower half back in. Oct'Tulommon locked eyes with one of the Fractured, calling out to him. Without hesitation, the wolf ran to his aid, not to get him out of the pit but offering his throat to be crushed instead.

Oct'Tulommon leaned down and took hold, killing him almost instantly. Ult'Ilinok was disgusted with the display of mindless loyalty. "Is this what you are?" He addressed the outland wolves.

"fuel for his bloodlust? Where do you think your flames go when he is done squandering it?"

They didn't seem phased. Using the stolen flame from the sacrifice, he slipped into the void again. Ult'Ilinok climbed from the pit, every hair on his body covered by white ash, his determination unwavering.

"You look like a ghost, Ult'Ilinok, but don't be in such a hurry. You will be one soon enough."

Oct'Tulommon stood at the other end of the circle, as far away from the pit as he could get, his lungs full of ash. He coughed and heaved until he vomited, gasping for air.

Once freed from the pit and the ash cloud, Ult'Ilinok looked down beside him to see the lifeless husk of the dead wolf. He found his footing again and sprinted into Oct'Tulommon head-on. The power knocked him clean off of his feet. Ult'Ilinok landed several bites on his opponent's chest and face. He tore large swathes of fur from his neck and a portion of his lower lip blood dripped from the fresh wounds. He tried his best to free himself from the flurry, but every time he landed a counterstrike, Ult'Ilinok flashed into the void and instantly freed his jaws. The fire in the center of the great hall faltered. Unable to provide enough power for Ult'Ilinok's void array.

"Haha. The fire falters Alpha. Whatever will you do now?"

Ult'Ilinok pulled himself away. Shocked that Oct'Tulommon wasn't defending himself.

"The void. It's so much more…reliable." Oct'Tulommon said as his eyes turned white. Ult'Ilinok looked to the right and witnessed a replica of the demon wolf just a few feet from his neck. Underneath him, Oct'Tulommon laughed as he faded out of existence.

"There are many useful ways to use it if you are willing to sacrifice."

Ult'Ilinok backed away. He spotted three Hesperus wolves move in silence to the opposite end of the great fire. Throwing cord after cord of wood in, as many as they could before Vog'Morlinok spotted them. He made his way over with the rifle, but before he could pull the trigger, the three wolves flung themselves into the flames. Ult'Ilinok felt anger surge through him. The needless death and destruction of the day on both sides of the conflict was overwhelming.

"Ha! That was noble!" Oct'Tulommon said sarcastically.

Ult'Ilinok felt the intensity of the flame grow higher and higher. His body pulsed with power. He sauntered toward Oct'Tulommon as his fur smoldered and smoked and his eyes burned brighter and brighter. Oct'Tulommon cowered in fear and hid his face from the fierce light in Ult'Ilinok's eyes. It was a turn of events he wasn't prepared for.

"Oct'Tulommon, stand up!" Vog'Morlinok yelled.

"STAND UP AND FACE HIM!"

The great hall vibrated with tension as Oct'Tulommon was reluctant to face the burning figure. The once confident and brutal wolf was now confronted with the ignited fury of a powerful Alpha rooted with the Awl'Fire and his ultimate purpose. The outcome of their battle hung in the balance, both sides watched with bated breath. Oct'Tulommon collapsed in fear as he looked up to see the Alpha burst into flames. His fur singed by the rolling flames that disappeared from the pit in the great hall and now surrounded Ult'Ilinok.

"Give me every last flame from him, and I will give you all you desire, Oct'Tulommon."

The voice grew into a presence that dominated every creature's attention. The sound of it pulsed with colossal strength. Oct'Tulommon's fur was consumed completely on the left side of his body his visible flesh had been boiled. Just before Ult'Ilinok reached a distance close enough for a strike, a single shot resonated through the great hall. It ripped through Ult'Ilinok's chest and stopped him in his tracks. He looked to see Vog'Morlinok with his gun raised in his direction.

"NOOO!" Oct'Tulommon screamed as Vog lined up the second shot.

It was perfect. Ult'Ilinok could not react in time. The bullet entered his left eye and exploded through the back of his skull before it lodged in the rocks behind him. The spray of his blood and brain matter covered them. His lifeless body dropped to the floor and the fire that enveloped it formed a vortex. Slow at first but quicker as the vortex wrapped tighter and tighter. It rose higher in the Great hall before it slipped through a small crack in the cavern above, a crack caused by the explosives. Every wolf and man around the great hall couldn't believe what happened. As Vog'Morlinok lowered the gun, Oct'Tulommon stood to see the focus turn away from him.

He had been forged...

"Elden Vog'Morlinok; The Brother of Oct'Tulommon, Deceiver of wolves and keeper of the Moon array. The Alpha of the Illnok territory."

A thunderous clap boomed from the stones above. A crack splintered across the length of the rocks above. Hulks of granite and quartz, some small, some large enough to break bones and pin bodies to the ground, rained down on the crowd below. Those that fell into the fire pit sent hot ash and red-hot coals in every direction. The constant rumble intensified as a chorus of wolves yelped with fear. From above, a cascade of tentacle-like appendages reached and clasped outcroppings and jutting rocks, easing its attached unformed body into a slow and calculated descent from the darkness above. A sentient collection of the void in a conscious state of darkness. It stretched and unfurled its body out after ages of imprisonment above the fire.

Vog'Morlinok's improvised explosive device, weakened the hold of the mountain, and with all the violence and bloodshed in concentration. The Axael; The fabled creature encapsulated in the stones above the fire for ages, was set loose.

Morgrim and the two Eldens that remained, Volcrim and Li'Illnok. Watched the Altapex from the balcony above, too occupied by attacking Feral wolves to have done anything to stop it from beginning. The four watched in shock and disbelief as Vog's perfectly aimed shot echoed through the great hall. They could only watch in horror as the Awl'Fire left the Alpha's dying body.

"What is that great thing?!" Volcrim exclaimed.

Li'Illnok was silent. *The Axael*... Shocked by the realization that all he thought was a myth was confirmed, and now loose.

"Still yourself Elden!" Li'Illnok warned him.

"There is nothing left here for us to do. We need to go. Save as many wolves as we can," he said as they dodged falling rocks.

"Let us go to the southern cliffs. El'Wren is with a regiment of battle wolves. They may be our last hope." Morgrim said. As the chaos of the great hall escalated around them, the group hastened towards a tunnel, secluded behind a rock wall in the Alpha's den, their hearts heavy with the burden of responsibility. The path before them was treacherous, lined with the remnants of a once-proud pack now devastated by Vog and Oct'Tulommon's actions. They knew they had to press on, for the future of their kind depended on their ability to rally the wolves that remained. From outside the mountain, a great exodus of all creatures, big and small, turned to watch as a solid column of darkness spewed from the base of the Alpha's mountain. The clear smoke-filled sky appeared to be split in half by it. A pillar pierced through the heavens above, an ominous sight that filled them all with dread.

"It's horrifying, but beautiful all at the same time." Li'Illnok expressed as he limped backward. "It broke through the floor of its prison. The balance is now in its favor...." Li'Illnok said with a sullen tone.

Inside the great hall, the remaining wolves, both of the Fracture and Illnok, retreated from underneath the massive creature, descended from the loose rocks above.

"Vog!!! What have you done!?"

Oct'Tulommon shouted in pain. His leg was pinned underneath massive chunk of slate. Vog was in shock. He dropped his rifle and watched the void take an enormous gulp of air into its folding chest.

"What have I done…" Vog said. He sank back into his wolf form and stood in the gathering of raw flesh and broken bones of his human skin.

"In the grand tapestry of existence, you creatures believed you could confine the embodiment of darkness? The Endless Void? Yet, you failed to comprehend the fundamental nature of the cosmos, where malevolence has a way of seeping through the very fabric of reality. Your faith in your world's flawed beliefs and secrets has led to this moment of reckoning,"

The Axael spoke with an eerie calm directly to Vog.

"Throughout the annals of time, I watched from above, through the breaks and cracks all around this mountain. False knowledge has been passed on, but only to a select few. The Elden Sayers of this…failed tribe of creatures, the keepers of stories and histories, withheld the truth from all, the truth about what their ancestors locked away above. I remained contained until now. Thanks to you and your efforts."

Vog's eyes brimmed with tears as the weight of his decision to conspire with his brother settled in. The devastation that unfolded in the great hall was only the prelude to the true dread that now jeopardizes the realm. They shattered the unity among all beings, and a new darkness loomed.

The creature, a living embodiment of the void, extended its long, sinuous arms and gathered the last flickers of fire from the dying wolves. He gathered it into a pulsating ball of energy that swelled into its chest. The power was absorbed, and the flames were snuffed out, leaving only lifeless husks in its wake.

"I have suffered this realm and all these creatures here for too long. You, Vog'Morlinok, will go to the world of man as my emissary. You will grow the void that is in their hearts, and when the time is right, I shall return to claim it all for The Endless Void."

Oct'Tulommon, realized the gravity of the situation. He wrenched his leg from its socket to free himself from the crushing rock. Desperate and defiant, he called out to the creature of the void.

"Look at me!" he barked to gain the Axaels' attention. "It was I who united this fractured pack of feral wolves and brought the Moon Array to life! I deserve the title of emissary, ancient one! Grant me this, and I will usher in the apocalypse in your name!"

The void turned its gaze upon him. Its eyes resembled the swirling darkness of the cosmos, cold and unfathomable. Oct'Tulommon grew weaker as his blood poured from the gaping wound where his leg used to be.

"You cannot be the one, wolf. Your heart is full of hatred, evil and anger, merely a precursor to what lives within your brothers. His heart is heavy with remorse and regret for the things he has done but cannot change—that is the true essence of the void."

Vog's face contorted with the unbearable weight of his new destiny and the understanding of the difference between him and his brother. Oct'Tulommon was evil, but Vog had transcended.

"Alpha Vog'Morlinok of the Void lands. I leave you to do your duties."

Chapter 30
Rabbit Tombs

"Hurry now, we must hurry; the others will be waiting for us on the other side of the mountain," Unis urged, doing her best to keep the younglings engaged in steady movement. Shepherding a herd of scarred rabbit younglings from certain death was not something Unis ever thought she would have to do.

"My legs are tired!"

"I'm hungry!"

"Are we almost there yet?"

"We are my mother and father?"

She had the same questions bounce around in her mind a million times, and they weren't even halfway to their destination. The scent of smoke wafted through the tunnel from behind her. It cast an edge of heaviness to the situation. She was terrified.

"Mulgris was right about everything." she thought. Hoping he and Burren made it out in time before they were swept up in the chaos by Oct'Tulommon and his fractured wolves. Behind her, she counted roughly twelve younglings and three adult rabbits as more swarmed in through the feeder tunnels above. They all shared Mulgris's plan: to head east.

"Unis! Has Nilian found you yet? I heard a rabbit say he left for the mountain; to warn the wolf Alpha. Did they know Oct'Tulommon was coming?"

"Have you heard from Mulgris, Unis?!"

"Will we be okay?!"

The adults had their own set of repetitive questions. She faced an endless barrage of inquiries with which she had no answer for.

"Stop! All of you! Just stop!" Unis shouted. Her patience wore thin. "I know as much as you about what's going on. Yes, Nilian left in a hurry to warn the mountain; that's all I can tell you. And yes! If you keep moving and stop holding everyone up to ask the same damned questions, we will be fine!"

The crowd in front and behind fell silent all at once.

"Now, let's keep moving, shall we? We have to be quick. And stay quiet!"

With that, the group resumed their journey, their resolve strengthened by Unis's words. The weight of their collective survival hung in the air, driving them forward with renewed determination.

They plodded, but soon they fell into a rhythm and moved more swiftly. The sound of their little feet pattering in the silence of the tunnels was rhythmic and soothing.

After a solid hour of darting through tunnels and burrows, the smoke from the borderline fires dissipated into a faint tinge in their small noses. In its absence, the fresh air from the mountainside swept in to take its place. Unis knew they were close to the mountain's eastern side when she caught the scent of magnolia trees and the lilac that bloomed in the rolling hills of the far side. She visited her grandmother there when she was a youngling, playing all day in the sun and watching the wind blow the dandelion spores into the air, catching them as they escaped into the sky.

"It smells like flowers here!" one youngling said, leading to a chorus of sniffling. Unis smiled. She could hear giggling over the sound of all the little noses.

"That's the li—" Just as she attempted to explain, a pulse of pressure from the explosion in the great hall collapsed the surrounding tunnel.

"RUN!" Unis yelled as the rabbits scurried out in every direction. She saw beams of light slice through the shifting dirt and rock above. Rabbit holes that led up disappeared as the earth choked them.

She watched as the younglings were suffocated under rocks in the ground all around her. She tried to push them to safety as she ran past, throwing the ones she could into burrows lined with bigger stone and denser packed dirt. With more rabbits ahead of her in the tunnel, she herself was caught in the cave-in.

Once the earth stopped falling around her, Unis found herself confined to a narrow tunnel section with five younglings and three adults. Two were injured. The dust choked air only added to the encroaching darkness. Despite looming panic and despair, Unis stayed resilient for the others' sake.

"We need to find a way out." Unis's voice was steady, despite the fear that gripped her. "Okay little ones, Let's search the walls for any cracks or weak spots. Together, we will make it through this."

With determination, the small group of rabbits set to work, hoping against all the odds that they would escape their earthen prison and reunite with their kin on the other side of the mountain.

"It must've been an earthquake?" one rabbit speculated.

"No, an earthquake? In these parts? That's unheard of." another disagreed.

"It was an explosion. I know because I've been through this before. The humans, they used explosives and blew apart my last burrow in the West. I was a youngling then. This was just like that," an older rabbit with an injured leg explained.

"What did you do to get out?" One youngling asked, eyes wide with curiosity.

"We did what rabbits do best; we dug!" the older rabbit replied. They had air from above and light to see. They were fortunate to be underneath a rabbit hole that had only partially caved in. But the stones that filled it from each side were too heavy and too big to move.

"What are you waiting for? Get to digging! You're going to be heroes when this is done and over!" he encouraged. The younglings' fear dissolved.

Unis watched as he grimaced. His leg had been struck by a falling rock that caused a compound fracture. He hid it from the younglings, knowing it would have only scared them. "Thank you," Unis said.

"Mal'Rey, Mal'Rey Orem Exula," He introduced himself.

"Ha!" she laughed. "Is there not a rabbit in the Illnok lands that isn't related to Finnick?!"

He joined in her laughter. "I don't suppose there is, my lady. Quite the lover, so I'm told… Charged by the pound."

Unis laughed harder than she had in a while, at least since the last time she saw Finnick. He was unquestionably related to him. "Seriously though, what are we going to do? We're stuck here."

Mal'Rey winced in pain, but somehow, he stayed optimistic, with a good sense of humor. "Stuck between a rock and a hard place, we are."

As the scent of damp earth filled their nostrils, the trapped rabbits dug, their tiny paws clawed through the soil with determination. The once quiet space now echoed with the sounds of their labor, and the air grew heavy with the smell of sweat and effort. Each moment that passed brought them closer to freedom, their hope and determination propelled them forward, and despite their dire situation, the camaraderie and laughter created a warm atmosphere between them.

Together, they faced the challenge head-on and refused to give in to despair. As they excavated, the once dimly lit tunnel glowed with a sense of hope and resilience.

Chapter 31
Of One Mind

"Mal'Rey? Are you awake?" Unis called out softly. It had been at least three hours since Unis and Mal'Rey had become trapped beneath the Earth, surviving the cave-in from the explosion in the great hall. Shortly after the younglings begun securing their freedom, another quake occurred among the tunnels. A result of the Void's escape from its prison above the fire in the great hall. It shifted more dirt and rocks on top of them but didn't hinder their resolve to escape. They were considerably luckier than their brothers and sisters from the Illnok burrows, but time was of the essence on the eastern side of the Alpha's mountain. Mal'Rey's injuries stopped bleeding, but the pain was still very present in his leg. "Mal'Rey! Are you okay? We need to show you something!" one youngling nudged him, barely moving his large body.

"Yes, I'm awake, youngling. Have you finished that tunnel yet?" He questioned, not expecting much.

"Well, we found something you should come and see. We think it may be important."

Mal'Rey stood the best he could on his wounded leg and walked to Unis to wake her. "Unis… Unis? Wake up; these younglings have something to show us again."

Unis slowly rose from the dirt. This wasn't the first time they were roused by the younglings to see something that they'd found encased in the Earth. They had been digging for a while in several directions, trying to tap into a tunnel that could lead them away safely. So far, they had only found air pockets. The Adult rabbits decided to forbid the younglings from digging back from where they were. Most of the younglings' loved ones were smothered to death in the collapse.

"This better not be another funny-shaped rock," she said to Mal'Rey. He snickered. "Don't get your hopes up my lady. If there's one thing I've learned about these younglings, if there's a funny-shaped rock beneath the mountain above… They will find it…"

Unis took the lead right behind the group of excited younglings. Mal'Rey lagged but did his best to keep up the pace. It hadn't been long since the last time the younglings summoned them to the end of their tunnel, but they made quite a bit of progress.

"Wow… I'm actually kind of surprised at the size of this tunnel. You rabbits are doing a swell job, better than I could do at your age," Unis was impressed by their efforts, as she bumped her head on a rock jutting down from the roof. "Watch it, my lady!"

Mal'Rey grimaced as he spoke. He felt the pain in his leg worsening.

"HERE! Come quick!" One of the younglings called.

The closer they got to the end of the tunnel; they saw the younglings lined up at the edge of a drop. The tunnel was dim, but there were beams of light reaching out from an opening further down from where they were standing. It looked like the river emptied into a shallow body of water.

"I hope you know how to swim, Unis… I think these younglings just saved our lives." Mal'Rey's eyes gleamed with hope.

Mal'Rey and Unis smiled, unable to believe their luck. "Well done, lads! Well done indeed! Haha!" Mal'Rey exclaimed, his laughter echoed through the tunnel. He sent one of the younglings to return and gather the remaining survivors. It would be risky, but it was their only chance of survival.

As the rest of the rabbits filtered in from the younglings' tunnel, they all stood at the cliff's edge and studied the water for a bit. It was ice-cold, most likely runoff from the mountain above. It was also moving extremely fast. The margin for error was minimal.

"Listen up, everyone. This is the plan. That light coming up from underneath is from a hole. A hole that most likely leads to–" "what do you mean? Most likely? You mean you're not sure?!" a nervous rabbit interrupted Mal'Rey. His voice quivered in fear.

"All I know is that there's a lot of light. Most likely, it's a hole at the bottom of a shallow spring. It's impossible to tell from here." "I'm… not going…" the nervous rabbit interjected again, defiance in his voice.

"Whoa, calm down there, friend. There's no need to be afraid. Rabbits are excellent swimmers. We'll just take it nice and slow." Unis implored, she looked at Mal'Rey and waited for him to take control of the situation.

"What if we get in there and there's no way out? What if we're trapped in the water?!"

The fear in the rabbit's voice was contagious and Mal'Rey could sense the younglings growing uneasy.

"Listen, friend, you need to calm down; you're scaring the—" "YOU THINK I CARE?! You're asking us to risk our lives on 'most likely?!"

Before anything else could be said, the bickering rabbits heard a splash behind them, followed by droplets of icy cold water spraying them. Unis took it upon herself to be the first to jump in.

"Bloody hell!" Mal'Rey exclaimed as he watched her in astonishment. "I like this rabbit! Haha."

They watched with bated breath as Unis effortlessly swam down with the current and up through the hole at the bottom. Once through, she disappeared for a while. They waited anxiously to see if she would return, but she never did.

"Well, that doesn't prove anything. Great job, Mal'Rey. Now what?" the nervous rabbit complained.

"Wait a damn minute! Quiet!" Mal'Rey hushed the others.

"Look!" One of the younglings exclaimed. Unis reappeared, gripping the side of the hole. She motioned for the rest to follow. One by one, the younglings jumped in, swimming like tiny, furry fish through the emerald light of the hole.

"Well! Would you look at that! See you on the other side, friend!" Mal'Rey called out, about to follow the others.

"Wait!" the nervous rabbit yelled out. "I can't... I can't swim."

Mal'Rey paused and hopped over the best he could to the nervous rabbit. "Well, you could've just said that friend!"

He tightly wrapped his front paws around the trembling rabbit and pushed off the rocks, sending both of them diving into the fast-moving current.

Mal'Rey; considerably bigger and more muscular than any other rabbit in the burrow, had no trouble making it through the hole, even with his injured leg.

Once through, they found themselves in warmer, still water. For a moment, it felt like they were floating through thin air. Fish swam by bright-colored anemones waved gently, and shelled crustaceans moved about peacefully. Above them, about thirty feet up, was the surface. They could see the tinged gray sky dotted with ash and puffs of smoke and dust. A shiver of relief and excitement ran down Mal'Rey's spine at the sight of the daylight, even though it looked like something terrible happened.

Once they broke the surface, the nervous rabbit gasped for air like he hadn't taken a breath in decades.

"What the hell Mal'Rey?! How dare you?!" the nervous rabbit said furiously. His legs buckled as he jerked away from Mal'Rey in an attempt to gain a footing on the spring's side.

"What? Not even a thank you!? I just saved your furry little a—"

"Mal'Rey!" Unis interrupted before the young rabbits could hear what he was about to say.

"This place is so nice." One of the younglings exclaimed as he smelled the flowers a little beyond the water's edge. The little sunlight that could seep through the clouds of smoke; beamed off all the different colored flowers blooming around the spring. The pleasant scent mixed with the smoke from the burning forest around the great hall's entrance. Mal'Rey didn't mention the hints of the other smell that lingered in the air, the same scent from the CDC burn pits in the west.

"I'll find you some wild lettuce before we go back down. It will help ease your pain. We need to leave this place as quickly as we can, though. Mulgris warned me not to show our faces topside until we got further south." Unis said nervously.

"Everyone, keep your heads down and watch your surroundings. We don't know what's lurking on this side of the mountain." Mulgris warned.

*

The rabbits continued south for the rest of the afternoon, searching for a place to duck back underground. Since the explosion crumbled the Earth, they didn't get far from where they started. It was not a good situation. The Fracture could be heard everywhere, barking and howling, hunting and killing anything they could to fill their insatiable appetites. The lush green forests and rolling hills of tall grass give way to flat plains. Hot, dried grass covered gritty limestone sand dotted with thickets of thistle weed and prickly bushes. Not a rabbit hole to be found.

"Mal'Rey, we have to find a hole soon. This is starting to worry me."

"Don't worry, we will soon enough. Those wolves aren't close, and we are downwind from the mountain. I don't suspect they even know we're here." He tried to comfort her, but even he was beginning to worry. Not of the wolves, but of the other creatures that called this part of the Illnok home.

"Look!" One of the younglings ahead of them spotted something in the distance.

Mal'Rey saw three or four tiny little mounds on the horizon, like miniature volcanoes.

"Those are rabbit holes! I'm sure of it!" one of the younglings exclaimed as he took off. Mal'Rey could sense something wasn't right; Those holes were not made by rabbits. Perhaps ground squirrels or prairie dogs." He said to Unis.

"Hey! Over here, you guys! I'm going in!" As the youngling stopped by the side of the hole, he turned his head down and looked

301

inside, only to find the remains of two dead baby ground squirrels. He gasped and backed away. Mal'Rey halted.

"It's just a hole full of fur and bones!" The youngling was disgusted.

"What? What is it, Mal'Rey?" Unis asked, her voice full of concern. Mal'Rey's nose twitched as he picked up a strong scent carried by the wind.

"Round everyone up and get under that thistle bush. Start digging as fast as you can. I'll distract them," Mal'Rey didn't break eye contact with the younglings that were now backing away from the hole.

"Distract what Mal'Rey?" Unis asked, but he didn't answer.

He took off quickly, racing to save the young rabbits. Unis watched him, shielding her face from the sand he kicked up. As the dust cleared, she saw a giant red-tailed hawk swoop and snatch one of the younglings up just before Mal'Rey could reach him. All the rabbits gasped, their eyes wide with disbelief.

"Everyone, get under the bush and start digging now!" Unis commanded; her voice trembled. Panic set in as the other rabbits heard the youngling's screams from above, gripped in the strong claws of the hawk.

The predator hadn't come alone to the prairie to hunt; two more hawks followed. They'd stalked the rabbits since they left the spring, waiting for the right time to strike. Mal'Rey was furious with himself. He had been too focused on Unis and potential threats from the ground that he forgot to look up.

"This is my fault, damnit!" He muttered as he turned back to the group. He zigzagged through the brush and the scattered rocks. Mal'Rey had outsmarted a hawk once before a long time ago, but never three. A plan needed to be devised and quickly, or he would lose more than just one youngling.

Under the bush, Unis and the panic-stricken rabbits made little progress in the soft, brittle limestone sand. Every time they pulled the dirt out, it would just widen the hole, filling it back in.

"I'm going to try for one of the other holes. Maybe I'll have better luck there. The ground could be sturdier further down," the same nervous who balked in the tunnel announced.

"No, wait! They're watching us from the sky!" Unis tried to reason with the frightened rabbit, but it was useless.

"Don't try to tell me what to do! We're all going to die under this bush!" he yelled, his brow furrowed. He was panting heavily, and his legs were shaking. This rabbit always preferred the safety of the burrow and the protection of larger, tougher rabbits. This was the first time his life had been in real danger and it showed.

"He's right… I'm going too," another rabbit chimed in, equally fearful of their current situation. As more rabbits considered following suit, Unis realized she needed to take control and keep everyone safe until Mal'Rey could return.

"Yeah! Me too! I'm not staying here underneath this bush!" another rabbit declared, clearly influenced by the nervous rabbit's actions. Unis was mortified; the panicked behavior stirred a wave of irrational thoughts.

"PLEASE!!!" she screamed as two younglings and the nervous rabbit sprinted toward the other holes.

"Sorry, Unis! Take care of yourself!" One of the younglings called out before being snatched from the Earth by another set of claws. The other youngling dodged a third hawk's swoop just in time. Diving into one of the other holes. The nervous rabbit reached his destination miraculously unharmed but found a fat rattlesnake coiled beneath exposed roots hiding inside the hole. When it spotted him, his tail shook, warning him to stay out. He backed away slowly so as not to startle it. Once out of sight, he turned to run to the other hole where the youngling was tucked in, narrowly dodging two separate attempts by the hawks.

To his surprise, the nervous rabbit made it to the other hole, but it was too shallow for him and the youngling to hide. As he watched the two remaining hawks circle and double back, he realized he had to make a choice.

"Get out! Now!" the nervous rabbit demanded of the youngling. Get out now, or I'll pull you out myself!"

The youngling cried. "No! I got here first! Just go!"

"Fine! So be it!" The larger, stronger rabbit grabbed the youngling by the ear and pulled him out into the open with his two front teeth. The youngling screamed in pain and terror as the panicked rabbit filled the bottom of the hole with his larger body.

Unis watched the entire scene from under the bush, along with three other rabbits and the last remaining youngling. She cried and held the little rabbit close, shielding his eyes from the horrifying fate of his tiny friend out in the open field. When it was all over, each hawk claimed a meal and retired to the tall pines in the east. Only seven rabbits remained in their group.

Mal'Rey felt useless, unable to draw the hawks' attention away because of the actions of the nervous rabbit he saved earlier that day. He felt responsible for the death of the younglings and harbored anger towards the rabbit he rescued.

Once the coast was clear, they met beside the hole where the nervous rabbit was cowering under neath some pieces of wood.

"It's your fault those two died. Especially the one you dragged from this hole to save your skin!" Mal'Rey accused the nervous rabbit. His voice dripped with anger and frustration.

Panic continued to ripple through the rabbits, enraged at the nervous rabbit's actions. Mal'Rey's once light-hearted demeanor vanished, replaced by a palpable anger that sent shivers down the spines of the other rabbits.

The nervous rabbit said nothing. Mal'Rey approached him, his robust frame radiating unsettling energy. In the distance, Mal'Rey noticed the hole where the snake lay coiled, the very reason the nervous rabbit couldn't stay there earlier.

"What is your name, rabbit?" Mal'Rey asked, his voice stern and unyielding.

"Me? My name, Mal'Rey? Why… Why do you need to know my name?" he replied nervously.

Mal'Rey looked to Unis as if seeking permission. She remained quiet and nodded before the rest of the rabbits turned their bodies away from the scene.

"My name is Santilian. Why? Why do you ask?" he said, his voice shaking.

"I just figured it would be polite to introduce you by name," Mal'Rey responded, his voice cold and detached.

"I don't understand." Santilian stammered.

"You will. Come on, let's go. I don't want to keep him waiting," Mal'Rey said, forcefully shoving Santilian towards the hole where the rattlesnake lay.

"...The interesting thing about snakes Santilian, which I don't think many rabbits know, is that they're all of one mind. Creatures who don't need the Awl'Fire in their hearts to sustain them. That doesn't make them evil thought as most would think. It makes them... one with the Earth. Like plants or trees. Snakes, lizards, fish, insects. Each kind of creature shares a mind. It's confusing, I know, but quite simple, really. Every spider you've ever seen, whether in a tree, a bush or grass, is the same spider as any other, just a different body." Mal'Rey explained. He watched as Santilian's face glazed over with confusion.

"Okay, if you've met one snake, you've met them all… Anyway, it doesn't matter much now to be honest." Mal'Rey continued, forcefully guiding Santilian closer to the snake.

Santilian could see the rattlesnake ahead. He made his way out of the hole and was coiled beside a tuft of weeds. At least five feet long. The sight of the snake made his heart race, and nervousness started seeping from his body.

"This is an old friend of mine. I've known him most of my life. I owe him a favor for something he did for me when I was young, and finally, I can repay him. Thanks to you, Santilian," Mal'Rey's voice dripped with sarcasm.

"Ssssantilian," the snake hissed. Its forked tongue flicked in and out as it fixed its cold, unblinking eyes on the trembling rabbit. The air was thick with tension, and the true gravity of the situation finally dawned on Santilian as he realized the price he would have to pay for his actions.

The snake repeated Santilian's name with a sinister whisper, sending chills down his spine. Desperate, Santilian attempted to flee, but Mal'Rey tripped him with his injured leg. He winced in pain. The snake swiftly closed in and sank its fangs into Santilian's thigh so fast that he barely realized what happened.

"You should've never done that to that youngling. I hope you spend eternity in the obsidian desert, you bastard." Mal'Rey seethed, and intently watched as the snake's venom took effect. Santilian's body swelled grotesquely. Blood oozed from his eyes and nose as the powerful coagulant coursed through his veins.

"Consssider your debt to me paid Mal'Rey. I hope we meet again sssoon." The snake hissed, tightly wound around the dying rabbit. Though he wanted to witness the end, Mal'Rey reluctantly turned away. "Until then." He whispered.

Upon his return to Unis and the rabbits that remained, Mal'Rey sensed their relief at Santilian's departure into the Void. He had been a deplorable example of their kind, and the world was now better off without him. Unis nestled her small frame against his to offer him comfort.

"I'm glad you're okay, Mal'Rey," she murmured.

He sighed deeply. "I want to apologize to all of you. I feel responsible for what has happened here today. I should have been more vigilant in watching the sky, and I don't think I can ever forgive myself."

Silence hung heavy in the air as the others respected his need for space to process his emotions.

"Let's go now. We still need to find a rabbit hole before something worse tries again for us," Mal'Rey finally said, his voice filled with determination. They suffered enough losses, and he was resolute in ensuring their survival.

Chapter 32
The Climb

n the chaotic aftermath of the Axael's escape, Vog knew that any
ffort to reason with his brother's anger and disappointment was
seless. "Vog! What have you done!?" Oct'Tulommon shouted as he
rantically clamored over corpses and broken stone.

"This was my plan, my destiny! And you stole it all from me!"
…I'm sorry, Oct'Tulommon. I... I didn't know!" "Liar! Do not insult
ny intelligence by downplaying your own! I know you are smart
nough to realize the implications of taking the life of an alpha!"
ct'Tulommon shouted as his Vog retreated. "Vog, listen to me! We
ust think of what to do next! Where are you going? Don't run from
e, brother!"

Vog knew no deal would save him; his brother would seize any
ance to take his life. Oct'Tulommon was notoriously incapable of
aring the spotlight. As Vog stumbled over a dead fractured wolf, he
und himself pinned beneath his brother, Oct'Tulommon's full weight
as bearing down on him.

"The power you wield is not meant for such a weak wolf as you
og! It was meant for me. I'm stronger, more vicious than any wolf! It
as my destiny! Give it to me! Or I will take it with your life. I don't
re if you are my blood!"

Vog strained as he tried to free himself from his brother's grasp.
e skin on half of his face was badly burned. He smelled like charred

hair and meat. The strength in his anger blinded him to the fact that he was bleeding out from his leg.

"I cannot give it to you, Oct'Tulommon! Even if I was inclined to! You heard the Void and what it instructed me to do. I can never escape what I have done! What you! convinced me to do! I'm sorry!"

Vog's eyes shimmered white as he teleported from under his brother and materialized amidst the smoke at the great hall entrance. It was his first walk in the void, but it didn't phase him. He shouldered his rifle and departed." Damn it, Vog! I'm coming for you!"

In a desperate attempt to stop the bleeding from his torn flesh, Oct'Tulommon grabbed a half-burned log with his mouth, the end still red hot from the fire. He placed it on top of his wound's mangled, hanging flesh and cauterized it to stop the bleeding. He writhed and howled, but temporarily gave himself a chance to continue his pursuit. After he gathered his thoughts and pushed back the intense pain, he went outside after Vog. He scanned every direction for clues as to which way he went.

Losing hope, the light from the sun through the smoke, glinted off a metal clip that bound the shoulder strap to the rifle hung over Vog's back.

"I see you, Vog, and I'm coming for you!" Oct'Tulommon called to his heart through the Void.

Oct'Tulommon, still in his wolf form, struggled to negotiate the rugged crags of the mountainside with a missing leg. Even though he knew it would be easier for him with Lennon's body, he thought it best to reserve what little power he had left for one last decisive change, only as a last resort.

Meanwhile, Vog established a great distance between himself and his brother. He meticulously calculated his every move and every step to conserve as much energy as he could with a slower approach. He intently focused on his ability to remain calm and collected. Oct'Tulommon did not know why he set out to scale the mountainside, but did not concern himself with anything other than retribution.

He is going to kill me; I know it, vog muttered to himself as he stopped on an outcropping of stone and scanned the rocks below for his brother's position. Just as Oct'Tulommon poked his head out from under the overhang, he saw Vog line up a shot. The bullet sparked and fractured the rocks below. It sent debris into his face. He backed away from the edge and started the transition from his mangled self into Lennon. It took a little longer and hurt considerably more than before, as he was depleted of his reserves of void power. Shocked that his new form materialized with a sore and slightly misshapen leg.

Well, that's better than nothing, I guess. He thought. Oct'Tulommon's lunge from the outcropping to another a little further over was more of a calculated fall. He continued his climb as Lennon, his skin tearing on the sharp rocks and his muscles burning from overexertion. It was a new sensation for him. After an hour, Oct'Tulommon was exhausted. The combination of Lennon Grenlow's body and determination was powerful, but it was no match for the challenging climb, especially now that his void power was gone. The altitude and the thinning air were difficult for even the strongest flesh. He gasped for air.

Once more, he climbed to the edge to see if Vog was in as much of a struggle as he was. But his brother was even further from him now than before and didn't seem to be exhausted. The peak was close, only a short climb ahead of him.

"Vog, where are you going?" Oct'Tulommon sent his words out as far as he could and hoped they would get through to him. "Can we not talk about this?" "What is there to talk about, Oct'Tulommon?" Vog replied, his tone cold.

Oct'Tulommon was surprised when he answered.

"Why are you pursuing me? If not, to kill me? You're too proud to let me live after what happened."

Oct'Tulommon's anger re-surged as he envisioned the bullet ripping through Ult'Ilinok's skull. "You did nothing but steal the Seat of Power from me! I held his faltering resolve in my grasp. The Altapex was mine, brother!"

"Stop calling me brother!" Vog shouted. "I am no more your brother than any other wolf. You decided that when you left us all those years ago. I am the one that stayed and watched our father's slow decline. I am the one who suffered those mindless wolves of the Illnok alone, and for what? For you to take it all? I have just as much right to that seat of power as you do, Oct'Tulommon."

"Ahh! I see the truth now. You and I are more alike than I thought. Vog! Haha! Except for one minor detail. I do not care about the seat of power. I don't want to rule over a pack of mindless, brainwashed wolves. No! I want to rule the world of man. That was the plan from the beginning!"

They were both tiring; the climb was becoming a battle of wills.

"Then I have nothing to offer you, Oct'Tulommon. Leave here. Your assault on man must be all on your own. I will have no part in it."

Oct'Tulommon stood and jumped as hard as he could, grabbing a stone a few feet above his head. He bent his waist and climbed over another outcropping just as Vog unleashed a volley of gunfire from above. A bullet clipped his thigh, sending a shockwave of pain through his entire body.

"Dammit, VOG! Put down the rifle!" Oct'Tulommon roared.

Vog laughed. "Ha! You are one of the most untrustworthy wolves I have ever known, Oct'Tulommon. You will not stop your pursuit if I do not kill you."

One last time, Oct'Tulommon leaped. Grasped a stone and pulled himself over. A volley of bullets rang out and struck the loose rocks. It sent jagged rocks once more into his face. The supple hairless skin of his human body wasn't as resilient as his wolf form. The nicks and cuts stung like bees and burned for much longer. *I can't take the weakness of this human skin!* Oct'Tulommon used the last of his void power to change back into his original form. There was no turning back. Vog reached the top.

As Oct'Tulommon stood, the steady cold mountain wind whipped the burned exposed skin on his left side. It sent needles throughout and hurt worse than the cauterized hanging flesh of his missing leg. He was broken, close to death, but still bent on blind retribution. He looked to the west and saw the path of destruction his brother and the Fracture made on their way to the mountain. It was like a scar on the land. Small fires spread to different spots, carried by embers on the wind, landing in the dry grass. He didn't care in the slightest.

Behind him; the summit. He was disappointed to see nothing of any value, no statues or piled rock features, ominous glowing fires, or remnants of any culture aside from one. An obsidian stone altar that stuck out of the ground in front of a set of crude steps leading down into a shallow featureless crater. Some markings lined the rocks on the outside pictures, with instructions on how to enter. It wasn't as simple as just passing through the threshold.

The small engravings depicted a wolf and a man standing before a sealed doorway. The picture that followed showed the doorway open and the two passing through. Vog stood defensively as his brother approached.

"What is this place, Vog? What do you make of these carvings?" Oct'Tulommon was so entranced by what the cryptic symbols could mean, he didn't acknowledge the gun Vog pointed straight at him. As Oct'Tulommon came closer, the earth rumbled to life underneath them. From the base of the shapeless crater rose a stone doorway that seemed to open as it rose from the ground.

"Vog! What have you found here? It thinks you are a real man. It's opening to us! We—" "Shut up, Oct'Tulommon!" he snapped,

"You knew this was up here? What is this place?... Vog?"

As Oct'Tulommon fell under the spell of the moving stones, Vog stepped back behind him with the gun still at his head. Just as his finger tensed, a massive object plummeting from the sky blocked the sun. Vog turned just in time and dove out of the way. The sound of the impact was deafening. It sent a shockwave that vibrated their hearts and stole the breath from their lungs.

Once the dust cleared, they stood in awe of the creature that descended from the heavens. It was a wolf three times the size of any earthly wolf. Instead of wiry fur to cover its colossal frame, it was draped in sharply edged white feathers that reflected the little sunlight in the smoke-filled sky. Its tail was razor sharp, gliding like a snake's body. The most unsettling attribute of the colossal creature were the two vast wings that stretched wide, catching the wind like the sails of a great ship. It was the Peregrine.

"Oct'Tulommon!" the creature called out in a booming voice, using its mouth like a human and speaking man's language. "You make false promises, wolf! So, I took matters into my own hands."

"Peregrine? Is that you?" Oct'Tulommon stammered, incredulous. Vog was still in shock, reeling from the sight of the divine being before them. Tears rolled from his eyes at the awe-inspiring sight. He slowly backed away, hoping the situation would not escalate.

"What do you mean, Peregrine?" Oct'Tulommon said with a nervous laugh. "We were simply..."

"You sound... scared, little wolf. Do I scare you? Haha, do I threaten you?" Oct'Tulommon could tell the Peregrine was relishing the sight of him cowering in fear. He was the creature he always yearned to be. As a bird, he wasn't any real threat to anything more significant than a raccoon. But now, everything would fear it, and the Peregrine was thriving on that fear.

"Bow to me! Bow your heads to the King of the skies!" Immediately, Vog took his place on his bare knees before the magnificent being. He groveled like a servant.

"Yes! That's right. Oct'Tulommon, take your place beside this one. He is your brother! Do not leave him to worship alone." Oct'Tulommon's response was a deep, threatening growl.

"This man has made his choice. A creature this weak is not of my blood," Oct'Tulommon declared defiantly. The Peregrine's expression turned to one of disappointment.

"Hmmm, that's sad, really, for both of you. I never had a brother," the colossal creature mused, its lips curling into a sinister smile. In one swift motion, he lunged for Vog and grabbed him by the back of his neck, lifting him up in front of Oct'Tulommon. Behind them, the ancient doorway started to close.

"Peregrine! No! He needs to stay alive!" Oct'Tulommon cried out.

"Ahhh! There it is, Oct'Tulommon! Beg me! Beg me to spare his life!" The Peregrine taunted him with Vog as he tightened his powerful grip around his tired, frail frame. Life slipped away; blood dripped down his chest. The door of the passage grew smaller and smaller.

Vog's eyes met Oct'Tulommon's one last time. "Oct'Tulommon, get inside before the door closes, brother." In an instant, Vog disappeared, leaving the King of the Sky bewildered.

"I will never beg for anything, bird!" Oct'Tulommon snarled. He watched the disappointment flood the Peregrine's eyes. Oct'Tulommon leaped and made it through the door just before it shut completely. He could hear the Peregrine on the other side, its massive talons scraping at the rock relentlessly. But it couldn't get in. After a while, the scratching stopped, and Oct'Tulommon's ears were silent as the darkness within the doorway enveloped him. He felt a ping of adoration for his brother as he took the last advice he offered before slipping out of the Peregrine's mouth. Not knowing that the entire game of cat and mouse up the mountainside was part of a quickly devised plan. A plan by a more intelligent wolf to imprison him for the rest of his natural life.

"All the secrets these bastard wolves have been hoarding here are mine." Oct'Tulommon didn't know that above him; the stones that formed the doorway slowly sank back into place, locking him in the same prison the Axael fought so hard and waited for so long to escape. Inside the great hall, the rocks above the fire started vibrating and shuffled back in to close the opening. The crater, where the Axael escaped, was gone as if nothing ever happened.

Chapter 33
The Cliffs

It took Nilian and El'Wren the better part of the day to journey from the Alpha's mountain to the southern cliffs. The battle wolves escorting them managed to save the lives of at least thirty others from that terrible day in the great hall. The group consisted of injured pack wolves and an assortment of bears, deer and other woodland creatures they picked up along the way. All hoped to find sanctuary in the south. Nilian felt uneasy, as he walked the distance flanked by hungry wolves; wolves that hadn't eaten for the entire trek. El'Wren noticed his anxiety and reassured him that the battle wolves would protect him while under their care, but it remained an experience that troubled him greatly.

When they arrived at the southern cliffs, they were greeted by two Border Wolves tasked by Ult'Ilinok to patrol the length of the cliffs, looking for signs of human activity. Oftentimes, the Illnok Alpha would assign newly appointed Border Wolves to circumnavigate the cliffs as their first duty. It was a task that rarely saw any action, given that humans could only breach the land from the south by sea. And even then, the beaches lay deep below the cliffs, rendering it virtually impossible to land a boat.

The southern cliffs were a sight to behold. Magnificent crystal blue water beneath churned and pounded against sharp rocks that jutted out from a foamy surf. Behind the cliffs, the landscape was flat and desolate, but closer to the edge were patches of dense brush and magnificent trees, their limbs heavy with ripe fruit.

"I never thought I would see this place, Nilian. I've heard stories about its beauty from the Hesperus wolves in the great hall, but to see it is a unique experience altogether." El'Wren admitted. Her eyes took in the stunning panorama. The sight of the majestic southern cliffs evoked a sense of awe and wonder. The beauty served as a reminder that despite their struggles, some places in the world still flourished.

Nilian sat with El'Wren as the cool air from the surf below cascaded over them.

"Hmm, the stories I heard when I was a youngling painted a much different picture of this place," Nilian mused. He hopped down from beside her and weaved through the rocks in search of clover.

"What do you mean, Nilian? What is it you heard?"

"Well, if I can remember correctly, it wasn't the place that was the problem; it was the wolves that called this place their home. They were called the Tunibog. A pack of wolves half the size of the Illnok in numbers. They tried and failed several times to negotiate a share of land from the Illnok, not a large piece, just enough to hunt on. The Illnok would not allow it. So they fought for years until the Alpha Awl At'Linok of the previous Alpha invaded and claimed all these lands for himself."

"I heard none of that," she chuckled, her disbelief clear. "Why would they not just want to help? It doesn't seem to be like the Illnok to be selfish."

Nilian stopped and looked out over the water. "What is the creed that the Elden Sayer recites on the night of the first rite of passage, El'Wren? You went through the rites, didn't you?"

El'Wren was silent. "If I must be honest, Nilian, I never got the chance. They gave me the role of a chamber wolf before I came of age. My father wolf died when my mother was carrying me; she died before I was three winters. I was taken into service by the Alpha. I never even left the Interior of the mountain before the age of five winters."

"Oh, I did not know, El'Wren. I'm sorry."

"It's fine, Nilian. That doesn't make me sad. It was a great childhood. I had friends, I was fed, and I was safe. My life has always had a purpose and a direction."

He relaxed again as the awkwardness passed. "Well, the Illnok believe that hunger keeps a wolf from starving. That means that the Tunibog would have been able to survive out here on the southern cliffs if they respected the lands and the creatures in them. Instead, they were over-hunted; the animals didn't have a chance to flourish, so they died out or migrated away from here."

"Oh…" El'Wren murmured, her understanding of the situation deepened. She was caught entirely off guard by the story.

"Alpha Awl At'Linok was kind to them, at least. He allowed most of the older Tunibog to live underneath the Alpha's Mountain and gave the other Tunibog a probationary period. The Border Wolves watched them closely. If they were caught taking more than their fair share, they were interned; put into service for the Alpha."

"The Hesperus Wolves?"

"… It's not just the Hesperus wolves that were Tunibog, El'Wren…." Nilian hinted, giving her the chance to read between the lines.

"What do you… oh, my mother and father wolves? They were Tunibog?"

"Most likely. It was so long ago; I don't think anyone knows." Nilian could tell he said too much. He had a habit of doing so. Just as El'Wren was coming to terms with her lineage, the Battle wolves that escorted them to the cliffs directed all the wolves to stay put while they went hunting and to scout the area before dark. Although the lands of the southern cliffs were breathtaking, it would not be possible to sustain as many creatures in their party.

"What are we going to do, El'Wren? We cannot stay here long; there won't be enough food."

She sighed, knowing Nilian was right. "Morgrim told us he would come for us; it would be best to wait it out here, at least for a while."

"Agreed, I think we can manage a few days," Nilian said as he sat beside her on the cliff side. "If I weren't so hungry, I feel this place would be perfect…."

It wasn't long before the next wave of refugees from the territory's Interior arrived. Darkness was closing in when Nilian spotted the battle wolves as they returned to camp. Everyone expected a meal, only to be met with more hungry mouths. The only consolation was that the mouths were tiny and didn't require any meat.

"Nilian!?" a familiar voice called out from the crowd of rabbits being herded to the cliffs by the battle wolves.

"Unis! How did you get here?"

El'Wren could see the relief on Nilian's face as he recognized Unis. The journey was difficult, but at least some familiar faces were still together. The rabbits huddled together, taking solace in their shared experience, and waited for the next step in their uncertain future.

"Oh, I'm so glad to see you, my love; I was worried about you." Nilian rubbed his head against Unis', both almost in tears.

"Unis, where are the others?" His smile faded, and her expression grew somber. "Well, I'm not entirely sure, love. Burren and Mulgris stayed behind and ensured the rest of the rabbits got out safely. We made it just below the mountain when a deafening noise caused the walls to cave all around us. We lost… we lost a lot." She paused and turned to look at the rabbits behind her. "These few are the only ones I made it out with."

"Unis, there must have been at least a hundred rabbits in the Illnok Burrow!" Nilian exclaimed, his little heart heavy with concern.

Tears welled up in Unis's eyes as she thought about all the loved ones they could have potentially lost. "I'm sure there are more scattered to the winds. Hopefully, Burren and Mulgris are with them."

"Nilian!?" Mal'Rey slowly hopped up beside Unis, his leg still in terrible pain.

"My old friend, I haven't seen you since your mother died." Nilian looked at him, puzzled for a moment.

"Mal'Rey? Is that you? Haha!"

"Yes, boy!"

"Oh! Mal'Rey! I'm so glad to see you; I have so much to tell you!"

Unis and El'Wren smiled as they watched Nilian jump around with excitement. Finnick would have been proud of his little brother. The small group of rabbits and wolves found solace in their reunion, their spirits lifted by the familiarity of old friends in the face of adversity.

"I assume the only thing left for us to do is wait out here until the Eldens come for us."

El'Wren said to her as both their smiles faded.

"Let's just pray to the Awl'Fire that we will have enough to eat until they do," Unis said as she looked at the Multitude of survivors still gathering behind them.

"Hunger keeps a wolf from starving is a lot easier to say when there's food to eat."

El'Wren said. Alluding to the fact that none of the wolves in the Illnok territory were ever close to starving.

Part VIII: Forgotten Reasons

Chapter 34
Nah'Hele and the Council of Wolves

A long time ago, before the age of the Illnok, a dwindling tribe of natives found themselves in the northern wildlands. Their exodus from the malice and tyranny brought upon them by white settlers in the region to the west, forced them to journey much farther than they had ever gone before, in hopes of finding refuge.

At the crest of a snow-capped hill, the chief of the tribe, Nah'Hele, which means "Forest," stepped forward to speak on behalf of his people. Safe passage through the lands in the North could only be granted by an ancient council of wolves seated on a massive obsidian stone. These majestic creatures were the keepers of the last remaining wildlands and the protectors of the hallowed mountain containing the fabled arrays of knowledge.

"My tribe is Tec'Tulomeh," the young warrior chief began. "Behind me are my people. We have come in search of a new beginning. The white man takes and does not give. The forest is angry, and the animals have no longer talk to us because of them. They have begun to see us as one of the same. We tried to make peace with them, tried to tell the story of the first man and the great dimming, but they did not feel the Awl Fire warmth. They do not value peace as your kind and my people do. Only greed, pain, and slaughter of our people and the animals. We are your brothers; we respect the bond we once shared and wish to share with you again."

The young Native boy, no older than the age of fifteen winters, standing in front of the ancient wolf council, was the bravest warrior of the Tec'Tulomeh tribe. Pleading for sanctuary from the depravity sweeping the lands in the South, they had no other place to go. The great northern wildlands were their last hope in a line of many failed attempts to rekindle the lost bond between the two species.

The ancient wolf council received the young boy's plea with open hearts. It had been a long time since they had seen a man. Set high in the mountains just past the Rimwoods, the council was challenging to find. In total, seven great wolves sat on the stone from various parts of the region, comprising a union of fiercely territorial wolves over the North. At this point in time, it was where they called home.

The Hunters' Den behind them rose high above the earth, shadowing most of the other peaks that comprised the Northern Skylands except one. Known to the wolves of the North as The Great Peak, it was an unfathomable distance from the Hunters' Den. But still the most prominent peak that could be seen in any of the four cardinal directions. So high the top reached well into the stratosphere, hidden away behind a thick sheet of gray clouds. No wolf had ever made it there and lived to tell the tale. It was so treacherous that it had been several winters since any wolf dared even try it.

The space between the two peaks was ripe with hunting lands. Valleys that dipped low and provided secluded areas of temperate climates for wildlife to thrive were stocked full of life and untouched by humans. Large lakes, both frozen and free flowing, adorned the landscape, and even a stretch of desert was rumored to wrap around the opposite side of the great mountain. The northern wildlands offered the promise of sanctuary and a chance for the Tec'Tulomeh tribe to rebuild their lives in harmony with the ancient wolf council.

The wolves atop the great stone sat in contemplation for a time, discussing both the good and the bad that could arise from reprising the bonds between the world of man and wolf. It was a decision that hadn't needed to be discussed for hundreds of years. The wolves had all but given up on the hearts of men and wrote them as a scourge upon the earth, destined to live out their days alone and broken.

"This man's aura is of a different color and size than the ones that have come before him. Ill'Rune, I say we shelter them, for a time, a grace period if you will, in order to weigh the embers glowing in their hearts,"

A wolf sat on the end with grayish hair and blue eyes opened the dialogue with the much larger wolf in the center. Ill'Rune was more or less the alpha among them, the one who was the oldest and much more trusted in decisions involving outsiders and interlopers in the lands.

"I would agree with Cer'Ulith, Ill'Rune. We have neglected our duty to maintain the bond between us as the first ones did. Are we not responsible for The Dimming in a sense?" another wolf chimed in.

Ill'Rune cut his head sharply at the wolf who spoke. The others in the council followed suit. "Bite your tongue, Mirth'Erin! We are no more responsible for the hearts of man than a fish is responsible for the current in the river! We did not leave for the warmth and comfort of an easy existence below the snow in the North!"

The wolves whimpered as Ill'Rune became increasingly agitated as he spoke. His lips curled as he growled and crossed the stone to meet Mirth'Erin. "I see the treacherous heart beating in your chest, wolf. As I have for quite some time. It would be best if it were torn out so all here could see how it beats for the men standing before us!"

"Please!" the young Native boy, Nah'Hele, suddenly interrupted, his voice full of fear and determination. The sudden plea caught the council's attention, silencing the growling wolves.

"Do not fight among yourselves because of us. We seek only peace and the chance to rebuild our lives in harmony with you. If you cannot trust us, we will leave and never return. But if you give us a chance, we will honor and respect the bond between our peoples and prove our worth to you," Nah'Hele implored. His eyes glistened with sincerity as he gazed upon the ancient wolf council.

The tension in the air slowly dissipated, and the council members looked at one another, then weighed the young boy's words. Ill'Rune, still glaring at Mirth'Erin, turned his gaze to Nah'Hele and then to the desperate faces of the Tec'Tulomeh tribe. The decision that lay before them was not easy, but the potential for a renewed bond between man and wolf was an opportunity that could not be overlooked

With a heavy sigh, Ill'Rune spoke, his voice now tempered with both wisdom and caution. "Very well. We shall grant you sanctuary for a time. Prove that your hearts are true, and perhaps we can rekindle the bond our ancestors once shared."

Nah'Hele stepped into the empty space between his tribe and the council's stone, determination shining in his eyes. "My heart is pure, as are the hearts of all my people. We do not wish to cause any hardship between you. We seek only to grow stronger together."

As Nah'Hele spoke, his eyes turned white and he disappeared into the Void and reappeared atop the stone between Ill'Rune and Mirth'Erin. He bowed his head to Ill'Rune. "We are here to reforge the bonds, not break them. I am descended from the first man and carry the void array, just as you are descended from the first wolf."

Ill'Rune could feel the Awl'Fire emanate from Nah'Hele's heart. The frozen ground beneath his bare feet slowly melted away. Snow fell harder than it had in months, yet each flake that landed on his bare skin melted and ran down as tiny droplets of water.

Ill'Rune noticed that Nah'Hele and his entire tribe were barely clothed, with no protection on their feet, yet they were unphased by the cold. His skepticism faded as the proof lay before him.

Ill'Rune stood silent, pacing between difficult decisions within his own mind. "I've heard of your tribe in the past, Nah'Hele. The stories of your fiercest hunters echo through the wilderness, and the obsidian spearhead atop your staff has collected many flames."

Nah'Hele stepped back and stood the staff on its end with the tip at the side of his face. "I only kill what I have to in order to feed the men, women, and children of my tribe. Never more. Many flames. Many thanks to the Awl'Fire for providing the strength."

Ill'Rune turned and sat back in the line of Council wolves, severing the conduit between his mind and Nah'Hele's.

"O'Rik, how have your battle wolves fared in the Endless Pines?" He shifted the conversation to the state of their own lands while he kept a watchful eye on the fate of the Tec'Tulomeh tribe.

"I ordered three to reinforce the five I have already sent. As of this morning, only one has returned: Rey'Zol. His jaw is broken, and the flesh from his right flank has been flayed. I do not see him surviving the night." O'Rik's voice was heavy with sorrow.

The council wolves bowed their heads, their ears sinking low. Ill'Rune sighed. "And when did you send the others??"

"...Before the first snow." O'Rik replied.

They all knew there was very little chance they would see them again. "And how many wolves does that make in total now?"

O'Rik took a moment to calculate the numbers in his mind. "...Twenty-one."

As the wolves continued to speak among themselves, Nah'Hele hopped down from the stone and returned to his wife's side. He wrapped his arm around his youngest son and waited. "Nah'Hele! What do you think is the outcome? They seem to be taking their time while we starve." Aha'Nu complained.

"Aha'Nu! Quiet. They only want what's best for the land. The same as us; they will know the right choice." Nah'Hele tried to reassure him.

Aha'Nu clicked his tongue against his cheek like a child. A few moments later, all at once, the seven wolves of the council stood. "Nah'Hele! Come forth," Ill'Rune called to him through the falling snow.

"It has been decided that the Tec'Tulomeh tribe will stay here in the northern wilderness for at least the coming snowstorm; the older generation, the younger generation, and the women. All will take shelter in the Hunter's Den."

As Ill'Rune's words settled, Nah'Hele and the others smiled. Relief washed over them. The snow fell more heavily, and the clouds looked swollen and full. By nightfall, the council wolves were expecting a full blizzard, which was not uncommon for the time of the season.

Ill'Rune stepped forward. "As the leader of your tribe, it is clear that you seek to protect your people above yourself. As do we, Nah'Hele. Please forgive us if we seem a little reluctant to accept that there is still goodness in man's heart after we have witnessed such terrible things."

Nah'Hele's smile faded as Ill'Rune reminded him of the past and all the evil things he witnessed men do. "I do not fault you for your hesitation, Ill'Rune. We have seen the wickedness in our kind as well, and like you, we are hesitant to trust."

As the other wolves in the council led the families to the Hunters' Den, Nah'Hele and Aha'Nu stayed behind with Ill'Rune to discuss the logistics of their settling in.

"I'm afraid you have come to the North at a dark time, Nah'Hele. There is something that I wish to speak to you about, something that the council and I believe you may be able to help with."

"Anything you ask, we shall do, Ill'Rune. We are not here to only take but to give as well. What do you ask of us?"

Ill'Rune continued to speak with a worried expression. Nah'Hele could see that it was severe, and he was afraid to ask. "Back in the summer season, I sent a party of wolves into the South to find a more temperate land for us to settle. These lands, I'm sure you know very well, considering it is where you come from. The winters in these parts of the North are very harsh; the older generation of wolves within our packs become stricken with pain in their bones and joints. Not to mention the food sources dwindle as they flee from the cold. In the previous winter, we lost five to the elements. This year, the temperature has fallen earlier than last, and we have already lost two. The South is not ideal for us since it is closer to the world of man, but something must be done. We cannot watch as our older generations dwindle in the cold winter while we do nothing."

Nah'Hele looked puzzled. "Ill'Rune, as I have said, the world is getting smaller, and men are dangerous. Large settlements in the South came after the slaughter of innocent life, both man and animal. I do not feel like that would be a wise choice. Ill'Rune, surely there are lands below the cold peaks of these mountains here in the North. What are these... Endless Pines, you speak of? Can this not be a place your pack can call home?"

Ill'Rune paused and considered Nah'Hele's suggestion. He walked to the edge of the snow-covered ridge and pushed his head through cedar branches as Nah'Hele and Aha'Nu followed suit. Outstretched in front of them is a green valley reaching off into the distance. "The Endless Pines is a vast and dense forest, rich with life and sheltered from the harshest winds. But it is not without its dangers. There is a creature somewhere down there that even we wolves have learned to avoid. However, with your tribe's help and our combined knowledge, perhaps we could find a way to rid the lands there of the scourge, and we can begin anew."

Nah'Hele nodded, determination shining in his eyes. "We will do everything we can to help you find a home for your pack, Ill'Rune. Together, we can overcome the challenges that the Endless Pines present."

"What is it?" Aha'Nu asked."...A monster?"

Nah'Hele elbows him in the side, trying to silence the sarcasm that leaked from his words. Ill'Rune looked out over the valley below. Nah'Hele could sense the sadness and fear emanating from the wolf's heart.

"We call it the Axael and have concluded that it is a collection of the Void. A saturation of it that has walked in our realm since before any other creatures of the earth. Much in the way, the great Rock Prism had, lying dormant under the earth until the Awl'Fire brought forth life. It seems that it cannot go any further than the moderate climate of the Endless Pines. Anything that breathes, it will kill and consume."

"...And then what?"

Ill'Rune turned to Nah'Hele and Aha'Nu with a solemn expression they'd not seen before.

"That's the part we have yet to learn about him."

Nah'Hele was not afraid of much, but sensed the fear in Ill'Rune's mind. It sent chills down his back. Aha'Nu, on the other hand felt that it was just a fable Ill'Rune spun so that fear would keep them in line. An effort to create a barrier of intimidation around the treasures that the North offered.

"Ill'Rune, we will help you defeat this…Axael. You say he kills plenty of wolves. Maybe a spear or arrow from a bow will kill him."

Aha'Nu's attitude quickly changed from smug to worried. He clicked his tongue again and stared at Nah'Hele.

"What!? You're not afraid, are you Aha'Nu?" Nah'Hele says. Ill'Rune didn't change his facial expression. It was a serious matter.

"You may be right Nah'Hele. Let us discuss more in the morning. For now, I'll show you to the Hunter's Den so that you may rest with your people."

Nah'Hele was never one to back down from a challenge, especially if it involved the safety of his tribe.

After a short climb up the mountain. Ill'Rune disappeared in between two junipers. To follow him to the other side, Nah'Hele and Aha'Nu had to crawl on their bellies through the snow and the wet ground beneath. Once they reached the other side, the mountain plateaued, revealing a rock entrance that led down into the mountain.

*

The entrance to the Hunter's Den had the shape of a simple rectangle, constructed using blocks of heavy granite—one on each side and one across the top. It was magnificent and old, much older than any of them realized. Down a short distance, the corridor turned into a reasonably decent-sized room with a fire burning in the center. The people of Nah'Hele's tribe were seated around it; some were asleep while others conversed with the wolves from the council. The children chased one another and played games in the light of the fire. They were happy. Nah'Hele's wife, Aro'Win, nursed his newborn son and rubbed the head of his eldest as he lay asleep in her lap. Nah'Hele's heart was whole at that moment. As he looked out over them; together with the wolves he thought to himself how this was the way it was meant to be. Once he joined her on a deer skin pelt and quickly fell asleep.

The morning came quicker than he expected. The fire in the center of the den was still burning bright, but the light from the morning sun was lost. The snow almost buried the entrance and was still falling, with no signs of slowing. He rose and instructed Aha'Nu to gather the two best Tec'Tulomeh warriors and meet him outside with Ill'Rune.

"Ine'Rah, Ol'Mah, wake up. Nah'Hele has asked us to meet him and the Council wolf outside," Aha'Nu stirred them from their slumber, each lying with their wives and children, comfortable in the heat.

"Ahhh… come back later Aha'Nu, it's too early…" Aha'Nu looked down and saw one of Ol'Mah's children stared at him and smiled. He motioned for the child to stand, then instructed him to jump on Ol'Mah to get him up. The little boy paused and lined up his body to not land on his little sister. He dove, but just before he made contact, Ol'Mah turned over and grabbed him midair and pulled him to his chest. He riddled his tiny little rib cage with tickles.

"Never! You're too slow, Papoose! Grow bigger and try again!" Ol'Mah said. Everyone in the den was awake now at the sound of the little boy's laughter – it was infectious.

"Ok! Ok! I'm awake Aha'Nu. Let's go!"

Outside, Nah'Hele stood with Ill'Rune on top of a boulder just across from the entrance next to the cliff. The visibility decreased, and nothing could be seen below. The Endless Pines were shrouded in a cover of thick morning fog. Only the tips of the tall, slender trees showed through the gray haze.

"In'Rah, Ol'Mah, and Aha'Nu, these are the best warriors the Tec'Tulomeh Tribe has to offer you. Together, we have faced many battles against the white-faced invaders. We will vanquish the Axael, and you can claim the Pines as your new home," Nah'Hele said with conviction.

Ol'Mah and Ine'Rah had no idea what they were talking about, but they didn't care. They would do anything Nah'Hele commanded of them – no questions asked, even if it meant certain death. It was the way of their tribe.

"Good, very good, Nah'Hele, but I'm afraid it isn't possible to make our way down this morning. We must wait out the storm before we can go," Ill'Rune said. "Let's give it two days, and we will reconvene. For now, stay warm in the den with your families. I will send two hunting wolves in the morning to help you hunt, if you wish."

The four of them bowed to Ill'Rune in a show of respect and commitment to the task at hand. Ill'Rune bowed back just before he disappeared in the opposite direction.

"You three can go back to the den. I'm going to find Har'Inuk. I need counsel for what we are about to do," Nah'Hele told them.

Har'Inuk was the Tec'Tulomeh's shaman, an old spirit who lived many lives before this one and would live many more lives after. They knew that if Nah'Hele was involved with him, it was serious, and they had better say their goodbyes to their families before they left.

Nah'Hele found Har'Inuk sitting atop a stump just past the ancient Hunter's Den. He had a large buffalo pelt drawn over his head. He must have been there through the night, as much snow covered the hide. Nah'Hele came close and called out to him. "Har'Inuk! It is me, Nah'Hele. I wish to seek counsel with you!"

The snow-covered pelt twitched slightly, sending clumps of powdery snow falling. The front opened, and a thick cloud of smoke billowed out. Nah'Hele could see the shaman sitting cross-legged on top of the old stump.

"Come closer, boy!" He said with a smile. The old man's face was painted white with greasy gray hair hung down on his face. His teeth were almost the color of dried wood, cracked and chipped across the front.

"Step under the pelt and come inside with me." The old man said. Nah'Hele grasped one side of the buffalo pelt and lifted it over his head. It fell behind him as he entered. At first, it was dark and smelled like wet dirt and wood. His stomach tightened as if he dropped from a high place. Har'Inuk laughed. Light filled the space underneath the pelt. Nah'Hele was standing upright. The space should have been cramped, crowded even. Instead, it was a vast expanse of blackness. The only light was a warm yellow glow emanating from Har'Inuk. He was still sitting on the stump but unencumbered by the weight of the pelt he had been holding when Nah'Hele found him.

"I was beginning to think you would go on without seeking my counsel first, boy. Your generation seems to jump first and ask why you broke your leg afterward," Har'Inuk chuckled as he drew smoke into his mouth from the pipe held loosely between his dry lips.

"Har'Inuk, these wolves have allowed us to take shelter here. I need to help with this problem; we need to repair the bonds to survive together again. This Axael is a great fear to the wolves here. I can feel it in them. What is it, Har'Inuk?"

Har'Inuk's smile faded as he dumped the burnet tobacco from his pipe into the dirt. The embers still glowed orange. "Duality… That is what the Axael is."

"I don't…understand, Har'Inuk."

"Night and day, summer and winter, love and pain. These are all opposing forces meant to keep the other in balance. You cannot have a night without day; you cannot have summer without winter and so on. This Axael is the harbinger of the Void; it only exists because its purpose is meant to balance the Awl'Fire or so we thought.

"...so, if the Awl'Fire is…good, then the void is evil?" Nah'Hele asked.

Har'Inuk smiled. "No, Nah'Hele, the Awl'Fire and the Void are neither good nor evil. It is the very concept of balance itself. The construct of good and evil only exists in perception." He gave Nah'Hele a chance to let the idea sink in.

"It is chaos. The Awl'Fire grows with experience; it helps to facilitate order in the universe and gives life to all, with no promise of anything in return. It's indifferent. The Void is just the absence of order. It feeds on pain and suffering, just as the Awl'Fire feeds on experience and love. It is what fills in the cracks of a broken heart. In the absence of happiness, it is sadness," Har'Inuk explained with intensity. The air around them seemed to shimmer with the weight of his words.

"It is the same amalgamation that rested for a thousand years behind the first precious gem pulled from a muddy riverbank. That's why it's so dangerous," he added.

Nah'Hele started to grasp the idea better. "Because of the Dimming."

Har'Inuk nodded. "Yes, Nah'Hele, the Dimming. Our ancestors unknowingly let their minds slip into calamity. The Void filled the spaces in our hearts that were once burning with the Awl'Fire. Our ancestors, the founders of the Tec'Tulomeh tribe, were direct descendants of the first man, so we have a certain immunity to it. Tell me, Nah'Hele, when you slip into the Void, do you feel the urge to stay?"

Nah'Hele nodded his head. "Yes, that is the darkness trying to take root. The call to stay would be too great for any other man." Har'Inuk Cautioned.

"They want me to kill it for them." Nah'Hele said.

"Ha! There is no killing it, Nah'Hele; it is an artifact of the natural order of things, just like the Rock Prism, who gave the arrays." Har'Inuk's eyes sparkled with a mix of wisdom and mischief.

Nah'Hele's mind ached "Then what can I do? These wolves need our help to get free of these snowdrifts. The South is under siege by the white-faced men, and the North—"

"Listen to me, boy. The Axael is weak. The wolves are under the impression that they can eradicate him, but they cannot. Once he has caused enough chaos, he will leave the Endless Pines and search until he finds the world of men. There are enough empty hearts and feeble minds in the lands to the west to make him unstoppable, tipping the balance in favor of the Void. When you get close enough, Nah'Hele, if your mind and heart are not in the right place, he will call you, and you will not be able to resist. You must find another way to fight it. You will not prevail if you do."

"Then, if what you say is true, it is just a matter of time before he is free of the pines. Eventually, this will be a problem for all, not just the council," Nah'Hele contemplated, the gravity of the situation weighing heavily on him.

Har'Inuk smiled and nodded as he packed another pipe with tobacco. "Your path has led you to this, Nah'Hele. I cannot tell you what it is you need to do. Have faith in the Awl'Fire, and you will know."

As Har'Inuk spoke, the light emanating from his body faded. Once it was gone, Nah'Hele found himself outside the buffalo pelt, standing knee-deep in the snow.

Back at the hunter's den, the children of the Tec'Tulomeh tribe were busy outside, digging through the snow, wrestling, and playing with one another. Although Nah'Hele felt overwhelmed, he couldn't help but laugh as he watched the kids throw snowballs at each other. It was a heartwarming sight to see. It had been long since they felt safe enough to let their guard down. Even some wolves were joining in and chasing them around in the tunnels.

Once the light of day burned out, the children and the wolves tucked themselves away by the fire in the den. The older native women sang and told the children stories while the men roasted rabbits over the fire. Nah'Hele watched as his fiercest warriors laughed and continued with their loved ones. He thought, "This is how it should have always been."

It didn't matter how content he felt; the threat of the Axael was still looming over them. He was nervous, scared that the answer to the problem would not be easy to find. After they had all eaten, the children quietly fell asleep one by one until everyone was silent.

"Nah'Hele! Wake up; it's Ol'Mah! He's missing!" Ol'Mah's wife I'Rah, was frantic, pacing about the den and waking everyone to see if they had seen him. The air was thick with worry, and the firelight flickered across the faces of the tribe members, casting eerie shadows on the den's walls.

"I'Rah, calm yourself down. The sun has been up for a while now; I'm sure he went to scout for a hunt. The Wolf council sent two hunting wolves this way; he must be with them," Nah'Hele reassured her.

Ine'Rah stopped and looked at the den's entrance and the snow piled high above it. "Nah'Hele, the snow hasn't been touched. No one has been in or out since yesterday," Aha'Nu stated as he walked from the entrance. Besides the main entrance into the den, there were no other openings for him to leave through. Nah'Hele tried to remember if he had seen him last night by the fire, but he couldn't recall.

"Ine'Rah, Aha'Nu, dig the snow back from the entrance. Maybe he left, and the snow-covered his tracks behind him," Nah'Hele instructed. Once they cleared the entrance, they could see that the snowstorm had grown more intense in the early hours. The snow reached above the den's entrance, covering almost every feature outside. If Ol'Mah did leave, it would be impossible to know where he went. Aha'Nu came back to Nah'Hele and pulled him to the side.

"If he left in the night, there's a good chance he may be lost out there. What do you think we should do?" Aha'Nu asked concern etched on his face.

Nah'Hele was silent, watching I'Rah cry as she held her children. "Do you think he slipped into the Void, Nah'Hele?" Ine'Rah asked.

"No, Aha'Nu, he can't walk in the Void; he's afraid of it. Always has been." They were all puzzled.

"I think the best and safest thing to do is to wait. See if he comes back; I cannot risk losing any more people in the snow," Nah'Hele said, his voice filled with determination.

"You don't think it's the wolves, do you, Nah'Hele?" Aha'Nu asked.

"I don't see why they would have any reason to want to hurt us; they have been nothing but good to us so far." He looked around to see the five different wolves, the same five that had been with them from the beginning. Nah'Hele interacted with them but felt no threat, if anything they were just a little inquisitive.

"Just to be safe, I think we need to keep watch. We will do it in shifts. I will take the first. Aha'Nu, you will be second, and Ine'Rah, last. Try not to let anyone know you are doing so; I don't want to create panic," Nah'Hele instructed, and they all agreed, ready to do whatever it took to protect their people.

By nightfall, there was still no sign of Ol'Mah. His wife cried herself to sleep before the fire was lit for the night. Everyone was worried but tried their best to keep the children occupied. Sleeping while their friend was missing wasn't easy, but they had no choice. The snow was beginning to slow, but it didn't matter; the people would not be able to leave the den until the temperature rose enough to melt the snow a little. Throughout Nah'Hele's watch, he saw nothing unusual. Everyone was asleep – all fifteen tribe members, young and old, and the five wolves. He threw a stone at Aha'Nu to wake him, signaling his turn to keep watch. Once Nah'Hele was confident that Aha'Nu was awake, he fell quickly asleep.

Two hours passed without issue until Nah'Hele was awakened by screaming. One of the tribe mothers woke to find two of her children and their grandmother was gone. Everyone was wide awake, searching the den, but it offered no hiding place. The snow was once again untouched, yet somehow, they vanished. Nah'Hele looked over to see Aha'Nu rubbing his eyes.

"Aha'Nu! Please tell me you saw something. What happened!?" Nah'Hele asked, panic evident in his voice.

Nah'Hele could tell Aha'Nu just woke up. "I… I don't know, Nah'Hele... I must've fallen back as–"

"Say no more! I trusted you," Nah'Hele interrupted, disappointment heavy in his words.

Aha'Nu's face turned into a scowl. Knowing that Nah'Hele was upset with him was unbearable. He stood up and joined the search, hoping to find some clue that would lead them to the lost. Nothing. No tracks, no blood, not even a scent. Aha'Nu looked over to see the five wolves huddled together in the corner.

"What are you saying, wolves?" Aha'Nu asked in a very demanding tone. "What are you saying in your hearts to each other so we humans cannot hear you?"

The wolves lowered their ears and whimpered. "Aha'Nu! Leave them alone; you have no reason to believe they could do such a thing as this. Don't blame them because you failed!" Nah'Hele scolded, his voice filled with frustration.

Aha'Nu locked his gaze into a stare, and the wolves knew this was not a good situation for them. But, like the tribe, the nervous wolves were stuck in the den. "In'Rah!" Nah'Hele called out. Ine'Rah was across the den, talking to his wife. "Yes Nah'Hele?" he responded, his voice tense as the situation grew more desperate." I will cross over and see if I can see anything from the Void. I need you to promise that if I don't come back, you will get everyone out of here and go south," Nah'Hele said, his eyes filled with determination.

Ine'Rah looked confused. "Why would you not come back?"

"Just promise me, Ine'Rah."

"…I promise," Ine'Rah replied solemnly, understanding the gravity of the situation.

"I need to take a few moments with my wife and children, and then I will go," Nah'Hele announced, his voice heavy with emotion.

Aha'Nu was deeply upset when he overheard Nah'Hele giving Ine'Rah the responsibility of protecting the tribe in his absence. He couldn't help but feel a sense of guilt for having fallen asleep during his watch and a pang of jealousy that Nah'Hele entrusted Ine'Rah with such an important task.

Nah'Hele's wife, Mer'Rah, held their youngest child in her arms as she paced anxiously by the fire. The air was thick with worry for her and all the other mothers with small children. They were terrified of losing their little ones, like the ones who already vanished.

"Mer'Rah, I must enter the Void. I need to witness what is happening from the other side. Perhaps I can unravel this mystery and stop it before it's too late," Nah'Hele said with determination.

Tears welled up in her eyes, aware of the gravity of the situation. "Then go and do it before one of ours is taken. I will not sleep until you return. Please come back to us, Nah'Hele."

He smiled at her, fighting back his tears. "I will, my love." He stepped closer and tenderly kissed her forehead before kissing his two sons. "Watch over Aha'Nu, my love. I fear he is angry with himself for falling asleep on watch."

She nodded as he walked away. Nah'Hele knelt down by the den's entrance, his back against the wall. Word spread of his intent, and a crowd of onlookers gathered. The mothers of the missing children begged him to find their little ones, but he made no promises. The Void did not offer guarantees, and only he and Aha'Nu knew what lurked on the other side.

"Listen, everyone! I will journey to the Void, seeking answers for our people. I cannot say how long it will take, but I promise to return as soon as possible. Ensure that at least one of you remains awake at all times if it is something using the Void; no one has been taken when we are awake.

"Nah'Hele, find my boy!" a mother from the crowd pleaded.

"Yes, mine too, Nah'Hele!"

As he prepared to cross into the Void, he closed his eyes and took a deep breath. The air felt colder, and a shiver ran down his spine. He knew that this journey was fraught with danger, but he had no choice; the lives of his tribe members were at stake. And so, with a heavy heart, Nah'Hele sat with his back against the stones of the hunters' den, his eyes shifting into bright iridescent white as he flashed out of the den. His wife and two children were huddled together. Doing their best to stay strong.

Chapter 35
The Void

The first time Nah'Hele found himself in the void, he was just a young boy. He had been playing with Aha'Nu and their friends on the rocks scattered about in a river's bend. They were leaping from one to the next, racing across the slippery, moss-covered stones jutting out of the water. It was during this game that Nah'Hele lost his footing. Just before his head made contact with the wet rocks, he disappeared, leaving his friends behind. They waited for him to return, hoping he would reappear before it got dark so they could all go home and avoid their parents' anger.

When Nah'Hele opened his eyes, he found himself in another place. He was cold, and his friends were nowhere to be seen. The sky was a muted gray above the river where he and his friends had been playing, but the water was gone, leaving a bed of dried silt and rock in various shades of gray. The wind that softly blew the leaves in the trees along the riverbank stopped altogether. The air was thick and heavy, carrying a faint, earthy scent. Nothing about this place was appealing.

Once on his feet, Nah'Hele found himself following the riverbed, hoping to spot some form of life, but nothing was present—only the feeling of loneliness that seemed to grow heavier with each passing minute.

"Hello!?" Nah'Hele called out, but his voice seemed to fall flat his feet as if standing in front of a rock wall. Further down the riverbank, he could see movement in the underbrush. Something reasonably large was causing the leaves to rustle and shake.

"Hello!" Nah'Hele called out again, the desperation in his voice falling flat in the dirt shrouded in the eerie silence of the void.

He tried again, but his words were lost just like before.

"Speak with your heart, boy. It's the only way anything will hear you in this place." The voice resonated within him like a thought or a dream. "Simply think of what you want to say and send it to me."

It took Nah'Hele a moment to get the hang of it.

"Whoo…Are y…you?"

A man stepped forward and hopped down from the riverbank. It was Har'Inuk, the Tec'Tulomeh shaman.

"You know who I am, boy. I sensed your Awl'Fire in the void as soon as you came through. Figured it best for me to find you first and show you the way out," Har'Inuk said, trying to keep his voice low.

"Who are you… hi…hiding from?" Nah'Hele asked.

Har'Inuk grabbed him by the arm and pulled him over to the riverbank, ducking beneath the old, exposed roots of a tree.

"Stay quiet, boy. You're not ready to know the meaning of this place just yet."

Nah'Hele could hear the sound of dead leaves crushed under the footsteps of something big above. Slowly he turned to try and look, but Har'Inuk quickly jerked him around.

"Don't, boy! The last thing you want is to let it know where you are. It will feed on your fears," Har'Inuk warned.

Nah'Hele puffed his chest and curled his thick eyebrow as if offended by the thought of someone questioning his resolve.

"But I'm not afraid, Har'Inuk!" Nah'Hele insisted, his curiosity growing unbearable.

Har'Inuk jerked his arm down swiftly, gritting his teeth with frustration. "Stupid boy! Hard-headed and weak! You may think you're strong, but wickedness can bend a resolute heart into something else! You are not ready!"

Nah'Hele finally heeded Har'Inuk's warning and settled in under the roots. The creature's sound continued for a while. It trundled above its footsteps grew more distant as Har'Inuk's grip on Nah'Hele's arm eased.

"Welcome to the void, Nah'Hele. This is the place between the world of the living and the dead."

"So… I died?" Nah'Hele inquired, a mix of confusion and fear creeping into his voice.

He asked as he pinched the skin on his arm and winced in pain.

"No, if you were dead, you would know. You are very much alive. Remember the story of the first man and the first wolf?" Har'Inuk questioned.

Nah'Hele nodded.

"Your presence here means you are a direct descendant of the first man. Only the first one's bloodline possesses the arrays, some more than others depending on the strength of their Awl'Fire."

Nah'Hele's excitement grew, realizing the implications of his new ability. "I have the void array?" He asked, inspecting his spirit form.

"You must be careful with this, Nah'Hele. It is not for the weak-hearted. The more time you spend in the void, the harder it will be for you to leave."

"But I feel fine, Har'Inuk. My heart and my intentions are pure!" Nah'Hele insisted.

Har'Inuk sighed. "Yes, boy, but… there are things you don't know, things your young mind may not grasp, things that take time to learn."

"Then let us go, and let me learn," Nah'Hele said, ripping his arm from Har'Inuk's grip. He smiled and started to walk down the river.

"Nah'Hele! No, you are not ready for this yet. Let us go, and I will explain everything to you when our feet are firmly back on the other side of the void."

"I feel incredible, Har'Inuk! Don't worry!" Nah'Hele insisted. But just as the words left his mouth, he turned in time to see a specter moving in the trees. It was white and flickering like a flame, faceless and frantically searching as if it were looking for something. Nah'Hele backed up and stopped beside Har'Inuk.

"Is that a… ghost?" he whispered, his previous confidence wavering in the presence of the mysterious entity.

"No, boy. It's a Voidwalker."

Har'Inuk could see Nah'Hele's fascination growing.

"What is a void walker? And what does want with us?"

"Nah'Hele, their stories remain veiled in mystery, known only to the spirits. These beings once walked among us, but their souls were ensnared within the void, stranded between life and death's realms. Tormented by their existence in this place, the darkness has molded them, making them both violent and unpredictable. A ravenous hunger for the remnants of the Awl'Fire drives them, and they relentlessly pursue any living being who enters their domain.

These Void Walkers can sense the Awl'Fire in those who venture into the void, drawn to it like a moth to the flame. Cunning and unyielding, they become formidable foes even for the mightiest warriors. Those who walk within the void must be vigilant, always mindful of the lurking dangers hidden within the shadows."

Just as he said it, the Voidwalker stopped and turned. Its white, ethereal body shimmered and glistened in the muted light of the void. Nah'Hele could see its muscular form tense up, ready to pounce. It was a massive, imposing creature with unpredictable strength.

"Close your eyes, Nah'Hele, and try to move your mind from here."

The Voidwalker jumped from the bank, put its face to the ground and sniffed the cold earth like a predator in the search of his prey.

"What? How?"

"You must close your eyes and think of the river with your friends. Take yourself back!"

The Voidwalker started to run.

"Do it NOW!"

Har'Inuk demanded before he flashed out, leaving Nah'Hele alone. panicked, he shut his eyes and held his breath. When he opened them again, he saw the Voidwalker sprinted toward him. Just as its long, wiry arm swiped to grab him, Nah'Hele's face hit the water in the river.

Above him, Aha'Nu's hands reached down to pull him up.

"Stand up! It's time to go, Warrior." He said as he pulled him out of the water. Nah'Hele had done it. He didn't know how, but he had. He could hear the other boys yelling for him, jumping into the water to save him before he drowned.

As Nah'Hele continued to grow and hone his skills with the void array, the other boys in the tribe couldn't help but feel a pang of jealousy. They heard the stories of the first man and the first wolf, and each secretly hoped they, too, might possess the unique ability to cross into the void. However, try as they might, they couldn't replicate Nah'Hele's incredible gift.

Whispers spread among the young warriors, some questioned whether Nah'Hele's power was a blessing or a curse. Others speculated about what he might be doing when he ventured into the void, their imaginations ran wild with tales of secret knowledge and hidden treasures. Some even accused him of using the void array for his benefit, seeking unfair advantage in battles and hunts.

But despite envy and suspicion. Nah'Hele remained loyal to the tribe and the commitment to using his gift responsibly. He understood the risks and the burden of his ability, and he never flaunted it or used it to belittle others. Instead, he often tried to share what he learned from the Tec'Tulomeh elders and the wisdom he gained during his visits to the void, hoping to benefit the entire tribe.

However, the jealousy of the other boys was not quickly quelled, and it continued to simmer beneath the surface, threatening to create rifts within the tribe. Nah'Hele knew that he must continue to navigate the delicate balance between harnessing his unique gift for the greater good and ensuring that his fellow tribespeople didn't feel left behind.

Chapter 36
The All-Consuming Fire

"Warrior of the Tec'Tulomeh, Go to them. They are waiting to be saved from this place."

Nah'Hele opened his eyes to a dark, empty den with only a pit full of ash where the fire once burned. The words rang in his ears and felt more like a memory of something he heard than something spoken to him. The snow that blocked the entrance vanished, and the strange gray light of the overcast sky seeped in from outside. The air was stale, and the smell of earth filled his nostrils. Once outside, he noticed the snow was gone, and the mountain trees were stripped of their foliage, bare limbs and trunks were exposed to the gray light.

He followed an old trail down into a place the ancient wolf council called The Endless Pines. It was a desolate land, with pine trees jutting out of the ground like wooden needles, stretched as far as the eye could see. In the distance, Nah'Hele spotted a huddled mass of creatures, moving sluggishly as if sleepwalking. Wolves, deer, bears, and even humans were aimlessly wandering.

As Nah'Hele drew nearer, the creatures took notice of him. A bear with a sunken face spoke as he walked past, "Hello, human. Have you also died?"

"No, friend, I am seeking answers to some important questions I have. Perhaps you can help me? What is your name, Great Bear?"

The Bear sat down and sighed. "My name?" it said, puzzled as if he struggled to remember. "...Cern? I think… it's been a long time since anyone asked what my name is or was."

"Well, it's good to meet you, Cern. I am Nah'Hele, a warrior from the Tec'Tulomeh tribe."

"Ahhh, a warrior. I remember others like you, warriors fighting for good causes, fighting against tragedy, fighting against bad things. Maybe I was a warrior. Tell me Nah'Hele of the Tec'Tulomeh tribe, do I resemble a fierce warrior? A… good warrior?" The Bear asks with a very slow childlike inflection.

"Cern, you look as mighty as any warrior bear, I have seen, Strong, with a good name and heart. Fearsome and celebrated by your kind, I'm sure…." Nah'Hele couldn't be sure what the outcome of this conversation would be. He never encountered a bear as long as he'd walked the void. Cern's tight scaly lips drew back, almost cracking as they changed into a smile that hadn't been used in an unknown amount of time.

"Good to meet you too, Nah'Hele," Cern replied, his voice tinged with melancholy.

"What must you know to help you on your quest here? From one warrior to another."

"My people have been disappearing from our den, just on the other side of the void, in the world of the living. With no clues as to where they have gone, something deep within tells me they have been brought here by a fearsome force. Something that I must try and stop."

"Hmmm…" Cern looked confused as he tried to unravel the mystery. "I have no concept of time. It may have been days, weeks, or even centuries, but I have seen a group of human children and men about your size and build. All of them didn't seem to belong here. Too addled to stop and speak to an old warrior bear. Nonetheless, I don't think they arrived here like I did."

Nah'Hele's heart raced.

"I was gathering food for my kin, preparing for the winter months in the caves, when I found myself sliding down the loose rocks of the hills into a stretch of pines, oddly similar to this place. That's when I was caught by a beast with giant arms, much bigger than me. It stood tall on two legs and pulled me into the blackness of its chest…."

Cern's voice trailed off, and he stared into the distance, lost in sadness and pain.

"That's terrible, Warrior."

"Yes, I would have to agree," Cern sighed and took a deep breath. "But that was a long time ago, I'm sure."

Cern rose onto his hind legs. He towered more than three times Nah'Hele's height. With a ragged arm and unkempt claws, Cern pointed toward several creatures that lumbered around and seemed to be an endless walk through the thick gray fog.

"Go further into the pines. I can't say for sure how far. Distance is just as odd a thing here as time. But I am fairly certain that if they are here, they went that way."

"Thank you, Cern. You have been a great help to me."

Cern's eyes flickered with the tiniest bit of color and light. At first, they were lifeless, gray with no spark behind them. But kindness and friendship brought back a little bit of life. Nah'Hele knew this was dangerous. The Voidwalkers were attracted to even the tiniest spark. Just his presence there, alive, was enough to bring them. He had to be careful to keep the spark from spreading.

"Please, Nah'Hele, find me again if time permits. I rather enjoy the company."

Nah'Hele walked away as Cern dropped to all fours and slowly walked in the same direction. To the left and on the right, several other creatures followed suit. Too slow to be problematic.

He continued into the crowd of creatures—squirrels, birds, and rabbits, all slowly moving but going nowhere. He forced himself to be unfriendly, not even giving a look in their direction. It was difficult; everything seemed so sad and lonely. Ahead, huddled around a fallen tree leaning over a large stone, he found the missing children gathered around Ol'Mah. Nah'Hele sprinted to them as the surrounding creature watched with curiosity.

"Ol'Mah! What happened?"

Ol'Mah held the children tight, trying to comfort them.

"I was scared, Nah'Hele. I let fear into my heart. The wolves in the den told me stories of the creature in the Endless Pines—the creature you wanted us to face. When I fell asleep that night, it came to me in a dream and took me into the Void, into this place. I tried to call out, but it was too late." Ol'Mah said as he started to cry. Nah'Hele placed his hand on Ol'Mah's shoulder. "Is it here now, Ol'Mah? When was the last time you saw the great beast?" Nah'Hele asked looking around. Ol'Mah was puzzled. Nah'Hele knew it was a long shot, as time didn't work the same way as it did on the other side.

"He took the children after me...then he was gone, and we haven't seen him since." Ol'Mah's eyes were wet and full of fear.

Nah'Hele knew this was what Har'Inuk warned him about—what would happen if the creature managed to collect enough Awl'Fire.

"...Are we dead, Nah'Hele?" one of the young boys asked. Nah'Hele could tell they weren't their eyes were not the same as Cern's or any other creatures that died.

"No, young warrior, you are not. We are going to get you out of here." The children lit up as fear in their hearts started to be replaced by hope. Ol'Mah stood up and pulled Nah'Hele to the side.

"...That thing that dragged us here was the Axael, wasn't it?" Nah'Hele could see the fear in his eyes. The story of the Axael was told to them as boys. A fairy tale of sorts to keep them on a good path. They could never discern whether it was truth until now.

"Yes, Ol'Mah, it was. Now we have to stop it before it tips the balance in the wrong direction."

"...How long have we been gone, Nah'Hele? I feel like it has been years, centuries even. Is my wife alive? My boys?"

Nah'Hele could see tears form in Ol'Mah's eyes. "Ol'Mah, it's okay. You were only gone two days. The children here were taken just last night."

As soon as Nah'Hele said it, he realized he was a little fuzzy on how long he'd been there. That's when he knew time was running out.

The tears collected in Ol'Mah's eyes fell. He was so happy. Nah'Hele turned to gather the young ones to prepare them to cross when he noticed the children engaged with the animals. They were speaking and laughing.

"Children! Get back right now! These animals are not like you! They are dead!"

All at once, they stopped and slowly backed away, still staring at him. It was too late.

"Children, come to me now. We have to go." Nah'Hele shouted. They heard the shrieks of the void walkers from over the ridge. In the blink of an eye, they came flooding down. They flickered and kicked up a cloud of gray dust behind them. They were fast and hungry for the sparks the children ignited within the creatures. The animals scattered about, trying to get away, but one by one, they fell. The void walkers pinned them beneath their claws, using their body weight to hold them down while they ripped open their chests and abdomens to find the spark in their hearts. "Nah'Hele! your spear, The tip it's... its glowing white!" Nah'Hele looked up to see the obsidian spearhead. It glowed with a vibrant white. So bright that it was almost hard to look at. In the distance, the haze that lingered over the pines was forced out. The Axael Stood tall with its giant arms clinging to a dead tree. He tore the dead tree from its roots with one swift pull and threw it at them.

"Nah'Hele, get the human cubs behind me!" Cern yelled as he stood tall. Nah'Hele, Ol'Mah, and the children huddled behind his massive body as he fought off the walkers. He grew stronger with each one he defeated, tearing their elongated, milky white heads off as they twitched and coiled up. The Axael reached out, caught several animals and squeezed, draining the tiniest little sparks from their hearts. Nah'Hele watched the light travel from the Axaels giant hand to his chest. "Embers, Sparks, give them to me!" He started in their direction, slowly closing the distance between them. It looked as if he was suspended in water. He was weak, and in need of power to sustain him.

"He cannot move fast but gets stronger with every spark. You have to get out of here, warrior. Go now! I will hold them off." Cern commanded as his claws tore into more Voidwalkers. Nah'Hele kneeled and gathered the attention of all the huddled children and Ol'Mah.

"Okay, all you must do is find yourself in the den with your mothers and fathers. It's that simple. Close your eyes, take a deep breath, and let your fear disappear. There's nothing left for you here,"

Nah'Hele said. He watched as one child vanished, followed by another, and then another.

"Nah'Hele! Hurry, I can't hold out much longer!" Cern shouted, his Awl'Fire growing more potent with each void walker he killed.

Only two children remained, the smallest of the group. "You can do this, young warriors. Your mothers are waiting. Think of their smiles."

Just as he spoke, one of them disappeared as the other was pulled away by a void walker that slipped past Cern. The child's arm was ripped loose, dislocated and badly torn. He screamed as the void walker pinned him down with one foot on his thigh and another on his neck. Putting an end to his screams.

"NOOO!" Nah'Hele shrieked as Ol'Mah held him back. Cern was paralyzed in shock, allowing another void walker to latch onto his massive arm. He jerked in pain as the creature tried to pull him down, but Cern planted his feet and became heavier than a boulder. His body combusted with Awl'Fire, setting the void walker ablaze. The creature stumbled backward, shrieking in pain. The Axael stuck his arm out and drew the flames from the burning beast. He gained more speed, closing even more distance.

"Go now..." Cern whispered softly through the flames of the Awl'Fire consuming him. The void walkers scrambled to him, trying to take the fire for themselves. Nah'Hele looked up to see a flood of void walkers pouring over the hills above like ants.

"They're drawn to the fire, Ol'Mah! We have to go now, or we'll be caught!" They closed their eyes and tried to leave, but it wasn't working. They were too distracted by the rush of void walkers screaming as the fire consumed them and grew larger. Ol'Mah was taken when a void walker pierced his back with its claws and drug him into the inferno. Nah'Hele screamed in horror. He watched a void walker lunge at him from the corner of his eye. Just before he made contact, Nah'Hele flashed out and flickered into the world of the living for a brief moment before flashing back into the void. He dodged the attack and opened a window of opportunity. He knew it would be over if he didn't stop the Axael now. The twisting inferno climbing higher into the sky of the void would be the source of power he would need to escape. He eyed the Axael in the distance. Not far away from the edge of the blaze. "The spearhead, use it, warrior!" Har'Inuk yelled. Nah'Hele sprinted, dodging void walkers like he was jumping from tree to tree, using the void to glide in and out of the living realm. It was working. He vaulted into the air and came down at a sharp angle. He flashed out one more time to dodge the Axael's giant arm. Just before he planted the spear in his foot. Immediately, Nah'Hele found himself back in the world of the living, staring at the snow. The Axael's massive foot was pinned to the ground. Nah'Hele succeeded in landing a mortal blow with the obsidian spear but didn't realize the power he gained from Cern's inferno on the other side was all he needed. The Axael reached down and pulled the spear from his foot as Nah'Hele fell into the snow and pushed himself backward. He stopped when he bumped into a pair of legs.

"Stand up warrior, it's time to go…"

Aha'Nu stood tall above him, with all the warriors of the Tec'Tulomeh and an army of wolves led by the council.

"You are the harbinger of the void. Are you not, creature?"

Vul'Rynth said as he stepped closer. The Axael raised his hand to catch the falling snow with a childlike demeanor."

"I am." The Axael's voice was almost soothing, reverberating through the snow-tipped pines.

"It is believed by both man and wolf that you seek balance. If that is true, why do you insist on destroying everything?" The Axael centers his stair on the Vul'Rynth. He shuddered with fear.

"I do not wish to destroy this…balance you speak of. It is my very nature to consume the Awl'Fire. It is only living creatures that find my nature destructive."

He puts his hand out and drains the Awl'Fire from Gmork, a member of the ancient wolf council. His bright green eyes fade quickly as his flame is sucked into the Axael's palm. "The Awl'Fire in your heart is never ending no matter if it is with you or with the nothing." He said as he lifted his hand to the sky and released a pillar of light, shooting far into the emptiness above.

Both human and wolves shriek in terror. They watch his lifeless body crumble in the snow.

"You are a demon! Not a deity!" Nah'Hele shouts.

"I fear your kind will come to learn in time, those concepts are one and the same."

From behind The Axael, Har'Inuk appeared with a bow. Slowly he crept around a group of evergreens with an arrow clasped between his rotting teeth; an arrow with an obsidian tip that glowed white a white aura like Nah'Hele's spear.

"The bird eats the insect; the lion eats the bird. Are they not evil in your eyes for this? It is merely a question of perspective. The Awl'Fire is the insect. You are the bird. I am the lion." The Axael raised his hand once more as Har'Inuk drew back the arrow and let it loose. The arrow missed its mark and stuck in the Axael's shoulder. In shock, he turned around to see Har'Inuk slip into the void.

"The spear!" Har'Inuk screamed from the other side. Once more, Nah'Hele Flashed into the void. Immediately, the inferno that rose into the sky, pulled the air from his lungs. It singed the flesh on his forearm as he shielded his eyes from the mass of heat. He fought desperately to stay upright as he ran to the other side and flashed back over. The wolves were in the flurry of a melee with the Axael. They bit and tore at its translucent flesh. Its black oily blood spilled the snow. Arrows and spears from the Tec'Tulomeh were doing very little to hinder him. Nah'Hele picked up the obsidian tipped spear and slammed into the lower left flank of the beast. It caused it to pull away and drain several Fires from the wolves latched on to him.

The bodies of the dead stacked up in the snow. The Axael wailed with pain as gallons of brackish liquid flowed from the wound. With the spear tight in his hand, Nah'Hele pushed hard once more and shoved the spear into his outstretched hand before he could siphon his Awl'Fire. No matter the effort made. The Axael was unable to slip into the void. Instead, it retreated over the hills and headed West.

The Wolves and Tec'Tulomeh warriors did their best to catch it before it reached the slanted snow. But its size and stride gave it the advantage it needed to make a breakaway. Har'Inuk reappeared beside Nah'Hele and Vul'Rynth. They watched the great Axael saunter its way to the hill, leaving a trail of black blood in the snow.

"Nah'Hele, you know what we must do," Har'Inuk said out loud. Vul'Rynth didn't know the words but understood the emotion behind them. They had to stop it, whatever it took.

"Let us gather our dead, then we will reconvene on the matter soon. We can't waste much time." Vul'Rynth headed off across the expanse of the snow. He howled for all the wolves to gather.

"I will stay back and bury the dead with the others. Go to your family, Nah'Hele and speak to the council. Whatever you decide, I will stand with you." Har'Inuk said as he grasped Nah'Hele's neck and placed his forehead to his.

Chapter 37
Gifts of Power

For Nah'Hele, mere hours had passed as he traversed the void. But back in the Hunter's den, five days had gone by for everyone else. The children who had slipped out of the void returned sporadically within a few days of one another, recounting the tale of a fierce bear named Cern. His great Awl'Fire drew the void walkers from the hills and into his flames.

They told how the Axael had only stolen their fires and left them to fend for themselves in the void's bleakness. He wasn't there to kill them, only to use them to get over the mountains. When the Scouting pack returned to the den to let the Tec'Tulomeh warriors know Nah'Hele was seen in the pines. They said their goodbyes and headed for the uncertainty out in the snow. That was the last time they saw their loved ones.

"Mer'Rah..." Nah'Hele whispered as he made it back to the Hunter's den. She clung to his body. He shivered when the fire inside slid over his skin. The mothers of the returned children fell to their knees in thanks to him for his courage in the void. Mer'Rah could see in his eyes that there was bad news. He was hesitant to divulge.

"What is it, my love? Tell us, Unburden yourself! We are all family here. The warriors met you in the field. Why?" she asked, as she wrapped her arm around him. The others still kneeled beneath and waited with bated breath.

"The creature in the void has crossed over. He slipped into our realm when I pierced his flesh with my obsidian spear." Nah'Hele said.

The tribe's people gasped in horror. "He killed many wolves and several of our warriors without impunity." Nah'Hele named the six and watched as each family fell apart. Mer'Rah's eyes spilled tears down his bare chest.

"The Axael was too strong and too powerful for us to take down. He made an escape over the hills of the endless pines and is headed west." After he recounted the story, he spent some time with each family and thanked them for their sacrifice.

"Nah'Hele. Vul'Rynth is ready for us now. He is waiting at the stone with the remaining council members." Aha'Nu whispered in his ear.

"My people!" Nah'Hele stood up to gather everyone's attention.

"The time has come for us to make a choice. Come with me to the stone so we can all make this decision together."

*

Nah'Hele and his tribe arrived at the council's stone just before sunset. Instead of the seven, there were only four. Ill'Rune, Vul'Rynth, Mirth'Erin and Minerva made it out of the pines. But Gmork and Cer'Ulith were not so lucky.

"We will remember this day as a great tragedy for humans and wolves. We are sorry for your losses, people of the Tec'Tulomeh. Your warriors will be remembered." Ill'Rune said as he stood on the stone.

"And we, the Tec'Tulomeh, give our condolences to the wolves your packs have also lost."

Both sides fell silent for a moment as Mirth'Erin stepped forward.

"The Axael has escaped the Endless Pines and is heading west as far as we know. We must go, hunt and destroy him before he can reach the world of man. I will volunteer." He said as he sat on the stone

Vul'Rynth stepped forth. "Mirth'Erin is right. The power he will gain from their densely populated encampments and villages will be more than he needs to bring the void walkers to our realm. He will spread the void; it is his only desire. I will also volunteer. To do what needs to be done."

Vul'Rynth sat beside Mirth'Erin.

"May I suggest something, Ill'Rune?"

He nodded to Minerva, the fourth council wolf,

"I will go as well, but I feel the Tec'Tulomeh will hinder us..." Nah'Hele and the remaining warriors turned sharply to the wolf on the stone. "We are strong, Minerva; have we not proven that to you? We will do whatever it takes to stop what has started."

Minerva stepped forward alongside them. "I do not disagree with you, Nah'Hele," Minerva came down from the stone and stood before the tribe.

"I feel you and your tribe have earned the right to use the Moon array."

"She is right, Ill'Rune. The Moon Array is the answer. If they can go to him as wolves, they will track better, move quicker, require less food, and be able to slip past the humans undetected."

Vul'Rynth agreed, Ill'Rune weighed the options in silence.

"It appears the majority is in favor of this. So, I will agree with it as well. Who among us will share their likeness with Nah'Hele and the Tec'Tulomeh?"

Before the words even left his mind. Every wolf who stood around the council stepped forward. They made their way to the individual members of the tribe and pressed their heads against theirs. Sharing their Awl'Fires with them. Vul'Rynth gave his to Nah'Hele, Ill'Rune gave his to Aha'Nu.

"These are gifts we shall never forget; we thank you, brothers," Nah'Hele said as Vul'Rynth and the others returned to the stone.

"Now. We know the Axael cannot be destroyed, so our best option is to trap it. I will leave the planning of this to your human minds. Let us take some time to familiarize you with the changing, and then we will go to the west. The longer the Axael spends cultivating the void in the west, the stronger he will become."

*

When the Tec'Tulomeh and the wolves arrived back at their old campsite, the Axael had taken the white settlers who had been there before. They climbed the mountainside, scaling the rocks to the summit quickly. Once at the top, they cleared the foliage and piled it high.

"Har'Inuk! It's time!" Nah'Hele called out to him. Har'Inuk had sat at the edge of a cliff on the opposite side of the summit, smoking his pipe, while the rest of the tribe worked tirelessly to clear the land.

Once the trees, bushes, and plants were all removed and piled in the center, Har'Inuk used a stone to draw a square in the dirt while the rest of the tribe sat around him in a circle. Har'Inuk reached into a leather satchel that hung on his hip and pulled out four black crystals and various bones and stones. The tribe locked their hands and closed their eyes as Har'Inuk commenced an ancient incantation. At first, nothing happened.

"Everyone! Close your eyes and think of the earth opening where the square is drawn. All you have to do is focus. I will do the rest," Har'Inuk instructed as he picked up sand and roots from the ground and packed them into his lower lip. He started the incantation again. This time, a deep rumble from within the mountain grew louder and louder as Har'Inuk spoke faster and with more intent.

The ground shook and spewed dust from the square, the land sinking and turning black. Around the perimeter of the square, flat stones poked through the dirt; they rose up to form a black and hollow entrance that led down into a hole. A hole that expanded more every second. Har'Inuk stood with his arms outstretched in front of the entrance as a fire burned symbols into the border of the door.

"All of you! Find your way down and use the Moon Array to stay out of sight. There's not much more to do here." Har'Inuk said as the Tec'Tulomeh hurried down.

Nah'Hele stayed back and watched Har'Inuk; this would be the last time he would ever see him.

"Nah'Hele, you will do great things with the power of the Awl'Fire. I am glad to have known you." Har'Inuk smiled as his eyes turned white. He climbed the woodpile in front of the stone doorway and with one last grin. He spoke words from a lost language and imploded into a great light. It ignited the wood beneath in a white fire. Nah'Hele could see down into the corridor behind the entrance, lit with torches that seemed to go on forever.

Once at the bottom of the mountain, the Tec'Tulomeh changed into wolves and disappeared into the forest to hide. Not long after the sun went down, the fire called to the Axael like a siren. It lured him up the mountainside.

As it trundled through the forest, it's massive body felled trees and uprooted stones. The power it claimed from the humans it devoured on the way to the mountain gave it folded wings that pulled tightly up against his back. it was as tall as a tree, with a sleek black form and a terrifying presence. The sound of its footsteps was like an earthquake.

It didn't take it very long to scale the mountainside as he twisted his body in ways impossible by any other creature they had seen. The fire atop the summit pulled towards it in a spiral that arced into its chest.

It consumed the fire and allowed it to grow even stronger with each flickering flame.

By the time it reached the summit, the fire at the top had been wholly consumed. Only the light from the corridor remained. The Axael couldn't resist its allure. It made its way down; each flame danced on the torches before they were snuffed out one by one as it descended the steps. It was so preoccupied with the fire lining the walls it didn't realize the door had closed behind. It sealed itself shut as the engravings on the outside dimmed into a steady white glow, which would persist for ages to come.

Down below, in the mountain's interior, Nah'Hele and Aha'Nu built a great fire in the hollow center. A fire that would hold the beast's attention for centuries to come.

The Axael's actions had cleared the lands of all the evil men and provided the Tec'Tulomeh tribe the opportunity they needed to flourish as they had for generations before. As time passed, Nah'Hele and his people became more comfortable surviving in the wilderness as wolves, so they discarded their Tec'Tulomeh banner and their human flesh in favor of a new wolf pack identity: The Illnok.

Over time, as more and more generations of wolves were born into the Illnok tribe, the Axael, entombed in the mountain above, became nothing more than a fable—a children's story to be told under the night sky, serving as a reminder of their past and the power of unity

Part IX: Order Among Chaos

Chapter 38
New Lands

For more than an hour, the peregrine circled above the peak of the Alpha's mountain, as the wind whipped through his new, coarse fur. From his vantage point, he could see Oct'Tulommon's path of destruction, a scar upon the once-pristine Illnok landscape. The peregrine found himself aloft in a sky he no longer desired to be in. The air streams on which he once rested his outstretched wings no longer gave him the lift he needed. Stealing away the sentiment of superiority over the beasts in the fields and the Unclean that flew much lower beneath him.

The once-clear skies seemed hostile towards him now, it rejected his presence among the fresh air and billowing clouds. His grisly transformation had left him with a body mass almost five times greater, it made his ability to maintain his preferred altitude in the stratosphere very taxing, even with the new dense muscle tissue stretched over his fame. So, with no sign of the demon wolf Oct'Tulommon from the mysterious corridors that swallowed him up, the peregrine descended upon the ravaged lands at the great hall's entrance.

Feeling the softness of the dirt below his massive paws was an invigorating fresh experience. As a falcon, his claws were only meant to grip and tear the flesh of his prey; now, he received sensory information throughout his new paws' sensitive pads and bones. The ground's temperature, the terrain's roughness, and the vibrations from deep within the earth were just a few of the sensations he now experienced.

His vision had always been impeccable, able to see the tiniest of movements from up to two miles away. Now, he could see over great distances and detect movement from every side of him, even in the dark. This newfound sight gave him the luxury of never having to fear a surprise attack. He scanned the trees around the mountain's perimeter and found no signs of life. Everything was still alive after the day's events had chosen to flee, hoping to stay clear of the fractured wolves roaming the wilderness.

As he walked inside the great smoke-filled hall, he found the smoldering remains of the fallen alpha amidst an endless sea of blood, rock, and bone. His extraordinary vision allowed him to take it all in with vivid detail, which filled his heart with anger—not because of the violence of what happened, but because he could not witness it firsthand. The fire in the center of the great hall was gone; nothing but ash and giant boulders lay in the pit where it once burned. It left the great hall in almost complete darkness. He could still take it all in, thanks to his new night vision.

Above him, around the rock ledges that overlooked the great hall, he spotted a murder of crows, perched in silence. Awestruck by a new creature they had never seen before. Yet felt oddly familiar.

"Crows! Why are you not down here pillaging the dead? There is nothing here to hurt you now," The peregrine called as he walked closer to the ledge. He could sense the reluctantcy in them.

"What do we call such a creature as you?"

One crow inquired. His beady eyes reflected the faint light that filtered into the hall.

"You have the scent of the stratosphere, but your coat suggests you are earthborn?"

"Yes, creature, what are you? We have flown far and wide throughout the world of man and the untamed wilderness and have seen nothing that looks the way you do."

The crows questioned, their voices trembled with curiosity and fear.

The peregrine stood on his hind legs and spread his wings. They blocked what little light filled the space in the great hall."

That's because I am the only one of my kind. I am..."

He paused for a moment as the realization sank in. He now had the power to be whatever he wanted, to be named anything he desired. No one could dispute his supremacy over the land, both in the heavens and on the earth. All except one, but he had watched from a great distance as the evidence of the Axaels' drift into the void disappeared into the sky above the Alpha's Mountain. He was at the apex now.

He vaulted his tremendous frame from the ground level of the great hall and landed hard behind the crows on the ledge. A gust of wind from his hard landing stirred the dust around them and forced them to spread their wings to keep their balance on the ledge. The beast thought hard about a name for the first time. He recalled a tale he had once overheard while in a tree high above a group of humans. They spoke of a mythical creature named "Vaigon," a malevolent and merciless being that was said to have once walked the earth in the darkest days of ancient history.

Vaigon was a creature born from the shadows, a dark force that fed on the fear and despair of those unfortunate enough to encounter him. It was said that Vaigon could assume many forms, each more terrifying than the last. The very mention of its name would send shivers down the spines of even the bravest warriors.

This sinister name resonated with him as it echoed the malice and power he now possessed, a perfect fit for his newfound might. And so, with an air of menace, he declared, "I am Vaigon, the Great Falcon Wolf, and it displeases me that you do not know me."

The crows cowered in fear, looking at one another, hoping that one among them would know who he was. "We are sorry, Falcon Wolf—"

"Great Falcon Wolf!" he corrected them.

"...We are sorry, Great Falcon Wolf. We are of the Unclean and have no lineage to learn our histories from. Tell us so that we may know whom we serve."

The crows were so terrified they didn't even have to be persuaded to swear their fealty to him. He laughed and wondered how such creatures made it through their insufferable existences, being so easily fooled. "You may not serve me until you have made offerings. This is what I require to be your deity."

They looked at each other, puzzled. "...Great Falcon Wolf, we are so small, we hardly think we can gather enough of a sacrifice for you to even quench your hunger."

"Yes, what is it we can offer you? To save our kind from your wrath?"

He pondered for a moment before he answered. They were right; there was nothing the little birds could scavenge that would fill his belly. Even his favorite rabbit meat would no longer be enough to satiate his giant stomach. In fact, he had developed a new craving the moment he sunk his teeth into Vog's back. Human flesh.

"Bring all the Unclean birds in the lands to this mountain. I will make this smoldering ruin of ashes into a new kingdom on earth, and you and all like you will bow your heads to me."

The Great Falcon Wolf jumped from the ledge back down to the great hall, spread his wings, and vaulted himself into the sky with his massive legs. The crows followed, scattering in all directions.

Once atop the mountain above, he perched on the ancient altar built by Har'Inuk and the other members of the Tec'Tulomeh. He longed to see the runes filled with light around the square in the dirt, but he didn't know how. Oct'Tulommon would have to wait until he could figure it out. Until that day, the great Falcon Wolf would spend his days building his new kingdom in both the Outlands and the Illnok territory, where both alphas had lost their seats of power.

Thus began the reign of Vaigon, the Falcon Wolf, king of the Unclean lands.

Chapter 39
The Traveler

"Evan! Evan, wake up! He's back!"

The urgent whisper pulled Evan from the depths of sleep, a tremor of excitement running through him.

It had been two months since the night Atticus Atuawee had filled Evan and Millie's minds with astonishment and knowledge of man's true history. Both had assumed they would never see him again, but Tulie had reassured them that this was Atohi's way. He was an interloper, coming and going when the time was just right to do so.

"It's 2 AM, babe! Send him away and come back to bed," Evan mumbled, reaching out in the darkness for Millie, feigning nonchalance though his heart raced with anticipation. As he glimpsed her face in the darkness, he saw her brow was heavy with concern.

"Tulie's crying. I think it's serious. Come on, get up." Her voice shook. Evan sprang to his feet.

He pulled on an old shirt he'd grabbed from a chest of drawers. The worn fabric bore the image of a red-haired singer in a black dress, "Reba" emblazoned beneath her in elegant cursive. Since Millie had invited Evan to stay with her in the master bedroom, they'd vowed to clean out the drawers, but never seemed to find the time.

As they hurried out the back door, they found Tulie kneeled down in the dew-drenched grass. Atohi's weakened body cradled in her arms. The ancient wolf's fur, once a vibrant tapestry of colors, was now dull and matted, his once-powerful frame reduced to a pitiful husk.

Atohi was dying.

From the day of his encounter with Oct'Tulommon to that very moment, a little over two months had passed.

"There's so much that has happened since the last time I was here," Atohi rasped, his voice barely audible. "In my weakened state, I couldn't use the void to communicate or travel to you... So, I had to come by foot."

"Who did this to you, Atohi? Who shot you?" Evan asked, his eyes filled with rage and concern as Millie dashed back into the house to retrieve her medical bag.

"...It was Oct'Tulommon Evan."

Atohi projected a vision of the melee into Evans' mind. It was brief but gave him a true sense of the brutality of it. He could feel the heat of rage boil in his body.

"I found him, Evan. I found the wolf responsible for your father's death. He's the Alpha of the Outlands, and his fractured wolves aim to take over the sacred Illnok Territory and your lands. I fear he won't stop until all that remains is ashes."

Millie returned with a few first aid supplies, but nothing that could dress a sucking chest wound.

"Tulie, I love you and always have," Atohi gasped, his breath grew more labored by the second. "Remember that for the rest of your life. You know—" "Stop it, Atticus! Stop! Millie's going to fix you!" Tulie choked out, her voice cracked with emotion.

Tears welled up in Millie's eyes as she realized she could do nothing to save Atohi. His life was slipping away.

"Tulie, feel inside my heart with yours and know I mean what I say. I'll always be with you, watching you from the void. I'm sorry it had to end like this," Atohi whispered. His body grew weaker by the second.

"Tulie, I want nothing more than to spend my last moments on this Earth in your arms. When I'm gone, bury my body here to be close to you."

Tulie's grief threatened to shatter her very soul. "No! Atticus!" she cried; her voice echoed in the still night air.

"Millie? What's going on?"

A tiny voice asked from the back porch. It was Steph, her eyes wide with.

"Steph! Go inside, okay? We'll be in just a moment." Millie's voice was firm yet gentle.

"What's wrong with Tulie?" Steph questioned, her eyes wide with concern as she tiptoed closer to the edge of the porch.

"Steph, go inside. We wi—" "It's the wolf from my dreams!" Steph said.

In that instant, all three turned to look at her, their expressions a combination of disbelief and shock. Despite their astonishment, Millie hurried to her side and guided her back inside. She knew no matter how surreal the situation felt, she couldn't let Steph bear witness to Atohi's last moments. "He told me this was going to happen."

Everyone, including Atohi, didn't know what Steph was talking about, but time had run out. They would have to find the answers themselves later.

Atohi's voice grew weaker. "Evan... clear your mind and heart. You must make room for the Void Array. It's yours now..."

The ancient wolf's breaths were shallow and strained, each word a monumental effort. "You must find the Illnok Elden Sayer Li'Illnok, and an obsidian wolf named Morgrim... They will help you. Together, you will form a new pack, as it is meant to be."

A sense of urgency and determination filled Evan's heart as he listened to Atohi's last instructions. He knew he must honor the dying wolf's wishes and ensure the balance between order and chaos remained intact.

As Atohi spoke his last words, he closed his eyes, and a faint smile graced his dry lips before he drew his last breath. Tulie's sobs filled the air, a mournful melody accompanying the ancient wolf's departure from the world.

Evan's breaths grew heavy as a white glow enveloped his eyes. It illuminated the surrounding darkness. The brilliant light seemed to sear his soul. He closed his eyes and willed the intense sensation to subside. In mere moments, the radiant energy dissipated and left a warm calm in its wake.

To Evan's astonishment, he saw Atohi stand up from Tulie's embrace, both his eyes clear and vibrant, his fur gleaming with vitality. Atohi's renewed form was a sight to behold, a testament to the power he had just passed onto Evan.

With a solemn nod to Evan, he acknowledged the immense responsibility now entrusted to him. Atohi turned and disappeared into the shadowy depths of the forest. He would never again be seen by mortal eyes except by those gifted with the mysterious power of the Void Array.

Evan's heart pounded in his chest, the gravity of his newfound purpose weighing upon him. As he gazed into the darkness where Atohi had vanished, he knew he must forge ahead, embracing his destiny as a guardian of the delicate balance between order and chaos.

Without knowing what was beyond the fence past Fern Gully, Evan was afraid he would risk the lives of the ones he loved most. But as he thought of all the tragedy befalling humankind, it seemed to be the lesser of the two evils.

Chapter 40
Barely Alive

After Vog'Morlinok escaped from the summit of the burning mountain, the new and rightful Alpha of the Illnok territory, wandered aimlessly through his new lands like a tormented specter. In many respects, he was emotionally dead, his heart shattered by the memory of all that he and his brother had expertly accomplished. The voice of the Axael was strong within his mind.

"The world of man awaits you Vog, do not hesitate."

Vog's depression and melancholy only deepened after he saw the realm of the void for the first time. Aside from the muted gray of the fog, it was indiscernible from the wasteland west of the Alpha's Mountain, the land that was scorched by Oct'Tulommon. There were no songs from birds or playful chatter from the woodland creatures in the burned trees and the scorched fields. Only the distant cries of pain and anguish from those left to fend for themselves against the feral wolves that now roved the area. It resonated through the barren landscape. The tranquility cultivated in the Illnok lands throughout thousands of years no longer lingered.

As he crossed the Border woods into the Outlands, where his brother's reign was now over, he wasn't surprised to see how the landscapes melded the two territories were now one in the same. The fractured wolves he had helped create had decimated everything of color and left nothing but ash and bloodstained dirt behind.

After more than a day's walk. Something caught his eye in the distance. A metal fence separated the Outlands from the world of man on the other side. Above the rusted chain link rose tall green trees that bordered a lush, green forest, with towering trees swaying gently in a light breeze. Reluctantly, Vog decided to cross the fence. He was no stranger to the cities of man, and he knew that in their realm, he might find some semblance of peace with alcohol.

"I feel a flicker of hope in your heart Vog, you mask it well with reluctancy." The Axael was relentless, a constant reminder beneath the surface that he was nothing, that he was only alive to serve one purpose. It was maddening. He felt himself becoming angry with his situation, as he looked out over the fresh green foliage in front of him, he knew he had to find a way to hide from him.

The forest gave Vog a slight sense of wonder, as being amongst the greenery reminded him of the Illnok lands before their fall—full of life and untouched by humans. After he stopped to rest his weary body, the evening turned to night and back into day. Not once did he sleep?

As he continued, he found himself on a long, empty stretch of highway. The machines men used for transportation were strewn everywhere, dilapidated and losing a battle against nature as vines and plant life crept over them. Houses hid in the foliage, while fences around what used to be front yards were now bursting with overgrown plant life that cared not for boundaries.

Vog finally felt another glimmer of intrigue when he heard the sounds of men — a small encampment cut out in a field lined with tents and campfires. The smell of hickory smoldering underneath pots of cooking meat and vegetables wafted through the air. He assumed the form of a man and made his way into their world, slipping undercover a wolf wrapped in a human flesh cloak.

As masked survivors steered clear of his unmasked face and his gaunt look. He felt indifferent.

The encampment people shared their stories of survival, rebuilding, and hope for a better future. He listened from a distance. Feigning surprise, laughter, sadness and anger when the social cues called for it. After a time, he stood by and watched as the Rasping fever took life after life. Until he was the only one left alive in the encampment. The Void fed. It used Vog as a siphon. It gained power through the melancholy surrounding Vog.

"Move along Vog, to the next gathering of me, watch them die," it commanded him.

More time had passed as Vog traversed the dying cities of men. Not wanting to reveal his true nature to the people who had accepted him along the way. Torn between the hints of a newfound purpose with the humans and his past responsibilities, Vog wrestled with the decision before him as the voice of the Axael called to him to do what he knew would eventually be commanded............

"Vog…. Kill them all……."

The End

Acknowledgments

Completing my first novel has been a journey of lessons, with patience standing as the most significant. The concept, shared first with my brother Michael, delved into creation, the essence of the spirit, and life's purpose. Despite my initial shortcomings in grammar and structure, I persisted, writing for long hours and gradually increasing my daily word count.

In my quest for improvement, I discovered several tools that helped refine my writing. Despite this, the early drafts were still clumsy and riddled with mistakes and fragments of ideas, making it hard for readers to engage. With the invaluable feedback I got from a handful of intrigued readers, I was able to refine my work further. (Amanda Mccain, Martha Crotty, Ciara Massingale, Tim Bass and Agatha Wells) thank you so much for sticking with the story all the way through. Your input helped me far more than I can express.

The search for a co-author yielded no results, and professional editing seemed prohibitively expensive. Finally, in 2023, two years into my writing journey, I found a solution: OpenAI and ChatGPT. This AI allowed me to take charge of the editing process myself, resulting in another, more polished draft.

Venturing into the realms of publishing and printing was initially daunting due to my lack of experience. After submitting the manuscript for "Wardens" to multiple publishers, I soon discovered that the offered hybrid contracts were not in my best interest as a writer. This realization led me to another conclusion. I was equipped with all the necessary tools to independently handle this process.

By formatting the text on my own and utilizing Stable Diffusion for cover art creation in conjunction with Google Docs, I successfully produced the book layout. This enabled me to print my very first trade paperback with a professional printing company, seeing my vision become a tangible reality. Together with my brother Michael Hogan, we designed to cover art and pushed on to find a distributor.

If this book brings even a single reader joy, I will be deeply gratified. Yet, even if it doesn't, I hope it stands as a testament to the power of determination. This book is proof that anyone, with enough resolve, can achieve their dreams, be it in writing, music, painting, design, photography, or any other field. Remember, don't let traditional methods constrain your creativity. Explore, innovate, and discover new ways to realize your aspirations.

A heartfelt thank you goes to my wife, Amber, and our two children, Elias and Walker. For two years, you've endured my non-stop chatter about plot twists and character arcs, all while I turned our kitchen table into an impromptu writer's den. Your constant love and support have been the support I've leaned on the most, even when I was possibly more attached to my computer than the Pac, the family cat.

-   Steven James Hogan

www.ingramcontent.com/pod-product-compliance
Lightning Source LLC
Chambersburg PA
CBHW021224060726
47590CB00005B/1630